Bridging the Unseen

Caroline Brooks

Published by Caroline Brooks, 2024.

This is a work of fiction. Similarities to real people, places, or events are entirely coincidental.

BRIDGING THE UNSEEN

First edition. October 8, 2024.

Copyright © 2024 Caroline Brooks.

ISBN: 979-8227210319

Written by Caroline Brooks.

Chapter 1: An Unlikely Encounter

The day I meet Ethan, I'm balancing two coffees in one hand and a stack of floral arrangements in the other. The air is fragrant with the scent of roses and jasmine, a heady mix that might as well be my personal perfume. I've always believed that a touch of floral magic could brighten even the most mundane day, but on this particularly chaotic morning, I'm feeling anything but enchanted. The coffee cups, precariously perched and steaming, threaten to spill at any moment. I weave through the crowded café, dodging tables and patrons as I head toward the exit, the weight of the morning's orders pressing against my arm.

Just as I push open the door, my elbow catches on the edge of his jacket, and in that split second, I realize that the universe has conspired against me. The inevitable happens: both drinks cascade down the front of a crisp, navy suit, sending rivulets of steaming liquid onto fabric that, until this moment, seemed as immaculate as a well-kept secret. My heart races, not just from embarrassment but from the way his blue eyes pin me in place, a stormy sea contrasting with the bright sun pouring in from the open door behind me.

"I'm so sorry!" I gasp, the words tumbling out of my mouth before I can process the horror of the situation. My cheeks flare up, warmth pooling at my temples as I brace myself for the confrontation that never comes. Instead, he's looking at me as if I've just delivered the punchline to an excellent joke.

"Coffee is overrated, anyway," he replies, his deep voice soothing the chaos I've caused. There's a wry smile tugging at the corners of his lips, and suddenly, the mess feels like something far less catastrophic—a shared moment of clumsy humanity rather than a disaster.

"I should have watched where I was going," I stammer, utterly flustered. I can feel the curious gazes of other patrons, a blend of sympathy and amusement, boring into my back like tiny pinpricks. "I promise I'll make it up to you. Let me buy you a new one."

He raises an eyebrow, a teasing glint in his eyes that suggests he's not entirely displeased by the interruption. "And risk another spill? I think not."

The tension in my shoulders eases slightly, and I can't help but laugh, a nervous little sound that feels oddly freeing. "Okay, maybe that was a bad idea." I take a step back, acutely aware of the way his gaze drags over me, weighing the floral apron tied around my waist, the wild curls escaping my ponytail, and the remnants of yesterday's mascara still lingering under my eyes. It feels as if I've stepped into one of those romantic comedies where the heroine, a floral designer, collides spectacularly with the dashing yet brooding businessman. My life, I remind myself, is decidedly less cinematic and more chaotic.

"Ethan," he introduces himself, extending a hand, a gesture both formal and strangely intimate. "And you are?"

"Cora," I reply, taking his hand and feeling a jolt of energy course through me, the kind of spark I hadn't felt in ages. The skin of his palm is warm, steady, and it sends an involuntary shiver down my spine. I glance down at the coffee stains blooming across his suit and wince. "I'm really sorry about your jacket. I can—"

"Cora, right? Let it go," he interrupts, his voice a playful melody. "I've spilled far worse on this suit."

A light-hearted banter begins to unfurl between us, an unexpected and delightful ease that makes me forget the haphazardness of my morning. "Well, I can at least offer you a cupcake," I suggest, feeling an odd urge to repay this stranger's kindness, as if he's taken a moment out of his day just to make mine a little brighter.

"Is that your secret weapon?" he asks, leaning closer as if sharing a joke. "Floral arrangements and sugary bribes?"

I snort, unable to hold back a laugh. "Something like that. Though, I have to admit, the arrangements tend to take precedence over the sweets. It's just me and my flowers trying to bring a little joy to the world." I gesture vaguely behind me, toward the café, the bustling street outside, the jumble of colors spilling from my floral cart.

"I can see the joy, but how about a little caffeine to go with it? The flowers might just be too sweet without some bitter to balance them out." He tilts his head slightly, his gaze pinning me in place once more, and for a brief moment, I feel as if the chaos of the world outside has melted away, leaving just the two of us suspended in this little pocket of time.

"I'll take you up on that," I say, more impulsively than I intended. I don't know why I'm so drawn to him, this stranger in a coffee-stained suit. Perhaps it's his charming grin or the way his eyes seem to reflect the sky—vivid and full of depth. Whatever it is, I'm intrigued. And just like that, I find myself contemplating the strangeness of life, how it can pivot on a single moment—a misstep that leads to an unexpected encounter.

We step outside, the sun filtering through the trees lining the street. As we walk side by side, the chatter of the café fades behind us, replaced by the sound of distant laughter and the rustle of leaves in the gentle breeze. I can feel the weight of my floral arrangements at my side, but the connection with Ethan makes the burden seem lighter. With every word we exchange, every teasing remark, I wonder what it is about him that holds me captive. Perhaps it's the promise of something unexpected, a hint of adventure in the air, or simply the fact that, for the first time in a long time, I don't feel alone.

As we near a nearby bakery, the rich aroma of fresh pastries fills the air, wrapping around us like a comforting hug. I steal a glance at Ethan, and he catches my eye, a spark of mischief dancing across his features. "What's your poison? Cupcakes? Or are we doing something extravagant, like éclairs?"

"Let's live dangerously," I reply, my heart quickening at the playful challenge. "Éclairs it is." I can hardly believe I'm here, exchanging witty banter with a man whose suit I just ruined. It feels like the kind of story I would write—except I can't write my own plot; it's happening in real time, right in front of me.

The bakery, with its sun-kissed windows and an intoxicating scent that could tempt even the staunchest dieter, greets us like an old friend. A charming little sign dangles above the door, proclaiming, "Eat Cake, Be Happy." The motto alone could spark a revolution, or at least a good excuse for dessert. I step inside, the bell above the door jingling like a cheerful greeting, and the ambiance shifts from the bustle of the street to a cozy cocoon of warmth and sugar. The walls are painted a soft pastel, adorned with photographs of indulgent pastries and happy customers, a scrapbook of sweetness that draws you in.

Ethan follows closely, and I can feel his presence like a warm glow beside me. It's both thrilling and terrifying, the way our banter has filled the space between us with something electric, something I can't quite put my finger on. The shop is surprisingly busy for a midweek morning, patrons seated at small tables, their laughter and chatter melding into a comforting backdrop. I glance at the display case, my mouth watering as I spot éclairs stacked high, their glossy chocolate tops glistening like promises.

"Is it too cliché if I say I want the chocolate one?" I ask, shooting a sideways glance at Ethan, who leans casually against the counter as if he owns the place. The warmth of his laughter bubbles up like the steam from a freshly brewed coffee, filling the air with something sweet and light.

"Cliché, yes, but also the right choice," he replies, his grin widening. "If you can't indulge in chocolate éclairs on a day like today, when can you? Besides, you've already ruined my suit; I feel we should both have a good excuse to make bad choices."

"Touché," I laugh, my cheeks warming under the combination of embarrassment and exhilaration. I can't help but appreciate his ability to roll with the punches. There's something disarming about how easy he is to talk to, how he seems to effortlessly draw me into a comfortable rhythm.

We move toward the counter, where a friendly baker with flour-dusted hands greets us. "What'll it be?" she asks, her smile as warm as the freshly baked goods behind her.

"I'll take two chocolate éclairs, please," I say, and Ethan leans in slightly, his expression playful.

"Make that three; one for me, and I can't let the floral artist suffer alone in her bad decisions," he adds, and I can't help but chuckle at the thought of being branded as a rebel because of pastry choices.

Once we've made our selections, we find a small table in the corner, sunlight streaming in through the window, illuminating the soft curls of steam rising from our coffees. I carefully set the éclairs in front of us, and for a moment, the world outside fades into a blur. Ethan picks up his pastry, eyeing it as if it holds the secrets of the universe.

"Here's to spontaneous encounters and messy beginnings," he says, raising his éclair as if it were a glass of champagne.

"Cheers," I reply, clinking mine against his with a mock seriousness, and we both take a big bite. The taste explodes in my mouth—a symphony of rich chocolate and airy cream that makes me forget about the earlier chaos.

"So," Ethan says, licking chocolate from his thumb and making my heart flutter in an entirely unanticipated way, "what's a floral designer like you doing in a café like this, spilling coffee and stealing pastries?"

"A floral designer like me?" I ask, arching an eyebrow. "Is that supposed to imply that I don't belong in a café like this?"

"Not at all! I just meant that you strike me as someone who prefers their mornings filled with flowers and sunshine rather than caffeine and chaos," he replies, a teasing glint in his eye.

I take a moment to consider his words, the unexpected warmth of his curiosity wrapping around me like the petals of my favorite blooms. "You're not wrong. I'm usually knee-deep in petals and arranging vases, but today seemed like a good day for a little adventure. Life can't always be about order and symmetry, right?"

His gaze sharpens, intrigued. "Adventure, huh? Is that what this morning has been for you? An adventure?"

"Absolutely," I say, leaning in slightly, my tone conspiratorial. "Every day I deliver flowers, I wonder if I'll stumble upon something extraordinary. Today, I just didn't expect to trip over a handsome man in a coffee shop."

He laughs, a sound rich and genuine, as he studies me through the remnants of chocolate coating his lips. "Well, I promise I'm not always this charming. You caught me on a good day, clearly."

"Oh, I'm sure it's not just the suit." I roll my eyes playfully, glancing at the dark stains still visible against the pristine fabric. "You're hiding a bit of mischief under that polished exterior, aren't you?"

"Me? Mischief?" His eyes glint with humor, but there's an intensity there, too—something deeper lurking just beneath the surface. "I prefer to think of myself as a man of mystery. You know, the kind who orders a double espresso and reads philosophical novels during lunch breaks."

I snort, unable to keep the amusement at bay. "You're a businessman, aren't you? What's your brand of 'mystery'? Suits and coffee stains?"

Ethan leans back in his chair, hands clasped behind his head, a self-satisfied grin spreading across his face. "You know, you're sharper than I expected. Yes, I am in business, but it's more than just suits. I run a tech startup. The 'mystery' part is figuring out how to keep everyone happy while wrangling algorithms that rarely cooperate."

"Tech, huh?" I say, pretending to mull over this revelation. "Does that make you an IT wizard or just a glorified coffee addict?"

He laughs again, this time a little harder, shaking his head. "I suppose a bit of both. But honestly, if I didn't find a way to enjoy the chaos, I'd drown in spreadsheets and server issues."

"Ah, so you're a fellow chaos navigator!" I tease, taking another bite of my éclair. "Let's call this meeting an exploration into the world of mishaps, then. Here's to both of us dancing on the edge of disaster."

"Indeed," he agrees, raising his pastry like a trophy. "And to finding unexpected allies in the most unlikely of places."

A comfortable silence stretches between us as we devour our éclairs, the mess and laughter of the morning gradually fading into a pleasant background hum. I find myself stealing glances at Ethan, intrigued not only by the ease of our conversation but by the way his laughter feels like a balm against the chaos of my day. There's a depth in those blue eyes, a flicker of something that suggests he's seen more than his share of life's messiness.

"Okay, Cora," he says, breaking the comfortable quiet. "Tell me, what's the most outrageous floral arrangement you've ever created? I want to hear about the moment that made you think, 'Yep, I'm definitely the crazy floral lady.'"

A grin spreads across my face, and I lean forward, ready to share a story that's been tucked away, waiting for the right moment to bloom. "You have no idea what you've just unleashed."

As I lean in, poised to share the story of my most outrageous floral arrangement, I catch the mischievous spark in Ethan's eyes, and for a moment, I forget the chaos of the morning. I take a deep breath, ready to unearth the wildest moment of my career. "Picture this: a wedding in the middle of a vineyard, sun setting in the background like it's auditioning for a painting, and I'm tasked with creating a centerpiece that could rival Mother Nature herself."

Ethan leans closer, his interest palpable. "Go on."

"I decided that no ordinary arrangement would do. I went for a living table—a massive spread of flowers and greenery that would make even the most jaded florist swoon. I had roses, peonies, eucalyptus, and—here's the kicker—grapes hanging from the vine as if they were part of the arrangement. You know, because vineyard," I explain, waving my hand in a dramatic flourish.

"Sounds ambitious. How did it go?" he asks, a teasing smile curving his lips.

"Well, it was all going perfectly until the moment I realized I hadn't accounted for the wind." I roll my eyes, remembering how naive I'd been. "It was like a scene from a disaster movie. The gusts picked up right as the guests were seated, sending half of my hard work flying like confetti."

"No," Ethan gasps, his eyes wide in mock horror. "Not the flowers!"

"Yes! The flowers! They were scattering everywhere! I had one bridesmaid trying to catch rogue peonies while the groomsmen looked on, amused, as I chased after a runaway vine. I was practically wrestling a bouquet while the photographer captured the entire debacle for posterity."

Ethan bursts into laughter, his joy filling the air around us like sunshine. "That sounds like an Instagram-worthy disaster! I can't believe you survived that."

"Survived? I thrived!" I laugh, leaning back in my chair, exhilarated by the memory. "The guests thought it was a performance art piece. By the end of the night, everyone was coming up to me, raving about how I'd turned an accident into the highlight of the event."

"I can't say I've ever been to a wedding where floral wrestling was on the agenda," he muses, his gaze still fixed on me with an intensity that makes my heart flutter.

The conversation flows naturally, and with every shared story, the atmosphere around us thickens with an unspoken connection. It's intoxicating—like the sugar in our éclairs. Just as I'm about to dive into another ridiculous floral tale, the bell above the bakery door jingles, interrupting the moment. A familiar face walks in, one I definitely didn't expect to see today.

"Cora!" My best friend Maya bursts into the bakery like a whirlwind, her hair bouncing in sync with her exuberant energy. "There you are! I've been looking everywhere for you!"

"Maya?" I respond, startled but also relieved. "What are you doing here?"

"I was just at the florist's picking up some arrangements for the gallery opening tomorrow, and I had this feeling you might be around," she says, her gaze shifting from me to Ethan, her eyes narrowing with suspicion. "And who is this?"

Ethan straightens up, adopting a mock-serious expression, his eyes glinting with amusement. "Ethan. Just a man she collided with, literally."

Maya cocks an eyebrow, a sly smile spreading across her face. "Ah, so you're the unfortunate soul who's had the pleasure of experiencing Cora's trademark chaos firsthand."

I shoot Ethan an apologetic glance. "Sorry about that. This is Maya, my best friend and professional distraction."

"Pleasure," Ethan says, extending a hand toward her, still playing along with the banter.

Maya shakes his hand, but there's a flicker of something behind her cheerful exterior—a protective instinct that I've seen in her before. "So, Ethan, are you planning on sticking around in Cora's life for a while, or is this just a one-time adventure?"

"Depends on how many more coffee spills and pastry disasters she can concoct," he replies smoothly, flashing a charming smile that would make any heart race. "So far, I'd say I'm enjoying the ride."

Maya's eyes narrow further, and I can practically see the gears turning in her mind as she sizes him up. "You're not just some random guy, are you? What's your angle?"

"Maya!" I exclaim, mortified by her directness. "He's just a client I spilled coffee on, for crying out loud!"

"Just a client, huh? We'll see about that," she says, still assessing Ethan, and I can't help but roll my eyes.

Ethan chuckles, unfazed. "I promise, I'm not here to steal her flowers—or her heart, for that matter." He shoots me a quick glance, his eyes twinkling with a hint of mischief.

Maya watches us closely, her expression a mix of curiosity and concern. "Well, I hope you know what you're getting into. Cora's flowers are her babies. Treat them right, or you might end up wrestling an arrangement yourself."

I snicker at that, imagining Ethan covered in petals and foliage, a sight that's both absurd and strangely appealing. "He survived one disaster; I think he'll be okay."

The atmosphere shifts slightly, as if the air has thickened with an underlying tension. Maya's presence brings a sense of reality crashing down around me, reminding me of the life I've built—a life that is orderly, chaotic, and predictable all at once.

"Speaking of disasters," Maya continues, her voice suddenly serious, "have you heard from Derek lately?"

The question lands like a lead balloon between us, sucking the air out of the joyful bubble we had just created. I wince, memories of my last relationship flashing through my mind like a lightning storm.

"No, and I'm not exactly itching to hear from him," I reply, forcing a smile that doesn't quite reach my eyes. "I think we're done here."

Maya's brow furrows, and she seems to be weighing her words carefully. "Cora, I just want to make sure you're okay. I know you put on a brave face, but—"

"I'm fine," I cut in, a little more sharply than intended. "Really." I turn to Ethan, desperate to steer the conversation back to lighter topics. "You know what? We should probably—"

Just as I'm about to change the subject, the bell above the door jingles again, this time heralding the arrival of a familiar face that makes my stomach drop—a face I'd hoped to avoid.

Derek steps inside, his eyes scanning the room before locking onto mine. His presence feels like an unwelcome storm cloud, darkening the sun-drenched space. "Cora," he calls, his voice dripping with feigned innocence. "Fancy seeing you here."

Ethan stiffens beside me, and I can feel the tension radiating off him like heat waves. This wasn't how I envisioned this morning going. The vibrant, joyful energy that had flowed between Ethan and me comes to an abrupt halt, replaced by a heavy, uncomfortable silence that blankets the air.

"Great," I mutter under my breath, watching as Derek strides toward our table, a confident smirk plastered on his face. This was the last thing I needed.

Ethan shifts in his seat, and I can sense the protective instinct bubbling just beneath the surface. "Do you want me to—" he starts, but I cut him off, panic surging through me.

"No. I'll handle it," I reply, even though the truth is, I'm not sure how. Derek's presence threatens to unravel the delightful chaos I had just found myself wrapped in, and I can feel the weight of expectation settling heavily on my shoulders.

As he approaches, a sense of urgency fills the air, pulling me into an unexpected confrontation. I take a deep breath, trying to regain my composure, but the words escape me. The last thing I expected today was to have my past collide with my present—and with Ethan right there beside me, a new element of complication that I hadn't anticipated.

Derek leans against the table, his eyes scanning my face as if searching for a reaction. "Looks like you've moved on to bigger and better things, huh? Coffee spills and mysterious strangers?"

His taunting words wrap around me like a vine, squeezing tight, and I fight against the instinct to flinch. I can't let him have this moment. Not now. Not when I've finally found a spark of something unexpected.

Ethan's gaze hardens, and I can see him weighing his options, ready to jump into the fray. I can almost feel the electric tension between us, like a live wire about to snap.

"Who invited you?" I shoot back, my voice steadier than I feel. "I thought we were done playing games."

Derek chuckles, a low, mocking sound that grates against my nerves. "Oh, but I didn't get the memo about your little café rendezvous. Care to introduce me to your new friend?"

I glance at Ethan, and in that moment, I know that everything is about to change. How I respond now could set the tone for not just the rest of this encounter but the potential for something real and meaningful with Ethan.

"Ethan," I say, my voice steady despite the chaos swirling in my head, "this is Derek, my ex."

The words hang in the air, thick with unspoken tension, as Ethan's expression shifts,

Chapter 2: The Invitation

The invitation, embossed with elegant gold lettering, feels heavier than a stack of lead weights in my hand. Ethan Whitmore. The name reverberates through my mind, striking chords of nostalgia that I'd rather leave undisturbed. Just two months until he ties the knot, and I, the ever-reliable wedding planner, am to orchestrate this grand event. My stomach knots into a pretzel as I think of the countless weddings I've managed, each with their own unique charm, yet none stirs the mixture of dread and excitement swirling within me now. This time, it's different. This time, it's Ethan.

I allow my eyes to roam over the delicate script again, tracing the letters as if they might lead me to some hidden understanding. The invitation isn't just an announcement; it feels like a shackle, binding me to the memory of that fleeting moment in the coffee shop. I can still recall the heady aroma of roasted beans, the soft clinking of ceramic cups, and the quiet hum of conversations drifting in and out like the steam from my espresso. He stood there, his dark hair tousled, his blue eyes alive with laughter, as if the world was just an amusing riddle waiting for the punchline. It was a serendipitous encounter that has since morphed into a persistent echo in my mind, impossible to ignore.

I push the thoughts away, clutching the invitation tighter as I walk to my office desk, a sanctuary littered with mood boards, swatches of fabric, and photographs of smiling couples. My laptop glows softly, the screen lighting up with reminders and emails, but for once, I'm distracted. My usual buoyancy dims under the weight of this assignment. I remind myself that I'm a professional—a wizard of matrimony, a conjurer of blissful celebrations. Planning Ethan's wedding should be no different than any other. But as I inhale the faint scent of jasmine from the candle burning on my desk, I know this isn't just another job. The knot in my stomach tightens as I realize it's Ethan's wedding. Ethan, who makes my heart race in ways I've long since buried under deadlines and checklists.

The morning drags on, each tick of the clock echoing the anxious drumming in my chest. I should be poring over venue options and floral arrangements, but my mind keeps wandering back to him. The moment when our eyes met, the laughter we shared over spilled coffee, and the peculiar connection that sparked so unexpectedly. Could it be that he felt it too, that fleeting warmth, or was I simply romanticizing a moment that was never meant to blossom?

By the time I arrive at our scheduled meeting, my palms are clammy and my heart is performing a rather frantic tango. The venue we've chosen—a sprawling estate with ivy-covered walls and manicured gardens—provides a stunning backdrop, but it does little to calm my nerves. I step inside, greeted by the soft rustle of fabric and the chatter of wedding planners already bustling about, their conversations swirling around me like leaves caught in a breeze.

I spot Ethan standing near the grand fireplace, his back turned to me, but I can feel the magnetic pull of his presence. It's ridiculous how a mere silhouette can conjure such vivid emotions. His laughter drifts toward me, warm and rich, as he exchanges pleasantries with a member of the staff. The sight sends my heart into a wild flutter, and I take a moment to gather myself, inhaling deeply, the scent of fresh blooms filling my lungs.

When he finally turns, that familiar grin lights up his face, and the world around us seems to fade. "There you are! I was beginning to think I'd have to plan this wedding without my planner," he teases, his voice smooth like velvet, wrapping around me and momentarily soothing my frayed nerves.

"Not a chance," I reply, forcing a confident smile. "I've got more enthusiasm for this wedding than I have for my morning coffee, and that's saying something."

"Coffee is life," he agrees, chuckling, his eyes sparkling with mischief. The warmth between us crackles, and I remind myself that I am here to be a professional. "Let's get started, shall we?"

As we dive into the details, I try to maintain a steady rhythm, flipping through the meticulously organized binder I've brought along. His opinions on florals and cake flavors flow freely, each suggestion colored with his charming wit. But as I speak, I find it increasingly difficult to ignore the lingering glances he casts my way. There's an electricity in the air, something more than mere camaraderie—a lingering heat that dances just at the edge of our conversation.

"Tell me you at least have a favorite flower, so I can try to work some of your preferences in," I say, trying to keep my tone light as I pull up options on my tablet. His brow furrows thoughtfully, and for a moment, the playful banter pauses.

"Honestly, I've never given it much thought," he admits, leaning back against the plush couch, his gaze fixed intently on me. "But I trust you to make the right choices."

There it is again—the way he looks at me, like I'm a puzzle he's eager to solve. I feel myself blushing, and I quickly glance down, pretending to examine the screen. How do I navigate this delicate dance, the one that straddles the line between professionalism and something far more dangerous? This isn't just about flowers or seating arrangements; it's about emotions I can't afford to entertain. Yet, with each passing moment, I can't shake the feeling that our connection is far more intricate than the plans laid out before us.

The meeting unfolds like a carefully choreographed dance, each detail poised to distract me from the simmering tension beneath our polished conversation. As Ethan leans back, his fingers absently toying with a pencil on the coffee table, I can't help but notice how the sunlight filters through the tall windows, casting a warm glow that outlines his features. He looks relaxed, yet there's an intensity in his gaze that catches me off guard. I glance down at my meticulously organized binder, flipping pages that suddenly feel meaningless.

"So, about the color palette," I begin, trying to steer the conversation back to business, but my voice trembles slightly, betraying my inner turmoil. "I was thinking soft pastels for the flowers, something that complements the venue's vintage charm. Maybe blush pinks, muted lavenders?"

Ethan's lips quirk up at the corners. "Blush pink? Is that the color of love? Or just the color of a toddler's birthday party?" His playful banter nudges me out of my spiraling thoughts, the corners of my mouth tugging into a reluctant smile.

"Hey now," I counter, feigning indignation, "blush pink is a timeless classic. It says, 'I'm sophisticated but also willing to eat a cupcake with sprinkles.'"

He chuckles, and the sound ripples through me, easing the tautness in my chest. "Alright, I'll concede. Let's go with blush pink, but I want a bold accent color—something unexpected, like electric blue. That'll really throw people off."

"Electric blue?" I laugh, shaking my head. "You want your wedding to look like a high school dance gone rogue?"

"Why not?" he replies with a devil-may-care grin. "Life's too short for boring weddings."

My heart skips at the challenge in his tone. Here is this man, on the precipice of a new chapter in his life, yet he is so comfortable, so effortlessly engaging. The back and forth, the playful jabs, are like a magnetic pull I can't resist. "Fine," I concede. "Let's leave the shocking colors to the actual dance floor. We can save the blue for the groom's socks."

As we continue to bounce ideas back and forth, I momentarily forget the reality of our situation—the wedding, the bride, the impending commitment. Instead, I'm lost in the thrill of collaboration. Our discussions meander through floral arrangements, cake designs, and even guest list drama, with Ethan sharing humorous anecdotes about his family that make me laugh until my cheeks hurt.

But as the conversation shifts toward his fiancée, a familiar knot tightens in my stomach. I can't shake the thought that I'm helping him plan a celebration for someone who isn't me. A dull ache settles in my chest as I contemplate the reality of my role, the professional façade cracking ever so slightly. I glance up to see Ethan's expression shift, and in that moment, the laughter fades, replaced by something deeper.

"Hey," he says softly, breaking the tension that has slipped between us like an unwelcome intruder. "Are you okay? You seem... I don't know, distant."

I force a smile, trying to dismiss the weight of his concern. "Of course! Just thinking about logistics. Weddings are complicated, you know?"

He studies me for a moment, his blue eyes searching mine as if trying to unlock a secret I'm unwilling to share. "Complicated, yeah, but I meant more than that. You look like you've just received some bad news."

The concern etched on his face tugs at my heartstrings. "I promise, I'm fine. It's just—weddings bring out a lot of emotions, and sometimes it's hard to juggle it all." The half-truth feels safe enough, yet I can't shake the feeling that he sees right through me.

Ethan nods slowly, the corner of his mouth twitching up again. "You should be the one getting married, you know. You clearly have a gift for this. You're like a wedding whisperer."

"Wedding whisperer?" I chuckle. "I think you've been drinking too much coffee. I'm just a planner trying not to turn into a bridezilla."

"Maybe I should just get a bridezilla shirt made for you," he teases, leaning closer, the teasing lilt in his voice sparking a different kind of heat between us.

"Only if you wear a matching one that says 'Groomzilla,'" I shoot back, grateful for the humor that lightens the weight of unspoken truths.

Our laughter mingles in the air, and for a brief moment, the chaos of planning fades into the background. But the reality creeps back in, heavier than before. "So, about the bride," I say, trying to reign in my spiraling thoughts. "Have you discussed the guest list yet? I have some ideas about how to manage seating arrangements based on, you know, family dynamics."

Ethan leans back again, running a hand through his hair as he sighs. "Honestly? It's a minefield. My family can be... intense, and my fiancée's parents are even worse. They have their own agenda. I just want everyone to get along, but I fear a showdown at the dinner table."

"You know what they say—keep the peace or end up with a food fight," I quip, trying to lighten the mood.

"Good advice," he replies, his tone turning serious again. "It just feels overwhelming. Sometimes I wish I could just elope and skip all the drama."

"Maybe you should," I suggest, my voice softer. "Focus on what matters—the two of you. The wedding is about your love, not about impressing everyone else."

He studies me for a moment, the weight of my words hanging between us. "What do you think would happen if I actually did that?"

My heart races, caught in the thrill of possibility. "Probably a lot of disappointed family members. But at the end of the day, who cares? It's your life, Ethan. Live it how you want."

His gaze flickers back to mine, and for a heartbeat, it feels like the world around us has faded into oblivion, leaving just the two of us in this fragile bubble of connection. "You're right," he says softly. "It's just hard to break tradition, you know? Everyone has expectations."

"Expectations can be exhausting," I agree, my heart pounding as I wonder if he realizes how deeply this conversation is resonating with me. How much I wish I were the one he was planning for, how much I long to challenge the traditions that bind us.

He leans forward, his voice low. "Sometimes, I think you'd be the one who could help me navigate it all if I did decide to elope."

The weight of his words hangs in the air, and I feel a flicker of hope blooming in my chest, unexpected and fierce. My heart races, but I quickly swallow it down, knowing this is all a mirage. "You'd have to leave me out of that—wedding whisperers don't elope. We stay and plan!"

"Right," he laughs, but his eyes remain locked onto mine, leaving me to wonder if he sees what I see. Or if he simply sees the planner, the professional dedicated to making his wedding a success, even as my heart silently screams for something more.

The laughter lingers like the fading notes of a song, but the air around us is thick with unspoken words. I can see the flicker of uncertainty in Ethan's eyes, a mixture of longing and hesitation that mirrors my own turmoil. It's as if we've crossed a line in our playful banter, one that separates friendly planning from something more profound, something that threatens to complicate everything.

"Anyway," I say, clearing my throat, "let's get back to the seating arrangements. We want to avoid a 'family reunion' situation that resembles a reality TV show, right?" I manage a half-hearted chuckle, trying to shake off the tension that now hangs like a veil between us.

He nods, but I can tell his mind is still dancing around the weight of our earlier conversation. "Yeah, I think we should try to keep my mother away from my future in-laws as much as possible.

Last time they met, it turned into a debate about the best way to prepare a Thanksgiving turkey, and I think the salad got involved somehow."

"Do I even want to know how?" I ask, amused and slightly horrified at the prospect.

"Let's just say the salad ended up as collateral damage," he replies, a wry smile forming on his lips. "We'll have to schedule the seating with military precision."

"Got it. So, strategically place your mother far enough away from the salad. Check." I scribble furiously on my notepad, pretending to take detailed notes when all I can think about is how effortlessly he makes me laugh. "Now, what about your friends? Are they the kind of crew that would turn a toast into a roast?"

"Oh, absolutely. If I don't have to wear a fireproof suit during the speeches, I consider it a success." He leans back, clearly enjoying the banter. "In fact, I think I'll have a running tally for every roast joke made. The winner gets a free round of drinks at the reception."

I laugh, the tension between us momentarily forgotten. "That could be your best idea yet. Just make sure to have a solid plan in place for the drink count, or the dance floor might turn into a circus."

"Trust me," he says, raising an eyebrow, "a circus is exactly what I'm hoping for. Who needs elegance when you can have a conga line with flamingo hats?"

The idea is ludicrous enough to make me snort. "Now that's a wedding I'd love to plan." I take a sip of water, grateful for the lightness he's infused into our discussion, yet I can't shake the feeling that this laughter is merely a temporary distraction.

As the meeting progresses, we delve into the specifics of floral arrangements and menu tastings. I revel in the details, crafting a vision that somehow feels impossibly vibrant and yet entirely out of reach. I steal glances at Ethan, who remains enthusiastic, his passion for this event as palpable as the growing tension in the air between us. Every time our eyes lock, my breath catches, and I wonder if he feels it too—the unspoken connection that simmers just below the surface.

"Okay," I say, gathering my thoughts. "Let's wrap up for today. I'll send you an email with the timeline and next steps, and we can meet again next week to finalize everything."

"Sounds good," he replies, his voice casual, but there's a flicker of something deeper there, an urgency that makes my heart race. "Hey, before you go…" He hesitates, running a hand through his hair, a nervous habit that makes my stomach flutter. "Can I ask you something?"

"Sure, shoot," I say, trying to sound casual even as my heart pounds in anticipation.

"What's your ideal wedding?" The question hangs in the air, heavy with meaning.

My mind races. "Um, I guess I've never really thought about it," I respond, fumbling for an answer. "But I suppose I'd want something intimate, maybe a cozy venue filled with twinkling lights. Lots of laughter, good food, and people who genuinely care about each other."

"Sounds perfect," he muses, his eyes narrowing as he studies me. "But what about the person? Who would you want to be standing next to?"

The question strikes a chord deep within me, and I hesitate, caught off guard. I force a smile, pretending the question doesn't sink into my chest like a stone. "Honestly? It's more about the day and the memories than the person. I believe it's the celebration of love that matters."

"Right," he says, though his tone carries a weight of disappointment. I see the light in his eyes dim slightly, and I instantly regret my guarded response. "But you're a romantic at heart, aren't you?"

"Maybe," I say, taking a breath. "Or maybe I'm just a wedding planner who's seen one too many relationship train wrecks. It makes you a bit cynical after a while."

"Cynical, huh?" He smirks, crossing his arms. "And here I thought you were just a wedding fairy godmother."

"Fairy godmother?" I scoff, raising an eyebrow. "Please. More like a wedding witch. I cast spells to make the day perfect, but I'm still left with all the chaos that comes afterward."

Ethan laughs, the sound rich and genuine. "Maybe I'll have to think of you as my wedding witch then. Do I get a wand with that?"

"Only if you agree to wear a matching hat," I tease, but the air between us shifts again, the playful banter giving way to an undeniable tension.

"Okay," he says suddenly, his voice dropping to a serious tone that pulls me closer to the edge of something monumental. "I need to tell you something, and I don't want you to freak out."

"Now you're just making me nervous," I reply, a laugh escaping my lips, though my heart races with trepidation. "What is it?"

He takes a deep breath, leaning in slightly as if the very act will solidify whatever revelation he's about to share. "The thing is, I think we need to talk about how my fiancée feels about... you."

I blink, the words sinking in with a mix of confusion and alarm. "About me? But why—"

"Let me finish," he interrupts, urgency lacing his voice. "I don't want you to misunderstand, but I've caught her making comments about how she thinks we're too close during the planning. She might think I'm developing feelings for you."

A chill runs down my spine, and I feel the blood drain from my face. "Wait, she thinks what?" My heart races as his words settle heavily between us, a realization hitting me with the force of a tidal wave.

"I don't know how to explain it," Ethan continues, his voice low but urgent. "She's been feeling insecure, and I don't want her to think that there's anything between us. I mean, there's nothing, right?"

Panic flares within me. "Ethan, it's just business! I'm your wedding planner, that's it. There's nothing between us!" But even as I say the words, I can feel the weight of my own heart's longing bearing down, twisting into something uncomfortable.

"I know," he insists, desperation creeping into his tone. "But it's complicated. I don't want to lose her, and I certainly don't want to lose you as my planner."

"Then what do you suggest?" I whisper, feeling a mix of dread and exhilaration at the chaos unfurling around us. "Do we just pretend this never happened? That we don't feel anything?"

"Maybe," he says slowly, uncertainty lining his words. "But how do we do that when every time we're together, it feels like this?"

The air crackles between us, charged with tension, and I can feel the ground shifting beneath me. I want to scream, to run, to ignore everything spiraling out of control, but I can't move. "Ethan, I..."

Suddenly, the door swings open, and in walks a woman with an air of confidence, an unmistakable presence. She has striking features, dark hair framing her face, and an expression that says she owns the room. It's obvious she's here for Ethan, and as she strides toward us, I realize with a sinking heart that I recognize her from Ethan's social media—the fiancée.

"Ethan, there you are! I've been looking everywhere for you," she calls, and the playful spark in our conversation is snuffed out, replaced by a cold wave of reality crashing in.

My heart thuds painfully in my chest as I turn my gaze to Ethan, who looks equally torn, caught between two worlds.

"Um, hey, Lila. We were just—"

She cuts him off, her bright smile faltering for a moment as she assesses the scene, her eyes narrowing slightly as they flicker between us. "Planning, I see?"

In that instant, the fragile tension bursts like a bubble, leaving me reeling, and I'm left with the uneasy realization that the secret between us might never see the light of day.

Chapter 3: Lines That Blur

The smell of fresh coffee mingled with the vibrant scent of lilies, filling the air with a sweetness that wrapped around me like a comforting blanket. The little café on the corner of Elm and Maple had become our unofficial meeting spot, a quaint sanctuary where laughter and chatter intermingled with the clinking of cups. I tucked a stray hair behind my ear, the slight warmth from the late-morning sun pouring through the window casting a golden hue over the polished wooden table where Ethan and I sat, deliberating the nuances of wedding flowers.

"Jasmine is too strong for a spring wedding," I said, trying to keep my tone light as I flipped through the pages of a glossy catalog. "You want something delicate, like peonies or daisies. They whisper sweetly instead of shouting." My gaze flicked up to meet Ethan's, catching the faintest glimmer of amusement in his deep brown eyes.

"I thought you liked bold statements," he replied, a teasing lilt in his voice that sent an unexpected flutter through my stomach. "Didn't you say once that life should be lived like a fireworks display?"

"Fireworks burn out," I countered, my voice a tad too sharp, "and sometimes they leave behind a mess." I glanced away quickly, feeling the blush creep up my cheeks. The way he was looking at me made it difficult to breathe, as if the air between us thickened, electrified with unspoken words and buried desires. Ethan's presence was magnetic; his charisma wrapped around me like a silken thread, weaving its way into my thoughts.

With a sigh, I closed the catalog and pushed it aside, feeling a pang of frustration. I had agreed to help him with the wedding plans out of friendship, a solid and uncomplicated bond. But the more time we spent together, the more I felt that friendship fraying at the edges. It wasn't just the way he made me laugh or the way he remembered the small things, like how I took my coffee—half and half with just a hint of sugar—but rather the magnetic pull I felt whenever he leaned in just a bit closer.

Ethan rubbed the back of his neck, a nervous habit I had grown accustomed to over our meetings. "What about these?" He gestured toward a particularly lush arrangement of white roses and greenery. "Classic and elegant, right?"

"Too predictable," I said, a playful smile breaking across my face despite the tightness in my chest. "A wedding should feel like an adventure, not just a checklist."

"Are you saying my wedding is going to be boring?" He feigned shock, raising an eyebrow, and for a moment, the tension dissipated into laughter that echoed against the walls.

"Not boring, just...traditional. You know that's not your style. You're more of a 'spontaneous road trip' kind of guy, not 'a neatly pressed suit' type."

His laughter faded, and for a moment, his expression shifted, becoming contemplative. "You think so?"

"I know so," I said, allowing myself to lean in slightly, drawn to the vulnerability that flickered across his face. "You need that spark, something that's uniquely you."

"And you think I can find that?"

"Of course," I replied, my heart racing as I noticed the way his gaze lingered on me, searching and open, as if he were attempting to read between the lines of an unspoken story.

The moment stretched, suspended like a delicate thread in the air between us, both thrilling and terrifying. I should have pulled away, reminded him of the fiancé waiting at home, but I couldn't. The longing in his eyes mirrored my own, and it ignited a flame of hope that danced at the edges of my consciousness, whispering sweet nothings that I dared not acknowledge.

"Can I ask you something?" he finally said, breaking the silence that felt thick with anticipation.

"Always," I replied, trying to keep my voice steady, though my heart was pounding in my chest, a wild drum echoing the conflict within me.

"Do you think it's wrong to want something different, something unexpected, even if it means stepping outside the lines?"

The question hung between us like a curtain waiting to be drawn back. I swallowed hard, suddenly aware of the stakes. "Different doesn't mean wrong, Ethan. But it can be complicated. Life isn't just a fairytale."

"Maybe it should be."

A flicker of something unnameable ignited in his eyes, and I felt my breath catch. Was he talking about the wedding or something much deeper, something that threatened to unravel the careful fabric of our lives? I looked away, focusing on the last dregs of my coffee, the bitter taste mirroring the chaos swirling in my heart.

"Lily," he said softly, and the way my name rolled off his tongue sent shivers down my spine. "You've always been different. You see the world in a way that's fresh and honest. That's what I admire about you."

His words sank in, filling the air with warmth, but a gnawing fear clenched at my insides. "You don't know what you're saying," I managed, though the hesitation in my voice sounded like a desperate plea.

"Maybe I do," he replied, leaning closer, his voice barely above a whisper, filled with the weight of everything unsaid. "Maybe I just don't want to ignore it anymore."

And that was when I realized: the lines we were dancing around were blurring into a haze of possibility, and it felt like both the most thrilling adventure and the most dangerous gamble I had ever faced.

I could hardly focus on the floral arrangements that day, my mind a chaotic whirlpool of thoughts and unbidden desires. The café buzzed around us, oblivious to the storm brewing at our table. Outside, a gentle breeze ruffled the leaves of the nearby trees, but inside, the air felt thick and charged, almost electric. Ethan leaned back in his chair, fingers steepled under his chin, his brow furrowed in concentration, and I fought the urge to reach out and smooth away the worry lines etched across his forehead.

"Okay, what if we did a pop of color?" I suggested, attempting to steer us back on track. "What about bright tulips against a backdrop of white?"

He seemed to consider it, though his eyes flicked to mine, and for a moment, I lost my breath. "I mean, tulips do have a certain charm. A whimsical vibe. But I always pictured you as more of a wildflower person—spontaneous and a little unpredictable."

My heart raced at the implication. "Wildflowers are beautiful," I replied, hoping I sounded composed rather than flustered. "They're free and a little chaotic, which is great if you don't mind a little mess."

"Mess can be good." He smiled, leaning forward, his elbows resting on the table, his expression serious yet playful. "Some of the best things in life come from a bit of chaos."

"Like this conversation?" I quipped, feigning nonchalance, but my pulse quickened. The air around us seemed to vibrate with unspoken words, each moment stretching like taffy, both tantalizing and terrifying.

"Exactly." He lowered his voice, a conspiratorial grin playing on his lips. "And maybe I'm just a little too good at creating chaos. You should see my apartment. It's a war zone."

"Are we talking socks on the floor or something worse?"

"Definitely socks, but also dishes that have formed their own ecosystem in the sink. It's a delicate balance, really." He laughed, the sound rich and warm, and I couldn't help but smile back, despite the growing tension.

"What about your fiancée?" I asked, trying to inject some logic into this surreal moment. The words tasted bitter on my tongue, but I pushed through. "Does she know about this chaos?"

The light in Ethan's eyes dimmed slightly, and I regretted bringing it up. "She thinks I'm 'quirky' in a charming way," he replied, the hint of sarcasm in his tone revealing a deeper frustration. "I'm not sure if that's a compliment or just a gentle way to say I'm a mess."

"It's both, I think," I replied, attempting to lighten the mood. "But it's one thing to be quirky and another to be chaotic."

He paused, a shadow crossing his face as he contemplated my words. "Maybe I'm both," he said quietly, and there was something in his tone that sent a chill racing down my spine. The laughter had faded, replaced by an unsettling gravity.

"Chaos can be beautiful," I offered gently, the moment tinged with a vulnerability that both scared and thrilled me. "But it's also a choice, and sometimes... choices come with consequences."

"I'm aware," he said, a flicker of something darker lurking behind his eyes. "But sometimes those choices are hard to ignore, you know? Like a moth drawn to a flame."

There it was, that weight again, a stark reminder of what hung in the balance. My heart pounded as I looked into his eyes, and I could see the struggle warring within him. We were standing at the edge of something profound, something that could either shatter our worlds or bind them together in unexpected ways.

Just then, the bell above the café door chimed, breaking the tension like a pin popping a balloon. In walked a couple, laughter trailing behind them, their joy infectious. I tried to reclaim my composure, but the sight of them felt like a stark contrast to the conflict simmering at our table.

"See?" I said, gesturing toward them. "That's what a real couple looks like—full of laughter, not tension."

"Maybe," Ethan replied, his gaze still distant, "but how many couples do you think sit in silence, wishing they could talk about something deeper than just the weather or dinner plans?"

"Point taken." I took a deep breath, desperately seeking to shift the energy. "So, flowers... tulips. They're bright and cheerful. We can get your future wife some funky, mismatched vases to accentuate that chaos."

Ethan chuckled, a hint of relief washing over his features. "Okay, let's go with that. But only if we can agree on one thing."

"What's that?"

"No daisies."

"Why not daisies?" I asked, genuinely intrigued.

"They remind me of grade school, and I had a really embarrassing crush on my teacher. It was traumatic," he said, a teasing glint in his eye.

"Traumatic? That sounds like a story worth hearing," I shot back, curious.

He leaned back, considering. "Alright, but only if you promise to share an equally embarrassing story of your own."

"Deal," I said, both excited and apprehensive about the prospect of peeling back the layers of our carefully constructed personas. "So, what happened?"

He paused, as if weighing the gravity of the moment. "It was during a field trip to the zoo. I was in love with Ms. Carter. I even made a 'Get Well Soon' card for her when she broke her leg, but the other kids teased me. They said I was her 'little boyfriend.' I was mortified."

I laughed, the sound bubbling up freely. "That is adorable! But why daisies?"

"Because when I see them, I just remember that cringeworthy moment and how I tried to impress her by bringing her a bouquet I picked from the schoolyard. Spoiler alert: they were mostly weeds."

"Aw, that's the sweetest worst story I've ever heard," I said, unable to suppress my grin. "You were clearly a romantic even then."

"Or just hopelessly naïve."

"Maybe a bit of both," I offered, but as the laughter faded, I felt the familiar tension creeping back in. The easy camaraderie was slipping through my fingers, and I was painfully aware of the line we were straddling.

"Lily..." he began, the softness in his tone pulling me back. I could feel the gravity of his gaze, and it took everything in me to maintain eye contact. "Do you ever wonder what happens when the chaos becomes too much to handle?"

The question hung in the air like an uninvited guest, an intruder in our dance. I didn't have an answer. What I knew was that the closer we danced to the edge of this abyss, the harder it would be to turn back. The world outside continued to swirl with colors and sounds, but inside that little café, we were suspended in our own private turmoil, unsure of how far we were willing to leap into the unknown.

Ethan's question hung like a dense fog, clouding my thoughts and choking out the laughter we'd just shared. The weight of it pressed against my chest, and I had to swallow hard to clear my throat. The walls of the café felt like they were closing in, the cheerful chatter around us muted by the storm brewing between us.

"Do you think it's really possible to ignore the chaos?" I asked, my voice barely above a whisper. I was acutely aware of how close we were sitting, the faint scent of his cologne—a hint of cedar and something warm—filling the small space between us.

He considered my question, his gaze drifting to the window where the sunlight filtered through the leaves, casting playful shadows on the table. "I think we're all trying to navigate a little chaos in our lives. Some of us do it better than others."

I let out a soft laugh, shaking my head. "You've seen my apartment. I can't even pretend to have it all together."

"That's not true," he countered, his eyes sparkling with mischief. "Your apartment has character, like a well-loved book. It tells a story."

"Yeah, a story of a woman who can't keep houseplants alive," I retorted, trying to mask the shiver that ran through me at the thought of him seeing my space—my mess. The very idea felt intimate, and I wanted to clamp down on that thought before it spiraled. "I prefer books to plants. They don't die on you."

"True," he said, his smile shifting into something softer. "But books can also get dusty. Just like people."

My heart raced at his words, at the layers of meaning behind them. Was he trying to tell me something, or was I reading too deeply into innocent conversation? I wanted to push back against the tide of emotion washing over me, but I felt myself being drawn deeper into his orbit.

Just then, the café door swung open, and a gust of wind burst through, bringing with it a small cascade of autumn leaves that danced across the floor. A chill enveloped us, breaking the momentary spell. I shivered, wrapping my arms around myself.

"Guess fall has officially arrived," Ethan remarked, glancing outside. "A fitting metaphor for... all this." He gestured vaguely between us, and I felt the weight of his words sink in.

"Yeah, changing seasons and all," I murmured, my thoughts a jumble of leaves swirling in my mind. "But I prefer spring. It feels more alive."

"Ah, the promise of new beginnings," he said, his voice laced with a wistfulness that made my heart clench. "But sometimes, I think fall has its own beauty. The colors, the crisp air—it's like the world is readying itself for a long sleep."

I wanted to argue, to tell him that even in rest, there was hope, but instead, I found myself leaning in, captivated by the intensity in his eyes. "Maybe we need both," I suggested, my breath catching in my throat. "To appreciate the beauty in every season, even the ones that seem to signal an ending."

Ethan nodded slowly, a serious expression crossing his face. "Sometimes endings can lead to the most unexpected beginnings."

My heart thudded as I realized how his words echoed the very tension between us. We were on the brink of something—something thrilling yet terrifying. I felt the urge to reach out, to bridge the gap that felt impossibly wide yet achingly narrow.

As if sensing the shift in energy, Ethan's gaze fell to our hands resting on the table, mere inches apart. I could almost feel the warmth radiating from him, begging me to close that space. Just as I opened my mouth to speak, his phone buzzed, shattering the moment like glass.

He glanced at the screen and sighed, visibly deflating. "It's Clara," he said, his voice tinged with resignation. "I should answer. She's probably wondering where I am."

"Of course," I said, trying to mask the disappointment. The last remnants of our connection evaporated, replaced by the familiar pang of reality crashing back in. I tried to focus on the sound of his voice as he answered, but my mind wandered, replaying the moments we'd just shared, the unspoken promises lingering like the scent of his cologne in the air.

"Hey, Clara," he said, his tone shifting to a more professional pitch. "Yeah, I'm at the café with Lily... No, we're just going over some last-minute details."

I watched his expression as he spoke, the way his smile faded slightly, how the warmth in his eyes dimmed under her scrutiny. The weight of expectation hung over him, and my heart twisted at the thought of him being trapped in a world that didn't fully embrace who he was.

After a moment, he ended the call, running a hand through his hair in frustration. "Sorry about that," he said, looking sheepish. "I'm trying to keep everything on track, but it feels like I'm constantly juggling."

"It's fine," I replied, forcing a smile, though the disappointment lingered. "I know how demanding wedding planning can be."

He nodded, but the lightness had shifted back into something heavy, something unsaid. "It's just... hard to balance everything sometimes, you know?"

"Especially when you're trying to please everyone," I replied, my voice barely a whisper. "Including yourself."

"Exactly." He leaned back, studying me for a moment. "And that's what makes it all so complicated."

The tension returned, thick and oppressive, wrapping around us like a vine. I could feel the weight of what remained unspoken, the yearning threading through our words, teasing at the edges of something real.

"I should probably get going," I said, reluctantly breaking the spell. "You have a wedding to plan, and I've got a plant rescue mission at home."

He chuckled, but his eyes were serious. "You know, if you ever need help with those plants—"

"Oh, please," I interrupted with a laugh. "If you walk into my apartment, you'll think you've entered a plant graveyard. I wouldn't subject you to that horror."

"Not even for a wildflower adventure?" he teased, but the hint of sadness behind his smile made my heart ache.

"Especially not for a wildflower adventure," I shot back, trying to inject some levity into the moment, though my smile faltered.

As I stood to leave, I hesitated, caught in the gravity of his gaze. "Ethan, can I—"

But before I could finish, the door swung open again, and a figure rushed in, breathless and flustered. It was Clara, Ethan's fiancée, her expression a mix of determination and something else—an urgency that sent a shiver down my spine.

"There you are!" she exclaimed, her eyes darting between us, the air thickening with the weight of unspoken truths. "I've been looking everywhere for you."

I felt my stomach drop as the moment I had been clinging to dissolved in an instant. Clara's gaze flicked to me, and I could see the tension ripple through her, a sudden awareness washing over her like a cold wave.

"Hey, I was just—" Ethan began, but Clara cut him off, her tone sharp. "We need to talk. Now."

I stood frozen, caught in the middle of a whirlwind that threatened to upend everything I had tried to ignore. The atmosphere shifted, crackling with tension, and I felt the fragile threads of our connection snap in an instant.

As Clara ushered Ethan away, her eyes lingering on me with a mix of suspicion and challenge, I was left standing there, my heart racing and mind whirling. I couldn't shake the feeling that the lines we had blurred were about to come crashing down, dragging us all into the chaos we had tried so desperately to avoid.

Chapter 4: Secrets in Shadows

Ethan and Madison had always seemed like the perfect couple, a polished duo against the backdrop of our small town, which was filled with whispers of anticipation for their impending nuptials. Madison, with her cascading blonde hair and radiant smile, glided through life like she owned it, an effortless embodiment of the dream wedding every girl planned in secret. Meanwhile, I watched from the sidelines, my own life a series of mismatched puzzle pieces, always struggling to find the corner pieces that would anchor my picture. As their wedding date loomed closer, the charm that usually enveloped them began to fray, revealing the jagged edges beneath their carefully constructed facade.

One evening, I found myself hiding behind a large potted plant outside the bakery, the tantalizing scent of freshly baked pastries wafting through the air. I had a job to do—deliver the latest batch of cupcakes to their planning meeting—but eavesdropping on their conversation became an unintentional indulgence. I could hear Ethan's voice, normally so full of warmth, now laced with an anxiety that struck a nerve within me. "Madison, we need to talk about the guest list again. There are people you've invited that I just—" He sighed, a defeated sound that hung in the humid air.

"Ethan, this is not the time!" Madison snapped, her voice sharp enough to slice through the tension. "You agreed to this, and now you're backing out? You're acting like a child. Just trust me for once." Her tone was deceptively composed, but the underlying current of desperation was impossible to miss. I leaned in a little closer, hoping to catch a glimpse of the chaos I could feel bubbling beneath the surface.

"Trust you? Madison, we can't invite people who will make my family uncomfortable," he retorted, frustration boiling over. I caught a glimpse of his expression—eyes wide with disbelief, mouth set in a grim line. He looked like he was grappling with something far beyond the seating arrangements. For a fleeting moment, I wondered if there was a crack in the veneer of their perfection, a fissure that could swallow them whole.

As I stepped back, I knocked into the terracotta pot, sending it wobbling precariously before I caught it with a gasp. The sound was enough to draw their attention, and I slipped behind the bakery door, heart racing, chastising myself for being a voyeur in their lives. I busied myself with arranging the treats, hoping the act would distract me from the unsettling feelings that were growing like weeds in my gut. What was supposed to be a joyful occasion was rapidly becoming a cauldron of tensions, and it felt as if I was slowly being pulled into the swirling depths of it all.

The next week unfolded like a series of muted whispers. I found myself exchanging messages with Ethan late at night, conversations that drifted from cake flavors to his ongoing doubts about the wedding. He texted me at odd hours, often while the world slept, his words forming a fragile thread connecting us amidst the chaos. "What do you think about using peonies instead of roses?" he asked one evening, his question hanging in the air like a lifebuoy tossed to a drowning sailor.

"Peonies would be gorgeous," I replied, biting my lip as I realized just how much time I spent pondering his messages. "They're romantic without being too traditional." I had never seen myself as the romantic type, yet here I was, scribbling poetic sentiments over floral arrangements in a flurry of excitement and concern.

"Madison loves roses, though. It's classic," he wrote back, and I could almost hear the weight in his sigh. "I feel like I'm losing her in all of this."

Those words hit me like a shot to the chest. The idea that he could lose her didn't just echo with an air of resignation; it dripped with an emotional honesty that pulled at something deep within me.

I had always viewed my role as a friend, the supportive sidekick to the sparkling couple, but now I could see the weight pressing down on him, the fatigue etched around his eyes when I glimpsed him during our meetings. Suddenly, the questions I had been wrestling with—was I falling for him? What did that even mean in the context of a wedding?—became sharper, more urgent.

One evening, while delivering cupcakes again, I spotted Madison alone on the patio, staring at her phone as if it held the secrets to the universe. I approached hesitantly, unsure of how to breach the sudden awkwardness that permeated the air. "Hey, Madison," I said, trying to keep my tone light. "Everything okay?"

She looked up, her expression shifting from one of frustration to a practiced smile that didn't quite reach her eyes. "Oh, just... wedding stuff, you know? It's overwhelming." Her words danced around the truth, and I sensed the brittle edges of her facade cracking beneath the surface. I wanted to reach out, to offer her an anchor in the chaos, but the tension between us had always felt like a tightrope.

"I can imagine. If you need any help or just someone to vent to, I'm here," I offered, my voice gentle, feeling as if I were throwing a lifeline into choppy waters.

Her smile faltered, and for a moment, her vulnerability shone through. "Thanks, but it's all supposed to be perfect, right?" She glanced away, as if the very word "perfect" burned her tongue. "Maybe it's just... not for me."

That admission hung between us, thick and heavy, and I could see the fractures widening in her carefully curated world. In that moment, a realization struck me: we were all performing, caught in a tragic play we never auditioned for, each trying to portray a role that felt increasingly foreign. I didn't know how to reassure her when I was still wrestling with my own feelings for Ethan, and the delicious thrill that came from our late-night exchanges felt like a betrayal to her anguish.

It was a dangerous game we were playing, one that could unravel all of us, and yet I found myself drawn deeper into the shadows. The wedding was meant to be a celebration, yet it felt more like a countdown to an inevitable explosion, a ticking time bomb cloaked in lace and flowers.

The weekend arrived with the scent of freshly mowed grass mingling with the sweet, sticky aroma of cotton candy from the fairground down the road. I found myself at the bakery, knees propped up on the cool metal stool, contemplating the lopsided cake I was decorating. The wedding was mere weeks away, and each fondant flower felt like a tiny representation of my tangled emotions. Ethan had insisted on a "traditional" wedding cake—three tiers of white frosting with pastel peonies carefully crafted from sugar. But the more I layered the cake, the more I felt the weight of it all, not just the confectionery creation but the emotional turmoil swirling around me.

As I worked, the bell over the bakery door jingled, and I looked up to see Madison striding in, an embodiment of grace wrapped in a floral sundress. Her hair cascaded down her back, catching the sunlight streaming through the windows, and for a moment, she radiated that ethereal bride energy that had enchanted everyone. But today, her smile was tight, as if she were forcing it into existence, and her eyes held a flicker of something that made my stomach twist.

"Hey, I just wanted to check in on the cake," she said, crossing her arms, her demeanor shifting from charming to wary. "Ethan mentioned you were working on it."

"Almost done!" I chirped, summoning every ounce of cheerfulness I could muster. "Just putting the finishing touches on the peonies." The words slipped from my lips like icing, and I motioned toward the cake, which stood, adorned but slightly askew. I chuckled, trying to lighten the mood. "It's more of a modern art piece at this point, really."

Madison's lips quirked up briefly before settling back into a serious line. "You know, it's okay to admit you're overwhelmed. This wedding planning has been a nightmare."

I paused, surprised by her honesty. The tension between us felt like a taut string, ready to snap. "Yeah, it can be a lot. But you're doing great! I mean, look at you. You have everything planned out."

Her gaze flickered, and for a moment, I saw the weight of her exhaustion reflected in her eyes. "That's the thing, though. It feels like everything's planned, but it's just... not right. I'm starting to wonder if I'm the problem."

"Madison, you're not the problem," I assured her, my heart softening. "You're just navigating a lot right now. Weddings are chaotic."

She stepped closer, her voice dropping to a whisper, "Do you ever feel like you're drowning in expectations? Like everyone has this image of who you should be, but you're not sure you fit into it?"

Her words resonated with me, hitting a nerve I hadn't realized was raw. I didn't expect to share this moment, this vulnerable glimpse of the person beneath the perfect exterior. "All the time," I admitted, leaning against the countertop. "I mean, it's like I'm a background character in everyone else's story."

Madison nodded, her expression softening, as if the mask she wore slipped just a fraction. "And yet, here we are, trying to play our parts in this production."

Our shared understanding wrapped around us like a warm embrace, dissolving the tension that had hovered in the air like a storm cloud. I dared to hope we might forge a connection in this chaotic world we inhabited. "Maybe we need to remind each other that we don't have to be perfect," I said, feeling a spark of camaraderie.

She chuckled, and it was a sound I hadn't realized I craved—a genuine laugh. "Right! Maybe we should start a support group for brides and wedding planners: 'Expectations Anonymous.'"

The laughter eased the atmosphere, a momentary reprieve in the whirlwind of wedding madness. But as quickly as it arrived, the lightness faded, replaced by the gravity of our circumstances. Just then, Ethan entered the bakery, a frown creasing his brow as he took in the scene.

"Madison," he said, his voice tight, "we need to talk."

Her smile vanished, replaced by a mask of professionalism. "About the guest list, right?"

"Yeah, about that..." His eyes darted between us, a mixture of concern and frustration etching deeper lines into his face. "Can we step outside?"

The shift in the air was palpable, like the moment before thunder crashes. I stood back, feeling like an intruder, yet anchored in place by the weight of their unresolved tensions. Madison shot me a glance, a flicker of uncertainty crossing her features before she nodded and stepped outside, Ethan following closely behind.

As they walked away, I could hear snippets of their conversation, the hushed intensity of their voices punctuated by sharp exclamations. "This isn't just about you, Madison!" "I'm trying to include everyone! Why can't you just trust me?" I fought the urge to eavesdrop, focusing instead on the delicate sugar flowers that seemed to mock me with their perfection.

The door swung open again, and Ethan returned, his expression a mix of frustration and despair. "Can we just... put a pin in the cake for a second?"

"Sure," I said, my heart racing. "Everything okay?"

"Not even close," he muttered, running a hand through his tousled hair, the very picture of a man caught in a tempest. "We're barely talking, and I don't even know how to fix it. She keeps shutting down."

I wanted to reach out, to tell him that sometimes, love meant navigating the messiness together. "Ethan, relationships aren't easy. Maybe she's just scared."

"Scared of what?" he shot back, frustration spilling over. "This is what she wanted—a perfect wedding, perfect life. It's all supposed to be perfect!"

"Ethan, no one's perfect. Not even Madison." The words slipped out before I could stop them, and his gaze narrowed, considering.

"I know that," he said, the fire in his eyes dimming slightly. "But what do you do when the person you love becomes someone you don't recognize?"

There was a raw honesty in his voice that made my heart ache. "You dig deeper. You talk. You listen."

He was quiet for a moment, a torrent of emotions swirling behind his eyes. "You're good at this. Why can't I be?"

I shrugged, the warmth of his gaze enveloping me. "We all have our strengths, Ethan. Sometimes it takes a little help to find them."

His lips twitched into a half-smile, a flicker of the Ethan I knew before the wedding chaos had begun. "Maybe I should have hired you as a therapist instead of a wedding planner."

"Only if you promise to take the late-night texts down a notch," I joked, and the lightness returned for a moment, allowing us both to breathe. But the undercurrent of tension remained, an invisible barrier that neither of us could quite name.

As the evening wore on, the bakery glowed under the warm light of the setting sun, casting shadows that danced playfully around us. We stood on the precipice of unspoken feelings and unresolved issues, the delicious scent of baked goods mingling with the weight of our unsaid words, each lingering in the air, begging for resolution.

The days slipped by, each one marked by the incessant countdown to the wedding, and with it, the tension escalated like an impending storm. I found myself caught in the eye of this swirling chaos, oscillating between the demands of my role as a wedding planner and the spiraling emotional lives of Ethan and Madison. With every late-night text from Ethan, our conversations grew more personal, layered with hints of frustration and shared secrets that bound us together like the strands of a wedding veil.

One afternoon, as the sun poured through the bakery's front window, illuminating the flour-dusted counters like a spotlight, Madison burst through the door, her usual air of grace replaced by a wildness in her eyes. "We need to talk," she said, her tone urgent, and for a moment, my heart raced in anticipation of the unfiltered honesty that hung in the air.

"About the cake? Or the seating chart?" I asked, trying to keep my voice light despite sensing the weight of her distress.

"More like about Ethan," she said, crossing her arms, an unconscious defensive posture that made me wary. "I don't know how to reach him anymore. It's like he's a stranger."

I nodded, a pit forming in my stomach. "I've noticed he's been… distant."

"Distant? That's putting it mildly. He's completely checked out. One minute, he's excited about our future, and the next, he's staring into space like he's in another universe," she confessed, her voice breaking slightly. "I don't know if it's the wedding or something else, but I can feel him slipping away."

The vulnerability in her admission took me aback. I had been so focused on Ethan's late-night messages that I hadn't considered how Madison felt, trapped in her perfect prison. "Have you talked to him about it?" I asked gently, unsure if my words would provide comfort or fuel to the fire.

"I've tried, but every time I bring it up, he deflects. It's like he's afraid to confront whatever is going on inside his head." She ran a hand through her hair, frustration evident. "And I don't know how to help him. I just want him back."

"Maybe he just needs to feel understood," I suggested. "Sometimes we need to peel back the layers. You're both going through a lot right now."

Madison sighed, her shoulders slumping under the weight of the world. "But what if he's not the same person I fell in love with? What if this wedding is just a cover for everything that's wrong?"

Her words resonated within me, igniting the embers of my own uncertainty. "What if he feels pressured to be perfect for you?" I countered, pushing away the thoughts of my own connection to Ethan. "He might be struggling with that expectation."

Madison looked at me, eyes sharp, searching for something—an affirmation, perhaps, or a lifeline in this swirling sea of doubt. "How do you know so much about relationships? You don't have a fairytale of your own."

Her words hung in the air, tauntingly close to the truth, yet far enough to remind me of my place in this intricate web of emotions. "I may not have a fairytale, but I see what happens when people try to be perfect. It rarely ends well."

Before Madison could respond, the door jingled, and in walked Ethan, his presence instantly shifting the atmosphere. He paused, eyes darting between us, a slight frown creasing his brow. "What's going on?"

"Just discussing wedding stuff," Madison said, a practiced smile plastered on her face. "You know, the usual."

Ethan's gaze softened as he approached her, a protective instinct rising within him. "You okay?"

Madison nodded, but I could see the cracks in her façade, the tension lurking just beneath. "Yeah, just a little stressed, that's all."

As Ethan reached for her hand, I felt like an intruder in their fragile moment. "We'll figure it out together, I promise," he said softly, and something within me twisted painfully at the intimacy of his words.

I busied myself with arranging cookies, trying to focus on the sweet distraction of chocolate chips and sprinkles, but their presence loomed larger than any confection. Every shared glance between them felt like an echo of a future I could only observe from a distance, and the invisible line of tension between us began to constrict further.

Later that evening, while I prepped for the next day's orders, my phone buzzed with a message from Ethan: "Can we talk tonight? I really need to sort some things out." My heart fluttered, a mix of dread and anticipation. I felt like a moth drawn to a flame, knowing the heat would hurt but unable to resist the allure.

Arriving at the bakery that night, I flicked on the lights and set up a makeshift seating area with mismatched chairs around the counter. The hum of the refrigerator was a comforting backdrop as I waited, heart racing with each passing minute. When Ethan finally stepped inside, the cool night air followed him, carrying with it a hint of rain.

"Thanks for coming," he said, running a hand through his hair, a nervous habit I had come to recognize. He looked at me, a storm of emotions brewing in his eyes. "I didn't want to do this over text."

"Of course," I replied, trying to keep my tone steady, masking the whirlwind of thoughts colliding in my mind. "What's going on?"

He took a deep breath, the kind that felt like he was bracing himself against a wave. "I don't know how to say this without sounding like a jerk, but I feel like I'm losing myself in this wedding planning. The pressure is unreal, and I don't know how to talk to Madison about it."

"Ethan, it's okay to feel overwhelmed," I reassured him, stepping closer. "You're allowed to be human."

"I just don't want to hurt her," he confessed, his voice low and heavy with sincerity. "I love her, but I feel like I'm being pulled in every direction, and I don't know what to do."

"It's not just about the wedding," I said softly, sensing the raw honesty spilling from him. "It's about who you are when all the bells and whistles fade away. You need to be honest with her, even if it's hard."

He nodded, the lines of worry etched on his forehead deepening. "I just wish it were easier."

We stood there, the silence stretching between us like a taut wire, thick with unspoken words and lingering feelings. Then, like a dam breaking, he took a step closer, eyes searching mine. "What if... what if I don't want to just be her groom? What if I want to be me, too?"

The words hung in the air, electrifying and terrifying. "Ethan," I whispered, the tension swelling around us, "you have to find a way to be both. You can't lose yourself in this."

Just then, the door swung open, and Madison stepped in, drenched from the rain, eyes wide with surprise as she took in the scene before her. "What's going on here?"

My heart raced, the air thick with unspoken truths as I exchanged a glance with Ethan. The precarious moment hung like a fragile glass ornament, teetering on the edge of revelation.

In that heartbeat, I understood that whatever path lay ahead would demand more from all of us than we were ready to give, and the shadow of impending change loomed larger than any wedding cake. The echo of Madison's voice shattered the stillness, and I knew that secrets could only be buried for so long before they forced their way to the surface.

Chapter 5: The Rain

The rain beat against the windshield in a rhythm that echoed the quickening pulse in my chest. Each drop seemed to punctuate the silence between us, as if the world outside had conspired to wrap us in an intimate cocoon. I glanced sideways at Ethan, his profile illuminated by the dim light of the dashboard, and for a moment, I forgot about the wedding designs, the daunting task ahead. Instead, I was entranced by the way the water trickled down the glass, blurring the edges of reality just enough to feel like we existed in a separate universe—one where the chaos of life outside melted away.

"What's the most ridiculous thing you've ever done?" I blurted out, an unexpected challenge hanging in the air like the humidity around us. It wasn't a typical icebreaker, but the weight of the moment needed a spark.

Ethan turned to me, surprise dancing in his hazel eyes. "Are we talking about the sort of ridiculous that involves poor life choices? Because I have a long list."

"Please, share the worst of it," I urged, my curiosity piqued. I leaned back in my seat, daring him to peel back the layers that cloaked his usually composed demeanor.

He smirked, the corners of his mouth lifting in a way that set off a flurry of butterflies in my stomach. "Alright, you asked for it. Once, I tried to impress a girl by pretending I could cook. Spoiler alert: I set my kitchen on fire. Not a full-on inferno, but definitely enough to smoke out the neighbors. And I wasn't even trying to make anything exotic—just scrambled eggs."

I couldn't help but laugh, the sound spilling out in bright bursts against the dreary backdrop. "I guess that's one way to make an impression! Did it work?"

"Not quite. I think she was more impressed by the fire department showing up than my culinary skills." He chuckled, shaking his head as if the memory still embarrassed him. "But hey, I learned two things that day: I'm terrible in the kitchen, and I should probably leave the cooking to professionals."

"Cooking is overrated anyway," I said, waving a dismissive hand as if the notion were as ludicrous as his tale. "What really matters is the presentation. I mean, no one ever talks about how good a dish tastes when it's Instagrammable, right?"

He raised an eyebrow, amusement dancing in his gaze. "Are you suggesting we base our life choices on aesthetics?"

"Only the important ones," I replied, grinning. "Like, should I buy the mint green dress or the peach one for the wedding? Mint green is trendy, but peach might make me look like a grapefruit."

"Definitely mint green. Unless you're going for a citrus-themed bridal party, in which case, I'd suggest you add a lemon hat."

Our laughter intermingled with the patter of rain, creating a soundtrack that drowned out the world beyond the car. It was in moments like these—when the conversation flowed so easily, when the laughter bubbled over like a warm cup of cocoa—that I felt the tension between us shift. There was something deeper lurking just beneath the surface of our playful banter, something we were both hesitant to name.

As the rain drummed against the roof of the car, we transitioned from lighthearted stories to more profound revelations. I shared snippets of my childhood, tales of my overbearing mother and her unending quest for perfection. "She had a vision for my life, you know? And it always involved a straight-A report card, a college acceptance letter, and an impeccable wedding. Nothing less would do."

Ethan listened intently, his gaze unwavering as he absorbed my words. "That sounds suffocating," he said softly, his tone laced with empathy. "Did you ever feel like you could be yourself in that environment?"

I paused, pondering his question as the rain continued its relentless assault. "Not really. I was always trying to fit into her mold, afraid that if I stepped outside of it, I'd disappoint her. It's like I was living my life as a performance, rehearsing lines that weren't even mine."

His expression darkened slightly, a shadow crossing his face as if he could feel the weight of my memories. "I can relate to that. My parents always had this expectation that I would follow in my father's footsteps, become a doctor, wear the white coat, and save lives. But I wanted to create, to explore. I didn't want to be a miracle worker; I wanted to be an artist."

"You're an artist?" The surprise slipped out before I could stop it. "I never knew."

He shrugged, a hint of vulnerability flashing in his eyes. "I guess I hide that part of myself. But I've dabbled in painting and photography. It's always been my escape, my way of expressing what I can't say with words."

A charged silence fell between us, thick with unspoken confessions and the kind of tension that makes the air shimmer. The weight of our shared secrets hovered like a storm cloud, and just as I thought it might burst, Ethan's hand brushed against mine. It was electric, an inadvertent spark that ignited the atmosphere around us.

I pulled away instinctively, the sudden distance between us a palpable ache. It wasn't just the warmth of his skin against mine that set my heart racing; it was the realization that we had crossed a line neither of us had intended to. The playful banter had shifted to something much more profound, and I was left reeling in the aftermath, caught between the thrill of discovery and the panic of potential loss.

"I should probably get out," I stammered, my voice barely above a whisper as I glanced out at the rain-soaked world outside. My heart thrummed in my chest, a frantic reminder of the sudden shift in our relationship. "The designs—"

"Wait." His voice, low and steady, cut through the chaos of my thoughts. I turned back to him, meeting his eyes that seemed to hold an entire universe of unspoken words. "Let's just... take a moment. Before we go in there and face all of that."

His words hung in the air, heavy with possibility. I nodded, uncertainty swirling in my mind, but a flicker of hope ignited in my chest. Maybe, just maybe, this rain-soaked moment could be the turning point I didn't know I needed.

Ethan's eyes locked onto mine, and the world outside faded into a blur of muted colors, the rain transforming the landscape into a watercolor painting, soft and dreamlike. My pulse quickened as I absorbed the weight of the moment, caught between exhilaration and the sharp edge of anxiety. The air was thick with unvoiced feelings, and for the first time, I felt the invisible thread that bound us—a connection that transcended our shared tasks and had begun to dip into something far more personal.

"Do you think it's always like this?" I asked, my voice a whisper as I gestured towards the torrential downpour outside. "I mean, do you think you can ever really know someone? Or do we just get glimpses, pieces of them?"

Ethan considered this, his brow furrowing slightly. "I think we see the highlights, the curated versions of each other. It's easy to put up walls and share only what we want others to know." He paused, his gaze searching mine. "But sometimes, you find someone who makes you want to take those walls down, you know?"

My heart raced at his words, a flutter of hope mingling with a tinge of fear. It was terrifying to think about baring my soul to someone, especially someone who had already become so integral to my life in such a short time. "And what happens if you let them in? What if they don't like what they see?"

Ethan's lips curved into a soft smile, the kind that radiated warmth. "Then you find out who they are, too. And maybe, just maybe, they surprise you."

A moment passed, where the air felt charged with potential, and I wondered if we were both standing at the edge of a precipice. But the heavy raindrops against the roof reminded me of the looming reality outside our bubble. I cleared my throat, redirecting the conversation to safer ground. "Alright, Mr. Philosopher, let's get back to business before we drown in our feelings. Do you have the final floral designs?"

Ethan reached for a folder on the back seat, his smile still lingering as he handed it to me. "I mean, I could pretend to be all serious and businesslike, but where's the fun in that? The flowers can wait. Let's keep chatting."

"Okay, but you know I need to nail down the centerpieces," I countered playfully, flipping through the pages. Each design reflected a vibrant aspect of our conversations: bold, daring choices that mirrored the laughter we shared. "This one looks amazing. I love how you combined the wildflowers with the more traditional roses. It's like you captured our chaotic energy."

"Chaos is my specialty." He laughed, and I caught a glimpse of the boyish charm that had made it impossible for me to stay aloof. "I figured we'd throw in some unexpected elements, like our lives, right? A little unpredictable, but totally beautiful."

"Beautiful chaos." I nodded, the phrase swirling around in my mind. "Sounds like a perfect metaphor for my life."

Ethan leaned back, his gaze thoughtful. "And what does that chaos look like for you? Beyond the flowers and wedding planning?"

I hesitated, unsure how much to reveal. "It's messy," I finally admitted, my voice barely above the rain's cacophony. "One minute I'm striving for perfection, and the next, I'm wondering why I even care about all these societal expectations. It's exhausting."

"Expectations can be like a weight on your chest, suffocating," he said softly, the seriousness of his tone catching me off guard. "But you're not just defined by those expectations. You can break free."

His sincerity wrapped around me, and I couldn't help but wonder if he understood my turmoil better than anyone else ever had. "You make it sound so easy," I said, shaking my head. "If only it were that simple."

"Maybe it is, in a way," he said, his voice low and steady. "What if you started making choices for yourself, regardless of what others think?"

"Like wearing the peach dress?" I teased, trying to lighten the mood, but his expression remained serious.

"Exactly. Wear the dress that makes you feel like you're stepping into the sun instead of hiding in the shade. Own your chaos."

His words settled into my heart, taking root in a way that felt both terrifying and exhilarating. "You make it sound so enticing," I replied, half-joking. "But stepping out of the shadows means taking a risk, right? What if I stumble?"

"Then you get back up, and you try again." His confidence was contagious, and I found myself leaning closer, drawn in by his unwavering resolve. "Life's about the messiness, not the perfection. It's the stumbles that make the best stories."

"Best stories, huh?" I mused, casting my gaze out to the rain-soaked street. "I suppose I've had my fair share of those."

Ethan turned to me, his expression softening. "Share one. I'm all ears."

I took a breath, my mind racing through a catalogue of misadventures. "Alright, but prepare yourself. This one involves a really bad karaoke night and a questionable choice of costume." I started with the story, recounting how I had convinced my friends to join me in an impromptu performance of a pop anthem, decked out in neon wigs and sequins.

"And of course," I continued, "halfway through the song, I tripped and landed right in front of the DJ booth, knocking over a stack of records. I thought I was going to die from embarrassment!"

Ethan was practically howling with laughter, his head thrown back as he leaned against the steering wheel. "Please tell me you went all in after that. Did you get up and finish the song?"

"Of course! I crawled back to the mic, threw my hands in the air, and just went for it. It turned into a dance-off with the DJ, and by the end, the whole bar was cheering."

"See? That's what I mean about chaos! You turned a potential disaster into a moment of glory." He smiled, a glint of admiration in his eyes. "You didn't let the stumble define you. You made it a part of your performance."

The rain continued to fall, but inside the car, the atmosphere felt lighter, charged with laughter and newfound intimacy. The walls I had built around my heart began to crack, allowing a flicker of hope to seep through. I realized, in that moment, that perhaps I didn't have to be the perfect version of myself. Perhaps I could embrace the chaos and let it guide me toward something beautiful.

"Okay, but you owe me a story now," I challenged, leaning in closer. "What's the most embarrassing thing you've ever done?"

Ethan's smile turned mischievous, and I felt a flutter of anticipation. "I'm glad you asked. But first, let's talk about the karaoke championship I may or may not have crashed."

As he launched into his tale, the tension shifted again, transforming into an easy camaraderie, and I found myself sinking into the warmth of his presence. Each word he spoke felt like a thread weaving us closer together, unraveling the fears I had harbored and revealing a space where laughter and connection could flourish. The rain might have blurred the world outside, but inside this small, intimate space, everything was beginning to crystallize into focus.

The laughter lingered between us, a fragile thread spun from the moments of connection that had blossomed during our rain-soaked car ride. Ethan's eyes sparkled with mischief as he recounted his karaoke debacle, complete with exaggerated hand gestures and dramatic reenactments that had me in stitches. I felt light, buoyed by the ease of our banter and the delicious thrill of shared secrets. It was as if the rest of the world had vanished, leaving just the two of us and the steady rhythm of the rain.

"Okay, okay, I have to admit," I said, wiping tears of laughter from the corners of my eyes. "You might actually be more entertaining than I initially gave you credit for."

Ethan leaned closer, a mock-serious expression painting his features. "Just don't tell anyone, or my reputation as a serious wedding planner might be at stake."

"Right, because the world is just waiting for a glimpse of your secret karaoke career," I teased, shaking my head. "What a loss that would be for mankind."

The car's interior felt charged with something electric, an awareness that crept up on me as I caught the way his gaze lingered on my lips for just a heartbeat too long. A small part of me thrived on that unspoken connection, but I wrestled with the caution gnawing at the edges of my exhilaration. We were walking a tightrope, balanced between friendship and something infinitely more complex.

"Speaking of reputations," he said, shifting the conversation in a way that made my heart race, "what's the most ridiculous thing you've ever done to impress someone?"

I hesitated, the question a double-edged sword. "Oh, there's a list," I replied, a laugh bubbling up, though my stomach twisted slightly. "But I think the highlight has to be when I attempted to bake a soufflé for a guy I liked. I watched every YouTube video, memorized the recipe, and when it came time to present it, I opened the oven door only to see a deflated disaster staring back at me. I still served it, though. With a smile."

"Did he eat it?" Ethan asked, the corners of his mouth twitching with amusement.

"Like a champ! I think he was just trying to be nice, but the look on his face was priceless." I laughed, but the memory was tinged with embarrassment. "Let's just say it didn't lead to a second date. I'm pretty sure he ran for the hills after that."

"I'm surprised you didn't throw in a bouquet of flowers to soften the blow," he joked, his voice low, rich with warmth. "Or maybe a heartfelt apology written in icing."

"Note to self: if you're ever baking for a guy again, consider the floral backup plan." I grinned, but my laughter faded as I felt an odd shift in the air, an unsteady moment where our playful rapport felt almost vulnerable.

"You know, it's easy to laugh about these things," Ethan said, his tone suddenly serious. "But sometimes, it's those moments that define us. They show us who we are, even when we're stumbling through life."

I held his gaze, the weight of his words sinking in. "What if I'm just a perpetual mess, then?"

"Maybe that's the best kind of person," he replied, his voice steady. "Life is a series of beautiful messes, and it's how we navigate through them that really matters."

His sincerity pierced through the lighthearted facade we had constructed. There was something about the way he spoke, the way he looked at me, that made my heart flutter and my mind race with possibilities. I felt stripped down to my core, and for a fleeting moment, I wondered if he could see right through my carefully constructed walls.

"Okay, enough of this deep stuff. We have a wedding to plan!" I said, attempting to redirect the conversation, though my voice wavered slightly. "Let's focus on those centerpieces before the bride decides she wants flamingos instead of flowers."

Ethan laughed, and the tension in the car lightened again, but something unshakable lingered beneath the surface. The rain had finally started to relent, the droplets now tapering off into a gentle drizzle that offered a momentary reprieve from the tempest outside.

Just as I reached for the folder to review the designs again, a loud crack of thunder boomed overhead, causing us both to jump. The car shook slightly, and for a second, the laughter faded into a startled silence.

"Okay, that was dramatic," I said, attempting to keep the mood light, but a nervous energy crackled in the air between us. "Maybe Mother Nature is telling us to get our act together and finish these designs before she unleashes the next round of chaos."

"Or maybe she's just trying to set the mood for our big reveal," Ethan quipped, his grin returning. "I can see it now: 'Welcome to the Wedding of the Century, complete with atmospheric sound effects!'"

"Perfect! Let's just hope the officiant doesn't get struck by lightning in the process," I replied, leaning into his humor. But as I flipped through the designs, I noticed a flicker of something in his expression, a seriousness that crept back into his eyes.

"What is it?" I asked, my curiosity piqued.

He hesitated, the weight of unspoken thoughts pulling at the corners of his mouth. "There's something I've been meaning to tell you," he said slowly, his tone shifting again, this time weighted with a gravity that sent a shiver down my spine. "About the wedding... and us."

"Us?" I echoed, a knot forming in my stomach. "What do you mean?"

Before he could respond, the car jolted, the sudden thud echoing through the air like a thunderclap. My heart dropped as the lights flickered, the engine sputtering as if it were alive and struggling to breathe.

"Uh-oh. I think we might have a problem," Ethan said, glancing nervously at the dashboard. The lights dimmed further, and then the car shuddered to a complete stop, enveloped in the heavy silence of the storm.

"Great," I muttered, casting a glance out the window where the rain continued to pour in earnest. "What are we supposed to do now? Sit here and wait for the tow truck while we drown in our unresolved feelings?"

He turned to me, a faint smile playing on his lips despite the tension in the air. "Well, we could either sit here in silence or make the most of this unexpected detour."

I swallowed hard, a mix of fear and excitement coursing through me. "What do you have in mind?"

"I don't know yet," he said, his gaze steady, challenging. "But I think it's time we really talked about what's been simmering between us."

The words hung in the air, a tantalizing invitation that sent my heart racing. I opened my mouth to respond, but the sound of the rain intensified, and another rumble of thunder cracked overhead, drowning out my thoughts and leaving us both suspended in a moment that felt both electric and terrifying. The storm raged outside, but the real tempest was brewing just a breath away from us, ready to unleash everything we had yet to say.

Chapter 6: Fractured Promises

The rain hammered against the window like a relentless drummer, each drop a percussionist determined to remind me of the world outside. I curled deeper into the couch, clutching my mug of chamomile tea like a life preserver in a turbulent sea. The dim light of my living room flickered as the wind howled through the cracks in the old window frame, and I took a sip, hoping the warmth would seep into my bones, dispelling the chill that had settled there since Ethan had stepped back from his own life.

Ethan's absence was palpable, not just in the quiet moments of the evening but in the spaces he used to fill with laughter and easy banter. He was my best friend, my confidant, and seeing him slip away was like watching the sun set, knowing it might not rise again. Our shared moments—those spontaneous adventures that used to punctuate our lives—felt like remnants of a dream I wasn't ready to wake from. But now, it was as if he were a ghost, haunting the edges of my thoughts, slipping away just as quickly as he appeared.

A sudden knock on the door jolted me from my reverie. The sound echoed through the apartment, breaking the spell of solitude that had cocooned me. My heart raced; I wasn't expecting anyone. I set the mug down, the tea's warmth still lingering on my fingertips as I approached the door. The sight of Ethan on the other side almost knocked the breath from my lungs. He was drenched, his shirt clinging to his skin, and his usually vibrant eyes were clouded with something darker—uncertainty, fear, or perhaps the weight of unspoken truths.

"Hey," I said, trying to inject some normalcy into the moment, though my voice trembled like a newly struck string on an untested guitar. "You look like you swam here."

"Funny," he replied, a weak smile flickering across his face, but it faded just as quickly. He stepped inside, leaving a trail of rainwater that mirrored the storm raging outside. "I, uh, I needed to talk."

The air shifted, thickening with tension, as if the universe had conspired to wrap us in a cocoon of impending revelations. I stepped aside, allowing him entry, my heart thumping a rhythm of its own as he crossed the threshold. The door clicked shut behind him, sealing us in a space that felt both familiar and foreign, the scent of wet earth and freshly brewed tea swirling around us like an aromatic embrace.

We settled into the living room, the space both comforting and suffocating. I motioned toward the couch, but Ethan remained standing, his posture rigid as though bracing for impact. The shadows cast by the flickering light danced across his face, highlighting the deep lines of worry etched into his brow. I wanted to reach out, to pull him close and shield him from whatever storm brewed inside him, but the air between us crackled with something unspoken, a fragile barrier that felt insurmountable.

"Are you okay?" I asked, my voice a quiet plea.

He ran a hand through his hair, the gesture so quintessentially Ethan that it made my heart ache. "I don't think I can do this anymore," he finally said, each word a nail driving deeper into the coffin of his engagement to Madison.

"What do you mean?" The question escaped my lips before I could filter it, my mind racing to piece together the fragments of this moment.

Ethan's gaze dropped to the floor, the wooden boards creaking beneath his weight. "I mean, everything. The wedding, the plans, Madison... I just feel like I'm suffocating. Like I'm trapped in a life that doesn't belong to me."

His honesty was both a relief and a torment. I felt the familiar pang of loyalty to Madison, her sunny disposition a stark contrast to the storm cloud hovering over Ethan. "But what about Madison? You two have been together forever. She loves you."

"I know," he said, his voice barely above a whisper. "But I don't think I can love her the way she needs. It's not fair to either of us."

The tension in the room thickened, the air heavy with the weight of unfulfilled promises and dreams slowly unraveling. I swallowed hard, searching for the right words, but all that came was silence—a deafening acknowledgment of the truth we both knew but had avoided facing.

"I don't want to hurt her, but every day I feel like I'm living someone else's life," he admitted, his eyes finally meeting mine, and I saw the desperation there, the flicker of hope mingling with despair. "I don't want to wake up five years from now, realizing I've wasted my life being someone I'm not."

I leaned back, my heart pounding a frantic rhythm. "So, what are you saying?" The question lingered between us, a fragile thread hanging over an abyss.

Ethan took a deep breath, his gaze piercing mine as if he were searching for some hidden truth within me. "I don't know. But I can't keep pretending everything's okay when it's not. And the truth is, I keep thinking about you."

The confession hung in the air like a fragile ornament on a brittle tree branch, ready to shatter under the weight of unsaid feelings. My breath hitched, a tumult of emotions swirling within me—excitement, fear, and a reluctant spark of hope. This was the line we had skirted around for years, and now it was crashing down like the rain outside, both liberating and terrifying.

"I care about you, Ethan," I said, the admission slipping from my lips like a secret I had been holding for far too long. "But we both know the mess this would create."

He stepped closer, the distance between us evaporating, the tension crackling like static electricity in the air. "Maybe we need to embrace the mess."

And just like that, the storm outside echoed the turmoil within, a perfect symphony of chaos and longing. The room pulsed with unspoken words, each heartbeat drawing us closer to a precipice we couldn't ignore any longer.

As the rain continued its relentless assault on the windows, the world outside faded into a blur, the rhythmic patter a symphony underscoring the tension between us. I could feel the weight of Ethan's confession hanging in the air, thick and suffocating. Each second felt like an eternity, every heartbeat drumming a nervous tattoo against my chest. He was standing so close that I could almost feel the warmth radiating from him, yet I couldn't shake the chill of uncertainty that settled deep in my bones.

"Embrace the mess," I echoed, as if the words themselves might illuminate some hidden truth. What kind of mess was I even talking about? The kind that could unravel lives, relationships, dreams? My thoughts raced, colliding like two cars at a red light—each one unyielding and unwilling to budge.

He stepped back slightly, running a hand through his damp hair, and I couldn't help but notice how the action seemed to ground him, the familiar gesture somehow calming. "Look, I'm not trying to create chaos here," he said, his voice a mixture of frustration and vulnerability. "But I feel like I'm suffocating in this picture-perfect life that's not mine. It's as if everyone expects me to fit neatly into a frame that doesn't even represent who I am."

The honesty in his words cut through the thick atmosphere, each syllable striking a chord within me. I wanted to wrap him in a blanket of comfort, but I also wanted to shake him and demand he take a breath. "Ethan, you know that life isn't about fitting into a frame, right? It's messy and complicated, but it's also beautiful when you stop trying to please everyone else."

He paused, searching my eyes for something I wasn't sure I could give him. "What if I want that beauty with you? What if I want to see where this goes?"

The air crackled, charged with a spark that danced tantalizingly between us. I had never considered what lay beneath the surface of our friendship—until now. The thought of crossing that line sent a rush of adrenaline through my veins, tinged with both excitement and fear. "You're engaged, Ethan. This isn't just some romantic whim. You're about to marry Madison. That's not a small thing."

"Marrying her feels like agreeing to a script I didn't write," he countered, his intensity unwavering. "I need to be honest with myself, and with you."

The implications of his words washed over me, a tidal wave of conflicting emotions that left me momentarily breathless. I glanced toward the window, where the rain blurred the world outside, mirroring the muddle of thoughts swirling in my head. I could sense the pull between us, the gravitational force that had been building over years of shared laughter and secret glances. But was I ready to explore this new territory? To navigate the potential heartbreak it could cause?

"What if this is just a moment?" I challenged, trying to regain some semblance of control. "What if you're feeling overwhelmed and this—whatever this is—just feels like a way out?"

Ethan stepped closer again, his gaze unwavering. "Then maybe I'm just tired of waiting for the right moment to be honest about what I want."

My heart raced, each pulse echoing his words. I could feel the walls I'd built around my heart start to tremble, but a small part of me still clung to the safety of friendship, unwilling to let it slip through my fingers. "But what about Madison?" I pressed, my voice trembling slightly. "She deserves the truth."

"I can't keep pretending," he said, the anguish in his voice clear. "I've been avoiding her calls, avoiding this whole situation. But every time I do, it feels like I'm erasing a part of myself."

I watched him, the battle within him evident, and I could sense how deeply he was hurting. It struck me then that I had always admired Ethan's strength, but right now, he was standing on the precipice, and I didn't want him to leap without considering the ground below. "You need to figure out what you want, Ethan. Not just for you, but for her too. Because once you say something, there's no going back."

He nodded, running a hand through his hair again, and I couldn't help but chuckle. "You're starting to sound like my therapist."

"Let's not go that far," I quipped, a smile breaking through the tension as he smirked back at me, the warmth of familiarity weaving itself into the moment. "I don't have a degree in emotions, just a lifetime of surviving them."

The laughter hung in the air, a fragile thread binding us closer, but I could see that underneath the surface, a tempest was brewing. "I know this is all sudden," he said, his voice softer now, almost as if he were afraid to break the spell of our newfound honesty. "But I can't shake the feeling that we're meant for more than just friendship."

"More?" I echoed, raising an eyebrow, half-amused and half-terrified. "What kind of more are we talking about? The kind that involves romantic dinners and candlelit confessions? Because if we're being honest, I can't cook to save my life, and I think I'd burn the candles too."

His laughter filled the room, and for a moment, the gravity of our situation lightened. "I'd take takeout any day if it meant spending time with you."

"Sounds like a plan, but let's not forget about the elephant in the room," I replied, crossing my arms in mock seriousness. "The fact that you're about to marry someone else. Did I mention she's not a fan of takeout? Or surprises? Or, you know, the thought of you breaking her heart?"

"Trust me, I'm acutely aware of how messy this is," he admitted, the humor fading from his eyes as the reality of the situation pressed in again. "But if I don't say something soon, I'm going to implode, and I don't want you caught in the blast."

My heart twisted in my chest, torn between the urge to reach out to him and the knowledge of what lay ahead. "You're going to hurt her, Ethan," I said softly, the weight of the words settling heavily between us.

"I know. But the worst part is that by staying silent, I'm already hurting both of us. And I can't live like that anymore."

The storm outside seemed to echo his turmoil, each thunderclap resonating with the tumult of our conversation. My mind raced with possibilities and fears, the world outside a blur of rain and uncertainty, while the storm within us mirrored it all—chaotic, unpredictable, and undeniably real.

The quiet between us seemed to stretch infinitely, a taut string pulled to its limit, and I couldn't tell if I was holding my breath or simply suspended in a moment of disbelief. I searched Ethan's eyes for reassurance, a flicker of hope or a sign that maybe we could find our way back to the friendship that had always anchored us. Yet all I found was a storm, swirling with uncertainty and a longing that felt dangerously close to love—a love that dared to tread into the territory we had both been so careful to avoid.

"Ethan," I began, my voice barely more than a whisper, "if you're thinking about leaving Madison, you have to be absolutely sure."

His gaze hardened, frustration mixing with vulnerability. "I've been sure for a while, but it took seeing you tonight for me to realize how much I've been lying to myself. Being around you makes me feel alive, and I can't remember the last time I felt like this with her."

A wave of warmth flooded through me, battling with the icy tendrils of guilt that crept in. The idea that I had been the catalyst for his awakening felt both thrilling and terrifying. "But what happens next? You can't just drop everything for a feeling. This is real life, not some romantic comedy where everything works out in the end."

Ethan stepped closer again, and I could see the determination in his eyes. "Maybe that's the problem. Maybe life shouldn't always follow a script. We've been dancing around this for too long, and it's time for me to make a choice. Do I keep pretending to be someone I'm not, or do I risk everything for something real?"

His words struck a chord deep within me, resonating with a truth I had kept locked away. The tension was electric, wrapping around us like a living thing, pulsing with the weight of unsaid desires and the inevitable heartbreak that could come from acting on them. I wanted to reach out, to bridge the gap between us, but the thought of ruining what we had—a friendship built on years of laughter and trust—held me back.

"So, you're saying I'm your option B?" I replied, forcing a laugh to mask the vulnerability I felt creeping in. "That's not exactly flattering."

His expression softened, the corners of his mouth turning up slightly. "You know it's not like that. It's just… I never realized how much I was holding back until I saw you again. You make me feel things I thought I had buried beneath layers of obligation."

"I'm not trying to be a temptation, Ethan," I countered, my heart racing at the prospect of what lay ahead. "You need to figure things out without dragging me into the middle of it. I care about both of you."

"Then care enough to help me find my way," he said, his voice barely above a whisper. "Help me decide what I truly want."

We stood there, caught in a moment suspended between past and future, the air thick with unsaid promises. I could hear the rain still hammering against the window, a rhythm that felt like the heartbeat of the world outside—wild, unpredictable, and exhilarating.

I turned away, trying to process the maelstrom of emotions swirling within me. "Ethan, if you go through with this—if you decide to break things off with Madison—you have to be ready for the consequences. For the fallout."

He took a step closer, closing the distance between us, and I felt the familiar pull of his presence, the magnetic force that had drawn us together time and time again. "I am ready. I have to be."

A flurry of thoughts raced through my mind, battling against the instinct to flee. The weight of his gaze felt like a warm embrace, wrapping around me and squeezing the last ounce of air from my lungs. "You're making a choice that could hurt everyone involved," I said, my voice wavering slightly. "What if you regret it?"

"I'd rather regret choosing happiness than regret a life of 'what ifs.'"

Just as I was about to respond, the room seemed to dim, the lights flickering momentarily. I glanced toward the window, momentarily distracted by the chaotic rhythm of the rain—each drop a tiny echo of the turmoil within us. When I turned back, Ethan had moved even closer, his expression a mixture of longing and fear, as if he were poised on the edge of a cliff, ready to leap but unsure of the landing.

"What if we—" I began, my voice trailing off as I hesitated, my heart pounding in my chest. "What if we're jumping into the unknown without a safety net?"

His breath caught in his throat, and I could see the weight of my words settling over him. "But what if the unknown is where we're meant to be?"

The moment hung between us, fragile and fleeting, before a loud crash outside shattered the silence—a nearby tree branch breaking under the weight of the rain, perhaps, or something more ominous. We both jumped, instinctively retreating from the sound, but the tension that had built up between us remained, thrumming like a taut wire ready to snap.

"I think," I started, my heart racing, "we should—"

Before I could finish my thought, my phone buzzed on the table, slicing through the charged air like a knife. I glanced down, my stomach dropping as I saw Madison's name flashing on the screen. My heart raced, caught between the impending conversation with Ethan and the urgency of the moment. I hesitated, my mind reeling.

"Should you answer that?" Ethan asked, his voice laced with apprehension.

"No," I replied, the weight of the decision pressing heavily on me. "I can't."

But as I stared at the screen, the buzzing intensified, and I felt an undeniable pull to pick up. It was the kind of tension that felt like a balloon stretched too tight, ready to pop. "But what if it's important?" I muttered, my thumb hovering over the screen.

"Maybe it is, or maybe it's a distraction from what we need to discuss," he said, the urgency in his voice unmistakable.

I opened my mouth to respond, but before I could say anything, I heard the unmistakable sound of a key turning in the lock. My heart dropped into my stomach as the door swung open, revealing

Madison—soaked from the rain, her expression a mix of confusion and concern.

"What's going on?" she asked, her gaze flickering between us, the tension in the room palpable as reality crashed in like the storm outside.

In that moment, I knew the fragile world we had been constructing was about to unravel, and everything we had danced around was about to be thrust into the harsh light of day.

Chapter 7: The Pull

Each day blurs into the next, the familiar rhythm of wedding planning morphing into something much more intoxicating. When Ethan walks into the café, the bell above the door jingles like a chime announcing the arrival of spring. There he is, all tousled hair and rumpled button-up shirts, exuding a charm that pulls at the corners of my heart. I had thought I'd be a fortress against distractions, but this man, with his easy smile and quick wit, is more than a distraction; he's a gravitational force pulling me closer, despite the glaring reality of our situation.

"Did you get the flowers?" he asks, plopping down across from me, his gaze unwavering and intense. It's a simple question, yet it sends an electric current through the air, crackling between us. The aroma of roasted coffee beans and sweet pastries fills the air, mingling with an undercurrent of tension that is impossible to ignore.

"I did," I reply, unable to suppress a smile as I think about the deep, velvety blooms I picked out—dark purple with a hint of silver, exactly what the bride envisioned for her dream wedding. "But I might have ordered a few too many. If the bride doesn't need them, I'm pretty sure I can find a good home for them. Maybe I'll start a side business selling overpriced bouquets to lonely hearts."

Ethan chuckles, the sound low and inviting, making my insides flutter like a thousand butterflies taking flight. "I bet you'd make a fortune. You could call it 'Bouquets for Broken Hearts.' It has a nice ring to it, don't you think?" His eyes twinkle with mischief, and for a moment, the world outside the café fades away. The chatter of customers, the clinking of cups, even the barista's cheerful banter become a distant hum as we bask in this bubble of shared laughter and unspoken connection.

The laughter dies down, leaving a comfortable silence, yet the air crackles with something unarticulated, a secret neither of us dares to name. I take a sip of my coffee, letting the warmth wash over me, but my gaze remains anchored to him. There's a storm brewing in those deep-set eyes, a swirl of emotions just beneath the surface that calls out to me. But I refuse to lean in, afraid of what might spill over.

"Have you thought about the rehearsal dinner yet?" I ask, shifting the topic, though my heart races in anticipation of what he might say next. The thought of any future without him is already unbearable.

"Yeah," he replies, running a hand through his hair in that way that drives me mad. "I thought we'd keep it simple. Just a nice dinner with the wedding party, maybe a few games to lighten the mood. But knowing this family, there will probably be a lot of unnecessary drama involved." His smirk returns, playful yet tinged with an edge of vulnerability.

"You could always hire a clown," I tease, my playful tone belying the deeper reality. "Someone to lighten the mood. Clowns are supposed to make everything better, right?" I bite back a grin, knowing full well how absurd that suggestion is.

He snorts, shaking his head. "A clown? Really? That sounds like a terrible idea, especially considering my family's talent for chaos. We don't need any more circus acts in the mix." The twinkle in his eyes reveals that he knows I'm being ridiculous, and for a heartbeat, we're not just a wedding planner and her client; we're two people sharing a moment that feels both electric and dangerously real.

"Fair enough. Just trying to offer some lightness," I respond, a hint of disappointment brushing my thoughts. I want him to see me as more than a professional, as someone he could lean on, someone who understands the weight of family expectations. "So what's the actual plan? Do we have a theme yet, or is it still 'let's throw it all at the wall and see what sticks'?"

"We're aiming for elegance," he says, his voice dropping an octave, adding a layer of seriousness to the conversation. "But I'm starting to think that my family's idea of elegance is actually just chaos dressed in fine silk." He leans closer, and the proximity makes my breath catch, a wild flutter of desire mixing with caution.

"Don't worry. I've seen plenty of chaos dressed in silk. It's usually just a matter of getting it to walk in a straight line," I say, unable to suppress the banter, though my pulse quickens under his gaze. "We'll find a way to tame the wildness."

Just then, a couple enters the café, laughing heartily, and the moment breaks, shattering the bubble we had wrapped ourselves in. I can feel the tension dissipate, replaced by the noise of the café and the pull of reality.

But the connection lingers like a fragrance that won't wash away, and as the laughter of the couple rises and falls, I can't help but wonder what life would be like if we were more than just wedding planner and client. What would it mean if we embraced this inexplicable pull? My thoughts race, wondering how easily the world outside could fade if only I dared to cross that line.

Ethan leans back, breaking the spell, and the sunlight filtering through the windows casts a warm glow on his face, revealing a vulnerability that makes my heart ache. "I know we're supposed to be just planning a wedding," he says, his voice a soft murmur, "but sometimes it feels like we're planning something else entirely."

"Something else?" I echo, my heart thudding in my chest, each word a fragile thread connecting us. "Like what?"

His gaze holds mine, and for a moment, the weight of everything hangs suspended between us. The laughter and chatter of the café fade to a dull hum, and it feels like the world is holding its breath, waiting for us to decide if we dare to take that next step into the unknown.

The chatter resumes around us, the vibrant café becoming a backdrop to the inner storm swirling between Ethan and me. A couple seated nearby raises their glasses, laughing with abandon, their joy a stark contrast to the tension creeping into our space. I take a deep breath, willing my heart to calm, but the air feels charged, like static before a thunderstorm, and I know the moment is upon us.

"Isn't this just so... ridiculous?" I finally say, breaking the silence that feels like a fragile thread about to snap. I gesture vaguely at the walls adorned with cheerful art and the table littered with wedding magazines, half-opened in an array of chaos. "Here we are, sitting in a coffee shop, planning someone else's happily ever after while our own lives hang in the balance. It's absurd, really."

Ethan raises an eyebrow, that familiar, playful smirk returning. "You're telling me. I'm basically the poster child for how not to navigate relationships right now. My ex-fiancée is planning a wedding, and I'm sitting here flirting with her wedding planner." He leans forward, and I feel the warm weight of his attention. "You know what that sounds like?"

"What?" I ask, unable to help the grin tugging at my lips.

"A bad rom-com waiting to happen." He chuckles, a rich sound that fills the space between us. "I mean, you can practically hear the laugh track in the background."

"Or the dramatic music as we grapple with our feelings," I add, the playful banter lifting some of the tension. "Picture it: a montage of us running through flower shops, arguing over napkin colors, and then—bam! A sudden realization at a wedding rehearsal dinner, where we both finally understand we're meant to be."

"Complete with a heartfelt confession," he replies, rolling his eyes dramatically, yet I can see the spark in his gaze, the amusement mingling with something deeper. "And, of course, a rain-soaked kiss on the last day of the wedding. Very original."

I can't help but laugh, but the laughter feels like a bandage over something raw and exposed. "You're right. It's all so cliché. But what if... what if we rewrite it? What if we make it our story instead?"

Ethan tilts his head, the humor fading from his eyes, replaced by a serious glimmer that sends my heart racing again. "You mean, like flipping the script entirely? Taking control of our own narrative instead of playing the part of the secondary characters in someone else's? That's bold."

"Or reckless," I counter, a nervous flutter taking up residence in my stomach. The implications of our playful banter hang heavy, wrapping around us like ivy. "But what if we have our own adventures along the way? We could discover the 'real' story beneath all the fluff."

"I'm not opposed to a little adventure," he says, his voice low, as if sharing a secret. "But I have to admit, I'm still trying to figure out if this is just an elaborate plot twist or if we're really onto something here."

"I think we're definitely onto something," I say, my heart thudding loud enough that I'm afraid he can hear it. The way his eyes linger on me makes it difficult to breathe. It's a dangerous line we're walking, teetering on the edge of something exhilarating and terrifying all at once.

Just as the air between us thickens again, the bell over the café door jingles, pulling my attention away. A familiar figure strides in, and my heart sinks. Emma, the bride-to-be, glides across the room like a summer breeze, radiating confidence in her flowy sundress and sun-kissed hair. Her face is lit with a smile, blissfully unaware of the storm brewing at our table.

"There you are! I was hoping to catch you both!" she exclaims, her voice bright as she approaches. "I've been dying to discuss the centerpieces!"

I can feel Ethan tense up beside me, and I force a smile, turning my attention to Emma. "Of course! Centerpieces are important! What did you have in mind?" I ask, my tone deceptively upbeat, masking the sudden swirl of conflicting emotions.

Emma leans closer, her enthusiasm infectious as she pulls out swatches of fabric and a notebook, blissfully unaware of the charged moment we just shared. "I thought we could incorporate more greenery. Something fresh and vibrant, you know? And I found these beautiful vases at a local shop. I think they'll add a really elegant touch!"

As she flips through her notes, I steal a glance at Ethan, who's now leaning back in his chair, the humor replaced by a brooding expression. It's a strange mix of longing and frustration in his eyes, and for a moment, I wonder if he feels as trapped as I do. We're caught in a loop of expectations—his obligation to Emma and my commitment to the wedding. It's as if we've slipped into a scripted dance, our real feelings hidden behind a facade of cheerful planning.

"Greenery sounds lovely," I respond, trying to keep my tone bright, though the knot in my stomach tightens. "Very on-trend and eco-friendly." My mind races with the unspoken words I wish I could say, the confession hanging on my lips.

"Right?" Emma beams, blissfully unaware of the shifting tides around her. "I want this wedding to feel alive, like we're celebrating something real. It's so important to me!"

Ethan shifts, the corner of his mouth twitching into a half-smile as he listens to her, and my heart aches at the sight. The way he looks at her is so different from the way he looked at me just moments before. The warmth fades, replaced by a chill of reality. It's a sharp reminder of the roles we're playing, the lines we can't cross.

"We can totally make that happen," I say, forcing myself to focus on Emma's excitement, even as my own heart feels heavy. "Let's brainstorm some more ideas! Maybe we can add string lights for that magical evening glow?"

"Yes! String lights are a must!" Emma claps her hands, her excitement palpable, and as she begins to share her vision for the wedding, I can feel the weight of Ethan's gaze lingering on me, full of things left unsaid. My pulse races, torn between the tension of this newfound connection and the duty I owe to Emma.

The rest of the meeting drifts in and out of focus, my thoughts swirling around the unspoken tension between Ethan and me. Each shared glance is a silent conversation, a whispered promise of something more that feels both thrilling and precarious. Even as we dive back into wedding logistics, a storm brews within, pushing us closer to a confrontation we've both been avoiding. As the details unfold and laughter fills the space, I can't shake the feeling that the real story is just beginning to unravel, and it's one we'll have to write together.

As Emma launches into a passionate description of her vision for the wedding—her animated gestures punctuating every word—Ethan's presence beside me feels more like a slow-burning ember than a comforting warmth. I smile dutifully, nodding along, but inside, a tempest brews, the walls of my self-imposed restraint beginning to crack. Emma's joy is contagious, and yet, with every passing second, I can't shake the feeling that the air between Ethan and me is thickening, charged with unspoken truths.

"So, about those string lights," I say, attempting to steer the conversation while suppressing the wild thoughts racing in my mind. "They'd look incredible draped around the trees at the venue. We could create a fairy-tale ambiance—like something straight out of a storybook."

"Exactly!" Emma exclaims, her eyes sparkling. "I want people to feel like they've stepped into another world." Her enthusiasm is admirable, but the way she looks at Ethan pulls at my heartstrings. It's a reminder of the impossible situation we're in, a tension I can't help but feel looming just out of reach.

"Another world?" Ethan quips, a teasing smile gracing his lips. "What about the world we currently live in? You know, the one where I'm trying to figure out how not to upset the delicate balance of my family drama?"

Emma laughs, oblivious to the undercurrents swirling around us. "You're fine! As long as you keep me happy, everything else will fall into place. Right, Ava?" She turns to me, her eyes expectant.

"Of course! Happy bride, happy life, right?" I reply, forcing a smile that feels as thin as a layer of icing on a poorly baked cake. In that moment, I wonder if Emma would still be so carefree if she knew how deep the shadows of my affection for Ethan run.

Ethan's gaze flickers to me, an unspoken acknowledgment passing between us, a silent agreement that we're treading dangerous waters. I can't help but feel an ache in my chest, an unsettling mix of longing and guilt. Just as I contemplate saying something to defuse the tension, Emma leans back in her chair, rifling through her notes.

"Ava, you have to see these inspiration photos I found online!" she declares, pulling out her phone and scrolling through her camera roll. "I want our wedding to feel warm and intimate, like everyone is sharing in something special."

As she thrusts the phone toward me, I glance at the screen, yet my mind drifts elsewhere. Each photo she swipes through seems to taunt me with the possibility of what could have been if things had gone differently—if Ethan and I had met under different circumstances, away from the looming specter of his impending marriage. I shake off the thought, forcing myself to engage with Emma's excitement.

"Oh, those are beautiful!" I exclaim, nodding along, even as my heart sinks. The rich hues and soft candlelight set a perfect scene, but the sight of Ethan, with his eyes caught in a battle between loyalty and desire, gnaws at me. "The colors are so inviting; they really set the tone for a celebration."

"Right?" Emma replies, her voice bubbling with enthusiasm. "And I want to incorporate personal touches—like those quirky elements you suggested! The family photos and maybe some fun trivia about the two of us at each table."

"Great idea!" I chirp, determined to keep the atmosphere light, but every time Ethan meets my gaze, the silence becomes a wall between us, laden with all the things we can't say.

The meeting stretches on, the conversation alternating between wedding details and trivialities that feel increasingly meaningless. I listen, nodding, but part of me is waiting for the moment when the dam breaks, when the carefully constructed façade we've all maintained can no longer hold back the flood of our intertwined emotions.

Finally, as Emma flips to another page in her notebook, I feel the tension between Ethan and me reach a boiling point. The air around us vibrates with unspoken words, an undeniable pull that seems to draw us closer, inch by agonizing inch. My heart races, and I catch a glimpse of his hand, resting on the table, fingers flexing as if they're reaching for something—someone.

"Ava, what do you think about including a 'wishing tree' at the reception?" Emma asks, snapping me out of my thoughts. "Guests can write their well wishes on little cards and hang them on the branches. It'll be so sentimental!"

"Absolutely!" I respond, feigning enthusiasm, though the idea feels like a thin veil for our reality. The only wish I want to write is for Ethan to finally admit the truth between us. I look at him, my heart pounding, and he meets my gaze, an intensity in his expression that sends a shiver up my spine.

"Hey, do you guys want to head out to the venue after this?" Ethan suddenly suggests, breaking the delicate tension. "We can check out the setup in the daylight. Maybe we can start mapping out where everything will go. I could use a break from this café."

"Great idea!" Emma jumps in, her excitement palpable as she nods eagerly. "Let's do it! I'll grab my things!" She rises from her seat, oblivious to the way the air feels electric around us, as if we're about to set off a chain reaction.

As Emma gathers her belongings, I can feel Ethan's gaze linger on me, heavy with anticipation. "Are you okay with that?" he asks, his voice low, filled with a mixture of hope and something unnameable.

I nod, unable to form words, my heart racing as I catch the unguarded look in his eyes. There's a flicker of longing that ignites the space between us, making my skin tingle. "Yeah, I think it'll be good to see it all in person. Get a feel for the layout."

The three of us step out into the bright afternoon sun, the warmth washing over us as we walk towards the venue. The chatter from the café fades behind us, replaced by the sounds of the bustling street. Emma prattles on about her ideas, but my mind drifts back to Ethan, who walks beside me, close enough that our arms nearly brush.

As we approach the venue, an old barn nestled among sprawling fields, the view stretches out in front of us like a dreamscape. The soft rustling of leaves dances in the gentle breeze, but all I can feel is the heat radiating from Ethan, a magnetic pull that draws me closer. I want to turn to him, to say something profound, something that acknowledges the wild current running through us both, but the words are lodged in my throat, heavy and unyielding.

Suddenly, as we step inside the barn, I catch sight of a massive bulletin board filled with images of past weddings, but one catches my eye—a photo of a couple that makes my heart drop. It's Ethan and Emma, smiling bright and carefree, a vision of happiness that feels like a punch to my gut. The laughter fades from Emma's voice, replaced by a deep silence that settles over us, heavy and suffocating.

Ethan glances at the photo, his expression faltering for just a moment before he composes himself, turning to Emma. "What do you think, Emma? Does this fit the vibe you're going for?"

Before she can respond, I take a step back, my heart racing with the weight of unspoken confessions and the reality of what I'm feeling. I can't stand here, caught between them, tethered to this confusion any longer. "I—I need a moment," I stammer, backing away from the warmth of their shared laughter.

As I slip outside into the open air, the sun shines down, but the weight of my heart feels like an anchor dragging me under. I breathe in deep, trying to calm the tempest within. Yet just as I feel the fresh air wrap around me, I hear footsteps behind me and turn to find Ethan, his expression a mixture of concern and urgency.

"Ava, wait!" he calls, reaching for me, but my pulse quickens, my mind racing. The moment is upon us, the precipice of something profound, yet terrifying. The question hangs in the air, unspoken yet omnipresent, and as I turn to face him, uncertainty and hope collide in a way that threatens to shatter the fragile equilibrium we've maintained.

"Ava!" he breathes, and in that moment, everything else fades away—the past, the expectations, the looming wedding—leaving just the two of us standing at the edge of everything we've been holding back. The storm is here, and I know that whatever happens next will change everything.

Chapter 8: Collateral Damage

The fluorescent lights in the conference room buzzed above us, a relentless drone that matched the tension spiraling in my chest. Madison sat across the table, her back straight and her demeanor unyielding, her dark hair framing a face that seemed to have been chiseled from stone. I felt a shiver skitter down my spine as she caught my eye, the sharpness of her gaze cutting through the chatter of our coworkers. In that instant, the air thickened, a web of unspoken words and secrets weaving around us. My fingers fidgeted with the corner of my notepad, the pen clicking anxiously in a futile attempt to drown out the cacophony in my mind.

Ethan leaned back in his chair, arms crossed, his face a mask of indifference. He used to laugh at my jokes, share secret smiles across the room, and now he seemed as far away as the moon. It was maddening, like standing on the edge of a cliff, the ground crumbling beneath my feet as I struggled to hold on to something solid. My heart raced, each beat a reminder of our stolen moments, the late-night conversations that felt too real to be mere fantasy. I didn't know what had changed, but whatever it was, it left an acrid taste in my mouth.

As the meeting dragged on, I could feel Madison's eyes boring into me, a silent accusation that sent heat creeping up my neck. My mind flickered back to last week, a memory of laughter spilling into the night, the warmth of Ethan's hand brushing against mine, so electrifying it felt like magic. Now that spark felt like a bomb, ticking down to a catastrophic explosion I could neither anticipate nor control.

Once the meeting finally ended, Madison made her move, her heels clicking against the tile floor with an unnerving precision. I attempted to slip out unnoticed, but her voice sliced through the crowd. "Lila, can I talk to you for a second?"

A knot twisted in my stomach as I nodded, forcing myself to follow her into the empty hallway. The noise of the meeting faded, replaced by a heavy silence that weighed on my shoulders. I braced myself against the wall, suddenly acutely aware of the scent of fresh paint mingling with the faint whiff of coffee lingering in the air.

"Stay away from him," she said, her voice low and dangerously calm. There was an intensity in her gaze, a ferocity I had never witnessed before. "Ethan isn't someone you can toy with. He's not yours to play with."

I opened my mouth to respond, but no words came. The accusation hung in the air, thick and suffocating. Was I toying with him? Or was it the other way around? A thousand responses flitted through my mind, each more desperate than the last, but all I could muster was a defiant stare.

"I don't know what you think you know," I finally said, forcing my voice to stay steady, "but Ethan and I are—"

"Are what?" She stepped closer, invading my space, her eyes narrowing. "Friends? Lovers? It doesn't matter. What matters is that you don't know what he's capable of."

Her words landed like stones, heavy and unsettling. I fought against the impulse to recoil, to retreat back into the safety of the bustling office. But something about her presence, the palpable rage simmering beneath the surface, made me stand my ground.

"What do you mean by that?" I challenged, my voice barely above a whisper, even as my heart thundered in my ears. "What are you afraid of?"

Madison's lips curled into a smile that was anything but friendly. "Ethan has a way of getting what he wants. You think he's just some charming guy with a winning smile? He's not. He'll ruin you, and when he's done, he'll leave you shattered and alone."

The warning sent a chill through me, the truth of her words brushing against the edges of my consciousness. But I couldn't allow that fear to dictate my choices. There was a part of me that was drawn to Ethan, the magnetism of his laughter, the weight of his gaze holding secrets I was desperate to uncover.

"Is that what this is about?" I asked, trying to keep my tone light despite the tension coiling between us. "You're jealous?"

Madison's expression darkened, her eyes glinting with an emotion I couldn't quite place. "Jealousy? No, Lila. I'm protecting you. There's a difference."

I wanted to roll my eyes, to scoff at the absurdity of it all, but instead, I found myself grappling with a gnawing doubt. Did she really have my best interests at heart? Or was this just a power play in the office's intricate social web?

"Why should I listen to you?" I retorted, crossing my arms defensively. "What do you know about me, about us?"

"More than you think," she shot back, a flash of frustration breaking through her cool demeanor. "Ethan's my best friend, and I can see the way he looks at you. It's dangerous. You're not ready for that."

The words hung between us, heavy with implications I hadn't considered. I had always viewed my relationship with Ethan as a thrilling adventure, a dance on the edge of a cliff. But perhaps I had been too naïve to see the deeper currents at play. Maybe Madison was right about one thing: I didn't know what I was getting into.

"Maybe you should talk to him," I suggested, a bitter taste creeping into my mouth. "If you're so worried about me, maybe you should be worried about him."

Madison's expression shifted, uncertainty flickering across her face. "You don't understand—"

"Then help me understand!" I interrupted, my frustration boiling over. "Tell me what I'm missing instead of standing here threatening me!"

For a moment, we stood in silence, the tension palpable as we stared each other down, each searching for cracks in the other's armor. But just as I felt a glimmer of hope that we might find common ground, her phone buzzed in her pocket, slicing through the moment like a knife.

With a frustrated sigh, she glanced at the screen, her expression shifting from fierce to anxious in the blink of an eye. "I have to take this," she said, her voice suddenly softer. "But think about what I said."

As she walked away, the distance between us felt impossibly vast, the weight of her warning clinging to me like a shadow. Alone in the hallway, I leaned against the cool wall, my heart racing with confusion. I didn't know who to trust anymore. The thrill of being with Ethan now felt fraught with peril, each moment laced with uncertainty. Would my heart survive whatever this was turning into?

The moment Madison turned away, leaving me alone in that sterile hallway, a flood of conflicting emotions surged through me. I leaned against the wall, letting the coolness seep into my skin, a desperate attempt to ground myself. The familiar chaos of the office hummed beyond the walls, but my world had shifted, tilted off its axis. My mind raced, a tornado of thoughts swirling around the warning she had just issued. Was I really in over my head?

I made my way to my desk, each step feeling heavier than the last, the weight of Madison's threat still pressing down on me. The muted sounds of keyboard tapping and low conversations enveloped me, but all I could think about was Ethan. I could picture him sitting in that conference room, the slight furrow in his brow as he listened to Madison. Did he notice the shift in the air? Did he feel the tension crackling between us like static electricity?

As I settled into my chair, I absentmindedly scrolled through my emails, but my focus remained elsewhere. Just then, the sound of laughter broke through my thoughts. I looked up to see a group of coworkers gathered around the coffee machine, sharing stories that spilled over with humor and warmth. I envied their ease, the way they seemed to glide through their day with purpose and connection. My own laughter felt like a distant memory, a fading echo of what once was.

The clock ticked slowly, each second dragging out the time until I could leave. I needed air. The suffocating atmosphere of the office felt too much, and the walls began to close in around me. I glanced at my phone, the bright screen lighting up with a message from Ethan: Hey, want to grab dinner later? My heart skipped a beat, a rush of excitement and anxiety mixing in a dizzying dance.

Sure, what time? I quickly typed back, my fingers moving faster than my brain could process. I needed to see him, to unravel the tight knot of worry that had settled in my chest since Madison's confrontation. He replied almost immediately, How about 7? My treat.

His casual confidence ignited a spark of joy, pushing away the shadows of doubt, even if only for a moment. Deal! I replied, the word bursting with optimism. As I clicked send, a wave of anticipation washed over me, momentarily pushing aside the nagging feeling that clung to the edges of my thoughts.

The rest of the day crawled by, each minute stretching like taffy, the hours a relentless loop of meeting reminders and half-hearted chatter. I found myself replaying our past interactions, the way his laughter ignited something deep inside me, the way his gaze lingered just a heartbeat too long. Yet, in the back of my mind, Madison's words echoed like a haunting refrain, a siren song warning me of the storm to come.

When the clock finally struck six, I felt a rush of relief mixed with anxiety. I hurriedly packed my things, the clattering of my belongings on the desk loud enough to attract curious glances from my coworkers. I plastered a smile on my face, nodding at their small talk as I made my escape. As I stepped into the crisp evening air, I took a deep breath, allowing the cool breeze to wash over me.

The city was alive with energy, lights twinkling against the darkening sky like a thousand little stars. I navigated through the bustling streets, the distant sound of laughter and music weaving around me, mingling with the chatter of people enjoying their evening. But the closer I got to our meeting spot, a cozy Italian restaurant tucked away on a quiet corner, the tighter my chest felt.

Upon entering, the rich scent of garlic and basil enveloped me, a warm embrace that made my stomach growl in anticipation. I spotted Ethan already seated at a small table near the window, his head bent over his phone, the soft light highlighting the sharp angles of his face. I could feel the flutter of nerves in my stomach as I approached him.

"Hey there, handsome," I greeted, a teasing lilt in my voice as I slid into the seat across from him. He looked up, his face breaking into a smile that sent a rush of warmth coursing through me.

"Look who finally decided to grace me with her presence," he quipped, his tone playful, but there was an undercurrent of something deeper in his gaze that made my breath hitch.

"Traffic was a nightmare. You know how it is," I said, trying to match his lightheartedness, though I could feel the weight of the day still lingering at the edges of my thoughts.

The conversation flowed easily as we dove into the menu, our laughter mingling with the clinking of dishes around us. He told me about a ridiculous incident at work involving a runaway cart of spaghetti that somehow ended up in the elevator, and I couldn't help but laugh until tears brimmed in my eyes. In those moments, the worries about Madison, about the secrets and shadows that seemed to loom over us, faded into the background.

But as our plates arrived, the conversation shifted, a heavy silence creeping in. I looked at him, trying to gauge his thoughts, his expression thoughtful, a touch of concern lingering in his eyes. "What's on your mind?" he asked, his voice low, the playful edge gone.

I hesitated, the words caught in my throat. I wanted to lay it all bare, to spill out the worries and fears that had haunted me since that meeting. "Just work stuff," I finally said, trying to keep my voice light, but I could see the flicker of disappointment cross his features.

"Lila, you know you can talk to me about anything," he urged, leaning forward, his sincerity wrapping around me like a warm blanket.

"I know," I replied, forcing a smile, even as the weight of Madison's warning threatened to crush me. "It's just... complicated."

"Complicated how?" he pressed, his brow furrowing in concern. "You've been distant lately. If something's bothering you, I want to know."

The sincerity in his voice tugged at my heart, and for a moment, I considered spilling everything. But the thought of revealing Madison's warning, of exposing our budding relationship to scrutiny, felt like too much. Instead, I opted for a diversion, my mind racing for a safe topic.

"Remember that time we got lost trying to find that coffee shop? I thought we were going to end up in the next county," I laughed, attempting to steer the conversation back to lighter ground.

Ethan chuckled, his eyes sparkling with a mix of nostalgia and amusement. "You mean the time you insisted on following that 'shortcut' that took us through the sketchiest alley in the city?"

"That was a great adventure!" I shot back, grateful for the way he fell back into easy banter. The atmosphere around us shifted, laughter bubbling up once more, and for a moment, I believed we could dance around the complexities of our situation, wrapped up in our own little world.

Yet, even as the laughter flowed, a small voice in the back of my mind whispered warnings. Madison's words lingered, like a shadow creeping into my happiness. I had chosen to forget, but I knew the truth remained, waiting for the moment when it would come crashing back, leaving me to pick up the pieces.

As the evening wore on, the laughter between Ethan and me flowed freely, masking the unease that lurked just beneath the surface. The rich flavors of the marinara sauce mingled with the warm scent of garlic bread, creating a comforting cocoon that wrapped around us like a soft blanket. I leaned back in my chair, taking a moment to savor the warmth radiating from the candle flickering on our table. It was so easy to forget the world outside, especially when his laughter echoed like music in my ears.

Yet, the happiness was fragile, teetering on the brink of something unresolved. I could feel the weight of the conversation hanging in the air, begging for attention. "So, what's really bothering you?" Ethan probed again, his voice gentle but insistent, pulling me back into reality with a subtle tug.

I could see the concern etched across his face, those blue eyes of his searching mine as if hoping to decode the mystery that was me. The vulnerability in his gaze made my heart ache with an overwhelming desire to share everything—the good, the bad, and the fears I didn't know how to articulate. But the memory of Madison's words clawed at the edges of my resolve, a reminder that some truths could unleash chaos.

"Honestly?" I finally replied, my voice steady as I forced a smile that felt like a mask. "I'm just trying to figure out my next move on this big project at work. It's all-consuming."

He tilted his head, skepticism evident. "You know, you're a terrible liar. I can practically see the wheels turning in your head. What's really going on?"

I tried to laugh it off, but the sound felt hollow, and the tension crackled in the air like static electricity. "You know me too well," I conceded, my heart thumping as I debated whether to let him in on my growing fears. "I just... I don't want to mess anything up with us."

His expression softened, a flicker of understanding shining through. "You won't. Just be honest with me."

In that moment, my defenses crumbled slightly, and I felt an urge to confess, to spill everything about Madison's warning and the web of emotions weaving between us. But before I could speak, a figure appeared in my peripheral vision, breaking the spell we had woven.

Madison strode into the restaurant, her heels clicking sharply against the tiled floor, a predator on the hunt. I froze, my heart plummeting into my stomach as her eyes scanned the room before landing on us. The smile she wore was like a wolf in sheep's clothing, too polished and too bright.

"Lila! Fancy seeing you here," she chirped, her voice dripping with saccharine sweetness that sent chills down my spine. "I didn't know you were a fan of this place. I suppose I should have guessed."

Ethan shifted in his seat, surprise flitting across his features. "Madison," he said, his tone curt. "What are you doing here?"

"Just grabbing a bite after work," she replied, her gaze locking onto mine with an intensity that made the air around us grow thick and oppressive. "Isn't it cute how you two are having a dinner date?"

The phrase felt like a slap, my cheeks flushing with embarrassment. I glanced at Ethan, who wore a look of irritation, his jaw clenched tight. "It's not a date, Madison. We're just catching up," he said, his voice steady but laced with tension.

"Oh, really? Because it looks like a date to me." She leaned closer, her eyes narrowing as she spoke. "You know, Lila, I think it's time for a little honesty. Ethan deserves to know exactly what he's getting into with you."

Every instinct in me screamed to stand up and walk away, but I was rooted in my seat, caught between a rock and a hard place. I could feel the heat rising in my cheeks as I struggled to find words, any words, that could diffuse the situation.

"Madison, stop," I said, my voice trembling slightly. "This isn't the place—"

But she wasn't listening. "You think you can just waltz in and charm him with your sunny disposition?" Her tone shifted, sharp and cutting. "You have no idea what you're up against."

"Why don't you enlighten me?" I shot back, my frustration boiling over, the simmering tension finally reaching a breaking point.

Ethan's eyes darted between us, a mix of confusion and frustration flickering in their depths. "Madison, can we not do this right now?" he implored, clearly wanting to restore the fragile peace that had been shattered.

"Why? Because you're scared? Scared she'll expose you for who you really are?" Her voice rose, echoing around the restaurant, drawing attention from nearby tables. A couple at the bar turned to watch, eyes wide with intrigue.

"Madison!" Ethan's voice was low and firm, but the fire in her eyes only intensified.

I felt like I was drowning, caught in a wave of panic that surged through me. "What are you talking about?" I demanded, though a sick feeling knotted in my stomach. I needed answers, but the words fell from my lips like stones.

Madison took a step closer, lowering her voice conspiratorially. "You really think you're special? That you're different from all the others?"

"Others?" I echoed, bewildered. "What do you mean?"

She smirked, her expression a mix of pity and malice. "Ethan has a type, and you're just the flavor of the month. Once he's done with you, he'll move on to the next—just like the others."

The world around me blurred as her words sunk in, each syllable a tiny dagger that twisted deeper into my chest. I glanced at Ethan, searching for any hint of confirmation, but his expression was unreadable, his gaze locked on Madison, eyes narrowed in a mixture of disbelief and anger.

"I can't believe you would stoop this low," he said, his voice low and laced with venom. "You know that's not true."

"Oh, is it not? You can't deny your track record, Ethan. It's just a matter of time before Lila finds out exactly how disposable she really is."

"Stop it!" I blurted, my voice louder than intended, desperation lacing my words. "This isn't fair. I came here to enjoy dinner, not to get ambushed."

Madison shrugged, an insincere smile still plastered on her face. "I'm just trying to save you from making a mistake, Lila. You're too good for him."

"Maybe I'm not looking to be saved," I shot back, my heart pounding as the words hung in the air, raw and honest.

"Is that so?" she challenged, crossing her arms, her demeanor almost smug. "What if he hurts you? You've seen how he operates."

"Enough!" Ethan erupted, his voice booming across the restaurant, silencing the murmurs around us. "This is between us, Madison. You need to back off."

Madison blinked, surprise flashing across her face, but I sensed an undercurrent of resentment swirling beneath her cool exterior. "Fine. Just remember, Lila, you've been warned." With that, she turned on her heel and strode away, leaving an awkward silence in her wake, the clinking of cutlery and murmurs of conversation resuming like the world had never shifted.

I took a deep breath, trying to steady the storm brewing within me, while the aftershocks of Madison's words echoed like a siren in my mind. The tension in the air was thick, and I could feel Ethan's gaze on me, searching, questioning.

"What was that all about?" he asked, his voice steady but concerned.

"Honestly, I don't even know anymore," I replied, my heart racing as I met his gaze, trying to gauge his reaction. "It was just... so out of line."

"I'm sorry you had to deal with her," he said, running a hand through his hair in frustration. "She's protective, but that was uncalled for."

I nodded, but doubts crept back in like shadows, clouding my mind. "I didn't think she'd come here. I just wanted a normal night."

Ethan leaned back, crossing his arms as his expression turned contemplative. "Lila, I promise you, I'm not like that. I want you to know that."

The sincerity in his voice pulled at my heart, but the echoes of Madison's accusation lingered like a dark cloud overhead. I wanted to believe him, to trust that our connection was genuine, yet the weight of uncertainty pressed down on me.

Just as I opened my mouth to respond, the restaurant door swung open, and a gust of cool air swept through, carrying a sudden chill. My eyes darted to the entrance, where a tall figure stood silhouetted against the warm glow inside. My breath caught in my throat as recognition hit me.

There stood Max, Ethan's older brother, his presence commanding and unexpected. Dressed in a tailored suit that seemed to mold to his athletic frame, he scanned the room with piercing eyes before locking onto our table.

"Ethan!" he called, striding toward us, a confident smile spreading across his face. "I didn't expect to find you here!"

A rush of anxiety coursed through me, a sense of foreboding wrapping around my heart like a vice. Ethan's expression shifted, and the tension between us crack

Chapter 9: Cracks in the Foundation

The rain pounded relentlessly against my window, a symphony of droplets that echoed the turmoil brewing in my chest. The clock on the wall ticked slowly, each second stretching into a miniature eternity as I sat on the edge of my couch, mind swirling with thoughts of Ethan and the fragile state of his engagement. The scent of damp earth drifted through the open window, mingling with the faintest hint of the lavender candle flickering on the coffee table, a feeble attempt at creating calm amidst the chaos. I could almost hear my mother's voice in my head, a mixture of admonishment and concern. "You can't plan love, darling; it's not a wedding checklist."

I squeezed my eyes shut, attempting to shut out the memories of Ethan and Madison, their laughter blending into a melodious harmony that felt painfully out of reach. A week had passed since Madison's warning, and each day had felt like walking on eggshells, the pressure mounting like a tempest just waiting to break. I had dedicated my career to making other people's dreams come true, crafting weddings that sparkled with joy, but now, I stood at the precipice of watching someone else's fairy tale crumble, and I was at the center of it all.

The doorbell rang, piercing the heavy silence. I froze, heart racing, knowing that any sense of tranquility I had tried to cultivate had vanished. It was late—too late for anything but bad news or unexpected visitors. I pushed myself up from the couch, each step feeling like a battle against gravity as I approached the door. When I opened it, the sight before me sent a jolt through my veins. Ethan stood there, drenched, his normally vibrant eyes now shadowed with distress, his usually charming smile replaced by a pallor that told me he had been wrestling with demons I couldn't see.

"Ethan," I whispered, taking a step back to let him in. The warmth of my apartment collided with the chill emanating from his body, a stark reminder of how the external world often mirrored our internal struggles. He walked in, shaking rain from his hair like a wet dog, and I couldn't help but smile at the absurdity of the moment. Despite the heaviness in the air, the image was endearing—an unwelcome reminder of how familiar we had become, like two errant characters in a romantic comedy who couldn't quite find their way to the happy ending.

But the levity faded as he turned to face me, and the laughter we shared before felt like a distant memory. "I can't do this anymore," he said, his voice a strained whisper that barely broke through the silence. "I can't go through with the wedding."

The thrill of his confession ignited a spark in me, a wild, reckless thing that danced dangerously close to the edge of despair. I wanted to scream with joy and sorrow all at once, but instead, I stood there, rooted to the spot, searching for the right words as if they were hidden behind my neatly stacked bridal magazines. "What do you mean? You're talking about Madison, right?" My heart hammered in my chest, each beat echoing the anxiety spiraling within me.

"Yes," he said, dragging a hand through his hair, wet strands sticking to his forehead. "I can't marry her. I just... I can't. It's not right."

"Is it because of me?" The question slipped out before I could reign it in, a clumsy confession hanging in the air between us. I cursed myself internally. This wasn't the time for me to take a selfish plunge into the depths of my emotions. This was about him, about what he needed, not what I wanted.

Ethan sighed heavily, pinching the bridge of his nose as if that would clear away the storm brewing behind his eyes. "I don't know, but I can't keep pretending everything is fine when it's not. And honestly, Madison deserves better than that. You both do."

His words struck a chord deep within me, resonating like a note plucked from a stringed instrument, raw and exposed. I had spent countless hours dreaming up perfect weddings, rehearsing vows and crafting the flawless ambiance, yet here I was, entangled in a web of heartbreak, realizing I might be the architect of my own undoing. "You can't just walk away from something like this. What about the plans? The family? The money spent?"

He looked at me, a mix of pain and confusion etched across his features. "You think I'm worried about the plans? I've spent too long worrying about everyone else's happiness. I'm the one who's miserable."

The walls of my carefully constructed world felt like they were trembling, as if the very foundation I had built my career upon was crumbling. I had never intended for any of this to happen, yet here we were, two souls caught in the maelstrom of emotions we had ignored for too long. I wanted to reach out, to comfort him, but the distance felt insurmountable. It was as if I were watching a slow-motion train wreck, horrified yet captivated by the unfolding disaster.

"I didn't mean for this to happen," I finally admitted, my voice barely above a whisper. "I never wanted to hurt anyone."

Ethan's eyes softened, the hardness melting into a vulnerability that sent a shiver down my spine. "Sometimes, hurting is a part of finding out what we really want." His gaze was penetrating, and I felt like he could see right through my carefully polished facade, unraveling the truth hidden beneath.

For a moment, the weight of our shared silence hung heavily in the air, charged with unspoken words and unrealized possibilities. We stood there, caught in a moment that felt suspended in time, a fragile thread connecting our worlds as the rain continued its relentless symphony outside.

The air thickened between us, a volatile concoction of vulnerability and unresolved tension. I watched Ethan, waiting for some flicker of resolve to ignite in his eyes, but instead, he looked more lost than ever. It was like he had stumbled into a maze of his own making, and I was stuck at the entrance, desperate to pull him back to safety. Yet, wasn't I the one who had crafted the blueprints of this very labyrinth? My heart sank with the realization that I could easily guide him through its twists and turns, but at what cost?

"I thought you were happy," I managed to say, my voice cracking like the fragile veneer of calm I was desperately trying to maintain. "I thought you loved her."

"I thought I did too," he replied, exhaling sharply as if he were releasing the air trapped in his lungs for too long. "But love is more complicated than just wanting to be with someone. It's about being true to yourself, and I haven't been true to myself in ages."

His honesty struck me. I often masked my own uncertainties with the bright, shiny illusions of weddings—the glittering aisle runners, the meticulously folded napkins, the laughter that masked the tears lurking behind closed doors. I could create a perfect day for someone else, but when it came to my own life, I felt more like a director struggling with a script I hadn't written.

"Then what do you want?" I asked, the words spilling out before I could reel them back in. A question that hung heavily in the air, glistening with the weight of everything unspoken between us. It felt almost reckless, like handing him a lit match and asking him to dance with fire.

"I want..." His voice faltered, and he stepped closer, the space between us shrinking, a void filled with unspoken dreams and regrets. "I want to feel free. I want to chase after what really matters."

"What matters to you?" I whispered, the question laden with a desperate hope I couldn't quite suppress.

"I don't know." He glanced down, his brow furrowed in contemplation. "Maybe it's not about chasing at all. Maybe it's about standing still for a moment and figuring out what I truly want."

I held my breath, the gravity of his admission pulling me closer to him, like a moth to a flame. And in that moment, standing under the soft glow of the living room lamp, surrounded by the remnants of my well-ordered world, I felt an urge to reach out and grasp the ephemeral connection between us, an urge to ground him, to ground myself.

Just as I opened my mouth to say something, anything that could anchor us both in this turbulent sea of emotions, a sudden knock at the door jolted us back to reality.

I jumped, the unexpected sound breaking the fragile atmosphere we had been weaving. "Who could that be at this hour?" I muttered, glancing at Ethan, who looked equally startled.

"Could be a wedding crasher, coming to collect an RSVP," he joked, attempting to mask the tension with humor. It almost worked.

With a cautious breath, I opened the door to find Madison standing there, eyes wide and hair wild, as if she had just stepped out of a storm. "I had a feeling I'd find you two here," she said, her voice edged with a mix of anger and confusion.

The moment hung in the air, sharp and charged. "Madison," I said, my voice faltering as I tried to gauge the depth of her emotions. "What are you doing here?"

"I came to talk to Ethan, obviously," she replied, her gaze shifting from me to him, her expression hardening. "I thought maybe you'd both figured out a way to fix this mess."

"Mess?" Ethan echoed, his voice betraying a hint of exasperation. "This isn't a mess, Madison. This is about being honest with ourselves. About what we really want."

Her eyes flared with indignation. "And what do you want, Ethan? To throw everything away because you're having a moment of doubt? We have a wedding to plan!"

"Not anymore," he shot back, a sharpness in his tone that sent a jolt through me. "I can't marry you, Madison. I thought I could, but I can't. I can't lie to you or myself."

Madison's expression shifted, the anger giving way to something deeper—hurt, confusion, maybe even a flicker of understanding. "So, what? You're just going to walk away from everything we built together?" Her voice trembled slightly, a crack in her bravado that revealed how much she cared, even amidst the chaos.

"We didn't build anything real," Ethan countered, the fight draining from him. "I've been living in this shadow of expectations, and I need to step out of it."

Madison's gaze flicked to me, suspicion mingling with a spark of realization. "And you—what part do you play in this? Are you the reason he's suddenly having an existential crisis?"

"I'm not the reason," I said quickly, the weight of her accusation heavy on my chest. "Ethan's feelings are his own, and he deserves to explore them."

The tension crackled between the three of us, a tangled web of unspoken words and raw emotions. I felt like an intruder in a narrative I had once thought I controlled. I wanted to stand up for Ethan, to defend the choice he was making, but there was an unshakable truth: this was his battle, not mine.

Madison crossed her arms, her posture radiating a mix of defiance and vulnerability. "And what about you? Are you really okay with this?"

I hesitated, the question piercing straight through the fragile barrier I had built around my heart. "I want him to be happy, even if that doesn't include me," I replied, my voice steadier than I felt. "That's what love is, right? Letting go when it's for the best."

Ethan's gaze flicked to me, a flicker of gratitude mixed with sorrow. It was in that moment that I realized the depth of my own feelings, tangled in a web of what-ifs and maybes. The truth hung heavily in the air: I cared for him more than I had allowed myself to admit, and watching him choose freedom felt like a bittersweet gift.

Madison opened her mouth to respond, but the words seemed to dissolve, caught in the tumult of emotions swirling around us. Instead, she simply shook her head, the storm of feelings swirling in her eyes. "I need to think," she finally said, her voice a whisper as she turned and walked away, leaving behind a lingering silence that echoed the gravity of our shared moment.

Ethan and I stood there, the door swinging slightly on its hinges, the remnants of a shattered engagement hanging like smoke in the air. The chaos had left us bare, exposed in ways we hadn't anticipated. And as the rain continued to drum against the window, a new kind of understanding washed over us, fragile and raw, yet somehow full of potential.

The silence left in Madison's wake felt like a taut string, vibrating with unspoken words and unanswered questions. Ethan and I stood together in the dim light of my living room, the air thick with unresolved emotions and an awkwardness that clung to us like the humidity outside. His expression shifted, caught between relief and regret, as if he had just stepped off a tightrope and wasn't sure how to find solid ground.

"What just happened?" he murmured, running a hand through his damp hair, the rainwater glistening like scattered stars in the soft light.

"Honestly? I think you just shocked the engagement out of her," I replied, a wry smile creeping onto my lips. "That was impressive. You should add 'emotional demolitions expert' to your resume."

He chuckled softly, the tension between us softening, if only just. "Great. Just what I always wanted. The first line of my cover letter: 'I am skilled at ruining other people's happiness.'"

"It takes a certain kind of talent," I teased, trying to lighten the mood, though my own heart was still heavy with the implications of what had just unfolded. "But really, you did the right thing. You have to follow your heart, even if it means breaking a few expectations along the way."

His gaze intensified, searching my face for something I wasn't sure I could give. "And what if my heart wants to be here with you?"

The words hung in the air like an echo, reverberating with the weight of possibilities. I felt a flicker of hope, a mischievous little flame that sparked in my chest, but just as quickly, caution pulled it back into the shadows. "Ethan, don't say things like that unless you're ready for the fallout."

"What fallout?" he asked, his voice low and sincere. "I mean, it's not like we have a wedding to plan anymore. What's holding us back?"

I bit my lip, grappling with the sudden rush of adrenaline that accompanied his question. The truth was a wild animal inside me, clawing at the bars of its cage. "You're still figuring things out. You just left Madison. You're in a vulnerable place right now."

He stepped closer, the distance between us dissolving in the warmth of his gaze. "And you're the one who makes me feel like I'm actually living, not just existing. I don't want to ignore that. Not anymore."

The gravity of his confession twisted in my stomach, both thrilling and terrifying. I wanted to lean into the moment, to dive headfirst into this new reality where we could be something more than friends. But the specter of Madison loomed large, her hurt still fresh and raw. "You're just feeling liberated. It's a rebound."

"Rebounds can be great, though." He leaned in, his voice dropping to a whisper, a playful spark dancing in his eyes. "Just look at all those sitcoms where the rebound ends up being the one."

I rolled my eyes, half-amused and half-frustrated. "Yeah, but sitcoms are scripted, Ethan. They don't account for the messiness of real life."

"But isn't that the point?" He edged closer, his breath warm against my skin, the scent of rain-soaked earth and his cologne weaving around us. "Life is messy. It's supposed to be."

I could feel the heat radiating from him, drawing me in like a moth to a flame, and suddenly I was acutely aware of everything—the gentle hum of the refrigerator, the soft patter of the rain, and the way his fingers twitched as if they longed to reach out and touch me. "Ethan—"

The doorbell rang again, interrupting the moment like a sudden gust of wind. My heart sank as the reality of our situation crashed back down on me. "Who now?" I muttered, irritation creeping into my voice. "It's like a soap opera out here."

Ethan chuckled softly, but the tension returned as we exchanged glances, both acutely aware of the delicate state of our emotions. "Should I answer it?" he asked, looking hesitant.

"Uh, maybe I should," I said, straightening my posture. "I don't want to make things worse. Not now."

But before I could reach the door, the ringing persisted, louder and more insistent, and a voice called out from the other side. "Open up! It's an emergency!"

I paused, my heart racing again, more from curiosity than fear. "An emergency? Who is it?"

"It's Madison! Please, I need to talk to you both!"

I exchanged a quick glance with Ethan, who seemed equally perplexed. "What does she want?" I asked, my voice barely a whisper.

"I don't know, but it sounds urgent," he replied, concern etching itself onto his features.

With a reluctant sigh, I opened the door. Madison stood there, her face a mix of determination and vulnerability, her hair wild from the rain, eyes glistening with unshed tears. "I need you both to listen," she said, her voice trembling slightly but laced with resolve.

I stepped aside, allowing her to enter, and Ethan's body stiffened beside me as he processed her sudden presence. "What's going on, Madison?" he asked, his tone cautious yet concerned.

"I realized something after I left," she began, her words tumbling out in a rush. "I don't want to lose you, Ethan. Not like this. I don't want to walk away from everything we've built without at least fighting for it."

Ethan's expression softened, but I could see the conflict within him. "Madison, I—"

"No, let me finish!" she interrupted, holding up a hand. "I thought I wanted the fairytale, but what if I've been chasing a dream that isn't mine to have? What if we need to take a step back and redefine what this relationship really means?"

"Are you suggesting an open relationship?" I blurted out, the absurdity of it all hitting me hard.

"No, not exactly." Madison's brow furrowed in frustration. "But maybe we need to talk about the fact that love doesn't fit into neat little boxes. I can't keep pretending everything is perfect when it's not, and I don't want either of you to feel trapped by what I expect."

I could see Ethan wrestling with her words, torn between the comfort of familiarity and the dizzying possibilities that lay before him. The air felt electric, a charged current that threatened to ignite whatever fragile hope had begun to form between us.

"Madison, are you really okay with this?" he asked, his voice barely above a whisper. "Because it feels like you're asking me to choose between you and... well, her." He gestured to me, the intensity of the moment swirling around us like the storm raging outside.

Madison looked back and forth between us, her expression earnest. "I want you both to be happy, even if it means letting go of my expectations."

The walls of my carefully constructed world began to tremble, and I could feel the ground shifting beneath my feet. "So, what now?" I asked, my heart pounding as I looked at Ethan, who stood on the precipice of an emotional cliff.

Before he could respond, another voice echoed from outside, cutting through the tension like a knife. "Ethan! You need to come out here!"

We all turned to the door, breath hitching in our throats.

The unmistakable figure of Ethan's mother appeared in the doorway, her face pale and drawn, eyes wide with concern. "There's been an accident! You need to hurry!"

My heart dropped, and the fragile moment of clarity we had built shattered like glass underfoot. As the storm continued to rage outside, another tempest brewed within our midst, and I could feel the storm of emotions crashing down around us.

"Wait! What do you mean? Who's been hurt?" Ethan's voice rose in panic, and I could see the fear flicker in his eyes, mirroring my own dread.

The reality of the situation hung heavily in the air, a cliffhanger that sent chills racing down my spine. Just as I reached for Ethan's hand, grounding him in the chaos, I knew we were about to be pulled into a whirlwind of decisions that would forever change the course of our lives.

Chapter 10: The Shattered Vow

I watch the raindrops race down the glass, a chaotic symphony of nature mirroring the tempest inside me. Ethan stands across the room, arms crossed tightly over his chest, the tension radiating off him like a storm ready to burst. His tousled hair, usually so charming, looks more like a battlefield today—disheveled and worn. Each droplet that splatters against the window seems to echo the unresolved questions bouncing around in my head. I wish I could say I was prepared for this moment, that I'd conjured up a script of understanding and acceptance, but all I have is a gnawing uncertainty that wraps itself around my heart like a vine choking the life from it.

"Do you want something to drink?" I ask, my voice teetering on the edge of steadiness. It's a mundane question, one that holds the weight of our shattered vows and my desperate need for normalcy in a world turned upside down. He shakes his head, but the corner of his mouth quirks up, a fleeting smile that doesn't quite reach his eyes. That smile, a remnant of better days, makes my stomach flutter and sink all at once.

"I think I need to process," he replies, his gaze drifting to the window, where the rain paints a blurry picture of the world outside. The streetlights cast an orange glow, giving the wet pavement a sheen that looks almost magical. It should be beautiful, but instead, it feels like a cruel joke, a reminder that life moves on even as ours hangs in limbo.

"Processing," I echo, as if the word is foreign on my tongue. I want to laugh, but the sound feels stuck somewhere in my throat, tangled with the pieces of our conversation and the weight of unspoken fears. "Is that what we're calling it? Because I think we might need a new term. 'Processing' sounds too serene for the disaster we've created."

Ethan chuckles softly, the sound breaking through the tension like a beam of sunlight, and for a moment, I can almost forget the impending storm. "Fair point. Maybe it's more like 'navigating the wreckage' or 'finding the light in the chaos.'" His eyes meet mine, and I see a flicker of the Ethan I fell in love with—the one who could make me laugh even on my worst days.

A comfortable silence settles between us, punctuated only by the rhythmic patter of rain against the window. I want to cling to this moment, to preserve it like a delicate flower pressed between the pages of a book, but the reality of our situation looms like a dark cloud. The wedding that had once sparkled with promise is now a distant memory, a shattered dream littering the floor like broken glass.

"Do you think we'll ever be okay again?" I finally ask, my voice barely above a whisper. It's a question that hangs heavily in the air, both vulnerable and terrifying. I watch as his brow furrows, the weight of the world reflected in his gaze.

"I don't know," he admits, his voice thick with emotion. "I want to believe we can be. But I also don't want to make promises I can't keep." His honesty is both a balm and a knife, soothing yet cutting deep into my heart. I nod, trying to mask the swell of disappointment. Promises were what we had, what made us believe in our future together.

"I thought we were stronger than this," I say, the words escaping me before I can reign them in. "That we could handle anything."

"Maybe we're not as strong as we thought," Ethan replies, his voice heavy with remorse. "Or maybe we just misread what strength really looks like. Sometimes it's not about holding on; it's about letting go."

His words hang in the air, mingling with the aroma of the coffee I had forgotten to brew. I can feel the pull of reality—our relationship in shambles, the painful truth that letting go might be the only way forward. But there's a part of me that clings stubbornly to the idea of us, like a child gripping their favorite toy as the world spins too fast around them.

"Letting go," I repeat, tasting the bitterness of it on my tongue. "Is that really what you want?"

His eyes search mine, seeking something unnamable, a connection that feels as fragile as spun glass. "It's not what I want," he finally says, "but maybe it's what we need. We can't keep pretending everything is okay when we both know it's not."

The admission cuts deeper than I expected. I can't shake the thought of Madison, the woman who had become a ghost in our lives, haunting every corner of our love story. She had been the shadow lurking behind the scenes, the secret that unraveled everything we had built. I should hate her, but instead, I feel a strange kinship—a shared experience of loss, a struggle for something unattainable.

As I gaze out at the rain-soaked street, I wonder what it would feel like to be free of this weight, to not have to look over my shoulder for shadows that no longer belong. But freedom often comes with a cost, and the thought of letting go of Ethan feels like signing a death warrant for my heart.

"Maybe," I whisper, the word slipping from my lips, uncertain yet heavy with meaning. "Maybe we can find a way back to each other. If we really want it."

The vulnerability in my voice resonates with him. He takes a tentative step forward, his expression shifting from guarded to hopeful. "What if we take it one day at a time? Just... see where it leads us?"

I nod, feeling a spark of resolve flicker to life amid the chaos. Perhaps this isn't the end but a chance for a new beginning—an opportunity to redefine us, to navigate the wreckage together. The rain outside begins to lighten, a sign that even storms eventually pass.

With Ethan beside me, I feel a glimmer of hope ignite, a fragile yet fierce determination to fight for the love that still lingers between us, just waiting to be rekindled.

The lingering scent of freshly brewed coffee fills the air, but it does little to ease the tension that hangs between us like a thick fog. I look at Ethan, his expression a mix of uncertainty and hope, and feel a strange urge to reach out, to close the gap that seems to widen with each passing moment. Instead, I turn back to the window, watching the rain diminish from torrential downpour to a gentle drizzle, as if the world outside is mirroring my own tumultuous emotions.

"Do you ever think about how life can feel like one of those terrible rom-coms?" I ask, trying to inject a hint of levity into the thick atmosphere. "You know, where you realize the plot twist is more like a bad punchline?"

Ethan's laughter, warm and genuine, wraps around me, soothing the frayed edges of my nerves. "Yeah, like when the lead character realizes she's been chasing the wrong guy all along while the right one stands in the background with a bemused expression."

I chuckle, despite the weight on my heart. "Exactly! The guy in the background is usually charming, wears glasses, and has the perfect sense of humor. And here I am, stuck in the middle of my own cliché."

His gaze turns serious as he steps closer, the distance between us shrinking, yet the gap of uncertainty remains. "Maybe this is our chance to rewrite the script. Maybe the guy in the background isn't so bad after all."

"Let's just hope there are no dramatic monologues about feelings," I retort, trying to mask the sudden flutter of hope in my chest with humor. "I'm not ready for that kind of intensity. I have a limit, you know."

"Then we'll keep it low-key," he replies, a spark of mischief lighting up his eyes. "How about a coffee date instead of a grand gesture? Just us, some caffeine, and no expectations."

"Caffeine sounds good," I concede, glancing back at the coffee pot, which now gurgles softly, begging to be poured. "But the last time we tried to keep things low-key, I ended up in a high-stakes game of emotional poker."

"True," he muses, running a hand through his hair. "But maybe this time we play with our cards face-up. No bluffs, just honesty."

I take a deep breath, steeling myself. "Alright, then. Face-up it is. But first, let's get that coffee before we dive into the abyss of our feelings."

With a determined nod, I pour two steaming mugs, the rich aroma swirling around us like a comforting embrace. I hand one to Ethan, our fingers brushing for a heartbeat, igniting a spark that sends a jolt of warmth coursing through me. It's a reminder that beneath the chaos, there's still something there, still a flicker of what we once had.

We settle onto my small couch, which has seen better days—stuffed with mismatched cushions and a throw blanket that's more frayed than fashionable. But in this moment, it feels like a safe haven. I take a sip of my coffee, allowing the warmth to seep into my bones, while Ethan watches me with a curiosity that makes my heart race.

"Okay," I say, placing my mug on the coffee table with a determined clink. "Let's get into it. What's really going on with you? The Ethan who called off the wedding isn't the same guy I know."

His eyes cloud with a flicker of something—guilt, perhaps? "I guess I was hoping you'd still see the good in me," he replies quietly. "But you're right. I'm a mess right now."

"Being a mess isn't a crime," I counter, leaning forward, eager to peel back the layers. "What's the root of it? Is it Madison? Or is it... us?"

He takes a deep breath, his fingers wrapping tightly around his mug as if it's a lifeline. "It's everything, really. I thought I had it all figured out, and then suddenly—everything was wrong. I felt trapped, and instead of talking to you about it, I made the wrong choice."

The raw honesty of his admission hits me like a wave. "Trapped how? Was it about the wedding, or was it about something deeper?"

"Both, I guess," he says, the honesty weighing heavily between us. "It felt like I was gearing up for a life I wasn't ready for. I was so focused on the wedding that I lost sight of why we were getting married in the first place."

"Are you saying you didn't want to marry me?" My heart races, and the question hangs in the air, a fragile balloon filled with sharp-edged uncertainty.

"No, that's not it at all!" He rushes to reassure me, his voice rising slightly. "I wanted to marry you. I still do, but I was terrified of becoming what everyone expected me to be—this perfect husband, this ideal partner. And the pressure of it all just... I panicked."

I sip my coffee, trying to process his words, my mind a swirling tempest of emotions. "But you could have talked to me. We could have worked through it together."

"I know," he replies, remorse lacing his tone. "I should have. I didn't want to drag you into my mess, but in doing that, I ended up creating an even bigger one."

There's a vulnerability in his eyes that softens my heart, but I can't help the sharp edge of fear creeping back in. "So what happens now? You say you want to rewrite the script, but how do we start?"

"By being honest, I think. By acknowledging that we're both scared, but that doesn't mean we're broken."

I study him, this man who once made my heart sing and now feels like a puzzle with missing pieces. "So, if we're being honest, what about Madison? You can't expect me to ignore that elephant in the room."

His expression falters, and I brace myself for whatever he might say next. "I don't want to hurt you, but I can't deny that she's a part of this. I got caught up in something I shouldn't have, and now I have to face the consequences."

I nod, the sharp sting of jealousy mingling with a deep sense of betrayal. "And what if she comes back? What if she wants to be with you again?"

"Then I'll deal with it. But right now, I want to focus on us," he says, his gaze intense. "I want to figure this out, but only if you're willing to fight for it, too."

The challenge hangs in the air, tantalizing and terrifying. It would be so easy to retreat into my safe shell, to distance myself from the storm that is Ethan. But beneath the uncertainty, I can see the flickering flame of what we once shared. Perhaps it's worth fighting for. Perhaps we can emerge from this wreckage, battered but unbroken, and write a new chapter together.

The silence that blankets the room feels both heavy and electric, as if the air itself is charged with unspoken truths and unacknowledged fears. I can sense Ethan grappling with the weight of his choices, the gravity of what we're trying to navigate together. The coffee, now tepid, sits forgotten between us, a relic of our attempt to find comfort in a moment that's anything but cozy.

"Okay, let's say we do want to fight for this," I begin, my voice steadier than I feel. "What does that even look like? Do we have a battle plan? A strategy for how to keep Madison at bay while we figure out the wreckage of our relationship?"

Ethan laughs softly, but there's an edge of nervousness to it. "I mean, I've never really been good at strategizing. My plans usually involve a solid escape route." He flashes a wry grin, and despite everything, it pulls at something deep inside me—a reminder of the laughter we used to share before the chaos set in.

"I can't believe you just admitted that," I retort, rolling my eyes playfully. "What kind of grown man has a solid escape route for romantic entanglements?"

"The kind who panics when faced with emotional commitment," he replies with mock seriousness. "But I'm working on it. I promise."

There's a softness in his voice that makes my heart ache, a blend of sincerity and vulnerability that pulls me in. I lean forward, resting my elbows on my knees, my gaze locked on his. "Then what's your plan now? Because I'd prefer not to be just another plot twist in your escape saga."

He takes a deep breath, his expression shifting from playful to contemplative. "Maybe the first step is to be real about everything—about us, about Madison, about what we both need. And that includes figuring out what I want, which seems to change every other day."

"Alright, let's break it down," I say, my tone shifting to that of a reluctant strategist. "What do you want?"

"I want to be with you, but I can't ignore the mess I made," he admits, his voice thick with emotion. "I can't pretend it didn't happen. I owe it to you to be completely transparent."

"Transparent? Now that's a novel idea," I reply, a hint of sarcasm slipping through. "But fine. I can handle the truth. Just give it to me straight."

"Fine," he says, a hint of a smile returning. "First, I need to tell you that Madison reached out to me last week."

My heart drops, plummeting into the depths of a stormy ocean. "What?" I can barely manage to utter the word, each syllable laced with disbelief. "You're serious?"

He nods slowly, his gaze never wavering from mine. "I ignored her. I swear I did. But she keeps popping up, like a bad penny."

"A bad penny?" I scoff, the metaphor sticking in my throat like a bitter pill. "More like a raging hurricane that threatens to tear apart everything in its path."

"Fair point," he concedes, scratching his head. "But I can't let her shake us. Not when I feel this..." He trails off, searching for the right words, a mix of frustration and sincerity etched on his face.

"Feel this what? Uncertainty? Fear? Guilt?"

"No," he says, his voice firm yet softening as he continues. "I feel this connection with you that I can't ignore. I want to figure this out, even if it's messy."

The raw honesty in his admission catches me off guard, and I can't help but feel a rush of warmth flood through me. "Then let's do that. Let's figure this out, together."

"Together," he echoes, and for a moment, the air between us feels lighter, filled with a hesitant hope that we might be able to navigate this wreckage after all.

But just as I start to believe we might find our way back to each other, the doorbell rings, shattering the moment like glass hitting the floor. The sound reverberates through the small apartment, echoing with a sense of dread that twists my stomach into knots.

"Who could that be?" I ask, instinctively rising to my feet. "If it's Madison, I swear—"

"It shouldn't be," Ethan interrupts, standing up beside me. "I didn't tell anyone where I was."

My heart races as I move toward the door, uncertainty gnawing at me. I peer through the peephole and my stomach drops at the sight of a familiar face.

"Is it Madison?" Ethan asks, his voice barely above a whisper, dread flooding his expression.

"No," I breathe out, relief washing over me for a fleeting moment. "It's just... my mom."

He blinks at me, his brows furrowing in confusion. "Your mom? What's she doing here?"

"Good question," I say, panic stirring within me. "I wasn't expecting her until next week."

Ethan glances back toward the kitchen, as if weighing his options, before shaking his head. "You should let her in."

I hesitate. "But we were just about to—"

"I know," he interjects. "But it's your mom. Maybe she has a reason for showing up unannounced."

Reluctantly, I step back and open the door, bracing myself for whatever whirlwind is about to blow into my carefully crafted space. My mom stands there, her bright smile dimmed by an expression of concern that makes my heart sink.

"Hey, honey! I was in the neighborhood and thought I'd stop by!" she chirps, but her eyes dart to Ethan, and suddenly, the air in the room grows thick with unspoken tension.

"Hi, Mrs. Daniels," Ethan says, his voice polite but tight.

"Ethan," she acknowledges, her gaze shifting back to me. "Can I come in?"

I exchange a quick glance with Ethan, the unspoken words lingering between us. "Um, sure," I say, stepping aside. "I was just making coffee."

She steps in, her gaze flicking around the living room before settling on us. "I hope I'm not interrupting anything important."

"Not at all," I say, my voice a bit too bright, trying to mask the turmoil bubbling beneath the surface. "Just some coffee and... life discussions."

"Life discussions?" she repeats, a hint of skepticism creeping into her tone. "Sounds serious."

"Just the usual," I reply, forcing a laugh that feels too high-pitched. "You know, the whole 'what are we doing with our lives' thing."

She raises an eyebrow, her intuition sharper than I'd like to admit. "It looks like there's more to it than that. Are you two okay?"

Ethan glances at me, and I feel the weight of his gaze urging me to share everything—the mess, the uncertainty, the love that still simmers beneath it all. But the moment hangs precariously in the air, as if the fragile hope we've started to build might come crashing down at any moment.

"Yeah, we're good," I say, a little too quickly, trying to brush it off. "Just some stuff to work through, nothing we can't handle."

My mom's expression doesn't change; she seems to sense the undercurrent of tension, and I can almost hear the gears turning in her head. "Honey, you know I'm here for you, right? Whatever it is, you don't have to go through it alone."

"Thanks, Mom," I manage, my voice tightening. But the truth is, I'm not sure I want to involve her in this mess—not yet, not when everything feels so fragile.

"Mom, you remember when I mentioned that Ethan and I were going to take a break from planning the wedding?" I venture, hoping to steer the conversation back to safer waters.

"Of course," she replies, her gaze softening. "But I didn't realize it was more serious than that."

The tension thickens as Ethan shifts uncomfortably beside me, the air crackling with unspoken words and unresolved feelings.

"Is there something I should know?" my mom asks, her tone suddenly sharp.

Before I can respond, my phone buzzes violently from the coffee table, interrupting the moment. I glance down, my heart racing as I see Madison's name flashing across the screen.

"Uh-oh," Ethan murmurs, his eyes wide.

I pick up the phone, my heart pounding louder than ever. As I look at the screen, my stomach twists with dread and anticipation. I know that whatever I choose to do next could alter everything—send us spiraling back into chaos or open the door to something new.

"Maybe I should take this," I say, my voice a whisper, the gravity of the situation heavy on my shoulders.

Ethan's eyes widen, uncertainty etched on his face, but my mom stands firm beside me, her gaze unwavering. The door that had cracked open for us now hangs in the balance, threatening to close just as swiftly as it had opened.

"Madison?" I finally say, my voice barely audible as I swipe to answer, unsure of what to expect.

And then the world tilts beneath me, a chasm of uncertainty stretching out before us, waiting to swallow us whole.

Chapter 11: A Town Divided

The bell above the door jingled as I stepped into the coffee shop, a sound that used to fill me with warmth. Now, it was a clanging reminder of the buzz around town. I could almost feel the eyes on me, hot and judging, like little needles pricking my skin. The aroma of freshly brewed coffee wafted through the air, mingling with the sweet scent of pastries. I had always adored this place, with its mismatched furniture and cozy nooks, but today it felt like I was stepping into enemy territory.

I approached the counter, forcing a smile at the barista, who had been a friend once—before the storm of gossip swept through. She busied herself with the espresso machine, avoiding my gaze as if I were the very embodiment of a storm cloud. I could hear the low murmur of voices behind me, snippets of conversation that twisted like vines around my heart.

"Can you believe she thought she could just step in like that?" one voice sneered.

I turned slightly, just enough to catch a glimpse of two women seated at a table, their heads bent together. One was holding a steaming cup, the other swirling a spoon in her half-finished latte, her expression a perfect mix of disdain and curiosity. It stung. I couldn't help but wonder how long they'd been waiting to pounce, sharpening their words like blades in anticipation of my arrival.

I pretended to be engrossed in the menu board, though I knew it by heart. My usual order, a caramel macchiato with a hint of vanilla, suddenly felt like a relic from a different life. Today, I needed something stronger—maybe an espresso shot to kick this overwhelming dread to the curb. "I'll have a double shot of espresso, please," I said, forcing cheer into my tone.

As I waited for my drink, I scanned the small café, my stomach twisting at the sight of familiar faces turned away from me. A group of college girls huddled together in a corner, their laughter ringing hollow. It used to feel like home here, this coffee shop, where I'd spend hours scribbling away in my notebook, lost in stories that bloomed like wildflowers in my mind. Now, it felt like a gallery of my shame, each corner a reminder of the life I had disrupted.

"Here you go!" The barista slid the cup across the counter, her smile strained, lacking the warmth that used to make me feel welcome. I clutched the hot cup, its heat seeping through the ceramic and warming my fingers. The bitterness of the espresso mirrored the sharp taste of betrayal that lingered in my mouth.

I stepped outside, the crisp autumn air a sharp contrast to the simmering tension inside. Leaves crunched beneath my feet as I walked down Main Street, their vibrant reds and yellows a mockery of the gray haze that clung to my thoughts. I had always loved fall, the way it wrapped the town in a cozy embrace, but today it felt like a funeral shroud.

With every step, I could sense the whispers following me, ghosts of my choices haunting the sidewalks. Ethan's broken engagement was like a thunderstorm brewing overhead—unpredictable and threatening. People loved Madison. They adored her. I was merely the backdrop to her fairy tale, a narrative thread plucked and tossed aside.

I crossed paths with Mr. Jenkins, the elderly man who owned the bookstore. He was adjusting his glasses, peering at me over the top of them as if I were a mystery he couldn't quite solve. "Morning, Clara," he said, his tone polite yet distant. "How are you holding up?"

I plastered on a smile, though it felt more like a mask than a genuine expression. "I'm doing okay, Mr. Jenkins. Just keeping busy."

He nodded slowly, and for a moment, I thought I saw a flicker of understanding in his eyes, a glimmer of sympathy before he turned and shuffled away. I felt my smile fade, leaving behind the bitterness that had settled like ash in my throat.

I reached the park, a place where children's laughter usually rang out, where picnics unfolded on sun-drenched grass. But today, it was empty, the swings swaying slightly in the wind as if echoing my own uncertainty. I sat on a bench, the wood cool beneath me, and took a deep breath, inhaling the earthy scent of fallen leaves mixed with the faint aroma of coffee still clinging to my clothes.

Ethan's name lingered in the air like a song I couldn't shake off. I had wanted to be the one to help him rediscover joy, to be a bright spot in the shadows of his heart. But I never intended to be the catalyst of chaos, the one who shattered the image of perfection that everyone else had created for him. I felt like a pariah in my own skin, a ghost haunting a place I once loved.

The sound of laughter broke my reverie, and I looked up to see a group of kids racing through the park, their faces alight with pure joy. For a fleeting moment, I envied their innocence, their ability to embrace life without the burden of expectations. But that envy quickly twisted into something sharper, a realization that I was the architect of my own undoing.

Just as I was about to rise and escape the suffocating silence, I spotted a figure approaching, someone I didn't expect but desperately needed. Ethan's tall frame cut through the haze like a lighthouse in the fog, his presence igniting a spark of something I hadn't felt in weeks. As he drew nearer, I could see the tension etched into his features, the weight of the town's whispers hanging over him like a storm cloud, threatening to unleash the rain of judgment upon us both.

"Clara," he said, his voice low and careful, as if testing the waters before plunging in. The way he said my name sent a rush of warmth through me, a reminder that beneath all this chaos, we were still connected—still tethered to each other in a way that felt both fragile and profound.

"Hey," I managed, my heart racing at the unexpected twist of fate. "What are you doing here?"

He sat beside me, the space between us heavy with unspoken words. "I came to find you. I thought we should talk."

My breath caught, a mix of hope and dread spiraling within me. This could be the moment that either shattered us further or began to rebuild what had been lost. I glanced at him, searching for signs of what he was feeling, and in that moment, I realized that no matter how divided the town might be, our hearts still beat in sync, both navigating the tumultuous waters of regret and possibility.

The wine glass trembles slightly in my hand, the deep red liquid swirling as I try to gather my thoughts. The room is dim, filled with shadows that seem to flicker with the ghosts of Ethan's past. I can't shake the feeling that we're standing on the edge of something vast and tumultuous, like the moment before a storm breaks. He leans back against the couch, his posture relaxed yet distant, as if he's physically here but mentally miles away. I wish I could reach into his mind, sift through the layers of his history, and pull out the pieces he's trying to hide.

"I never wanted to be the good son," he admits, his voice low, almost a whisper, laced with the bitterness of unfulfilled dreams. "My father always had plans for me—law school, the family firm. It was as if I was a project he could shape into his perfect image." He runs a hand through his hair, frustration rippling through him. "I wanted to be an artist, you know? To create something that was just... mine. But every time I picked up a brush, he'd remind me of my responsibilities, of what was expected."

Chapter 12: A New Perspective

It's a revelation that hits me like a bucket of ice water. I had assumed Ethan was the architect of his life, each choice deliberate and defiant. The thought of him being molded by someone else's dreams makes my heart ache. I shift slightly on the couch, feeling the heat radiate from his body, a comfort and a torment all at once. "So, you just... gave up?" I ask, struggling to comprehend the depths of his surrender.

His gaze flickers to mine, and for a moment, I see vulnerability etched across his features, a raw honesty that draws me closer. "It felt like survival. I didn't want to disappoint him. But that meant sacrificing my own happiness." He takes a long sip from his glass, the tension thick in the air. "Now, I don't even know who I am without those expectations looming over me."

The silence stretches, pregnant with unspoken words. I want to reach out, to comfort him, but the weight of his revelations hangs heavy between us. I've spent so long navigating my own labyrinth of disappointments that I can hardly bear the thought of stepping into his. "Ethan," I begin, my voice barely a whisper. "You're not defined by someone else's vision of you. You're allowed to be... you."

He snorts softly, a sharp sound that cuts through the darkness. "And who is that? I'm a mess, full of shattered dreams and regrets."

"You're also talented, intelligent, and kind," I counter, feeling a surge of defiance. "Just because you haven't found your path yet doesn't mean you're not worth knowing."

He turns to me then, those stormy eyes searching for something—maybe hope, maybe understanding. "You're just saying that because you're here with me now. You don't know the real me."

"Then let me," I challenge, leaning forward. "Let me in, Ethan. I'm not afraid of the mess."

His expression softens, and I think for a moment that I might have pierced through the armor he's built around himself. But as the moment stretches, it becomes clear that the walls are too high, too thick. The conversation weighs heavily, an anchor dragging us down into deeper waters.

We finish the bottle in silence, the room becoming a cocoon of intimacy tinged with tension. I can feel the air crackling between us, the unspoken thoughts pressing against the surface, begging to be released. Finally, he stands, moving to the window, the city lights casting a soft glow around him. "It's like I've been living someone else's life," he says, his voice barely above a murmur. "And now, I don't even know how to begin to unravel it."

I rise to join him, standing side by side, gazing out at the streets below. "You start small," I suggest, finding my footing in this uncharted territory. "Maybe by picking up that brush again. You could paint a self-portrait, a real one. Show the world who you are, flaws and all."

He laughs, a sound that's equal parts disbelief and relief. "A self-portrait? What if I'm not ready to face that version of myself?"

"Then you do it anyway," I reply, surprising even myself with the conviction in my voice. "You owe it to yourself. And I promise I'll be here, cheering you on."

He looks at me, his expression a mixture of gratitude and confusion. "You make it sound so easy."

"Easy?" I scoff, crossing my arms as I lean against the wall. "Not at all. It's messy and terrifying, but that's where the magic happens. It's the first step toward finding out who you really are."

His gaze softens, the shadow of uncertainty lifting slightly. "You really think I can do that?"

"Of course. You just need to start believing it."

As he turns back to the window, I can see the wheels turning in his mind, the glimmers of possibility igniting in those deep-set eyes.

But the truth lingers, like a specter hovering just out of sight—the undeniable fact that while I can encourage him, I'm struggling with my own ghosts.

As the evening wears on, the city outside remains vibrant and alive, a stark contrast to the heaviness in my chest. I know I'm asking him to confront his demons, yet I can't help but feel that I'm inching toward a reckoning of my own. My relationship with Ethan, the unspooling thread of his past, and the shadows of my own life intertwine in ways I'm not yet ready to unravel.

Time slips away, and I watch as Ethan paces, his mind racing. It's a dance of sorts, one where neither of us is quite sure of the steps. The fear and uncertainty have become familiar companions, lingering in the corners like well-intentioned yet annoying houseguests. And as the hour grows late, I realize that the journey ahead isn't just about Ethan's healing—it's about my own willingness to dive into the chaos of our shared existence, to confront the specters that haunt us both.

And while the past may be a weight that pulls us under, I can't shake the belief that perhaps it can also be the catalyst for our resurgence, our eventual rediscovery of self.

The weight of Ethan's revelations hangs in the air like a forgotten tune, one I can't quite recall but can feel reverberating through my bones. The bottle of wine sits empty on the table, a testament to our uncharted territory—a space fraught with raw honesty and unspoken fears. As he stands by the window, lost in thought, I grapple with my own vulnerability, the fragile threads of my heart exposed in the dim light. I can't help but wonder: what have I signed up for in this intricate dance between us?

"Tell me more," I venture, my voice steady but laced with curiosity. "What does it mean for you to find yourself again?"

His fingers trace the cool glass, and I can almost see his mind racing, sifting through memories like an archaeologist unearthing forgotten relics. "It means... I don't know, really. It means taking risks, maybe? I've spent so long trying to meet everyone else's expectations that I've forgotten what I want." He turns to face me, and for a moment, the vulnerability in his eyes is almost palpable. "I'm scared, you know? Scared that if I break free from all of this, I won't know who I'll be on the other side."

A nervous chuckle escapes me. "Welcome to adulthood. It's like a never-ending existential crisis wrapped in a burrito of confusion."

He cracks a smile, the first genuine one I've seen in ages, and it lights up his face. "A burrito of confusion, huh? I can get behind that. Can we add some guacamole?"

"Only if you promise to keep your existential dread away from my chips," I retort, reveling in the small flicker of warmth that sparks between us.

But the lighthearted banter doesn't fully chase away the lingering shadows, and soon silence descends again, heavier this time. I take a deep breath, gathering the courage to tread deeper into the murky waters of his psyche. "You know, I've spent a lot of time figuring out what I want, too," I confess, shifting the spotlight just slightly. "After my last relationship, I thought I had it all figured out. But then... life happened. And suddenly, I was just as lost as you."

He steps closer, intrigued, the tension in his shoulders easing slightly. "What happened?"

"It's a classic tale of running headfirst into someone who seemed perfect but turned out to be a beautifully wrapped disaster," I say, my tone dripping with sarcasm. "It was a whirlwind romance that felt like a dream until I woke up to find that I'd built a life around someone who didn't really exist. He was a mirage in the desert of my hopes."

"Did you ever confront him about it?" Ethan asks, his curiosity piqued.

I snort, folding my arms tightly across my chest. "Confronting him was like trying to get a cat to take a bath. It was messy, futile, and left me feeling drenched in disappointment."

"Sounds like you learned a valuable lesson," he muses, tilting his head as if weighing my words.

"More like a thousand valuable lessons." I lean against the window frame, mimicking his earlier stance, allowing the conversation to take root in the fertile ground of shared pain. "And you? What have you learned from all this?"

Ethan pauses, the flicker of uncertainty returning as his eyes darken. "I guess I've learned that I've let fear dictate my choices. It's kept me from pursuing what I really want, and now it's like I'm waking up from a long sleep."

The vulnerability in his admission draws me closer, and I can't resist the urge to reach out and touch his arm. "You're not alone in this. It's okay to feel scared. It just means you're human."

He nods, but the doubt still lingers in the corners of his eyes. "And what if I mess it all up again?"

"Then you mess it up," I reply, the words tumbling out more assertively than I intended. "You're allowed to stumble. The real mistake would be to stand still out of fear. You deserve to chase whatever it is that lights your fire."

The atmosphere shifts, charged with a new kind of energy—one that feels both exhilarating and precarious. We stand inches apart, the tension humming in the air, thick enough to cut. The moment feels pregnant with possibility, yet I can sense the storm clouds gathering again, the shadows creeping back in as uncertainty looms like a specter.

"Can we try something?" Ethan's voice breaks through the tension, and I blink, surprised by the earnestness in his tone.

"Sure. What's on your mind?"

"Let's make a pact. A commitment to dive headfirst into whatever comes next, no matter how terrifying it may be." He steps closer, his gaze locked onto mine, and I can see the determination flickering beneath the uncertainty. "But only if we promise to be honest—like, brutally honest. No more hiding behind façades."

I swallow hard, the weight of his proposition settling over me like a heavy blanket. "Are you sure you want that? Honesty can be a double-edged sword."

"Absolutely," he replies, his voice resolute. "I'd rather face the truth—however messy it is—than dance around it forever."

"Okay, let's do it," I agree, surprising myself with the conviction in my own voice. "We'll strip away the layers, face our fears, and see what lies beneath."

He holds out his pinky, a whimsical gesture that momentarily cuts through the tension. "Pinky swear?"

"Pinky swear," I reply, intertwining my finger with his. It feels like a fragile thread binding us together, a promise of solidarity as we plunge into the unknown.

But just as the weight of our pact settles in, the air shifts, thickening with something unnameable. I glance over at him, my heart racing, as I notice a flicker of discomfort flash across his face. "Ethan?"

He suddenly pulls away, a look of apprehension replacing the previous warmth. "I think... I think we need to talk about something else."

The shift sends a ripple of dread through me. "What do you mean?"

"I've been keeping something from you," he admits, his voice barely above a whisper, the weight of his confession palpable. "Something about my past that could change everything."

My stomach drops, and the world around us feels like it's tilting, threatening to unravel at the seams. "What is it?" I urge, the urgency in my voice betraying my mounting anxiety.

He hesitates, his gaze darting to the floor, and the seconds stretch like an elastic band, ready to snap. "I... I can't keep it buried any longer. But you need to understand, once you know, there's no going back."

The cliff of uncertainty looms before us, and as I take a step closer, my heart pounds in my chest, drowning out the chaos around us. "Ethan, just tell me."

His eyes search mine, and for a brief moment, the connection between us flickers, fragile yet electric. "I was engaged before," he finally admits, the words falling like stones into the abyss between us, each one echoing with the weight of secrets yet untold.

I gasp, the air suddenly feeling thin, and I struggle to comprehend the implications of his revelation. The very ground beneath us shifts, and I realize that everything I thought I knew about him—and us—has just been thrown into question.

Chapter 13: The Ghost of Her

There's a chill in the air, one that sends a shiver down my spine, as I sit at the kitchen table, a steaming mug of chamomile cradled between my hands. The world outside my window is awash in the colors of early autumn: golden leaves drift down like little whispers of change, twirling on the breeze as if they're reluctant to let go of the branches. I watch them with an odd sense of longing, the way they dance effortlessly, unfettered by past attachments. If only I could be as carefree, unburdened by the specter of Madison that shadows every moment spent with Ethan.

Ethan's laughter echoes through the hallway, bright and warm like the sun breaking through clouds on a dreary day. I can't help but smile, though that smile feels hollow, echoing the emptiness in my chest. I remind myself that laughter can be an escape, a momentary reprieve from the heaviness of the heart. Still, it's hard to forget the way his face lights up when he talks about her—the way his eyes glimmer with nostalgia, a bittersweet concoction of fondness and regret that slips through the cracks of our time together.

"Hey, what are you thinking about?" His voice slices through my reverie, and I glance up to find him leaning against the doorframe, arms crossed, a playful smirk dancing on his lips. There's a hint of mischief in his expression, like he knows a secret that I don't.

"Just admiring the leaves," I say, keeping my tone light, hoping to mask the weight pressing against my lungs. "They look so free, don't you think?"

Ethan moves closer, pulling out a chair and plopping down across from me. "If only we could all be as free as the leaves, floating on the wind without a care in the world." He leans back, fingers tapping rhythmically on the table, a habit of his I've come to find oddly endearing. "What's holding you back? You're not tied to any branches, are you?"

"Maybe I'm just waiting for the right gust of wind." I manage a smile, but it feels more like a mask than anything genuine. I take a sip of my tea, the warmth spreading through me, but it does little to chase away the chill creeping back in. I can't help but wonder if I'm just the temporary breeze in his life, a momentary distraction before he returns to the solid ground of his past with Madison.

The air grows thick with unspoken thoughts as Ethan watches me, his gaze penetrating, searching for something I can't quite articulate. "You know," he starts, his voice steady but laced with an undercurrent of hesitation, "you can talk to me about anything. I'm here for you."

I want to believe that, but the weight of my insecurities settles over me like a heavy blanket. "I know," I reply, forcing the words past the lump in my throat. "It's just... sometimes I feel like I'm competing with a ghost."

The silence that follows hangs in the air like a taut string, straining against the inevitable snap of reality. Ethan shifts slightly, and I can see the tension ripple across his shoulders. "Madison isn't a competition," he says slowly, his tone thoughtful but firm. "She was a chapter in my life, not the whole story. You're part of my present."

I want to believe him, but doubt gnaws at me, relentless and cruel. "But what if she's still part of your future? What if you're just waiting for the right moment to turn the page back to her?"

His expression hardens slightly, and I can see the frustration simmering just beneath the surface. "Why do you keep bringing her up?" His voice sharpens, not in anger, but in an urgency that rattles me. "I thought we were past this."

My heart races, a familiar feeling that often accompanies our conversations about her. "I can't help it! Every time I see her name pop up on your phone or hear people talk about her, it's like she's right there, sitting between us." I gesture around the kitchen, my hands animated, betraying the emotional storm brewing inside. "It feels like I'm trying to build something with you while you're still holding on to pieces of her."

Ethan runs a hand through his hair, a gesture of frustration and exasperation. "Look, I can't control how other people see us. I can't change the past. But I'm here with you, right now. Can't we focus on that?"

His sincerity pierces through my defenses, and for a moment, I want to let it wash over me, to wrap myself in the comfort of his words. But the nagging voice in the back of my mind won't quiet down. "What if your heart is still somewhere in the past?" I whisper, my voice barely above a breath.

Ethan's eyes narrow, and a flicker of anger passes over his face before he schools it back into calm. "You don't get it, do you? I chose you, not her. I want to build a future with you." The intensity of his gaze holds me captive, his sincerity an anchor amidst the tempest swirling inside me.

"I just... I don't want to be the rebound," I confess, feeling exposed and vulnerable, my heart laid bare on the table between us. "I want to be your choice, not just the one you picked when she wasn't available."

His expression softens, and I can see the understanding flood his eyes. "You're not a rebound. You're the one I want to be with, the one I choose every day." He leans in closer, his voice dropping to a whisper that wraps around us like a secret. "I need you to trust me. Trust that I'm not going anywhere."

For a fleeting moment, I want to let his words sink in, to allow them to dissolve the fear that clings to my heart. But Madison's ghost hovers, a persistent reminder of the past, and I can't shake the feeling that she's lurking just out of sight, waiting for the perfect moment to slip back into his life.

I try to shake off the remnants of our earlier conversation, but the ghost of Madison lingers like an unwelcome guest at a party. Ethan moves around the kitchen, making a show of rummaging through the cupboards as if searching for the perfect snack could somehow distract us both from the palpable tension hanging in the air. The clatter of dishes fills the silence, an orchestra of mundane sounds in stark contrast to the turmoil swirling inside me.

"Do you want some popcorn?" he calls over his shoulder, pulling out a bag from the back of the pantry, the corners crumpled like a forgotten promise. "Or should I whip up something more adventurous, like a cheese plate? We could pretend we're classy."

"Popcorn sounds great, but let's skip the cheese plate. Unless you're planning to impress me with your artisanal selections." I attempt to inject a note of humor into my voice, but it falters, hovering awkwardly between us.

He flashes a grin, the kind that momentarily chases away the clouds hanging over us. "Ah, so you're saying my cheddar and gouda aren't up to your standards? I'll have you know, I have an impeccable taste in cheese, thank you very much."

"Impeccable? Please. The last time you attempted to impress me with a charcuterie board, I swear I saw some expired salami in there."

"Hey, that salami had character," he retorts, feigning offense as he tosses the popcorn bag into the microwave. "Besides, the secret to a great cheese plate is really about confidence. You just have to believe in your selection, no matter how questionable it might be."

As the microwave hums to life, filling the room with the scent of buttery goodness, I can't help but admire the way Ethan effortlessly switches gears from serious to playful. Yet, as much as I want to join him in this banter, the weight of my insecurities clings to me, dampening the moment. It's like trying to swim with weights strapped to my ankles; every attempt to break the surface leaves me gasping for air.

"What do you really want, Ethan?" The question slips out before I can catch it, raw and unfiltered. I can't disguise my desperation, the desire for clarity amidst the confusion. "I mean, what do you want from us? Because sometimes it feels like you're here but not really all in."

He pauses mid-motion, turning to face me, his expression shifting from playful to serious. The lightheartedness drains from the room as the weight of my words settles over us like a fog. "I want you. That's not up for debate."

"Is it, though?" My voice shakes slightly, and I fight against the tremor, determined to hold my ground. "Because if Madison is still hanging around in the corners of your mind, how can you fully commit to us?"

He opens his mouth, then closes it again, like he's grappling with the truth. "I thought we were moving past this."

"Maybe I'm not ready to move past it. Maybe I'm stuck in this limbo, and I need you to help me find my way out." I'm surprised by the honesty that spills forth, fueled by a mixture of fear and frustration. "If you want me, I need to know that I'm not just the consolation prize."

The microwave beeps, breaking the tension, and Ethan's expression softens. "You're not a consolation prize. You're the prize. But I can't erase my past with a snap of my fingers. It's messy and complicated."

"Life usually is, isn't it?" I lean back in my chair, folding my arms, a defensive gesture I can't help. "So why not lay it all out? If we're going to build something together, we need to start with a solid foundation."

He looks thoughtful for a moment, a frown creasing his brow. "You're right. I need to be honest about Madison and what she meant to me."

I nod, urging him on, though my heart races at the prospect of what he might say. "Okay, then. Tell me."

He takes a deep breath, the air thick with tension. "Madison was a huge part of my life. We were each other's first love, and we thought we could build forever together. But life had other plans. We grew apart, and when she left, it shattered me. It took a long time to pick up the pieces."

"Do you still love her?" I brace myself for the answer, the very question I've been avoiding, hoping to dance around it like we were kids again, playing hide-and-seek in the summer sun.

Ethan exhales sharply, his shoulders slumping slightly. "I loved her, yes. But it wasn't a healthy love. It was a version of love that kept me trapped in the past. It took a while, but I realized that we were not meant to be. When I met you, I saw a future that I didn't think I'd ever have again."

His words hang between us, heavy and poignant, but still, doubt creeps in like a slow tide. "But what if she comes back?" I ask, my voice barely above a whisper.

Ethan leans in closer, his expression intense. "If she comes back, I'll deal with it. But right now, I'm here. With you. I'm choosing you."

There's a vulnerability in his gaze that sends a jolt of warmth through me, yet the fear doesn't completely dissipate. "I need to believe you," I admit, my voice softening. "Because I'm all in, but I can't keep holding on to this fear that I'm just a placeholder."

"I promise you're not. I want to explore this, explore us." He reaches across the table, fingers brushing mine, grounding me in that moment. "We can create something beautiful together. But it requires trust, and I know that's hard when you're dealing with ghosts."

I nod slowly, letting his words settle within me. "Trust takes time. But maybe, just maybe, we can start rebuilding, one popcorn kernel at a time."

The microwave pings, and Ethan jumps up, the momentary levity returning as he retrieves the popcorn. "Popcorn kernels, huh? That's how you want to build your future?"

I can't help but laugh, the sound bubbling up unbidden. "What can I say? I'm a connoisseur of cheesy metaphors."

"Good to know," he quips, tossing a handful into his mouth. "Just remember, if you're serious about being a part of my future, I will make the best cheese plate you've ever seen."

I chuckle, the tension between us easing ever so slightly, leaving room for something new to bloom. As we settle into a comfortable silence, the smell of buttered popcorn wafting around us, I realize that while the ghost of Madison may always linger at the edges, our connection is vibrant, alive, and worth fighting for.

Ethan and I settle into a rhythm, laughter threading through the kitchen like a familiar melody. The aroma of popcorn envelops us, a comforting backdrop to our playful banter, yet a weight still hovers in the air. It's a strange juxtaposition, this lightness laced with shadows, but for now, I'm determined to focus on the here and now, on the man across from me whose smile could easily melt my worries away.

"So, what's on your agenda this week?" I ask, eager to shift the conversation to safer territory, one free from Madison's specter. "More gourmet popcorn tastings, or are you planning to elevate your culinary skills to a Michelin star level?"

He leans back in his chair, an exaggerated look of contemplation washing over his face. "Well, I was thinking about entering the Great Popcorn Championship. You know, honing my skills with buttery precision," he jokes, his eyes sparkling. "But in all seriousness, I've got a meeting on Thursday. The marketing team wants to discuss some new campaign ideas, and I'm leading the presentation."

"Look at you, Mr. Big Shot!" I tease, pretending to fan myself dramatically. "Do you have a PowerPoint ready, or are you going to charm them with your dazzling personality?"

He chuckles, the sound warm and genuine. "I might just wing it. Who needs slides when you can dazzle them with wit and a killer smile?"

"Ah, yes, the killer smile," I reply, a smirk playing on my lips. "The same one that got you into this mess of a love triangle in the first place."

He raises an eyebrow, feigning offense. "You're not going to let that go, are you?"

"Not until I'm convinced that I'm not just a plot twist in your rom-com life," I retort, my tone light but my heart racing with the familiar anxiety.

"Okay, fair point. But I promise you, I'm invested in this story." His voice grows serious, the teasing fading as he meets my gaze. "You're not a side character in my life. You're the lead."

The sincerity in his words wraps around me like a warm blanket, and for a moment, I let myself bask in it, letting go of the doubts that clung to me like shadows. But as the moment lingers, I can't help but wonder how long this bliss can last when the past looms so close.

"Have you heard from Madison recently?" I ask, trying to keep my tone casual, though my pulse quickens.

Ethan's face tightens slightly, and I can see the flicker of tension in his posture. "No, and honestly, I'd prefer it stays that way."

"Good. Because if she tries to come back into your life, I don't think I can just stand by."

"Let's cross that bridge when we get to it," he replies, attempting to sound relaxed, but I catch the edge of worry in his voice.

I nod, but the unease lingers. "I don't want to be the person who drags you back to a past you're trying to escape. I want to be the reason you look forward."

"Trust me, you are." His eyes soften, but I can see the flicker of uncertainty there, and it ignites a pang of fear in my chest.

The microwave beeps again, the popcorn now perfectly popped, and Ethan jumps up to retrieve it. As he pours the fluffy kernels into a bowl, a thought hits me, sharp and insistent. "What if she shows up? I mean, physically comes back?"

He freezes mid-pour, and the popcorn spills over the sides, scattering across the counter like tiny reminders of my fears. "I don't know. I'm not sure how I'd handle that."

"Do you think you'd want to talk to her?" My heart races, the question hanging between us like a pendulum, swinging dangerously close to the edge of what I'm afraid to hear.

Ethan stares at the bowl, a frown creasing his brow. "It's complicated. I can't deny that a part of me would be curious. But I'm not the same person I was when we were together."

I take a deep breath, trying to swallow down the rising tide of jealousy. "Curiosity can be a slippery slope. Once you start talking, who knows what might happen?"

He turns to me, an earnest look in his eyes. "And what if you're the one I want to talk to about this? What if I choose to share my thoughts with you, rather than her?"

The sincerity in his voice does little to ease the knot in my stomach. "I want to be that person, but I need to know I'm not just a temporary fix."

His phone buzzes on the counter, the screen lighting up with a name that sends a chill through me. Madison. My heart plummets as Ethan hesitates, glancing from the phone to me, the tension palpable. "It's... it's just a group chat," he says quickly, but I can hear the lie hanging in the air, heavy and oppressive.

"Go ahead, answer it," I say, my voice steady, even though I can feel the ground shifting beneath me. "It's fine. I mean, it's not like I'm hanging on your every word or anything."

He narrows his eyes at me, a mixture of frustration and concern flashing across his features. "It's not like that. You know it's not like that."

"Then prove it." I challenge him, my heart racing as I brace myself for whatever is coming. "If she's just a ghost, why does her name still have the power to haunt you?"

With a deep breath, he picks up the phone, glancing at the message, then back at me. "It's not what you think."

But I'm already standing up, the chair scraping against the floor as I move closer, my pulse pounding in my ears. "Ethan, please. Just be honest with me. I'm tired of the secrets."

He looks down at the screen again, hesitation etched across his face, and in that moment, I feel the air shift, the room tightening around us. "Okay," he finally says, voice low. "I'll open it. But I need you to promise me that you won't freak out."

"Freak out?" I echo incredulously. "Ethan, I think I've already earned my freak-out points."

He presses the screen, and as he reads the message, the blood drains from his face. "It's... it's her. Madison wants to meet up."

My heart drops, and I swear the world tilts on its axis, leaving me suspended between dread and disbelief. "What?" The word escapes me like a gasp, barely managing to stay grounded in the whirlwind of emotions threatening to engulf me. "You have to be kidding."

"No, it's real," he whispers, eyes wide. "She says she needs to talk. It's important."

"Important? What could possibly be important enough to drag you back into her world?" I'm nearly trembling, rage and fear twisting inside me, and I can't help but feel the walls closing in.

Ethan's expression is unreadable, a mixture of concern and something else I can't quite place. "I don't know," he admits, voice barely above a whisper. "But I think I need to hear what she has to say."

And just like that, the air between us feels electric, charged with an unspoken challenge, leaving me teetering on the edge of uncertainty, my heart racing with the realization that everything is about to change.

Chapter 14: Storms on the Horizon

The room buzzed with laughter and the clinking of glasses, a small-town fundraiser for the community center blooming with vibrant chatter and the mingling of familiar faces. I stood near the entrance, cradling a glass of sparkling cider, the bubbles fizzing cheerfully against the rim. Beneath the warm glow of string lights, I could see people crowded around tables draped in white cloth, the silent auction items glimmering under the low-hanging lights. There were art pieces that made me squint in confusion—abstract colors smeared haphazardly together—and homemade baked goods in jars that looked like something out of a Pinterest fail. Yet, amidst the quaint chaos, a sense of normalcy surrounded us, fragile but hopeful. Little did I know, a storm was brewing, one that could wash away all semblance of peace.

Ethan stood in a corner, arms crossed, a glimmer of tension etched across his face as he observed the room. I could feel the weight of his uncertainty, heavy like the thick summer air before a thunderstorm. He was handsome in a way that felt both familiar and infuriating, with tousled dark hair that seemed perpetually windswept and those brooding eyes that looked deeper than any ocean. A part of me wanted to wade into that depth, but the other part warned me of the tides. I knew that whatever was brewing between him and Madison had reached a boiling point, and tonight would be pivotal.

Then she appeared. Madison entered the room like a whirlwind, all confidence and charisma, her presence eclipsing everything else. She wore a fitted navy dress that hugged her curves, the fabric shimmering under the lights. The moment she spotted Ethan, her lips curled into a smile that felt more like a challenge than a greeting. I instinctively shrank back, slipping into the shadows, the crowd swirling around me like leaves caught in a gust.

I watched as Madison approached him, her voice low but laced with a venom that cut through the jovial atmosphere. They stood close, and I could see the tension crackling like static electricity between them. A few heads turned, glances exchanged among the guests as curiosity began to mount. My heart raced as I caught snippets of their heated conversation, though the specifics eluded me. I could sense Ethan's discomfort, his brows knitting together, the muscles in his jaw tightening as she pressed on.

Suddenly, his expression shifted, fury flashing in those deep-set eyes. He took a step back, his hands moving through his hair in frustration, a gesture that felt almost primal. The air thickened with unspoken words, and it felt as though everyone in the room held their breath, waiting for the inevitable explosion.

"Just leave me alone, Madison," he spat, voice low but harsh, as if each word was a stone hurled into a still pond, causing ripples of tension that spread throughout the crowd. I could see it in his stance, the way he clenched his fists—he was done playing this game.

Madison didn't back down; instead, she leaned closer, her eyes blazing with something dark and desperate. "You can't walk away from this, Ethan. You think you can just forget everything we had?"

Their argument escalated, fueled by hurt and frustration, words spiraling out of control like a wild fire. I felt like an intruder in a private war, each barb they exchanged striking me like arrows. The laughter faded, replaced by a heavy silence that hung over the gathering, like a cloud ready to burst. I shifted from foot to foot, unsure of whether to intervene or simply watch as their lives collided in such an explosive manner.

Then, with a final furious gesture, Ethan stormed out of the building. His exit felt like a gust of wind ripping through the crowded room, sending a chill racing down my spine. I stood frozen, the crowd murmuring, glancing between Madison and the door through which he'd vanished. There was an ache in my chest, a nagging fear that this moment would shift everything for him—everything for us.

As soon as I could gather myself, I slipped out of the hall, following him into the night. The streetlights flickered against the darkening sky, casting long shadows on the pavement. Ethan was pacing like a caged animal, his breath visible in the cool air, hands raking through his hair as if trying to wrestle his thoughts into submission. The weight of his anger radiated off him, palpable and almost infectious.

"I can't do this anymore," he muttered, his voice barely above a whisper but laden with an intensity that felt like thunder rumbling in the distance. I could see the tension coiling in his muscles, a storm contained but ready to unleash. "I'm tired of it all. The expectations, the drama... everything."

His frustration echoed in my chest, and the words hung in the air between us. I hesitated, not wanting to add to his burden but feeling an overwhelming need to reach out. "Ethan, talk to me. Please." My voice was softer than I intended, a thread of hope woven into the desperation of the moment.

He turned to me, his eyes alight with a tempest of emotions. "What's there to say? I'm just... I'm so exhausted."

A part of me wanted to shake him, to implore him to see beyond the storm brewing in his heart. "You don't have to face this alone," I replied, stepping closer, hoping my sincerity would reach him through the chaos.

He dropped his gaze, the anger giving way to something deeper, more vulnerable. "What if I'm too far gone? What if I can't pull myself out?"

In that moment, I felt the weight of my own uncertainty pressing down, a reflection of his struggle mirrored in my soul. I wanted to pull him back from the edge, to remind him of the light he brought into the world—even if he couldn't see it right now. "You are stronger than you think. And I'll be here, ready to help you find your way."

He looked up then, a flicker of something unnamable in his eyes, a connection that felt both fragile and fierce. In the midst of uncertainty, we stood together beneath the weight of impending storms, and I hoped that somehow, together, we could weather whatever chaos lay ahead.

The air was thick with the smell of rain, an omen of the brewing storms beyond the horizon, but it felt all too fitting for the emotional tempest unfolding in front of me. Ethan's frustration coiled tightly around us, each syllable he spoke cutting through the evening with a sharpness that startled even the nearby cicadas into silence. I stood close enough to see the conflict etched into his features, the way his brow furrowed like he was trying to read the impossible, and I wished I could draw closer without shattering the fragile tension that hung between us.

"Ethan," I said softly, stepping into the light, where the glow flickered like a heartbeat. "I know it's hard. But you're not alone in this." My voice felt small against the backdrop of his storm, yet I hoped it would carry the weight of my sincerity.

He paused, eyes darting to mine, searching for something I wasn't sure I could give him—a lifeline or perhaps just an anchor. "You don't understand," he said, the words barely above a whisper, the storm still brewing in his chest. "It's not just about Madison. It's everything—this town, my family, the pressure to be someone I'm not."

I wanted to reach out, to touch his arm and assure him that the pressure could break, that the expectations suffocating him weren't his to bear alone. But the thought of crossing that invisible line—the boundary between comfort and the unknown—made me hesitate.

"Tell me what you want, Ethan. What do you need?" I asked, each word a stepping stone through the murky waters of his emotions.

"I want..." His voice faltered, and for a brief moment, vulnerability seeped through his anger. "I want to feel free."

The way he said it, like a prayer whispered into the night, ignited a fire in my chest. Freedom was a heady concept, like a wild horse roaming unbridled across the plains. "Then let's find that freedom together," I suggested, trying to keep the hopeful quiver from my voice.

"Together?" His tone shifted, tinged with skepticism, as if the very word felt foreign to him.

"Yes, together," I affirmed, my heart racing with determination. "We can carve out a space where you can breathe—where you can be who you really are."

He met my gaze, and for a heartbeat, the world shrank down to just the two of us, surrounded by the sounds of the night and the gentle whispers of the leaves rustling above. "What if I don't know who that is?" he asked, his eyes searching mine, a mixture of hope and despair swirling together.

"Then we'll figure it out," I replied, feeling a warmth spread through me as I recognized the depth of my own commitment to him. "You can start with a clean slate. No expectations. Just you."

A small smile tugged at the corners of his lips, a flicker of something that reminded me of the sun breaking through clouds after a storm. "You really think I can do that?"

"I know you can," I replied, surprised by the conviction in my own voice. "You just need to take the first step."

Ethan ran a hand through his hair, visibly shaken but clearly intrigued. "What's the first step?"

"Let's get out of here," I suggested, glancing back toward the community center where the chatter had resumed, oblivious to the chaos that had just unfolded. "Let's find a place where you can breathe and think without the pressure of this town."

He considered my words for a moment, and then, almost imperceptibly, his shoulders relaxed. "Okay," he said finally, a hint of a challenge in his tone. "Let's do it."

Together, we stepped into the night, the cool air wrapping around us like a comforting blanket. As we walked, I could feel the weight of his uncertainty slowly lifting, each step away from the fundraiser a step toward something unknown and exhilarating. The moon hung low in the sky, casting a silver glow on the cracked pavement, illuminating our path as we strolled through the quiet streets of our small town, the familiarity of the setting juxtaposed against the unpredictability of our choices.

"What do you normally do when you want to escape?" I asked, wanting to draw him out, to help him explore the parts of himself he'd kept locked away.

"I usually just go to the lake," he replied, glancing sideways at me, the moonlight glinting in his eyes. "It's peaceful there, away from... everything."

"Then let's go to the lake," I proposed, my heart racing at the idea. The lake was a place of solace, the kind of spot that held memories of summers spent laughing and splashing in the water, an idyllic backdrop for the storm we were trying to navigate.

As we walked, the tension began to dissipate, replaced by a buoyant energy that crackled in the air. I decided to push the boundaries of our conversation, seeking lightness amidst the heaviness. "So, are you a boat person or a swim-in-the-lake kind of guy?"

He chuckled, the sound light and unexpected. "Definitely a swim-in-the-lake person. I like feeling the water wrap around me. It's... freeing."

"That's a good answer," I teased, nudging him playfully. "I'd like to think I'm a bit of both. But swimming just sounds better when you say it."

Ethan laughed again, the sound echoing against the quiet surroundings. "What's your favorite thing to do at the lake?"

"Make terrible attempts at skipping rocks," I admitted with a grin. "I can never get them to bounce like everyone else does. It's like the rocks have a vendetta against me."

"I'll have to witness that," he replied, amusement dancing in his eyes. "Maybe you can teach me your terrible technique."

As we reached the lake, the water shimmered under the moonlight, a blanket of silver stretched out before us. We paused at the water's edge, the gentle lapping of the waves against the shore filling the silence between us. "This place feels different at night," I remarked, peering into the depths of the lake as if it held answers to questions I hadn't yet asked.

"Yeah," he agreed, his voice dropping to a whisper, as if speaking too loudly would break the spell. "It feels like anything could happen."

I turned to him, the moonlight illuminating the angles of his face, making him look more vulnerable than I'd ever seen. "What if we let it happen?"

His gaze held mine, the weight of the world still lingering between us, yet in that moment, we stood on the precipice of something new, something thrilling. And as the wind whispered secrets through the trees, I felt a spark ignite between us, a promise that whatever storms lay ahead, we would weather them together.

The lake stretched before us, a vast expanse of shimmering darkness under the moonlit sky. The soft sound of water lapping at the shore wrapped around us like a cozy blanket, as if inviting us to leave our troubles behind and dive into its depths. I felt an electric charge in the air, an undercurrent of possibility humming between

Ethan and me, mingling with the whispers of the trees swaying gently in the breeze.

"Do you ever think about just running away?" I asked, my voice barely above a whisper, but the words hung in the air, heavy with the weight of their implications. "Just leaving everything behind?"

Ethan considered this for a moment, his brow furrowed in thought. "I've thought about it more than I care to admit," he replied, a hint of longing lacing his tone. "Sometimes it feels like I'm just treading water, waiting for the next wave to hit."

"What if we found a place where the waves couldn't reach us?" I challenged, a playful smile creeping onto my face. "Somewhere tropical, with palm trees and no expectations?"

He chuckled, the sound rich and warm, dispelling some of the heaviness of the moment. "You mean, like, a permanent vacation?"

"Exactly! I could see us lounging on a beach somewhere, sipping coconut water, while you try to teach me how to surf."

"I can't even surf," he admitted, his laughter bubbling up again, mixing with the night air. "But I'd gladly take the plunge with you, if it meant avoiding Madison and whatever mess I've gotten myself into."

I sensed the way he'd steered the conversation back to the reality we were both trying to escape. "Maybe we don't have to make a permanent decision tonight. Maybe we just need to carve out this little moment for ourselves."

"Just this moment?" he echoed, tilting his head, a challenge glimmering in his eyes. "That sounds dangerous."

"Dangerous is where the good stories lie," I quipped, stepping closer to the water, the coolness radiating from it wrapping around my ankles. "After all, what's the point of living if we're afraid to dip our toes in?"

He studied me for a heartbeat, and I could see the gears in his mind turning, contemplating the allure of this shared spontaneity.

"You make it sound so simple," he said finally. "But what happens when we have to go back to reality?"

I shrugged, trying to maintain the levity of the moment. "We'll cross that bridge when we get to it. Right now, it's just you and me, and the lake. And I'm pretty sure this is the most fun I've had in ages."

"Okay, then," he said, taking a deep breath, as if inhaling the very essence of the moment. "Let's enjoy this while it lasts."

Just as the laughter faded, a distant rumble of thunder rolled across the sky, a reminder that storms were looming. I glanced up, noticing how the clouds began to gather, swirling ominously overhead. "It looks like we might be in for some actual storms," I remarked, an edge of concern creeping into my voice.

"Maybe it's just a sign," he mused, a playful glint still in his eye. "A warning that we should get out of here before we're caught in the rain."

"Or maybe a sign that we should dive in, metaphorically and literally," I countered, a defiant smile on my face. "What do you say? Let's jump into this lake and shake off our worries?"

Ethan laughed, but his eyes held an unmistakable spark of adventure. "You're ridiculous, you know that?"

"Absolutely. But aren't ridiculous moments the best?"

"Okay, fine," he relented, his smile widening. "You're on. But if we get struck by lightning, I'm blaming you."

"Deal!" I declared, excitement bubbling up inside me as I prepared to run toward the water's edge. "On three! One, two—"

Before I could finish, a blinding flash illuminated the sky, followed by a crack of thunder that echoed like a drumroll. My heart leapt into my throat, the playful atmosphere morphing into something more serious. The moment felt electric, charged with adrenaline and the realization that we stood on the brink of something huge.

"I think that was a little too close for comfort!" I laughed nervously, my pulse racing as I glanced toward the horizon where dark clouds billowed ominously.

"Maybe we should take this as our cue to go," Ethan suggested, laughter fading into the distance, replaced by an uneasy tension.

"Yeah, probably," I agreed, though I didn't move immediately. My feet remained planted at the water's edge, where the waves kissed the shore. "But I'm not ready to leave just yet."

He stepped closer, the water reflecting the chaos of the sky above us. "What are you saying?"

"I'm saying I want to dive into this moment, whatever it means, even if it's fleeting."

His expression softened, and for a moment, I saw something in him that resembled yearning—a desire to break free from the chains that bound him. "What if we're jumping into something we can't control?"

"Good!" I exclaimed, my heart racing as I faced the uncertainty head-on. "If we can't control it, that just means we can embrace whatever comes next."

He hesitated, a flicker of uncertainty crossing his features. "Okay, then."

And just as we stepped toward the edge, ready to plunge into the unknown, a torrential downpour unleashed itself from the heavens, the rain cascading down like a waterfall, soaking us instantly. The cold water shocked me, and I gasped, laughter spilling from my lips as I looked up at the darkened sky. "Talk about dramatic timing!"

"Seriously!" Ethan laughed, shaking his hair like a drenched dog, sending droplets flying. "Now we really have to go!"

But instead of retreating, I felt a rush of exhilaration, a wildness sweeping through me as I faced the tempest head-on. "No! Let's do it! Jump in!"

As if propelled by my words, I took off, dashing into the lake, the cool water embracing me in a rush of sensation. Ethan followed, his laughter echoing against the storm. We swam, splashing each other, our laughter melding with the rain, a symphony of chaos that felt like liberation.

And just as I turned to see Ethan swimming closer, a crack of lightning struck the water nearby, illuminating the night sky with a blinding flash. My heart raced, and I felt the thrill of both fear and exhilaration.

But it was the expression on Ethan's face that sent my heart plummeting. He froze mid-stroke, eyes wide with shock, and suddenly I realized, as the air thickened with tension, that we were not alone. Emerging from the darkness of the trees lining the shore was a figure, shadowy and menacing, watching us with an intensity that sent chills racing down my spine.

"Ethan," I whispered, my voice barely rising above the pounding rain, as I pointed toward the figure. "We need to get out of here."

His gaze followed mine, and as the storm roared around us, I felt a surge of dread. Whatever storm was brewing in Ethan's life was nothing compared to the one that had just materialized on the shore.

Chapter 15: Love and Lies

Ethan and I lingered in the quiet aftermath of what had become our routine—stolen glances across crowded coffee shops, laughter too loud for the space around us, and whispered conversations that danced just out of reach of prying ears. But that evening, the air hung heavy with something unspoken, a taut line stretched between us, fraught with the weight of words we weren't saying. The vibrant clinking of mugs and the rich aroma of freshly brewed coffee swirled around us, yet the warmth felt distant, like sunlight filtered through heavy clouds.

"Do you think we could get away for a weekend?" I asked, my voice barely rising above the hum of chatter. The idea hung between us like a balloon on the verge of popping, filled with hope and apprehension. I could almost see Ethan's thoughts spiraling behind those stormy gray eyes of his, the flicker of a smile battling with the clouds of his uncertainty.

"Where would we go?" His tone was light, but I caught the undercurrent of hesitation. We'd talked about adventure—about going to that quaint little beach town with the bright blue shutters and the sand that felt like warm sugar beneath your feet—but the conversation always seemed to fizzle out before we could make plans.

"Anywhere," I replied, shrugging with exaggerated nonchalance, as if the world was ours to seize. "A little cottage by the sea. Just you and me, with nothing to worry about." The thought of our toes in the sand, the taste of saltwater on our lips, made me yearn for the carefree days that felt like a lifetime ago. But reality hovered over us like a menacing shadow, reminding me that our lives were bound by complications and unspoken truths.

Ethan's brow furrowed slightly, his gaze drifting toward the window, where rain splattered against the glass, blurring the city's skyline into a hazy watercolor painting. "I can't just disappear, you know? There's—" He hesitated, the words caught in his throat. "There's too much going on."

I knew what he meant. The unrelenting pressure of our lives weighed heavily on both of us, but it felt different for him, like a stone lodged in his chest that refused to budge. There was Madison, his estranged sister whose return felt like a ticking clock set to explode. The whispers of her past still haunted our conversations, echoing through every corner of our lives. And I couldn't help but wonder if his inability to confront those ghosts was pulling him further away from me.

"Maybe we can just..." I started, trailing off as I searched for words that might bridge the gap growing wider between us. "Maybe we can figure this out together?" My voice softened, laden with the hope that he could hear my sincerity. "I'm here for you, Ethan. I want to help."

He turned his gaze back to me, and for a moment, I saw the flicker of the boy who had danced into my life with an effortless charm, the one who made everything feel possible. "I know," he whispered, his vulnerability a raw edge I wanted to wrap in comfort. "But sometimes, I feel like I'm just dragging you down."

"No," I said firmly, leaning closer, my heart racing at the possibility of reaching him. "You're not a burden. You're—" My words hung in the air, suspended like the mist outside, heavy with significance. "You're everything."

His lips twitched into a hesitant smile, but the shadows lurking in his eyes remained. I reached for his hand, entwining my fingers with his, grounding myself in the warmth of his touch. "Let's take a small step. Just us, no pressure. What do you say?"

"Okay," he replied, and for a fleeting moment, it felt like we were stepping back from the precipice. But then his gaze shifted, drifting again toward the rain-soaked window, as if seeking refuge in the world outside. I felt the pang of his retreat, a reminder that the storm within him was far from over.

A sudden gust of wind rattled the glass, and I pulled back, creating a space between us that seemed to grow in volume. "Ethan..." I began, trying to capture his gaze again. "We can't keep living like this, in shadows and whispers. I need you to meet me halfway." The words tumbled out, raw and unpolished, but they felt necessary, like stripping away the layers that had built up between us.

He nodded, but the distance in his eyes deepened. "I want to, I do. It's just..." His voice faltered, a crack in the armor he wore so effortlessly. "I don't want to pull you into my mess. You deserve better than that."

"Who says what I deserve?" I challenged gently, a playful tilt in my tone. "Besides, my mess is as colorful as yours, so we'd make quite the masterpiece together." I flashed him a grin, hoping to cut through the heaviness, but the spark of laughter that should have ignited between us flickered and faded.

He looked away, brow furrowed, and I knew he was battling demons I couldn't quite understand. "You don't know what you're asking for, and I don't want to hurt you. I can't do that to you."

"You're not hurting me. You're pushing me away," I countered, frustration bubbling under the surface. "Every time you say things like that, it feels like a wall. We need to break it down together." The urgency in my voice surprised me, but I couldn't stand idly by while the man I loved retreated into the shadows of his fears.

The rain continued to pelt the window, each drop a reminder of the chaos outside, a chaos that mirrored the turmoil swirling within. I could see him wrestling with his thoughts, the unvoiced fears thrumming between us like a pulse. I leaned in closer, trying to bridge the emotional chasm that had grown with each unspoken word.

"Let me in, Ethan," I whispered, my voice a tender plea that hung in the air like smoke, fragile yet insistent. "You don't have to do this alone." The connection between us felt electric, a frayed wire waiting for the right spark to ignite it. The challenge now lay in the intricate dance of trust, one I hoped we could navigate together without losing our footing.

The rain had softened to a drizzle, the world outside our little café transforming into a watercolor painting smeared by the gentle patter of drops. I stared at the rivulets racing down the glass, imagining each one carrying away pieces of the tension that had taken root between us. I yearned for that lightness, for laughter to erupt between us like the sound of popcorn popping, but the silence hung heavy, the kind that clung to the walls like damp air.

"Let's not let this turn into an episode of a really bad drama, okay?" I quipped, trying to inject some levity into the moment. "I mean, it's either that or we start wearing matching tracksuits and throw ourselves a pity party."

Ethan chuckled, the sound rumbling deep in his chest, a brief flash of the man I adored, and I clung to it like a life raft. "Tracksuits, huh? I think you'd rock the look, but I'm not so sure about myself."

"Oh, come on. You'd be the picture of athleticism. We'd be the envy of the neighborhood, tearing up the streets like the dynamic duo of mediocrity." I waggled my eyebrows, pleased when he smiled wider, but the shift was fleeting, like a butterfly landing for a moment before flitting away.

As the banter faded, the air between us crackled again with unspoken thoughts. I searched Ethan's face for clues, wondering what masked layers of emotion he was wrestling with. Was I the only one feeling like we were both standing on a precipice, unsure of whether to leap or step back?

"What if we actually went somewhere?" he suggested, the weight of the suggestion curling his lips into a half-smile. "Not necessarily a weekend, but maybe a day trip? Just to shake things up."

I leaned forward, excitement blooming like wildflowers in spring. "Are you serious? That could be fun! We could go to that little town you love, the one with the giant rubber duck in the harbor." The thought of escaping the weight of our reality felt like a breath of fresh air. "We could take silly pictures with it and pretend we're on a wild adventure."

He nodded slowly, the gears in his head turning as he considered it. "Yeah, maybe. It'd be a nice distraction. Just the two of us away from everything."

"Exactly!" I could feel the energy shifting, the potential for laughter and lightness threading its way through the fog of our conversation. "Let's do it. We'll grab coffee, hit the road, and let the world fade away for a bit." I could picture it—the wind in our hair, the sun breaking through the clouds, and the taste of freedom that had been eluding us for so long.

A glimmer of hope danced in Ethan's eyes, but before he could respond, the bell above the café door jingled, and my heart sank as Madison swept in, her presence like a sudden gust of cold wind. She was stunning, with her perfectly tousled hair and a style that seemed effortlessly chic, the kind that made you wonder how she managed to look like she'd just stepped off a fashion runway while the rest of us were still fumbling with our wardrobes.

"Hey, Ethan!" she called, her voice a melodic chime that carried across the crowded room. I felt the color drain from my face, and I quickly tried to compose myself. I hadn't seen her since she returned to town, and the fact that she was interrupting our fragile moment felt like a cruel twist of fate.

"Madison," Ethan replied, his tone flat, a stark contrast to her exuberance. I caught the flicker of discomfort in his expression, and it stirred something in me—jealousy, maybe, or a protective instinct. "What are you doing here?"

"I came to grab a coffee and thought I'd see if you were around. This place has the best chai lattes." She waltzed over to our table, a confident smile plastered on her face as if the tension in the air didn't exist. "And I see you brought a friend!" Her eyes flicked to me, a momentary spark of recognition clouded by something I couldn't quite place.

"Yeah, this is Mia," Ethan introduced me, his voice stilted. "Mia, this is my sister Madison."

I forced a smile, extending my hand. "Nice to meet you." The moment our hands touched, I felt a jolt, an unsettling mixture of warmth and coolness. Madison's grip was firm, but her eyes betrayed a sense of scrutiny that made me uneasy.

"Likewise," she replied, her smile wide but her gaze sharp, assessing. I wondered how much she truly knew about us, about the secrets hiding behind our laughter and stolen moments. "Ethan's told me a lot about you." The emphasis on his name felt heavy, almost accusatory, and I fought the urge to shrink into my seat.

"Good things, I hope," I said lightly, attempting to smooth over the prickly tension. I was met with silence, the air thick with unspoken words, and I cursed myself for inviting a potential landmine into our fragile bubble.

"Absolutely. Just that you're... special." The way she emphasized the word made it feel like a pointed barb aimed at me. I shot a glance at Ethan, who was now staring intently into his coffee as if it held the answers to the universe.

"I didn't know you two were hanging out," Madison continued, a casualness that felt rehearsed. "Are you having fun?"

"Yeah, you know, just trying to survive," I replied, my tone sharper than intended. I felt Ethan's eyes dart toward me, a silent plea to keep things light, but my nerves were fraying. The last thing I wanted was for Madison to see the cracks forming between us.

"Survival mode is no way to live," Madison chimed, her tone overly cheerful, but the glint in her eyes was anything but warm. "Maybe you could join me sometime. I could introduce you to some people, show you the local scene."

"Thanks, but I'm good," I said, an edge creeping into my voice. "I'm kind of busy." The thought of being thrust into a world where I had to navigate Madison's social circle felt overwhelming, like diving into an icy pool without warning.

Ethan's gaze shifted from his coffee to me, concern etched across his features. "Mia's been helping me with—"

"No need to put me on a pedestal," I interrupted, forcing a light laugh to diffuse the tension. "Just a casual friendship. Nothing to see here." The words tasted bitter on my tongue, and I could see Madison's interest piquing, her attention honing in on the fissures forming.

Madison's smile faltered for a brief moment, and I could sense her assessing us, weighing the pieces of a puzzle she was determined to solve. "Oh, casual friendships can be tricky," she remarked, her voice smooth like honey but laced with an edge that made me bristle. "You never know when someone might want more."

"More?" I echoed, feeling a flare of defensiveness ignite within me. "What do you mean by that?" The stakes felt higher, the air electrified as our gazes locked. I could almost feel Ethan's tension radiating across the table, a silent warning to back off.

Madison shrugged, feigning innocence. "Just an observation. It's easy to get tangled up in feelings when you're trying to keep things casual." Her words dripped with implication, and I could see Ethan's discomfort deepening.

"Maybe we should go," he suggested, cutting through the charged atmosphere with an abruptness that surprised me. "We were just about to leave." The urgency in his tone sent a ripple of alarm through me. I didn't want to appear weak or as if Madison was getting under my skin, but there was a truth buried within her words that unsettled me.

"Oh, come on! Don't run off just because I showed up," Madison countered, her tone bright but her eyes cold. "I'm just being friendly."

"Yeah, we should definitely get going." Ethan's voice had that tightness again, like a rubber band stretched too thin, ready to snap. I felt the weight of his unease, the invisible chains tying him to his sister, and my heart raced at the thought of what might lie ahead.

As I stood, ready to leave this café of unspoken truths, I felt a sense of foreboding wash over me. Whatever fragile ground we'd gained in our conversation had been shaken, and I knew we were no closer to finding our way through the shadows looming over us. Each moment felt like a step closer to a cliff, and I couldn't shake the feeling that we were teetering on the edge, the drop beneath us both exhilarating and terrifying.

The moment we stepped out of the café, the drizzle had transformed into a light mist, the air thick with the earthy scent of rain-soaked pavement. I pulled my jacket tighter around me, feeling as if the world had shifted slightly off-kilter with Madison's unexpected arrival. Ethan walked beside me, his silence louder than any words we might have exchanged. I stole glances at him, searching for a glimpse of the man I had known before all of this—the one who made me feel as if we were the only two people in a crowded room.

"I didn't mean for her to come between us," he finally murmured, his voice low as if he feared the mist might carry his words to her. "I thought she'd be busy."

"Busy with what? Spreading chaos?" I retorted, my tone sharper than I intended. I didn't want to paint her as the villain; that would be too easy. Yet, the lingering unease she left behind felt heavy, like a lead weight in my stomach. "It's not your fault she popped in. It's just... the timing, you know?"

He nodded, but his gaze remained focused ahead, as if he were trying to outpace his own thoughts. "I should've told you more about her."

"Should have? Or could have?" I tossed back lightly, attempting to ease the tension creeping into our conversation. "You've been guarding secrets like a dragon hoarding gold. I mean, who knew we were in a reality show called 'Family Drama: The Ethan Edition'?"

He chuckled, a low rumble that momentarily broke through the clouds hovering between us. "If I were on a reality show, I'd at least have more than one outfit to wear." His smile faded quickly, replaced by a seriousness that settled like a fog. "Madison isn't just anyone, Mia. She's... complicated. And I don't want her complications to spill over into our lives."

"Like a bad rash?" I teased, trying to bring back the lightness, but I saw the flicker of pain in his eyes, and it stung like a bee.

"More like a storm," he replied, a hint of vulnerability coloring his voice. "She brings a whirlwind with her. I just didn't want you to get caught in it."

"Ethan, you can't keep me sheltered from everything," I urged, my heart pounding in my chest as we walked. "I can handle your sister. I've handled worse."

He turned to me then, his gaze piercing. "Do you really think you can? Because I'm not sure I can even handle her. I've spent so long pretending she doesn't exist, pushing the memories aside, and now—now I have to face it all over again."

"Then we face it together. But I can't be kept in the dark. I don't want to be the 'other' in your life." My words felt like an ultimatum, but there was a tremor of truth in them. I wanted to stand beside him, not behind him, fighting battles I didn't even know existed.

As we reached the edge of the park, the familiar warmth of our surroundings began to creep back in. The lush greens glistened under the mist, and the laughter of children playing in the distance reminded me of simpler times. "I like it here," I said, trying to draw him back to our earlier moments. "It's peaceful."

He sighed, a resigned sound that echoed the shifting tension in his shoulders. "It can be. But peace is fragile, and I'm not sure how much longer we can maintain it."

"Then let's not waste any more time," I said, determination bubbling within me. "Let's talk to Madison. Set the record straight."

Ethan paused, looking out over the expanse of the park. "You really want to do that?"

"Absolutely. I can't let her shadow loom over us like this. I refuse to let her dictate how we feel or what we can have together."

He studied me for a moment, as if weighing the sincerity of my words. "Okay, let's do it. But promise me you won't take anything she says to heart. She can be... persuasive."

I grinned, feeling the spark of challenge ignite within me. "Oh, I thrive on persuasion. Just ask my marketing professor."

Ethan chuckled, and I felt a rush of warmth. But as we turned back toward the café, the atmosphere shifted again, like the clouds above us gathering for a storm.

Madison was outside, her figure silhouetted against the soft glow of the café's lights, arms crossed, the very picture of casual confidence. But there was something unsettling in the way she stood, an intensity radiating off her that set my nerves on edge.

"Mia!" she called, her voice carrying through the evening air like a melody with an undertone of discord. "I was just looking for you two. I thought we could all talk, you know, like a family reunion."

"Isn't that sweet?" I shot back, my heart racing. The last thing I wanted was to engage in some half-baked version of family therapy with her, but I held my ground, steeling myself for whatever was about to unfold.

Ethan took a step forward, placing himself between Madison and me. "What do you want to talk about, Madison?" His tone was firm, the protective instincts kicking in, and I felt a rush of gratitude mixed with frustration.

"I just think it's time for some honesty, don't you?" She pushed her hair back, her smile unyielding. "After all, you've been keeping secrets, Ethan, and I'm not sure how much longer you can keep that up."

Ethan's body stiffened at her words, and I could sense the crackle of tension in the air, like static before a storm. "What do you mean?"

Madison took a step closer, her eyes narrowing with intrigue. "Oh, come on. You really think I didn't notice? You and Mia have been playing house like it's some sort of game. But what happens when the truth comes out? People will talk. They always do."

"What truth?" I interjected, refusing to be sidelined in this game. "What are you implying?"

"Let's not play coy, shall we? We all know about your little arrangement, how you've been trying to keep this under wraps." Her voice dripped with mock sympathy, and I could feel the blood rushing to my cheeks. "What happens when Ethan's other life comes crashing in? Do you think you can handle it?"

Ethan stepped forward, anger flashing in his eyes. "Stop it, Madison. This isn't helping anything."

"Am I wrong?" she shot back, her voice rising, turning heads of the few passersby lingering nearby. "The truth will come out eventually, and when it does—"

"That's enough!" I exclaimed, stepping forward, fueled by an urgency I hadn't felt before. "If you have something to say, just say it! What's the secret?"

Madison's gaze flicked between us, a smirk creeping onto her lips. "Oh, it's not my secret to share, darling. But trust me, it's a doozy. And you'll want to know before the curtains are pulled back."

Ethan's breath hitched, and I could see the uncertainty wash over him like a wave. "Madison..."

The air grew heavy with unsaid words, the weight of impending revelations thickening the atmosphere. My heart raced as I looked at Ethan, desperate to bridge the widening chasm. "What is she talking about?"

Madison's smile widened, and for a moment, the air crackled with anticipation, as if the world had stopped to listen to whatever she was about to drop. "Just remember, love can be blind, but lies? They're a different story. So buckle up, sweetheart. The ride's about to get bumpy."

With that, she turned on her heel, walking away with a confidence that felt more like a departure from the truth than an exit. I stood frozen, the weight of her words pressing down on me, unsure whether to follow her or to confront Ethan, who looked just as lost, his expression a storm of confusion and fear.

"Ethan, what does she mean?" My voice broke the silence, the urgency palpable as I grasped his arm. "What's happening? What does she know?"

His eyes searched mine, and I could see the battle raging within him. "I don't know," he finally whispered, the shadows deepening in his gaze. "But I have a feeling it's about to change everything."

The air crackled again, but this time it felt like a warning, a storm gathering on the horizon, ready to unleash chaos. And as I stood there, caught between love and uncertainty, I couldn't shake the feeling that the ground beneath us was shifting, ready to give way, leaving us teetering on the edge of something far beyond our control.

Chapter 16: Crossroads

The soft hum of the streetlights outside wrapped around us like a thin blanket, casting flickering shadows across the room where we stood, the air thick with tension. Our living space, which had once brimmed with laughter and the hopeful light of new beginnings, now felt claustrophobic, the walls pressing in like a reminder of our unresolved issues. The dinner table was still set for the meal I had planned, a romantic affair with all the trimmings, but the elaborate spread sat untouched, just as we had left it during our heated exchange moments before.

"Maybe we rushed into this," I said, my voice barely above a whisper, the tremor betraying my certainty. The words tumbled out before I could catch them, like a wave crashing on the shore, and as they hung between us, I wished I could reel them back. Ethan's gaze locked onto mine, and for a heartbeat, I thought he might meet my vulnerability with his own. The silence stretched taut, filled with the sound of our breathing, and the weight of unspoken truths loomed larger than ever.

"No. We didn't rush. I just need to figure out who I am without her," he replied, his voice steady but tinged with a vulnerability that struck me like a bolt of lightning. His words sank into the room, a stone thrown into the still water of our relationship, rippling outward into every corner. I felt the punch of his admission as if he had pulled the air from my lungs. In that moment, I realized the impossibility of being everything he needed while he was still tethered to a past that refused to let him go.

I wanted to reach out and hold him, to reassure him that I would be his anchor through the storm, but the truth curled around my heart like a vice. I had stepped into this relationship, a whirlwind of passion and dreams, but now I was left standing in the aftermath, facing the reality that his past was a shadow I could never chase away.

It was a crossroads we never anticipated arriving at, the kind that made you question every choice you had made up to this point.

"Ethan, I—" My words faltered, caught in the tangled mess of my emotions. What could I say that would convey the confusion swirling within me? I didn't want to be the one holding him back, yet I also didn't want to be the one left behind, wondering what might have been.

He ran a hand through his tousled hair, the gesture filled with frustration. "I didn't mean to bring this up now, not like this," he said, his tone softening. "But every time I think I'm moving forward, she pulls me back." His admission was raw, a glimpse into the battle waging within him. I could almost see the memories flickering behind his eyes, like old film reels playing scenes of a life that once was. "It's not that I don't care about you. I do. You're everything I didn't know I was looking for. But I need to be whole again before I can give you all of me."

There it was, the haunting truth I had feared all along. Love, as exhilarating and intoxicating as it could be, often required more than just passion—it demanded clarity, independence, and sometimes, the painful acknowledgment of what had come before. I took a step back, the distance between us growing wider, as though physically manifesting the chasm of uncertainty that had opened up between our hearts.

"Maybe we should take a break," I suggested, the words tasting bitter on my tongue. The notion felt like a surrender, yet it was also a lifeline I had to throw, a necessary step toward healing. "Not a permanent one. Just... time to figure things out." I watched his expression shift, the flicker of surprise in his eyes quickly giving way to something deeper—concern, perhaps, or understanding. It was hard to tell.

"Is that really what you want?" he asked, his voice strained, as though the very idea pained him. The tension crackled in the air, an electric charge that held us both captive. "I don't want to lose you, not like this."

The sincerity of his words struck a chord within me. My heart ached with the realization that losing him would feel like losing a part of myself, but holding on too tightly might smother whatever flicker of hope remained between us. "Ethan, I don't want to lose you either," I said, my voice trembling again. "But I also can't keep pretending that everything is fine when it's not."

The truth lingered between us, heavy and unresolved, like a cloud hanging over the horizon, threatening rain but never quite releasing its burden. Ethan's jaw tightened, the flicker of indecision playing across his features. "I'll find a way to work through this, I promise," he replied, a fierce determination edging into his tone. "But I can't do it without knowing that you're okay too. You deserve that much."

A spark ignited within me at his words, a flicker of hope amid the uncertainty. "I just need to know that you're willing to try," I said, my heart pounding in my chest. "That you'll fight for us."

He nodded slowly, the tension easing ever so slightly as we stood in the dim light of our home, caught in a moment that felt simultaneously like an ending and a new beginning. "I will. I promise," he said, and the sincerity in his voice gave me a glimmer of hope, a lifeline amid the chaos.

Yet, even as the warmth of his words enveloped me, I couldn't shake the feeling that we were standing on the edge of something monumental, teetering between the thrill of love and the harsh reality of our intertwined pasts. And as we lingered in the quiet space, the decision loomed above us like a storm cloud, reminding me that every choice we made from here on out would shape the future we so desperately desired.

The next few days unfolded like a kaleidoscope of uncertainty, every color more vivid than the last, yet none quite blending harmoniously together. Ethan and I shared the same space but drifted like ships passing in the night, each carrying the weight of our separate thoughts, the silence between us thick enough to cut. I found myself meticulously rearranging furniture, convinced that if I could just shift the couch a few inches to the left or maybe hang that one painting I loved from the second-hand store, everything would right itself, as if my interior decor could mend our fraying relationship.

Every corner of our apartment seemed to echo the unresolved tension, from the kitchen where I once imagined us cooking together, to the living room, now a battleground of unspoken words. The coffee pot became a morning ritual of avoidance, our polite exchanges reduced to monosyllables and the clinking of cups. Each sip tasted bitter, as if brewed from the frustration swirling in my mind. I longed for the ease we once had, the easy banter that sparked joy between us like fireflies on a summer night.

One evening, I decided to break the silence, to dredge up a conversation that could lead us back to solid ground. We had both retreated to our respective corners of the couch, a chasm of air separating us, when I turned to Ethan, my heart racing as I summoned the courage. "Remember when we used to play those ridiculous games in the park?" I asked, trying to evoke a smile. "Like that time we played charades and you acted out a potato? I think that's when I realized I was definitely in trouble with you." I laughed, hoping he'd catch on, but his eyes remained clouded, lost in thought.

"Yeah, the potato. My finest hour," he replied, but the humor in his voice was feeble, just a shadow of what once felt effortless. "I just... I'm trying to figure things out." He shifted in his seat, running his fingers through his hair, a habit I had come to associate with his anxiety. "I thought time would help, but it feels like I'm just drifting."

"Drifting," I echoed, frustration bubbling within me. "Is that really all we're doing? Just waiting for clarity to wash over us?" I leaned forward, gripping the edge of the couch as if anchoring myself to the moment. "We need to face this, Ethan. You can't keep hiding behind the idea of what we could be while clinging to who you were."

The vulnerability in his eyes sparked a flicker of hope in my chest, but it was quickly extinguished as he looked away, the distance between us yawning wider. "I don't know how to let go," he confessed, his voice a raw whisper. The confession hung in the air like a thick fog, enveloping us in a cocoon of shared pain. "She was a part of my life for so long. I don't even know who I am without that version of me."

The honesty of his admission struck me, sharp and clear, like the crisp air of early autumn. "You're not that person anymore, Ethan. You've changed. We've changed." I could feel the frustration boiling beneath the surface, a simmering pot on the brink of boiling over. "You can't expect me to wait indefinitely while you sort through your past."

"I know!" His voice escalated, reverberating against the walls of our apartment. "I know, and I hate that I'm putting you through this. It's just... complicated." His hands moved in frantic gestures, as if he were grasping at something just out of reach. "I thought we could just... skip over this part. The messy part. But it's not working that way."

A fragile silence settled between us, thick enough to choke on. I felt like I was navigating a tightrope, each step carefully measured, unsure if the next would lead to safety or a dizzying plunge into uncertainty. "Ethan," I started, searching for the right words to articulate the fear settling in my chest. "I can't keep pretending that I'm okay with this limbo. I need to know you're all in or... or not at all."

His expression shifted, a flash of panic crossing his features as if I had suddenly unleashed a storm. "What are you saying?" His voice trembled, the fear evident in his tone. "You're not talking about breaking up, are you?"

I exhaled, the weight of my decision pressing heavily on my heart. "I'm saying we need to either choose to move forward together or be honest about where we stand. I don't want to end up resenting you for holding me back." The words felt like stones, heavy and laden with meaning, but they had to be said. I refused to let the fear of losing him dictate my life any longer.

He turned away, the muscles in his jaw clenched, and for a moment, the room echoed with the sound of his silence. "I don't want to lose you either," he finally said, his voice softer, more broken. "But I don't know if I'm ready for what you want."

A part of me felt relieved; at least we were finally saying what needed to be said, peeling back the layers of unspoken thoughts that had suffocated our connection. But another part of me quivered with uncertainty, aware of the precipice we teetered on. "Then let's take a step back," I suggested, my heart pounding. "Let's take the time we need to sort through this mess."

The look on his face was a mix of relief and dread, and I could tell he was weighing my suggestion against his fear of the unknown. "And what if we find that it's too much to fix? What if we discover that we were never meant to be?" His voice cracked, exposing the raw vulnerability beneath his bravado.

"Then at least we'll know," I replied, my tone steady, even as my heart raced. "We won't be left wondering what could have been. Sometimes, it takes losing something to appreciate what you had."

A moment passed as we absorbed the gravity of our situation, and slowly, I saw the flicker of acceptance in his eyes. "I don't want to lose you," he repeated, the words a mantra now, a lifeline amid the chaos. "I want to be whole for you. I will figure this out."

I nodded, relief flooding through me, though it was tempered by the uncertainty that lingered. "Then we take this time apart," I affirmed, my voice steady. "To breathe, to think. And if we're meant to find our way back, we will."

Ethan reached out, his fingers brushing mine, a fleeting touch that sent a shiver up my arm. "Okay. Okay, let's do that," he agreed, his voice heavy with resignation yet imbued with a hint of hope.

In that moment, the air shifted, infused with the possibility of new beginnings, as we took the first tentative step toward understanding what it truly meant to love someone, even when it hurt. As I looked into his eyes, I knew we were standing at a crossroads, a moment that could define us for better or worse. And while the journey ahead was fraught with uncertainty, the choice to face it together, even apart, felt like a leap of faith—one I was finally willing to take.

The days that followed felt like I was living in a half-light, a constant haze of uncertainty that clung to me like a second skin. The apartment became a labyrinth of memories—every corner turned brought flashes of our shared laughter and moments that felt eternal. Yet, those echoes were now tinged with a bittersweet quality, a reminder of what was at stake. I had given him space, an unspoken promise to respect his journey, but that didn't mean the silence didn't gnaw at my insides.

I threw myself into work, diving into my projects with an intensity that bordered on obsessive. The glow of the computer screen became my comfort, the rhythms of deadlines and meetings serving as a temporary balm for my restless heart. I told myself it was a good distraction, that it was helping me heal, but deep down, I knew I was merely postponing the inevitable confrontation with my feelings.

One afternoon, while knee-deep in a particularly challenging report, my phone buzzed with a message. I glanced at the screen, half-expecting it to be one of my coworkers, but my heart lurched when I saw Ethan's name. He hadn't reached out in days, and seeing those two familiar words made my stomach twist with both excitement and dread.

Can we talk?

I hesitated, fingers hovering over the keyboard. My mind raced through a thousand scenarios, each more anxious than the last. What if he wanted to end things? Or worse, what if he wanted to reconcile only to falter again at the first hurdle? Against my better judgment, I replied.

Sure. When?

The response came almost instantly. How about now?

I swallowed hard, glancing at the clock. I had twenty minutes before my next meeting. Panic fluttered in my chest, an unwelcome reminder of the unresolved tension between us. I took a breath, steeling myself for whatever this conversation would bring.

When Ethan arrived, I was perched on the edge of my chair, heart racing as he stepped through the door. The moment he entered, the atmosphere shifted, an electric charge sparking between us. His hair was tousled, as if he had been running his fingers through it in frustration. The vulnerability in his eyes felt like a lifeline—and a weight.

"I didn't mean to just drop by like this," he started, running a hand through his hair again, a gesture that sent my heart fluttering. "But I needed to see you."

His words wrapped around me, both comforting and alarming. "Okay," I replied, my voice a mere whisper, hesitant and fragile. "What's going on?"

He took a deep breath, as though gathering courage for the words that were about to follow. "I've been thinking a lot about everything. About us, about what I need to do."

"Good. That's good," I said, eager to maintain some semblance of optimism, even as anxiety twisted in my stomach. "I'm glad to hear that."

"I don't want to lose you," he said, a sincerity in his tone that made my heart clench. "But I also can't keep dragging you into my past. You deserve better."

The heaviness of his confession settled between us like a fog, suffocating and yet oddly soothing. "I just want you to be happy, Ethan," I said, the words spilling from my lips before I could stop them. "And I want you to be whole, whether that includes me or not."

His eyes locked onto mine, the weight of his gaze enough to break down the walls I had carefully constructed. "You're not just an option for me, you know that, right? You're my choice."

I felt the warmth flood my cheeks, a mix of relief and hope mingling with the ever-present tension. "Then what's stopping us? We can work through this. Together."

He hesitated, his expression flickering with uncertainty. "I want to. I really do. But there's still so much that I'm wrestling with. I feel like I'm standing at the edge of a cliff, and I'm terrified of what lies below."

"Then let me help you," I urged, my heart pounding. "We can figure this out together. I believe in us."

His lips curled into a hesitant smile, but it quickly faded, replaced by a look of apprehension. "What if I can't let go of her? What if I keep getting pulled back?"

"Then we take it one step at a time," I replied, trying to keep the frustration at bay. "It won't be easy, but nothing worthwhile ever is. Just promise me you'll be honest, no matter how hard it gets."

"Okay. I promise."

As the words left his mouth, a sense of resolve settled between us, a fragile hope that flickered like a candle in the dark. The tension shifted, an unspoken agreement forming in the air. But just as I began to feel a glimmer of optimism, a sudden knock at the door jolted us both.

I glanced at Ethan, confusion flickering across his features. "Who could that be?"

"I don't know," I replied, my heart racing again. I stood up, glancing through the peephole. My breath caught in my throat. "Oh, no."

"What is it?" Ethan asked, a mixture of concern and curiosity in his voice.

"It's... it's Claire."

His expression shifted, a cocktail of emotions crossing his face—surprise, anxiety, and a hint of panic. "What does she want?"

"I have no idea, but she looks... frantic."

Ethan's hands balled into fists at his sides, and I could see the conflict warring within him. "Should we let her in?"

A part of me screamed to run away, to hide from whatever storm was about to break. But another part, the part that cared for him and wanted to understand, pushed me forward. "Yeah. We should. We can't just ignore her."

As I unlocked the door, my heart raced, each beat echoing the trepidation coursing through me. I swung the door open, bracing myself for whatever was to come. Claire stood on the threshold, her eyes wide and frantic, as if she had been running.

"Ethan, I need to talk to you," she blurted out, breathless and desperate, as if she had just crossed a great distance.

In that moment, everything shifted. The fragile thread of understanding that had begun to weave itself between Ethan and me felt like it was unraveling before my eyes. I could sense the air thickening, the tension coiling tighter as I exchanged a glance with Ethan, who stood frozen beside me.

"Claire," he said, his voice barely above a whisper, laden with uncertainty.

The look in his eyes told me everything: we were standing on the precipice of a decision that could change everything. And as the door creaked open wider, it felt as if the world around us was holding its breath, waiting for the next chapter to unfold.

Chapter 17: Falling Apart

The days stretch out before me like a gray blanket, heavy and suffocating. Each sunrise feels like a muted reminder of what once was, a cruel joke played by a universe that knows how to toy with my emotions. I find solace in the rhythm of my daily routine, the mundane tasks that once felt comforting now seem like hollow echoes of a life I can't quite grasp. Coffee becomes my only companion in the quiet mornings, its rich aroma swirling in the air, though even that fails to ignite the warmth I crave.

I dive into my work with the fervor of someone trying to outrun their demons. My fingers race over the keyboard, creating reports and drafting emails, each click a feeble attempt to drown out the nagging emptiness gnawing at me. The fluorescent lights buzz overhead, illuminating a world that feels artificially bright. My colleagues buzz around me, their laughter a distant hum, while I sit ensconced in my own cocoon of solitude, painfully aware of the chair across from me that now feels unbearably empty.

"Hey, you okay?" Claire asks one afternoon, her brow furrowed with concern as she leans against my cubicle. The sweet scent of her vanilla lotion fills the air, a stark contrast to the sterile environment of the office. I look up, forcing a smile that feels more like a grimace.

"Yeah, just busy," I reply, trying to sound casual, though I know the truth is etched across my face like a neon sign. "You know how it is."

Claire's gaze sharpens, and I know she sees right through the façade. "You haven't been yourself lately. If you need to talk or if there's anything—"

"I'm fine, really." I cut her off, the words tumbling out a bit too hastily. I can't bear the idea of opening up, of exposing the raw, aching void that Ethan's absence has left in my heart. I glance at my computer screen, where numbers blur together in an indecipherable mess, and I wonder if this is how life feels without color—like being stuck in a black-and-white film.

The truth is, every moment without Ethan feels like wandering through a fog, the world around me dulled and muted. The laughter of my friends, the warmth of the sun, even the taste of my favorite chocolate cake—all seem tinged with a bittersweet longing. It's as if I'm stuck in a never-ending loop of memories, each one pulling me deeper into a well of nostalgia that I can't escape.

Evenings have become the worst. I retreat to my tiny apartment, walls painted a cheerful yellow that now feels mocking, each corner filled with the ghost of what used to be. I sink into my sofa, its cushions familiar yet cold, and allow myself to drift through thoughts of Ethan. The way he'd throw his head back and laugh at my terrible jokes, or the way his eyes sparkled when he was deep in thought, as if the world outside faded away and it was just us, suspended in our own little universe.

I scroll through my phone, tempted to text him. My heart races at the thought of hearing his voice, but I can't shake the nagging doubt that fills the air between us. What if he doesn't want to hear from me? What if I'm just a lingering memory, a shadow that won't quite fade? I tuck my phone back into my pocket, the weight of it feeling like an anchor in my gut.

As days bleed into weeks, I discover a rhythm to my melancholy. I fill my weekends with spontaneous adventures—tasting new cafés, wandering through art galleries, pretending to be the carefree person I once was. But each outing is laced with a sense of longing, an itch that no amount of distraction can scratch. My friends rally around me, pulling me into the vibrant social tapestry they weave, yet I can't help but feel like an outsider, watching from the sidelines as life unfolds without me.

"Let's go hiking this weekend!" Jenna suggests one Friday night, her eyes sparkling with enthusiasm. "We'll leave the city behind and just breathe, you know? It'll be fun!"

The idea lingers in the air, and despite my reservations, something within me stirs. Maybe I need this. Maybe I need to breathe again. "Okay," I agree, a flicker of excitement breaking through the fog. "That sounds good."

On the day of our hike, the sun bathes everything in golden light, and I can't help but feel a twinge of hope. The forest is alive, leaves rustling with whispers of secrets, the scent of pine intoxicating. As we walk, laughter bounces off the trees, and for a moment, I allow myself to feel free, unburdened by the weight of my thoughts.

But as we reach a clearing, Jenna's laughter cuts through me, sharp and unyielding. "Look at that view!" she exclaims, and I turn to follow her gaze, heart dropping as I spot a couple standing hand in hand, lost in their own world. It's like a punch to the gut—an image that freezes me in place, a reminder of what I've lost. The warmth of the sun suddenly feels cold against my skin, the laughter around me fading into a dull roar.

"Hey, you okay?" Jenna's voice pulls me back to reality, her brow creased with concern. I nod, but it feels hollow. I force a smile, the effort of it draining, and try to focus on the beauty around me. Yet all I can think about is Ethan—how he would have loved this, how his laughter would have blended with the symphony of nature, and how it all feels so profoundly wrong without him.

In that moment, a seed of determination plants itself within me. I can't keep running away from what I feel. I need to confront this aching void, to find a way back to the colors of my life, to rediscover the laughter that once came so easily. As the sun dips lower in the sky, painting the horizon in hues of orange and pink, I realize that while the ache of absence is a part of me now, it doesn't have to define me.

I can choose to reach out, to find my way back to the light, one step at a time.

The following weekend arrives with the promise of adventure, a faint light creeping into the corners of my heavy heart. My friends are buzzing with excitement, and as we pull into the hiking trail parking lot, I feel the first flicker of something that resembles hope. The air is crisp and fragrant with pine, and I breathe deeply, trying to inhale courage along with the scent of nature.

"Remember, this is not just any hike," Jenna calls out, her hair bouncing in the wind as she jumps from the car, "this is a healing hike! If you fall, we'll document it for posterity and laugh about it for years to come!"

"Great, now I'm under pressure," I quip, rolling my eyes as I grab my backpack. Inside, I have water, granola bars, and an emergency stash of chocolate—a necessity for any journey. "No pressure at all!"

"Honestly, it wouldn't be a proper hike without a little near-death experience," Claire chimes in, shooting me a mischievous grin. "Just don't die before we get to the summit, okay? I need you to carry my gear."

The camaraderie wraps around me like a warm blanket, yet the laughter feels fragile. I chuckle along with them, but a part of me remains cautious, like a wary animal on high alert, unsure if it can truly let its guard down. As we set off down the trail, the sun filters through the leaves, casting dappled shadows on the ground, and I find my rhythm with each step.

We ascend, our chatter bubbling up and cascading down the mountain like a gentle stream. Jenna talks about her latest crush, her voice animated as she reenacts an awkward encounter at a coffee shop. Claire chimes in, rolling her eyes and offering unsolicited advice that is both absurd and endearing. "If you're going to flirt, at least have the decency to not trip over your own feet, Jenna!"

"Hey, tripping is part of my charm!" Jenna retorts, sticking her tongue out as we climb higher. I can't help but smile, their banter a distraction from the storm brewing inside me. But with each mile we conquer, I feel the ghost of Ethan linger in the back of my mind, reminding me of the warmth that once filled my days.

As we reach a particularly steep part of the trail, the laughter fades into heavy breathing, the effort required pulling us into a comfortable silence. I glance over at Jenna and Claire, their faces flushed but determined, and I admire how effortlessly they manage to find joy even in exhaustion. "We should do this more often," I say, surprising myself.

"Absolutely," Jenna agrees, wiping the sweat from her brow. "Nature is like therapy but with better views and less judgment."

"Unless you run into a bear, then you're judged for your poor life choices," I add, feeling the familiar pull of humor, hoping to lighten the mood.

"Noted," Claire replies, "next time we'll bring a guide to fend off the bears. Or at least a whistle."

With the conversation flowing again, I feel a sense of liberation, but it's fleeting. As we crest the hill and the landscape opens up, my breath catches in my throat. Before us lies a breathtaking vista, the valley sprawling out like a patchwork quilt—each color vivid and alive, a contrast to the grayness that had become my world.

"Wow," I breathe, taking it all in, my heart swelling. "This is incredible."

Jenna and Claire step beside me, their eyes wide with awe. "This is what I was talking about!" Jenna exclaims, throwing her arms wide as if she could embrace the entire landscape. "See? Nature cures all."

"It does feel a little magical," I admit, gazing at the horizon painted in hues of blue and gold. For a moment, the ache in my chest loosens its grip, and I find myself smiling genuinely, almost forgetting the heartache that clung to me like a second skin.

As we settle on a rock to catch our breath and take photos, Claire pulls out a thermos of coffee, the rich scent wafting through the air. "Anyone want some liquid motivation?" she offers, pouring steaming cups. The warmth seeps into my hands as I take a sip, the bitter richness grounding me in this moment of connection.

"Liquid therapy, indeed," I murmur, savoring the taste.

Suddenly, a rustle in the bushes nearby grabs our attention, and Jenna jumps, her eyes wide. "What if it's a bear?"

"Then we'll throw you to distract it," Claire replies, laughter spilling over her words.

"I knew I was expendable!" Jenna exclaims dramatically, clutching her heart.

Just then, a small dog bursts forth from the underbrush, bounding toward us with an enthusiastic bark. Its scruffy fur catches the sunlight, and it seems utterly unfazed by the dramatic tension in the air. "Oh my gosh, you little fluffball!" I exclaim, bending down as it leaps at me, tail wagging like it's just won the lottery.

"Someone's happy to see us!" Jenna laughs, crouching down to pet the dog, whose energy seems to infect us all.

"Looks like we've got a new friend!" Claire smiles, reaching for the dog's collar. "No tag. Where did you come from, buddy?"

I scratch behind the dog's ears, feeling the warmth radiate from its tiny body. "Maybe he was just wandering around, looking for some adventure," I suggest, the idea sparking something inside me. "Just like us."

For the next few minutes, we indulge in dog antics, the little creature jumping and spinning as if it's the happiest being alive. It chases after sticks we toss, and as I watch it frolic, a sense of peace settles over me. The worries about Ethan feel momentarily dulled, the presence of this small creature reminding me of the joy that exists in simple things.

But the bliss is short-lived. As I stand to stretch, I catch sight of movement on the trail below. My heart skips a beat when I realize who it is—Ethan, making his way up the hill, his strides confident yet somehow hesitant, as if he's grappling with an internal battle.

"What the hell?" I mutter, my breath catching in my throat. My heart races, a mixture of joy and panic swelling inside me.

"Who?" Jenna asks, following my gaze.

"Ethan," I whisper, unable to tear my eyes away from him. The weight of our silence stretches between us like a taut string, and for a moment, it feels as though the world has paused, holding its breath in anticipation of what comes next.

My heart is a runaway train, racing down the tracks of uncertainty as I watch Ethan approach. Time stretches, and suddenly I'm acutely aware of every detail—the way the sunlight dances off his dark hair, the determined set of his jaw, and the faint sheen of sweat glistening on his brow. My breath hitches as if the universe has conspired to throw us together at this very moment, each beat in my chest a question waiting to be asked.

"Uh, are we going to pretend he's not climbing toward us?" Jenna whispers, eyes wide with disbelief. Claire stares too, her mouth slightly agape, as if she's just seen a celebrity emerge from the crowd.

"I can't believe it," I murmur, half in awe and half in dread. My legs feel rooted to the ground, a strange combination of excitement and fear making it hard to move.

"What's the game plan here?" Jenna prompts, her eyes narrowing with curiosity. "Do we play it cool or go full fan club?"

"Definitely not fan club," I reply quickly, glancing at the little dog still frolicking at my feet, oblivious to the tension threading through the air. "I don't even know what to say."

"Maybe just say 'hi' and not make it weird?" Claire suggests, her tone light but her eyes serious. I can tell she's gauging my reaction, assessing how this meeting could tip me back into the whirlpool of emotions I've been struggling to navigate.

Taking a deep breath, I finally manage to lift my hand in a half-hearted wave, hoping to convey something between nonchalance and sheer terror. "Hey," I call out, the word falling from my lips like an unexpected confession.

Ethan stops, surprise flickering across his face, and I can't help but notice the way his lips curl into a smile, a warmth that spreads through me despite the uncertainty knotting my stomach. "I didn't expect to see you here," he replies, his voice smooth yet tinged with an underlying tension.

"Yeah, just... you know, a healing hike," I reply, gesturing vaguely, as if this impromptu outing somehow justifies my presence. "I mean, you're not the only one who likes nature therapy, right?"

He chuckles softly, that familiar lilt to his laugh coaxing a flutter in my chest. "Right. Though I didn't know it came with an adorable dog."

"Meet Scruffy," I say, crouching down to ruffle the dog's fur, which instantly draws Ethan's attention. "He's our unofficial mascot for the day. He's practically a therapy animal."

"Good choice," Ethan says, kneeling down to scratch behind Scruffy's ears, and I can't help but feel a pang of nostalgia for the way he once fit seamlessly into my life. "I could use a little therapy myself."

For a moment, the world around us fades, leaving just the three of us in a cocoon of warmth and shared laughter. But then the reality of our situation crashes back, the walls of silence that have built up between us suddenly feeling insurmountable. "So, um, what brings you out here?" I finally ask, my voice quivering slightly.

"I needed to clear my head," he admits, shifting his weight uncomfortably. "Things have been... complicated lately. I thought some fresh air might help."

"Complicated is one way to put it," I say, my heart racing at the weight of his words. "I get that. It's been... well, different for me too."

He meets my gaze, those deep eyes searching mine for something unspoken, and for a heartbeat, I wonder if he feels it—the magnetic pull that lingers between us. "You look good," he finally says, breaking the moment and making me feel both seen and vulnerable. "How's work treating you?"

"It's keeping me busy, which is nice. I could use the distraction," I reply, avoiding the raw emotions simmering beneath the surface. "You know, running away from my feelings like a professional."

Ethan laughs, a rich sound that makes the tension ease just a little. "I've been doing my fair share of running, too."

Before I can respond, Jenna leans in, clearly trying to be helpful yet somehow making everything more awkward. "So, are we going to ignore the elephant in the room, or is this the moment we all break down and have an emotional chat?"

"Wow, way to kill the vibe, Jenna," Claire mutters, shooting her a warning look.

"What? I'm just saying what everyone's thinking!" Jenna insists, hands on her hips. "This is like a rom-com moment waiting to happen!"

I shoot her a look that I hope conveys my desperate need for subtlety. "Thanks for that, Jenna," I say dryly, but I can't deny that her words hang in the air like a loaded gun, waiting for the trigger to be pulled.

Ethan shifts slightly, the warmth in his expression replaced with a cautious curiosity. "What do you mean, exactly?"

"Just that things have felt a little... off lately," Jenna replies, feigning innocence. "Like there's a tension that needs to be addressed. Right, guys?"

I shoot her a look that could curdle milk, and Claire, sensing my embarrassment, hastily interjects, "Let's focus on the beautiful view!

How about that?" She gestures to the sprawling landscape below us, desperately trying to redirect the conversation.

But the moment has already shifted, the air thick with unsaid words and unaddressed emotions. I can feel Ethan's gaze lingering on me, and I'm torn between the urge to lean into the openness of this conversation and the instinct to retreat into the comfort of silence.

"Maybe we should sit down," I suggest, feeling a swell of anxiety knotting my stomach. "Catch our breath?"

"Good idea," Ethan agrees, his voice steady, though I sense an undercurrent of something deeper. We find a flat rock to perch on, Scruffy curling up at our feet, oblivious to the tension threading between us.

As we settle into an uneasy silence, I feel the weight of everything I haven't said, and I can't shake the feeling that this moment might be the tipping point, the edge of a precipice from which there's no turning back. "You know," I start, my voice barely above a whisper, "I've missed you."

Ethan looks up, his expression shifting, something unguarded flickering in his eyes. "I've missed you too. More than I realized."

Before I can respond, a rustle in the bushes nearby grabs our attention. My heart pounds as I glance over, an instinctual worry curling in my chest. "What was that?" I ask, my voice tinged with uncertainty.

Suddenly, the underbrush parts, and out bounds a figure I never expected to see. My breath catches, and the world around us seems to tilt on its axis. Standing there, looking as bewildered as I feel, is someone from my past—a person I thought I'd never have to face again.

"Surprise," they say, a smirk playing on their lips as they step forward, shattering the fragile moment that had begun to take shape between Ethan and me. My mind races, confusion swirling as the weight of their presence settles like a storm cloud overhead.

Chapter 18: When Everything Breaks

The office felt like a fishbowl, sunlight pouring in through the floor-to-ceiling windows, illuminating the dust motes swirling in the air. I had always loved this space; the light brought a warmth that seemed to foster creativity and ambition. But on that particular afternoon, as I sat at my desk staring at the glaring screen of my laptop, the warmth felt more like a spotlight, illuminating every flaw, every imperfection. Madison's arrival shattered the comfortable silence I'd wrapped around myself like a security blanket.

She swept into the room with an air of authority, her heels clicking on the polished floor like a countdown clock to doom. Her presence radiated a chill that froze the vibrant chatter of the office around me. Madison had always been someone who commanded attention, and today was no exception. The crispness of her tailored blazer matched the sharpness in her voice as she wasted no time on formalities. "We need to talk," she announced, cutting through the layers of small talk and niceties that normally cushioned such encounters.

As the door clicked shut behind her, I felt the air grow thick and heavy, as if the universe itself held its breath. I braced myself, fingers curling around the edges of my desk as she launched into a tirade about Ethan—my Ethan. Each word she spoke was wrapped in a honeyed venom that twisted my stomach into knots. It was as if she had studied every weak point I had, and now she was armed and ready to attack.

"Ethan's life has been spiraling since he left me," she said, her voice smooth, yet laced with the kind of triumph that made my skin crawl. "He's a wreck, you know. The rumors are flying. People are saying it's because of you."

I blinked, struggling to maintain my composure. Madison had a talent for making every sentence feel like a revelation. She could weave a story out of thin air, and somehow, I felt caught in her web, flailing and gasping for clarity. "You don't know what you're talking about," I finally managed, my voice surprisingly steady, though the knot in my stomach was tightening.

"Oh, but I do," she replied, an infuriatingly smug smile playing at the corners of her mouth. "He's not enough for you, you know. You never were." The finality of her statement hit me harder than I expected, echoing in my mind like the toll of a bell. I wanted to fight back, to declare the strength of what Ethan and I had built, but the confidence in her words made my own certainty waver.

I remembered the way Ethan had looked at me, the warmth of his hands entwined with mine, the hushed moments shared beneath the starlit sky. Hadn't we carved out a space that felt like ours? I wanted to scream that our love was real, tangible, a vibrant color splashed across the grayscale of Madison's manipulative machinations. But there, in that moment, doubt snuck in, slinking around my mind like a shadow. What if she was right? What if I was just a fleeting distraction, a pretty face that could never fill the void left by her?

As she droned on, recounting the whispers she'd heard and the pitying glances thrown my way, I felt the walls of the office closing in. Each accusation felt like a blow, and I clung to my chair, gripping the armrests as if they were my only lifeline. "He deserves someone who understands him," she continued, her tone dripping with false sympathy. "Someone who isn't going to pull him into her chaos."

A fire ignited within me, a spark of rebellion against the suffocating grip of her words. "Ethan chose me," I said, my voice gaining strength. "He's not a toy for you to manipulate. We are building something together, something real."

Madison's laughter was low and disbelieving, a sound that grated against the walls of my confidence. "Oh, sweetie, that's cute. But it doesn't change the fact that he left me for a reason." The way she pronounced the word "reason" made it feel heavy, weighted with unspoken truths that clung to the air like smoke. "He's lost, and trust me, he's not looking for a replacement."

Each word dripped with the satisfaction of someone who reveled in the pain of another, and it took every ounce of willpower not to crumble under her gaze. I fought to keep my expression neutral, to present a facade of unwavering resolve. Inside, however, I was a storm, a whirlwind of conflicting emotions.

"Why are you even here?" I shot back, the frustration bubbling up like a geyser threatening to erupt. "Isn't your life perfect? Why come and stir up trouble for both of us?" The question hung in the air, heavy with accusation, and for a moment, a flicker of uncertainty crossed her face. But it vanished as quickly as it came, replaced by a mask of icy determination.

"I want Ethan to be happy, and if that's not with you, I'll make sure he knows it," she replied, her eyes narrowing as she took a step closer, invading my personal space with the confidence of someone who believed they were untouchable.

As she left, I felt hollow, a vacant shell of who I had been just moments before. The office, once a sanctuary, now felt like a prison, the walls echoing with her words. "You're not enough." I leaned back in my chair, staring at the sunlight that flooded the room, but the warmth felt far away, replaced by an icy dread that wrapped around my heart.

Maybe Madison was right. Maybe I wasn't enough for Ethan. The thought gnawed at me like a persistent ache, relentless and consuming. I wanted to scream, to shake the doubt from my mind, but it lingered, clawing at the edges of my resolve. What if everything I believed in was a fragile illusion, ready to shatter at the first sign of pressure?

The minutes dragged by like molasses, each tick of the clock an unwelcome reminder of Madison's chilling visit. I sat in the office, the air thick with unspoken tension, feeling as if I were suspended in some kind of limbo, neither here nor there. My laptop remained open, the cursor blinking at me mockingly, like it was in on the cruel joke. I wanted to dive into work, lose myself in spreadsheets and project timelines, but all I could focus on were the remnants of Madison's words echoing in my mind.

My phone buzzed, pulling me from my spiral of self-doubt. I glanced at the screen and saw Ethan's name lighting up in bright blue. My heart skipped, a sudden rush of hope pushing through the suffocating weight of despair. I hesitated, finger hovering over the answer button. What could I say? Would it be a relief to hear his voice, or would it deepen the fissures that had already formed between us? After a moment that stretched too long, I pressed the button.

"Hey!" he said, his voice bright and warm, washing over me like a sunbeam breaking through storm clouds. But there was an undercurrent of weariness, the kind that seeps in after a long day, and I felt my heart clench.

"Hey," I replied, trying to sound casual, as if I hadn't just been interrogated by his ex in my own office. "How's it going?"

"Better now that I'm talking to you," he said, and there was a hint of sincerity that made me smile, despite the heaviness in my chest. "I missed you. Can I come by later?"

"Of course!" The enthusiasm came too easily, but I pushed the creeping dread aside. I would show him that whatever doubt Madison had planted could not take root in the soil of what we shared. "I've got some new wine I've been saving for a special occasion. Consider tonight our 'everything is fine' celebration."

"Wine and fine?" Ethan chuckled, and I could picture him, tousled hair and the soft smile that made my heart race. "Sounds perfect."

As the conversation flowed, I felt the barriers I had unconsciously erected begin to dissolve. We talked about everything—his latest project at work, a ridiculous mishap at the office where a team member had spilled coffee all over the quarterly report, and his upcoming weekend plans. Each laugh exchanged was a small victory, a shield against Madison's doubts. But beneath the laughter, my heart still thudded uncomfortably, like a warning drumbeat.

After hanging up, I moved through the motions of preparing for his arrival—setting out the wine glasses, lighting a couple of candles to create a cozy atmosphere. I filled the air with the soft hum of music, hoping to drown out the insistent whispers of insecurity. Yet with each flicker of the flame, a new wave of anxiety washed over me. What if I put too much pressure on tonight? What if the very air crackled with the tension of unaddressed doubts?

When the doorbell finally rang, I almost dropped the bottle of wine in my hands. I took a deep breath, straightened my back, and opened the door to find Ethan standing there, looking effortlessly handsome in a faded T-shirt and jeans. He grinned, and for a moment, it felt like everything was perfect.

"Surprise! I brought snacks!" He held up a paper bag with a flourish, and I laughed, the sound genuine and bright.

"You're a hero," I said, stepping aside to let him in. "I was about to pour myself into an existential crisis. What's in the bag?"

"Only the finest selection of overpriced cheese and crackers," he declared, placing it on the counter. "I figured it's the least I could do for someone who's been so busy saving the world."

"Is that what I'm doing? Saving the world?" I smirked, pouring two glasses of wine. "I thought I was just trying to survive another week of deadlines."

"Surviving is the first step to saving, right?" he teased, raising his glass as I handed him his. Our eyes met, and in that moment, the world outside faded.

We settled onto the couch, and as we munched on the snacks, the conversation flowed easily again. We spoke of dreams and future plans, each word laced with a sweetness that felt intoxicating, making me forget the chilling weight of Madison's words. I shared a silly story about my childhood obsession with collecting stickers, and he laughed, his eyes sparkling with delight.

But the laughter faded as I caught sight of his expression, the way it shifted subtly when I mentioned Madison. His brow furrowed slightly, and for a heartbeat, the atmosphere thickened. "You know, she's been reaching out to me," he admitted, and my heart sank.

"About what?" My voice was steadier than I felt, but a tight knot began to twist in my stomach.

"Just... you know, checking in," he replied, avoiding my gaze as he took a sip of his wine. "She's trying to figure things out."

A silence stretched between us, heavy and oppressive. I could feel the shadows creeping back, the tendrils of doubt wrapping around my heart. "Ethan, you don't have to feel obligated to engage with her," I said, my voice softer, tinged with the vulnerability that threatened to spill over. "You made a choice to be with me."

"I know," he assured me, but there was a hesitation in his tone that sent alarm bells ringing in my mind. "But I can't just ignore the past. It's a part of me, you know?"

I nodded, though my heart felt heavy. "And I respect that. Just... don't let her pull you back in. We have something real here, don't we?"

"Of course we do." His words were warm, but there was a flicker of uncertainty in his eyes that I couldn't shake. "You're incredible, you know that?"

"I try," I said, attempting to inject some levity into the tension. "But I'm not going to try harder than you, right?"

His laughter was a balm, but I could still feel the shadows lurking. We talked some more, and the evening danced on, a waltz of laughter and lingering touches. Yet, every time his phone buzzed with a notification, my heart dropped, anticipating a message from her.

As the night wore on and the wine flowed, the moments felt fleeting, like grains of sand slipping through my fingers. Each laugh felt like a fragile crystal, beautiful but precarious, and I couldn't shake the feeling that it was all teetering on the edge of something I couldn't quite define. I needed to anchor this evening, to carve it into my memory as a testament to us, but the lurking uncertainty made it feel as if the ground was shifting beneath me.

Just as the tension seemed to break, his phone buzzed again, and the moment shattered like glass, scattering my heart across the room. I could feel the shift in his energy as he glanced at the screen, and my breath caught in my throat.

The tension in the room thickened like fog, and as Ethan stared at his phone, a tightness gripped my chest. I watched him, the familiar comfort of his presence now feeling like a carefully balanced act on a tightrope. His fingers lingered over the screen, hesitating, as if he were weighing the consequences of whatever message had just appeared. I wanted to scream at the phone, demanding that it stop meddling in our fragile moment, but I merely shifted, leaning forward, desperate to catch a glimpse of his expression.

"Who is it?" I asked, attempting to infuse my voice with nonchalance, but it came out as more of a plea than I intended.

"It's...just a notification," he replied too quickly, his eyes darting away from mine. "Nothing important."

I raised an eyebrow, skeptical. "Nothing important? Your 'nothing important' notifications could very well be the reason we're not getting our happily ever after."

Ethan chuckled, but the sound was strained, lacking its usual warmth. "I swear, it's just work-related."

"Right," I said, feigning a roll of my eyes, but I could feel my heart racing. "Because nothing brings couples together like work notifications. Truly romantic."

"Okay, you've got me there." He placed the phone face down on the coffee table, a clear signal of his intent to focus on me. "Let's forget about it for a bit."

And for a moment, we did. We sunk back into our conversation, but I could sense the unease lurking beneath the surface like a shark circling its prey. I laughed at his jokes, leaned into the warmth of his shoulder, but with each shared smile, a part of me remained on high alert, poised for the next intrusion.

"Let me ask you something," Ethan said suddenly, his tone shifting. "How do you feel about relationships? You know, the deep, existential stuff."

I took a sip of wine, the familiar taste swirling with the uncertainty in my gut. "Is this your version of relationship therapy?"

"Maybe," he admitted, a glint of mischief in his eyes. "But I want to know what you think. Do you believe in soulmates? Or do you think they're just a fairy tale?"

"Hmm," I mused, feeling the weight of the question settle on my shoulders. "I think soulmates are like your favorite song. Sometimes you hear it, and it hits every note just right. Other times, you realize it's just stuck in your head and sounds better in theory than reality."

Ethan's laughter filled the space, a buoyant sound that momentarily lifted the heavy fog of anxiety. "That's beautifully tragic, actually."

"Thank you! I aim for beautifully tragic," I shot back, smirking. "But really, I guess it depends on the context. I believe that some people just click in a way that feels effortless, and others...well, they're like that one song you can't skip fast enough."

He studied me for a moment, and I could see the gears turning in his mind. "So what does that make us?"

"A ballad? A duet?" I ventured, my heart racing as the vulnerability crept in.

"More like an epic rock anthem," he declared with exaggerated flair. "Full of energy, unexpected solos, and perhaps a few lyrical mishaps."

"An anthem? I can live with that," I laughed, but my heart thudded uncomfortably as the implications of our banter sank in. What if this moment of levity was just a distraction from the storm brewing outside?

Just as the mood began to lighten, his phone buzzed again, a sharp reminder of the outside world crashing into our bubble. This time, Ethan's expression faltered, and I couldn't ignore the feeling that the air had shifted, thickening with the weight of unspoken words.

"Can you just ignore it?" I found myself saying, my voice barely above a whisper, as if raising it too high would shatter the delicate atmosphere.

"It's probably just a group chat," he replied quickly, but the tension in his shoulders told me it was more than that.

"Group chats don't usually make people look like they've seen a ghost," I snapped before I could stop myself. "Ethan, what's going on?"

He hesitated, eyes flicking between me and the phone, an internal battle waging behind those striking green eyes. "I just... it's from Madison," he finally admitted, and my heart plummeted.

"Great," I managed to say, forcing a smile even as dread washed over me. "What's she saying now? How she misses you? How you were her great love?"

Ethan sighed, pinching the bridge of his nose. "She wants to talk. About us."

"Us?" The word fell from my lips like a stone, heavy and cold. "What more could she possibly want to say? She left you, remember? Why does she suddenly care about our relationship?"

"Maybe because she sees me happy," he said, his voice steady but his eyes betraying a flicker of uncertainty. "Maybe she feels like she has a right to voice her concerns."

I could feel the edges of my heart crumbling, the jagged pieces cutting deeper than I anticipated. "Concerns? Is that what we're calling them now?"

"I don't want to hurt you," he replied, his voice low. "But I need to be honest. I didn't expect her to reach out, and I'm not sure how to handle it."

"Right, because keeping me in the dark has always been your strong suit," I said, my voice sharper than I intended.

"Don't twist my words!" he shot back, the frustration rising in his tone. "I'm trying to navigate this, just like you."

"Navigate what?" I challenged, my pulse quickening. "Your ex throwing darts at our relationship? Because that's all I see here—her throwing rocks, trying to see if she can make us crumble."

Ethan's eyes narrowed, and for a moment, I saw a glimpse of anger flash across his face. "I'm not going to let her dictate what we have," he said firmly. "But I don't want to ignore the fact that she's still a part of my life, whether I like it or not."

"That's rich," I spat, my hands clenching into fists. "Maybe you should have thought about that before diving headfirst into a relationship with me."

"Is this about you being insecure?" he countered, the heat in his voice mirroring my own. "Because it feels like you're ready to throw in the towel without even trying."

I opened my mouth to retort, but the words caught in my throat as the weight of the moment crashed over me. I could feel the tears stinging my eyes, a raw vulnerability that felt foreign and uncomfortable. "This isn't just insecurity," I finally managed. "This is about trust—trust that you won't let her worm her way back into your life when she sees you're doing well. Trust that I'm enough for you."

His gaze softened, but the moment of tenderness was fleeting. The tension in the room reached a breaking point, and as if sensing the unease, my phone buzzed beside me, startling me out of our escalating argument. I glanced down and froze, the message lighting up my screen.

It was from Madison.

"Come on, don't read it," Ethan urged, his voice sharp with urgency. "Whatever it is, it doesn't matter."

But I couldn't help myself; my fingers trembled as I opened the message. The words jumped out at me, a haunting invitation that wrapped around my heart like a vice.

"Let's talk. I know you're there with him. Just know, he's not yours yet."

The air thickened, the walls felt as though they were closing in, and the weight of the world bore down on my shoulders. I looked up, meeting Ethan's gaze, both of us suspended in a moment of realization.

"What does that mean?" I whispered, my voice barely a breath.

The tension shifted again, this time more palpable, crackling like electricity. In that moment, I knew that whatever was about to unfold could change everything.

Chapter 19: The Aftermath

The next time I see Ethan, he's different. It's like the light behind his eyes has dimmed, replaced by shadows that stretch across his face like dark clouds ready to burst. We sit on the edge of the old wooden dock, the paint peeling off in large, sun-bleached chunks, an ironic metaphor for the way I feel inside. The lake glistens beneath a shy sun, its surface rippling with the whispers of a gentle breeze, yet all I can focus on is the weight of the silence wrapping around us.

I glance sideways at him, hoping to catch a glimpse of the boy who once laughed so easily, who would toss rocks into the water just to watch the splashes bloom like flowers. Instead, I find him staring out at the water, as if it holds the answers to questions he can't articulate. His fingers drum against the weathered wood of the dock, a nervous rhythm that only accentuates the tension.

"I don't know how to fix this," he finally murmurs, his voice barely rising above the rustling leaves. There's a hitch in his tone, a fragility that slices through me like a knife. My heart sinks further into the depths of my stomach as I realize that the sadness isn't just in him; it echoes through me as well.

"Fix what?" I manage to ask, even though I already know. I want to tell him that he doesn't have to fix anything, that sometimes life is just about weathering the storm. But the words feel heavy on my tongue, entangled in my own uncertainty.

He turns to me, and I see it—the regret etched across his features, the way his brow furrows as he struggles to hold onto something. I want to reach out, to comfort him, but I'm frozen, trapped in this moment where everything feels impossibly fragile. "Us," he replies, each syllable weighed down by the gravity of his thoughts. "I keep replaying everything in my head, and it just doesn't make sense. We were good, and now..." His voice trails off, swallowed by the expanse of the lake before us.

The sun dips slightly, casting long shadows that stretch across the dock, mirroring the shadows that loom over our conversation. I swallow hard, searching for the right words, but all that comes is a sigh. "Maybe it doesn't have to make sense," I say, my voice steady, though inside, I'm a jumble of nerves and thoughts. "Maybe we just need to... breathe."

He looks at me then, really looks, as if trying to dissect the layers of my words. "Breathe," he echoes, a hint of bitterness curling the edges of his lips. "How do you breathe when everything feels broken?"

"By reminding ourselves that broken things can still hold beauty," I say, a flicker of hope igniting in my chest. "Like this dock. It's weathered, sure, but it's still here. It still holds us up."

Ethan scoffs lightly, the sound a mix of disbelief and something softer, something that makes me wish I could pull him into the warmth of a better memory. "I'm not a dock, though. I don't want to just hold on. I want to feel whole again."

His words hang in the air, a desperate plea wrapped in vulnerability. I can't help but reach out, my hand brushing against his in a gentle, tentative gesture. "You're more than just a dock, Ethan. You're a whole damn ocean. And oceans have depths that aren't always visible from the surface."

He stares at our hands, our fingers barely touching, and for a moment, it feels like the entire world has narrowed down to this singular point of connection. But then he pulls away, the movement almost instinctive, as if my words have made him uncomfortable. "You don't get it. The ocean can drown you, too."

A lump forms in my throat, and I fight back the surge of emotion that threatens to overwhelm me. "I know," I reply, my voice softer now, tinged with understanding. "But we're in this together, right? We can learn to navigate the waves."

Silence envelops us again, but this time it's different—charged with an unspoken agreement, a flicker of hope mingling with our uncertainty. As we sit side by side, I can almost feel the layers of tension peeling back, revealing the rawness beneath.

"Do you ever think about how easy it is to get lost?" he asks suddenly, his gaze returning to the lake, where the surface is now dappled with reflections of the clouds overhead. "One minute you're floating along, and the next, you're struggling to find your way back to the surface."

I nod, the truth of his words resonating deep within me. "All the time. But that's why we need each other. To help pull one another up."

A ghost of a smile flits across his face, a glimmer of the Ethan I used to know. "You're right. I guess I just don't want to drag you down with me."

"Too late for that," I quip, a teasing smile breaking through my own melancholy. "You've already gotten me lost in your sad, oceanic thoughts."

He chuckles softly, the sound a balm against the weight of our conversation. "You're insufferable."

"Only when I'm with you," I shoot back, warmth blooming between us. "But you love it."

"Maybe," he concedes, a spark igniting in his eyes as he shifts his weight to face me fully. "Or maybe I just don't have a choice."

"Choice?" I arch an eyebrow, intrigued. "Are you saying I'm like quicksand? You just can't escape me?"

His laughter bubbles up, filling the space around us, and I realize that for the first time since we sat down, the weight in the air has lifted just a bit. "Something like that," he replies, amusement dancing in his eyes.

In that moment, I find a renewed sense of hope. The path forward may be uncertain, fraught with challenges we can't foresee, but perhaps together we can learn to navigate the unpredictable currents of our lives. And maybe, just maybe, we'll find a way to stay afloat.

As the afternoon stretches lazily into evening, the sun begins its slow descent, drenching the lake in hues of orange and gold. Each ripple reflects a sliver of light, mirroring the bittersweet nature of our conversation. Ethan remains quiet, still processing the weight of our earlier exchange, and I find myself lost in thought, tracing patterns in the wood of the dock with my fingers, as if seeking answers etched in its grooves.

"Do you remember the last time we were here?" I finally ask, breaking the silence that's become almost suffocating. The memory springs up like a well-worn photograph—a sunny day filled with laughter, ice cream dribbling down our hands as we tried to out-paddle each other in those silly kayaks.

His lips twitch at the corners, just enough to suggest a flicker of the boy I used to know. "How could I forget? You practically capsized us both trying to prove you could paddle faster."

"Hey, you were the one who dared me!" I retort, feigning indignation but unable to suppress my smile. "Besides, you were the one who fell in first."

"I was also the one who pulled you back in," he replies, and I can see it now—the glimmer of fondness that sparks momentarily before fading into a shadow of regret.

"Yeah, well, maybe you were just trying to save your own skin," I tease, nudging him playfully with my elbow. "You wouldn't have wanted to be seen as the loser who lost to a girl."

Ethan shakes his head, but there's a warmth in his gaze, a familiarity that brings a strange comfort amidst the turmoil. "I wouldn't say that," he says softly. "I just didn't want to drown."

"Drowning seems to be a recurring theme," I reply, the weight of his words sinking in. "And yet here we are, still afloat."

The silence settles again, but it's not as heavy now. Instead, it's laced with shared memories and unspoken understanding. But beneath the lightness, I can feel an undercurrent of tension, like a storm brewing just out of sight. I want to ask him what's really going on, what's behind the sadness etched in his features, but every time I open my mouth, the words get tangled in my throat.

"Can I ask you something?" Ethan breaks in, his voice suddenly serious, piercing through the veil of nostalgia.

"Sure, hit me," I say, trying to sound nonchalant, but my heart skips a beat.

"Why do you always deflect?" His question hangs in the air, sharp and cutting, and I feel my breath hitch in surprise. "You make jokes, you laugh, but you never let anyone see what's really going on inside."

I blink at him, caught off guard. "I'm not deflecting. I'm just... trying to keep things light. There's enough heaviness in the world, don't you think?"

"Maybe," he replies, his expression serious, "but pretending doesn't help anyone. Not you, not me."

His honesty hits me like a cold splash of water, and I shift uncomfortably, searching for the right words to defend my façade. "It's just easier that way," I finally admit. "People expect me to be the one who keeps things upbeat. If I start spilling all my worries, who's going to lift them up?"

Ethan studies me for a moment, and I can see the wheels turning in his head. "You're wrong. Lifting each other up doesn't mean you have to hide how you feel."

The intensity of his gaze ignites something in me, a longing to open up, to shatter the walls I've built. "And what if I fall?" I ask, my voice barely a whisper. "What if I let you in and it all crumbles?"

He leans closer, the space between us shrinking. "Then we'll fall together. At least we won't be alone."

My heart races, the vulnerability of his words both terrifying and exhilarating. It's terrifying because what if he really sees me? What if I shatter into pieces? But it's exhilarating because maybe, just maybe, we can rebuild something stronger together.

Before I can respond, his phone buzzes loudly in his pocket, shattering the moment like glass. He winces, pulling it out and glancing at the screen. "It's my dad," he mutters, his shoulders tightening.

"Answer it," I urge, even though a part of me is reluctant to break this fragile connection. "You should take it."

Ethan hesitates, then sighs deeply. "Yeah, okay." He swipes to answer, his voice slipping into a more practiced tone. "Hey, Dad... Yeah, I'm at the lake."

I lean back, giving him space, my heart pounding in the quiet, a drum echoing my rising anxiety. I can't help but eavesdrop, the fragments of his conversation spilling over like water from an overturned cup. "I told you I'm fine... No, it's not about that. It's just... complicated."

His expression shifts, the shadows returning like dark clouds. "I don't want to talk about it right now," he says, a sharp edge creeping into his voice. "I need time."

I glance away, the ache of sympathy mixing with my own concerns. I wish I could dive into his mind, untangle his thoughts, and pull out the pieces that hurt him the most. But instead, I sit in silence, watching the sun dip lower, feeling the warmth of the day slowly dissipate into the chill of the approaching evening.

After a few minutes, he ends the call, tossing his phone onto the dock with a soft thud. The weight of whatever conversation just unfolded hangs heavy between us, and I can see the frustration and sadness mingling in his eyes.

"Sorry about that," he murmurs, running a hand through his hair, the gesture both familiar and heartbreakingly vulnerable. "He just doesn't get it."

"Get what?" I probe gently, desperate to understand.

Ethan shrugs, his vulnerability quickly retreating behind a wall of frustration. "Everything. The way I feel. Why I don't want to just fall back into the routine."

"What routine?" I ask, hoping to peel back those layers he keeps guarded.

"The routine of pretending everything's fine, of living up to everyone else's expectations. I'm tired, you know? Tired of feeling like I'm constantly wearing a mask."

The honesty in his voice is striking, and it draws me in like gravity. "But that's what makes you... you," I reply softly, searching for the right words to comfort him. "What if we just... took off the masks? Just for tonight?"

He looks at me, the question hanging in the air between us. "You think we can?"

"Why not?" I say, emboldened by the connection we've forged. "Let's be real. It's just us and this old dock. What's the worst that could happen?"

Ethan's lips curl into a small smile, but I can see the uncertainty lingering in his gaze. "You might regret it."

"Doubtful," I counter, flashing him a teasing grin. "Besides, I'm pretty sure I've done worse things in life than share a little honesty."

The corners of his mouth lift, the tension beginning to ease, and I realize that perhaps this evening will be the catalyst we need to unravel the threads of our complex lives. Together, we can navigate the depths of our fears and insecurities, and for the first time in a long while, I can see a glimmer of hope emerging through the murky waters.

The air grows thicker as the sun continues its descent, and a blanket of twilight begins to stretch across the sky. The colors deepen into rich purples and blues, as if the universe is trying to paint over our unease with beauty. I sit beside Ethan, contemplating the weight of his earlier confession, wondering if this moment of honesty might be the turning point we both need.

"You know," I say, attempting to lighten the mood, "if we keep this up, we're going to end up being the poster children for emotional dysfunction." I can't help but grin, hoping to coax a laugh from him.

Ethan lets out a breath that's half-laughter, half-sigh. "That's a pretty niche market, but hey, I'm willing to take one for the team."

"Team Dysfunction," I reply, shaking my head with mock seriousness. "We could host workshops. How to Navigate Your Emotional Tsunami: A Practical Guide."

He chuckles, and the sound warms me like the fading sun. "I'd sign up for that," he says, his eyes glinting with a mix of mischief and vulnerability. "But what if the main lesson is that there are no lifeguards in this metaphorical pool? Just a bunch of people flailing around."

"Then we'd hand out floaties," I counter, determined to keep this lightness between us. "You know, for support. Everybody needs a little buoyancy now and then."

His laughter fades, but he looks more relaxed, as if I've unwound a few of the knots tied around his heart. "That actually sounds nice. Floating aimlessly without worrying about drowning."

"Exactly. A free-for-all of emotions and questionable decisions." I pause, then add, "Wait, that sounds like college."

"Right?" Ethan rolls his eyes, but there's a warmth there, a spark of connection that feels tangible. "The good old days of questionable decisions. I wonder what kind of floaties we could've used back then."

"Probably ones shaped like cartoon characters," I say, grinning. "You know, to soften the blow when we inevitably crash into the pool wall."

He shakes his head, but there's a genuine smile on his lips. "You know, I really miss those days sometimes. When our biggest worries were exams and hangovers."

I nod, understanding. "Back when everything felt... simpler. Maybe we should try to find a bit of that simplicity again."

"Or maybe we just need to redefine what 'simple' means," he says, a thoughtful look crossing his face. "Because right now, my life feels like a never-ending jigsaw puzzle missing half the pieces."

The sincerity in his voice strikes a chord within me. "Same here," I admit, the laughter fading into a contemplative silence. "I think we all feel that way sometimes. Like we're trying to fit together fragments that don't quite belong."

As the last rays of sunlight dip below the horizon, casting the world into a twilight haze, I can't shake the feeling that this moment is pivotal. Ethan's presence beside me feels both comforting and electric, charged with an undercurrent that both frightens and excites me.

"What if we tried to find those missing pieces?" I suggest, my voice barely above a whisper. "Together?"

He meets my gaze, and the moment stretches between us like a taut wire, buzzing with unspoken possibilities. "Are you suggesting a road trip? Because I'm all in for getting lost in the middle of nowhere with you."

"Why not? We could use a little adventure," I say, my heart racing at the thought of freedom beyond this lake, beyond our troubles. "Plus, I'm pretty sure we can get away with singing badly in the car."

Ethan's eyes light up, the heaviness of earlier moments slipping away like shadows in the light of dawn. "We'd have to make a killer playlist, though. Something to accompany our car karaoke sessions."

"I'm sure I can whip something up," I say with a wink. "I mean, my musical tastes are impeccable, if I do say so myself."

"Impeccable? Is that what we're calling it now?" He raises an eyebrow, feigning disbelief. "I distinctly remember your atrocious taste in 90s boy bands."

"Okay, I might have gone a bit overboard with my NSYNC phase," I admit, laughing. "But it's all about nostalgia! Those harmonies were magical."

"Magic or a crime against music, you decide."

As we banter back and forth, a new energy envelops us, lifting the weight of our earlier conversation. We exchange stories of old music crushes, each anecdote revealing a layer of ourselves that we'd kept hidden away, much like the emotions we've been tiptoeing around.

But as the sun sinks lower, the fun fades, leaving the night air tinged with an uneasy tension. It's as if the universe is holding its breath, waiting for the inevitable crash that comes after moments of levity. I can sense it—a storm brewing just beneath the surface of our laughter, dark clouds gathering with every word unspoken.

"Do you ever think about what happens when the music stops?" Ethan asks, his tone suddenly serious again. "When we can't ignore the things we're running from?"

I feel the gravity of his question settle between us. "All the time," I admit, my heart racing. "But I think we owe it to ourselves to find out what's there. Maybe facing the music could lead us somewhere new."

"Or it could be terrifying," he counters, the uncertainty flickering in his eyes like the fireflies beginning to dance around us. "What if it reveals something we're not ready to handle?"

"That's a risk we have to take," I reply, my voice steady even as my insides churn. "We can't keep floating forever, can we?"

Ethan takes a deep breath, and I can see the cogs in his mind turning. "No, we can't. But sometimes I wish we could. It feels safer."

"Safer isn't always better," I insist, leaning closer. "Sometimes the scariest paths lead to the most beautiful destinations. What if we find something worth holding onto?"

He searches my face, as if looking for reassurance in the depths of my sincerity. "And what if it tears us apart?"

Before I can respond, a rustling from the trees behind us breaks the moment, jolting us both back to reality. I turn, heart racing, as a figure emerges from the shadows, their silhouette unfamiliar and ominous against the backdrop of fading light.

"What the hell—" I start, but the words die in my throat as I see the flash of a knife glinting in the twilight.

Ethan reacts faster than I can think, stepping in front of me, a protective instinct surging through him. "Hey! Who are you?" His voice cuts through the tension, firm yet edged with fear.

The figure pauses, uncertainty flickering across their features, but the knife remains raised. "You need to come with me," they say, their tone low and gravelly. "It's not safe here."

My pulse pounds in my ears, drowning out everything else as adrenaline courses through me. What was once a moment filled with hope and promise suddenly twists into a nightmarish reality, the air thick with dread and uncertainty.

Chapter 20: The Long Road Back

The evening air wraps around me like a familiar, if slightly frayed, quilt as I park my car on the gravel lot overlooking the lake. I'm greeted by a scene painted in dusky shades of lavender and gold, the water shimmering like a spilled treasure chest under the soft caress of the setting sun. I can almost hear the echoes of our laughter, the gentle splash of our toes in the water, and the whispered confessions that floated between us like dandelion seeds on the breeze. But tonight, the nostalgia is heavier, a palpable weight pressing against my chest.

I step out of the car, the crunch of gravel beneath my sneakers grounding me in the present, yet the memories swirl around my mind, taunting me. How did we end up like this? How did I let a rift grow so wide that it felt impossible to bridge? My gaze drifts to the horizon where the sun slowly sinks, and for a moment, I wonder if I can outrun the ache in my heart.

I tread along the familiar path that winds down to the water's edge, the smell of damp earth and wildflowers pulling me deeper into reflection. I can picture us here, Ethan with his tousled hair catching the light, his laughter ringing out like a bell—pure, untainted. He had that way of making the world feel expansive, as if we were the only two people who mattered in a universe that otherwise felt far too large and indifferent. But now, the lake looks like a mirror reflecting the chaos of my thoughts, and I can't help but feel like a ghost haunting a place where I no longer belong.

Taking a seat on a weathered log, I draw in a deep breath, the crisp air filling my lungs like a long-forgotten song. It feels as if I'm inhaling the memories of us, weaving them back together, thread by delicate thread. A soft breeze tousles my hair, and for a moment, I close my eyes, trying to catch a glimpse of him in the fading light.

But the serenity doesn't last long. My phone buzzes in my pocket, jarring me from my reverie. I pull it out, half-hoping it's him, a flicker of hope igniting before I glance at the screen. It's a work email, mundane and devoid of any emotional resonance. I groan, tossing my phone aside as if it's a hot coal. How did I let work take precedence over everything else? The projects I had buried myself in felt like an escape plan—one that backfired spectacularly when I realized that avoidance wasn't a solution.

I lean back on the log, gazing up at the twilight sky. It's beautiful, but beauty is a cruel reminder of the things I've lost. With every star that begins to twinkle, I'm reminded of how Ethan and I used to spend hours stargazing, our fingers entwined, speaking of dreams and futures that felt tangible. And yet, here I am, standing on the precipice of uncertainty, teetering between wanting to reach out and the fear of being met with silence.

"Staring into the void again?" a voice calls from behind me, and I turn, startled. It's Liz, my best friend, her expression a mix of concern and amusement. She leans against a tree, arms crossed, her auburn hair catching the last glimmers of sunlight. "I thought I might find you here, sulking like a romantic in a bad novel."

I can't help but laugh, even though the sound feels hollow. "I'm not sulking. I'm... contemplating life. Existential dread, you know?"

"Sure, sure," she replies, her eyes sparkling with mischief. "Just don't forget to breathe while you're at it. Want to talk about it, or are you planning to drown in your thoughts?"

"I just... I don't know where to start," I admit, gesturing helplessly toward the lake, the surface now a deep, inky blue reflecting the first stars of the night. "Everything feels like a mess, and I keep waiting for him to come back and fix it."

"Ah, the age-old dilemma of the waiting game," Liz replies, taking a seat beside me. "But what if he's waiting for you to make the first move? Sometimes, you have to take a step forward, even if it feels scary."

The weight of her words hangs in the air, mingling with the evening chill. "I'm scared, Liz. What if I reach out, and he doesn't want to talk? What if everything has changed?"

"Or what if it hasn't?" she counters, her voice firm yet gentle. "You'll never know until you try. Maybe he's just as lost as you are."

A silence envelops us, filled only by the soft lapping of water against the shore. I study the way her expression shifts from playful to serious, and for a moment, I see the glimmer of hope she's trying to ignite within me. It's tempting, the idea that there's a way back, a way to untangle this mess we've found ourselves in.

"What if I do reach out?" I whisper, more to myself than to her. "What do I even say?"

"Tell him the truth," Liz replies, her tone now tender. "Tell him how you feel, how much you miss him. Sometimes vulnerability is the bravest thing we can do."

As the stars start to blanket the sky, I feel a flicker of determination spark inside me. Maybe it's time to be brave, to take a leap of faith, to claw my way back from the edge of uncertainty. For the first time in weeks, I can almost see a path forward.

The silence that stretched between us felt like a taut wire, ready to snap at the slightest provocation. I sat in my car, the engine humming softly, the warmth of the leather seats cocooning me like an embrace I hadn't realized I missed. My fingers drummed nervously on the steering wheel as I stared at my phone, willing it to light up with a message from Ethan, some sign that he was thinking of me too. But the screen remained dark, an inky void reflecting my own uncertainty.

Liz's words echoed in my mind—"Tell him the truth." I could almost hear the casual lilt in her voice, the way she always managed to strip away the layers of my anxiety with a single, piercing statement. She had a knack for pushing me just enough to coax out the parts of myself I often kept hidden, even from my own reflection. Yet here I was, wrestling with the fear that had wrapped around me like a heavy fog.

"Just do it," I murmured to myself, glancing at the time. The sun was almost gone, the horizon bleeding colors I'd once thought were exclusive to paintings. I took a deep breath, feeling the cool air slide into my lungs. The world was quieter now, the kind of silence that felt thick and alive, full of unspoken possibilities. I could either continue to sit here, waiting for a sign, or I could become my own catalyst for change.

With a resolute nod, I picked up my phone and opened my messages. My heart raced, pounding against my ribcage like it was trying to escape. I began to type, the letters forming words that felt both foreign and deeply familiar at the same time.

"Hey, Ethan. I've been thinking about you." Simple, direct. But the moment I hit send, my stomach dropped, a flurry of anxiety spiraling through me. What if he didn't respond? What if he had moved on, a distant thought I was desperately clinging to like a life raft? I bit my lip, staring at the three little dots indicating he was typing. Time stretched out in front of me like a vast ocean, each second a wave of uncertainty crashing over my resolve.

When his response finally came, it was like a jolt of electricity—"I've been thinking about you too." The words danced across the screen, igniting a flicker of hope that had long been extinguished. I could practically hear the echo of his voice, the way he would say my name with that hint of wonder, as if he couldn't quite believe I was real.

"Do you want to talk?" I typed back, my heart racing as I hit send. The reply came swiftly, as if he had been waiting for the signal to respond. "Yes, let's meet at the old café. 7 PM?"

As the clock inched closer to seven, anticipation knotted in my stomach, twisting tighter with each passing minute. I drove the familiar route to the café, a cozy little place that smelled of coffee and cinnamon, the kind of warmth that seeped into your bones. It was where we'd spent countless evenings, lost in conversations that felt like they could last forever. But now, as I parked and stepped inside, everything felt different. The air was charged, crackling with an energy I hadn't felt in weeks.

I spotted Ethan almost immediately. He sat in our usual corner, the soft light casting shadows that danced across his features, making him look both familiar and achingly distant. The sight of him sent a wave of nostalgia crashing over me, but it was quickly tempered by the reality of our situation. I approached cautiously, every step feeling monumental, as if I were traversing a tightrope suspended above a canyon of unresolved emotions.

"Hey," I said, forcing a casual smile even as my heart threatened to leap out of my chest.

He looked up, his expression shifting from surprise to something softer, almost relieved. "Hey. I wasn't sure if you'd actually come."

"I almost didn't," I admitted, sliding into the seat opposite him. "But I realized I'd rather face the awkwardness than continue pretending everything is fine."

A brief silence followed, thick with unspoken words. His gaze flicked to the table, then back to me, and I could see the wheels turning in his mind, calculating the risk of what he was about to say. "I've missed you," he finally confessed, his voice low and steady, a balm against the uncertainty I'd felt for weeks.

"Really?" I asked, surprised at the sudden rush of warmth blooming in my chest. "Because it sure felt like we were both dodging each other like we were in some kind of bizarre game of tag."

Ethan chuckled, a sound I'd been craving. "You have no idea how hard it was to keep my distance. I thought maybe giving you space would help, but all it did was make everything worse."

We fell into an easy rhythm, the initial tension melting away like snow under the spring sun. With every shared laugh, every subtle nod, it felt like we were rebuilding the bridge that had collapsed between us, stone by stone. But as we reminisced, I noticed the shadows in his eyes—fleeting moments where vulnerability peeked through the cracks, revealing the depths of his own struggles.

"Can I ask you something?" I ventured, leaning in a little closer, the warmth of his presence wrapping around me. "What really happened? Why did we end up so far apart?"

Ethan sighed, his expression turning serious. "I was scared, honestly. I let my insecurities get in the way. I didn't think I was good enough for you, and instead of talking about it, I just pulled away."

My heart ached at his words, the honesty slicing through the fog of doubt that had settled over me. "I thought you didn't want me anymore," I admitted, feeling the weight of our misunderstandings settle in the space between us.

"I never stopped wanting you," he said, his gaze intense. "I just didn't know how to make it work without feeling like I was dragging you down."

We shared a moment of silence, the gravity of our admission hanging in the air. I reached across the table, my hand brushing against his, and the contact sent a thrill through me, igniting a spark of the connection we'd once had.

"We're both pretty messed up," I said with a wry smile, trying to lighten the mood. "But maybe that just makes us more compatible."

Ethan chuckled, a genuine laugh that lit up his eyes. "You always know how to turn a heavy moment into something bearable."

"Hey, it's a skill," I said, grinning. But underneath the banter, a realization began to settle within me. This was the first step back toward something that felt real. We were still tethered by the past, but perhaps we could redefine what lay ahead.

"Let's start over," I suggested, my voice steady. "No more hiding. Just... us. Whatever that looks like."

He nodded, a slow smile breaking across his face. "I'd like that. I really would."

In that moment, as the café buzzed around us, I felt the flicker of hope grow into a flame. It was a small beginning, but in this dance of uncertainties and fears, we were both willing to step forward into the light.

The air between us crackled with the remnants of old wounds and new beginnings as we sat in the café, our fingers lingering just long enough to ignite sparks of possibility. Ethan leaned back, a thoughtful look crossing his face, as if he were weighing the gravity of this moment against the backdrop of our tangled history.

"Starting over," he repeated, a smile creeping onto his lips. "I can do that. Just one thing, though."

"What's that?" I asked, raising an eyebrow, my curiosity piqued.

He leaned in, lowering his voice as if to keep our conversation a secret, even in the busy café. "No more running. If we're doing this, we have to promise to talk things out. No more dodging the hard stuff."

"Agreed," I said, feeling a rush of relief wash over me. This wasn't just a hollow promise. There was a weight to his words, a sense of seriousness that made my heart swell with hope. "It's about time we stopped pretending everything was okay."

As we began to discuss what a fresh start might look like—setting boundaries, exploring what we wanted from each other—I felt a weight lift off my shoulders. I hadn't realized how heavy my heart had been, burdened by uncertainty, until I was free to express my feelings openly.

"And, hey," Ethan added with a playful grin, "I make a mean cup of coffee. If we're being real, you might want to consider my barista skills as part of the deal."

"Mean, huh?" I laughed, the sound bubbling up easily now, each note a reminder of how effortlessly we'd connected before. "I've tasted your cooking, remember? Mean is one way to describe it, but 'disastrous' might be more accurate."

"Touché," he retorted, a mock pout forming on his lips. "But we can't all be culinary geniuses. I bring charm to the table. Well, that and takeout menus."

"Fair enough. Charm can get you pretty far," I conceded, feeling the warmth of affection wash over me. But beneath the humor, I sensed the fragile nature of our rekindled connection. It was like walking on a tightrope—one misstep could send us tumbling back into the chasm we'd just begun to cross.

Our conversation flowed easily, oscillating between light-hearted banter and deeper reflections. I discovered that Ethan had taken up photography during our time apart, capturing fleeting moments that felt eternally beautiful. He spoke passionately about his recent project—a series of portraits capturing the faces of our town. "Every picture tells a story," he explained, his eyes lighting up. "I want people to see the beauty in the ordinary."

"I love that," I said, genuinely impressed. "But how does that translate to mean coffee?"

He feigned a serious expression, resting his chin on his hand. "You see, the secret ingredient in my coffee is always—"

Suddenly, his phone buzzed on the table, interrupting our playful banter. He glanced at it, the smile fading from his face as he read the message. "Sorry, I need to take this," he said, the shift in his tone sending a ripple of unease through me.

"Of course," I replied, trying to keep my voice steady. But as he stepped outside to take the call, I felt the air grow thick with uncertainty, like the calm before a storm.

I took a sip of my coffee, the warmth a comforting reminder of our conversation. But as the minutes ticked by and Ethan remained outside, a gnawing anxiety crept into my chest. I shifted in my seat, feeling out of place in a world that had started to feel right.

Just when I began to contemplate whether I should go check on him, he returned, his expression unreadable. "Sorry about that," he said, his voice slightly strained. "It was my dad. He wants me to come over for dinner this weekend."

"That sounds... important?" I ventured, but a sliver of doubt cut through the warmth we'd just rekindled.

"Yeah, it is," he replied, running a hand through his hair. "He's been asking to see me more often, and I think he's worried about me. Maybe he senses I've been a bit... off."

"Is that a good thing?" I asked cautiously, sensing the tension lurking behind his casual tone. "I mean, the fact that he wants to connect?"

"I guess," he said, his brow furrowing. "But it also means I'll have to face some uncomfortable truths about my life lately. You know how parents can be."

"Yeah, it's like they have a sixth sense for when you're struggling," I said, attempting to lighten the mood. "Or when you're dodging their questions about marriage and grandchildren."

He chuckled, the sound genuine but tinged with an edge of apprehension. "Right? But it's more complicated than that. I don't want him to worry, but I also need to be honest with him about where I'm at, especially with everything that happened between us."

My heart tightened at the reminder of our complicated history. "You don't have to tell him everything, you know. Just enough to keep the peace," I offered, wanting to ease the pressure that had settled between us.

"Maybe you're right," he said, his eyes drifting to the window where the evening sky had deepened to a rich indigo. "But I can't shake this feeling that I need to be upfront with him. It's just... terrifying."

"Facing our fears usually is," I replied, feeling a kinship in our shared vulnerability. "But if you're going to do this, I'll be here for you. We can take it one step at a time."

"Thanks, that means a lot," he said, a grateful smile playing on his lips. "But I also need to be honest with you. I don't want to drag you into my family drama."

"Ethan," I said, shaking my head, "we're in this together, remember? I'm not going anywhere."

Just then, his phone buzzed again, a stark interruption that sliced through the moment we were trying to reclaim. He glanced at it, and I noticed the change in his demeanor—his brow furrowed, lips pressed into a thin line.

"Sorry, I should—" he started, but I reached out, gripping his hand gently.

"Ethan, wait. What's wrong?"

His gaze flicked to mine, and I could see the storm brewing behind his eyes. "It's just a message from work. I thought I could handle things, but they want me to go to a meeting tomorrow. An important one."

"Okay, but we can figure that out," I said, trying to keep my voice steady, even as my pulse quickened. "Is this something that could wait until after dinner?"

He hesitated, his thumb brushing against my hand, a fleeting connection that sent shivers up my spine. "I wish it were that simple."

In that moment, the café felt too small, the walls closing in as the weight of uncertainty threatened to engulf us again. I didn't want to be the reason he felt torn between two worlds, but something in the air had shifted, tension stretching like a taut bowstring, ready to snap.

"I just want to make sure we're on the same page," I said softly, my heart racing. "I want us to work, but it feels like every time we take a step forward, something pulls us back."

He opened his mouth to respond, but before he could find the words, the café door swung open, and a figure stepped inside—a woman with striking red hair and a confident stride. My heart sank as I recognized her, the weight of past encounters crashing over me.

"Ethan!" she called out, her voice like a bell ringing in the stillness, a sound I never expected to hear again.

He turned, shock flooding his features, and as my heart sank, I felt a sudden coldness seep into the warmth we had just begun to reclaim. The world shifted on its axis, leaving me grappling with the realization that the past was not done with us yet.

Chapter 21: A Fragile Reunion

I stand on his doorstep, my heart racing like a runaway train, an unwelcome gust of cold wind tousling my hair. It's been far too long since I felt the familiar weight of this moment—an uninvited guest at a party where I wasn't sure I'd even be welcome. The door swings open, revealing him in a worn T-shirt that clings to his lean frame, the faint scent of something comforting wafting from inside. He looks like he's been through the wringer, dark circles under his eyes, hair tousled as if he just rolled out of bed. I can almost hear the cogs in his mind turning, processing my unexpected arrival.

"Hey," I manage, my voice wavering, a fragile whisper against the backdrop of a world that feels far too loud.

"Hey." His reply is just as soft, a quiet invitation that seems to pull me over the threshold. I step inside, and the air wraps around me, thick with the scent of stale coffee and old books. It feels like home, yet haunted by echoes of laughter and arguments left unresolved.

The living room, littered with reminders of his life—crumpled takeout menus, a half-empty mug that stubbornly clings to the remnants of its last brew—reflects a chaotic beauty that makes my chest ache. We settle onto the couch, a familiar fortress of worn cushions that once cradled our laughter and whispered secrets. The silence blankets us, heavy and expectant, not quite comfortable but familiar enough to be disarming.

I glance at him, searching for the boy I once knew—the one who could conjure joy from thin air and paint our conversations with vivid strokes of imagination. But what stares back at me is a man shadowed by weariness, eyes reflecting the weight of too many days spent in solitude.

"I've missed you," he finally says, the words slipping from his lips like a fragile promise. The vulnerability in his tone slices through the quiet, stirring something deep within me, something that feels like both hope and heartbreak.

"I've missed you too," I confess, feeling the warmth of those words wrap around us, the fragile thread of connection pulling taut. "Things have been..." I hesitate, searching for the right words to bridge the chasm between us. "A little overwhelming."

The corners of his mouth twitch, a ghost of the smile that used to come so easily. "Overwhelming seems to be the theme of the year."

I chuckle softly, the sound almost foreign in the charged atmosphere. "You could say that again." The laughter feels good, a tentative step into the warmth of our past, where laughter danced around us like fireflies on a summer night. But even as the words slip out, I can feel the weight of the unspoken pressing against my chest, the truths we've both skirted around looming like a storm cloud.

"What's been going on?" he asks, leaning in slightly, curiosity mingling with concern.

I take a deep breath, the air thick with the dust of old memories and the scent of his aftershave that lingers like a ghost. "It's hard to explain." I fidget with the hem of my sweater, the wool soft against my fingertips. "After...everything, I just felt lost. Like I was floating through life without a direction."

His gaze sharpens, and I can see the flicker of recognition. "Yeah, I get that. It's like we were both tossed into this wild sea, and I didn't know how to swim." The honesty in his admission hits me squarely in the chest, a mirror reflecting my own struggles.

"I tried to find my footing," I continue, "but every time I thought I was getting somewhere, life threw me another curveball." The words tumble out, raw and unfiltered, each syllable a step closer to uncovering the layers of my vulnerability. "I didn't think I'd feel this disconnected from everything—like I was watching the world through a foggy window."

He nods slowly, the lines on his forehead deepening as he contemplates my words. "I think I've been living in that fog too. It's exhausting."

An unexpected silence fills the space, and for a moment, I let my mind wander through the tangled web of memories we've spun together—late-night drives, inside jokes that only we understood, the warmth of shared dreams. But those moments are tinged with bittersweet nostalgia, a reminder of the distance that's crept between us.

"What do we do?" I ask, my voice barely above a whisper. The question hangs in the air like an unresolved chord, full of longing and uncertainty.

"I don't know," he admits, his gaze drifting to the window, where the sky has begun to gray, clouds gathering like anxious thoughts. "But I think we need to try. I want to try."

His words settle over us, a fragile promise wrapped in vulnerability, stirring a flicker of hope within me.

"Trying sounds good," I reply, feeling the tightness in my chest loosen just a little. "Maybe we can take it one day at a time."

His smile returns, a small spark of light amidst the shadows. "One day at a time. I can work with that."

As we sit together, the silence feels less daunting, more like a shared understanding, two souls navigating the rocky terrain of their past in search of something solid to grasp. I can't help but wonder if maybe—just maybe—this fragile reunion is the first step toward stitching together the pieces we thought we had lost forever.

As we linger on the couch, the weight of shared memories fills the air, mingling with the faint smell of coffee and something distinctly him—like a well-worn sweater that has been cradled against a warm chest for too long. I can see the flicker of emotion behind his eyes, a storm brewing, and I wonder if we're both trying to navigate the choppy waters of what comes next. There's a certain intimacy to this moment, as if we're unwinding the tangled thread of our connection, one delicate strand at a time.

"So," he begins, shifting in his seat, "what's the wildest thing you've done since we last... talked?"

I raise an eyebrow, surprised by his sudden playfulness. "Are you expecting me to tell you I've taken up skydiving or become a world-renowned cheese sculptor?"

"Cheese sculptor would definitely be more interesting than the last thing I did, which was watch a three-hour documentary on the mating habits of pigeons," he deadpans, his eyes dancing with mischief.

"Pigeon love? Sounds riveting," I reply, laughter bubbling up despite the heaviness of our earlier confessions. "But I'll take the cheese sculpting any day. I've just been trying to figure out how to adult without losing my mind. Turns out, adulthood is a lot like trying to fold a fitted sheet—nobody really knows how it works."

"Ah, the eternal struggle," he agrees, a grin breaking through the remnants of his fatigue. "You need an advanced degree in origami just to tackle laundry."

"Or maybe a support group," I add, "for people who can't seem to keep their lives organized."

"Hello, my name is [his name], and I'm a master procrastinator," he quips, falling into the rhythm of our repartee. "I have a collection of half-finished projects that could rival a local museum. Like my dream of building a treehouse. Spoiler alert: it's still just a dream."

I chuckle, picturing him sprawled on the floor, surrounded by blueprints and bits of wood. "I can see it now. You, the architect of a disaster, with squirrels as your only inhabitants."

"Hey, they would appreciate the effort," he insists, his smile infectious. "And I would have the best friends in the neighborhood."

The laughter eases some of the tension, like a gentle balm on a wound that has yet to fully heal. I shift on the couch, feeling the warmth of his presence seeping into me, a reminder of what once was and what might still be. But as the laughter fades, an uninvited thought creeps in, dark and heavy, threatening to shatter the moment.

"What about you?" he asks, genuine curiosity lining his voice. "Have you found anything more productive to do than dissecting the complexities of adulthood?"

I bite my lip, the playful facade crumbling. "I've thrown myself into my work, mostly. It's... comfortable."

"Comfortable?" He raises an eyebrow, his gaze intense. "Or are you just avoiding something?"

I feel the heat rise in my cheeks, the truth curling around my tongue like a stubborn vine. "Maybe a little of both."

"Care to elaborate?" His voice softens, coaxing me out of the shadows.

I glance at the clock on the wall, its steady ticking almost mocking. "It's just that everything feels so... uncertain. I thought that by immersing myself in my projects, I'd find some clarity. Instead, I've just become a professional busybody."

"Sounds like a classic case of running in circles," he remarks. "What do you think you're trying to escape from?"

The question hangs in the air, weighty and expectant. I look into his eyes, searching for the courage to share my truth. "I guess... I've been avoiding the fact that I've felt really alone. Even when I'm surrounded by people."

His expression shifts, concern washing over his features. "I know that feeling. It's like being stuck in a crowded room but still feeling invisible."

"Exactly," I say, feeling a surge of gratitude that he understands. "I thought finding work would fill the void, but it only seems to highlight how disconnected I feel."

He nods, the understanding in his gaze anchoring me. "Maybe we can help each other find our way out of that fog. I'm tired of being lost."

I smile softly, the warmth of his words settling around me like a snug blanket. "Me too. It's exhausting pretending everything is okay."

A moment of comfortable silence settles between us, the unspoken bond weaving tighter. But then, as if the universe has a penchant for irony, the front door swings open.

"Hey! Sorry I'm late!" A voice booms, and I turn to see Jake, his roommate, bouncing in with the kind of exuberance that could wake a sleeping bear. "I brought pizza! You two won't believe the deal I scored."

The momentary warmth is interrupted by the sudden intrusion, and I can't help but exchange a glance with him. It's a look that speaks volumes—a combination of amusement and exasperation.

"Jake, we were having a moment here," he says, his voice dripping with mock seriousness.

Jake blinks, clearly oblivious. "A moment? Like a romantic one? Should I come back later?"

"Is there such a thing as a romantic pizza party?" I quip, shaking my head. "If so, I'm in."

"Great! I'm all for a three-way date with pepperoni," Jake replies, unfazed as he sets the pizza box down on the coffee table, steam curling into the air. "Who needs a table for two when you can have a table for three?"

I can't help but laugh, the absurdity of the situation peeling back the layers of tension. Jake's presence, while a little intrusive, acts as a welcome distraction, an unexpected twist that lightens the mood.

But even amidst the laughter and the chatter about toppings and cheese pull, I can feel the connection between us simmering just beneath the surface, a fragile thread that remains unbroken, waiting for its moment to shine. And I realize that in this strange reunion, perhaps the moments we're crafting together—even if interrupted—are still the ones worth savoring.

The laughter from Jake fills the room like a warm wave, washing over the remnants of our heavy confessions. He leans against the doorframe, a pizza slice dangling from his fingers as he grins, blissfully unaware of the delicate atmosphere he's stumbled into. "So, are we going to sit around talking about feelings all night, or are we diving into this cheese?"

"Why not both?" I counter, shooting him a playful glare. "A cheese-filled therapy session sounds like my kind of evening."

"Perfect! I'm always here for emotional breakthroughs and carbs." Jake plops down on the armrest, positioning himself like a self-proclaimed life coach, oblivious to the gravity of the previous conversation.

I catch a glimpse of him from the corner of my eye, his expression shifting as he tries to navigate this unexpected party. The momentary tension dissipates, giving way to a more relaxed atmosphere, the kind that feels reminiscent of all those late-night hangouts where laughter and food intertwined with the glow of friendship.

"So, pizza—what's your topping of choice?" Jake continues, tossing me a slice as though it were a golden ticket to happiness.

"Pineapple," I declare, half-serious, as I bite into the cheesy goodness. Jake makes a face that's so exaggerated I nearly snort my drink.

"No one should be allowed to enjoy that abomination," he declares, feigning horror. "Pineapple belongs on a beach, not a pizza."

"Ah, yes, the great pizza debate of our time. How profound," I tease, taking another bite while enjoying the ridiculousness of the moment.

"Debate all you want, but that's a slippery slope to topping an ice cream sundae with pickles. You have to draw the line somewhere."

As we banter back and forth, I can't help but glance at him occasionally, finding solace in the comfort of the familiar. The laughter feels like a reprieve, allowing me to forget, if only for a moment, the emotional weight still lingering between us.

Amid the lightheartedness, I notice him sneaking glances my way, his expression oscillating between amusement and something deeper, something unsaid. Each fleeting look ignites a tiny spark of anxiety within me, the unaddressed feelings hanging in the air like an uninvited guest at a dinner party.

"So, what's next for you two? You're not about to start a pizza restaurant, are you?" Jake asks, his gaze shifting back and forth between us with curiosity.

"Believe it or not, I'm aiming for world domination through the power of cheese," he replies with a wink.

"Hey, cheese is a powerful ally," I laugh, but beneath the humor, my thoughts flicker back to the conversation that had simmered just moments ago.

Jake, sensing the shift, lifts a slice to his mouth, blocking his own face in a comical manner, as if he could distract us from the gravity of the moment. "Well, if we're doing this therapy thing, I'm all for it. Let's dig into our feelings over some greasy goodness. What's the biggest elephant in the room?"

The question hangs there, bold and brazen. It's as if he's thrown a grenade into our lighthearted bubble, and the air instantly feels charged.

"I think I've tackled my elephant, thanks," I reply lightly, shooting a glance at him, but he knows me too well to let it slide.

"Sure, because avoiding it worked so well the last time," he teases, but there's a hint of concern in his tone, an unspoken understanding that we all grapple with our own baggage.

"I'm not avoiding," I insist, the defensiveness creeping into my voice before I can rein it in. "Just... pacing myself."

"Pacing? More like tiptoeing on a tightrope," he quips, eyes narrowing playfully.

"Okay, fine, maybe a little bit of avoidance is happening," I concede, the words tumbling out before I can fully grasp their implications.

"I think we all have things we're dodging, but ignoring them doesn't really help." Jake says this with the kind of sincerity that makes me want to recoil, yet I know he's right.

"Is this a therapy pizza party or a self-help seminar?" I counter, unable to suppress a grin as I pull the cheese away from my slice.

"Why not both? There's always room for a little introspection with your cheese."

Before I can respond, I notice him—a flicker of something dark crossing his face. It's brief, almost imperceptible, but it feels significant.

"Jake?" I ask, catching the way his smile falters, revealing the thin veneer of his carefree attitude.

"Nothing, it's nothing," he insists, but his tone lacks conviction. "Just, you know, life and its curveballs. You two have been through a lot."

The unspoken words linger between us, thickening the atmosphere with something more than just cheese-induced camaraderie. I feel a strange tension rising in my chest, and suddenly the pizza seems to lose its flavor.

"Speaking of curveballs," I say cautiously, my heart thumping in my chest as I glance at him. "What about you? Have you been okay?"

Jake's expression shifts, his humor faltering for the briefest of moments. "I'm fine. Just dealing with my own stuff," he mutters, but it's not convincing.

"That doesn't sound like 'fine,'" I press gently, my voice steadying despite the tremors of unease brewing within me.

"It's just... you know how it is. Trying to make sense of everything when the world feels like it's spinning out of control," he replies, his eyes darting away from mine.

"What do you mean?" I ask, and even I can hear the anxious edge creeping into my voice.

"Just work stuff. It's all manageable," he brushes off, but I can sense the anxiety churning beneath his surface.

"Jake," I start, but the tension crackles, and before I can press further, a loud bang echoes from the front of the house, jolting us all to attention.

"What was that?" I gasp, my heart racing as the mood shifts from lighthearted banter to an unsettling uncertainty.

"I don't know," he replies, his brow furrowing. "It sounded like it came from the back."

We all exchange uncertain glances, the laughter of moments ago hanging in the air like an unfinished melody. The lighthearted pizza party evaporates, replaced by the charged silence of anticipation, the kind that makes your skin prickle and your heart thud loudly in your chest.

"What if it's...?" I begin, but the thought trails off, and the tension coiling in the air seems to thicken around us.

"Let's check it out," he suggests, but even as he says it, I can see the concern shadowing his features.

"Together?" I ask, an involuntary shiver of apprehension running down my spine.

"Of course," he assures, though his voice is steady and firm, I can feel the unspoken question hanging in the air: what could possibly be waiting for us just beyond that door?

As we stand up, pizza forgotten, the weight of the moment sinks in. I take a deep breath, and suddenly the atmosphere feels charged with unknowing, teetering on the brink of something unsettling, something that could shatter this fragile reunion forever.

Chapter 22: Whispers of the Past

Sunlight filtered through the tall, arched windows of Ethan's family estate, casting long shadows that danced across the polished hardwood floors. The air was thick with the scent of freshly polished wood and something else, something faintly floral and nostalgic. Each step I took echoed in the silence, amplifying the tension that wrapped around us like a thin veil. Ethan walked a pace ahead, his shoulders squared, the weight of a thousand expectations pressing down on him, yet I couldn't help but admire how the light caught the angles of his face, highlighting both his vulnerability and resolve.

The grandeur of the estate was undeniable. Paintings adorned the walls, each frame filled with expressions frozen in time, their subjects staring down at us with a mix of disdain and curiosity. I caught a glimpse of one portrait—an austere-looking man in a dark suit, a severe frown carved into his face. I glanced at Ethan, who seemed unbothered by the judgments of long-dead ancestors, but I wondered how many of their silent gazes had shaped his life.

"This place is… something," I said, trying to break the ice. My voice felt small against the vastness around us, but I pressed on. "It's like stepping into a museum."

Ethan chuckled softly, the sound somehow both warm and hollow. "Yeah, a museum of my family's failures and regrets. A real treasure trove of disappointment."

I caught a glimpse of a flicker of something—was it amusement or bitterness?—but it disappeared as quickly as it had come. I wanted to reach out, to touch his arm, to reassure him that whatever weight he felt pressing down on him, he didn't have to carry it alone. But I could feel a barrier between us, one that had grown thicker every time we tried to peel back the layers of our past.

As we wandered deeper into the house, we passed a room filled with ornate furniture, each piece a conversation starter of its own.

A massive chandelier hung overhead, its crystals glinting like a thousand tiny stars. It was beautiful, yes, but also a reminder of the grandeur that defined his family—a legacy he felt obligated to uphold. The opulence seemed to smother him, each ornate detail a reminder of how far he had to go to measure up.

"Your parents are... interesting," I said carefully, my words tumbling out before I had a chance to think them through. "Do they come here often?"

"Only when they want to remind me how I'm not doing enough," he replied, his tone sharp, laced with frustration. "It's easier for them to come here than to acknowledge that I'm not the perfect son they wanted."

I could hear the unspoken words in his voice, the deep-seated fear of disappointing them. "You know, Ethan, being perfect is overrated. Besides, who's to say what that even means?" I attempted to sound lighthearted, but my heart felt heavy for him.

He turned to me, a flicker of surprise crossing his face. "And what about you? You're not a perfect person either. I've seen your mistakes." His brow furrowed, and for a moment, I thought he might actually be angry.

"Touché," I said, raising an eyebrow. "But I'd like to think my flaws make me more relatable. Perfection is just a good filter and a lot of luck."

We paused, the tension slowly dissolving into something more tangible. A thin line of understanding connected us, one that shimmered in the air like sunlight on water. "You know, it's okay to not have everything figured out," I said softly, my voice carrying the weight of sincerity. "No one does."

His lips twisted into a half-smile, and I couldn't help but feel that I'd struck a chord. We resumed walking, our pace synchronizing as we moved through the ornate rooms. As we entered a library, the shelves lined with books created an oasis of calm. The smell of aged paper mixed with the faintest hint of leather, filling the space with a sense of history and knowledge.

"Wow, this is impressive," I said, tracing my fingers along the spines of the books, each title whispering secrets of lives lived and lessons learned. "Do you ever read any of these?"

"Not really," Ethan admitted, his voice barely above a whisper. "They're more for show. Like the house."

His admission hung in the air, heavy with the truth of it. I could see him standing at the crossroads of expectation and identity, and the juxtaposition was painful. "It's sad, isn't it? That something so beautiful could feel so empty?"

"More than you know," he replied, running a hand through his hair, frustration brewing just beneath the surface. "I spend so much time trying to fit into a mold that I've forgotten what I actually want."

"And what is that?" I asked, my curiosity piqued, eager to peel back another layer.

He paused, the weight of the question hanging between us like a fragile glass sculpture—beautiful yet precarious. "I don't know yet. I think I'm still trying to find out."

I wanted to tell him it was okay to take his time, to explore his own desires rather than those dictated by others. The air felt charged, like a storm was brewing, and I held my breath, waiting for the lightning to strike. Would he choose to break free, or would he remain tethered to a past he didn't choose?

As if reading my mind, Ethan stepped closer, a flicker of resolve igniting in his eyes. "Maybe today could be a start," he said, his voice steady now, tinged with a newfound determination. "Maybe we can stop letting the past dictate our choices."

The words hung in the air, thick with possibility, and for the first time in a long while, I felt the fragile thread of hope weaving its way through the shadows that had long loomed over us. It was a small step, but in that moment, it felt monumental.

The warmth in the library seemed to seep into the crevices of my heart, and I took a deep breath, reveling in the sudden ease that settled between us. As we stood surrounded by the quiet wisdom of the countless books, I couldn't help but wonder what stories each spine held. They were treasures, each one a portal to a world beyond the suffocating expectations of the estate.

"Do you have a favorite?" I asked, gesturing toward the shelves, hoping to peel away some of the layers he kept so tightly wrapped.

Ethan shrugged, an endearing mix of shyness and defiance flickering in his eyes. "Not really. I've always been more of a comic book guy. Less pressure."

"Ah, the glorious world of superheroes," I grinned, imagining him perched on a couch, clad in a worn T-shirt, flipping through the colorful pages, immersed in battles between good and evil. "You've got to have a favorite superhero then."

"I suppose I've always leaned toward the underdogs," he said, a hint of mischief dancing in his gaze. "The ones who have to work twice as hard just to be noticed."

I felt a pang of recognition. "So you're telling me you relate to Spider-Man? The guy who balances being a student and a superhero? You're practically living that life right now, Ethan."

His laughter echoed off the high ceilings, a sound that danced like sunlight on water, warm and refreshing. "Yeah, but Peter Parker didn't have a legacy to uphold," he replied, his grin fading slightly. "He was just trying to do what was right, not live up to family expectations."

"Maybe it's time to swing into your own version of being a hero then," I suggested, my voice light but sincere. "You don't have to save the world all at once, just take one leap at a time."

Ethan looked thoughtful, his gaze drifting to the window where the sun began to dip below the horizon, casting a golden hue that spilled into the room. "Leap, huh?" he murmured, his tone contemplative. "Maybe I should take that more seriously."

"Not to mention, you have your very own sidekick right here," I said, nudging him playfully. "I promise I won't let you fall."

He turned to me, eyes brightening, and for a brief moment, the shadows receded, giving way to a flicker of hope. "You really think I could do that?"

"Of course! Just think of it as stepping off a ledge into the unknown. Admittedly, I don't know where that leap might take us, but it beats standing here, caught in a web of expectations."

He chuckled, and it felt like a victory. "Okay, okay. Maybe I'll try it. After all, my parents can't exactly control how I feel about superheroes. That's just wrong."

The air buzzed with the kind of energy that makes you want to dive into the moment and hold onto it forever. But just as the light began to shine a little brighter, shadows crept back in. The heavy thump of footsteps echoed from the hallway, and suddenly, the warm air felt a touch too oppressive. My heart raced. Ethan's expression shifted, a fleeting glimpse of panic flashing in his eyes.

"Stay close," he murmured, his voice low and tense, like a coiled spring ready to snap.

Before I could respond, a tall figure entered the library, all sharp angles and cool composure. His father. The man exuded an air of authority that was both intimidating and suffocating, and I felt the hairs on the back of my neck stand up.

"Ethan," his father said, his voice smooth as silk but edged with an undercurrent of disappointment. "I thought I might find you here, wasting time instead of preparing for your meeting tomorrow."

"Not wasting time, Dad," Ethan replied, his voice steady but strained. "We were just discussing—"

"Discussing what? Your comic books? I expected you to be more productive."

The dismissal hung in the air, heavy and bitter, the kind that curdles the milk of ambition. I could feel my chest tightening, a mix of protectiveness and indignation boiling within me.

"Actually," I interjected, surprising even myself, "we were talking about the importance of following one's passion, rather than being stuck in someone else's narrative."

The room fell silent, the weight of my words reverberating off the walls. I could see the flicker of surprise in Ethan's father's eyes, quickly replaced by irritation.

"Who are you to lecture my son about passions?" he snapped, his voice cool and dismissive.

"Someone who believes that people shouldn't be judged by their family's expectations but by their choices and aspirations."

Ethan's gaze darted to me, surprise mingling with gratitude, and in that brief moment, I felt a surge of strength. I could sense the tightrope we were walking—one misstep and the ground could crumble beneath us.

"Passions are exactly what he needs right now," I continued, emboldened by the spark in Ethan's eyes. "He should be able to explore them without the burden of your disappointment looming over him."

"Careful, young lady. You don't know what kind of pressures he faces," his father replied, icy calm. "You might think you understand, but you're not the one carrying our family name."

I couldn't help but roll my eyes, crossing my arms defiantly. "And yet here we are, in a room filled with books, and the real story seems to be how you value legacy over individuality. You might be surprised how much he could achieve if he wasn't drowning in the weight of your expectations."

Ethan's father opened his mouth, no doubt ready to launch into a tirade, but Ethan stepped forward, a newfound resolve sparking in his eyes. "Dad, I'm tired of living in your shadow. I need to find my own way, and that's going to take time."

The tension snapped like a tight string. His father's expression darkened, but I could see the tension in Ethan's shoulders ease, just a little. "If you cannot meet our standards, then I fear you're going to disappoint not just me but everyone else in this family."

The air thickened again, the looming specter of disapproval overshadowing our moment of defiance. But as Ethan's gaze met mine, I felt a silent promise pass between us—a mutual understanding that this was just the beginning of a much bigger fight. Whatever storms were brewing outside the walls of the estate, we would face them together.

The silence that followed Ethan's declaration was suffocating, as if the walls themselves were waiting for his father to unleash a storm. I held my breath, ready for the thunder to crash, but instead, a tension-filled moment hung in the air like a thick fog. Ethan's father seemed to be re-evaluating his stance, the challenge hanging between father and son almost tangible.

"Disappointment? Is that what you think this is about?" His father's voice, typically a well-rehearsed cadence of authority, cracked just a bit, revealing a flicker of something deeper—fear, perhaps. "I expect you to succeed. Is that so wrong?"

"Maybe success looks different for everyone," I interjected, the words tumbling out before I could reconsider. "Maybe for him, it means being allowed to explore his own path without judgment."

Ethan shot me a grateful glance, and I felt a rush of warmth, an unspoken bond solidifying in the face of adversity. His father's eyes flickered between us, suspicion and annoyance swirling like a tempest in a teacup. "You are not part of this family's legacy," he said, the words sharp as glass.

"Perhaps not," I replied, my heart racing but my resolve steady. "But I care about him, and that counts for something."

"Care? You think that matters when the name on the door is what people remember?" he scoffed, turning his back to us, the dismissiveness rolling off him like a wave. "You'll learn, young lady, that sentiment doesn't pay the bills or secure a future."

Ethan's hands clenched at his sides, a storm brewing behind his calm exterior. "Then what should I do? Stop caring? Stop dreaming?" His voice was thick with the weight of his family's expectations, but there was a defiance in it that sent a thrill through me.

"That's not what I'm saying," his father replied, frustration creeping into his tone. "I'm saying you need to be realistic. This is a business. There are standards to maintain."

"And what if those standards don't reflect who I am?" Ethan shot back, stepping closer, his voice gaining momentum. "What if I don't want to be part of a business that suffocates creativity and passion? Is that too much to ask?"

The silence stretched out again, taut as a tightrope. I could sense the shift in the atmosphere—the way the room buzzed with the tension of unspoken words and long-held grievances. Ethan's father opened his mouth as if to respond, but then seemed to reconsider, his brow furrowing as he surveyed the landscape of his son's face. "This isn't a conversation I want to have in front of... her."

I bristled at the dismissal, feeling the familiar sting of being an outsider in a world where familial loyalty trumped all else. "I may not be family, but I won't stand by while you dictate his happiness," I said firmly, my voice cutting through the tension like a knife.

Ethan stepped between us, his presence suddenly more significant, like a lighthouse guiding us through turbulent waters. "Dad, she's right. You need to understand that I can't keep living this way."

For a moment, it felt like we were standing on the edge of a precipice, the wind howling around us as we teetered on the brink of something life-changing. But then the moment slipped away, as his father's expression hardened. "You will do what is expected of you. We will not be the laughingstock of this town because of your whims."

"Whims?" Ethan's voice was a low growl, a protective layer wrapping around every syllable. "This isn't about whims. It's about my life."

Without warning, Ethan's father pivoted, storming out of the library, the door slamming behind him with a finality that reverberated in the air. We stood in the aftermath, the silence now heavy and thick like fog rolling in over the sea.

"Wow," I breathed, the adrenaline still coursing through me. "That was intense."

Ethan exhaled slowly, the corners of his mouth twitching up into a reluctant smile. "Intense is one way to describe it. I thought he was going to explode."

"Honestly, I thought he might call in the cavalry. But you, my friend, you stood your ground." I nudged him playfully, feeling buoyed by the moment. "It's nice to see you fight back."

His smile widened, and for a fleeting second, the tension lifted, replaced by a shared understanding. "Thanks for that. I really needed someone to back me up."

"Anytime. I'm like your personal superhero sidekick, remember?" I winked, the moment a tiny thread weaving us closer together. But even as the lightness returned, I could feel the shadows lingering just outside the library door.

"Do you think he'll come around?" Ethan asked, his voice quiet now, the bravado slipping away like the last rays of sunlight.

"Eventually, maybe. But it's going to take time." I hesitated, contemplating the complexities of familial bonds and expectations. "And it's going to be hard."

"I'm ready for hard," he replied, determination threading through his words. "It's time I figured out who I really want to be, not who my parents think I should be."

"Exactly," I said, feeling an unshakeable warmth bloom in my chest. "And whatever you decide, I'll be right here, cheering you on."

We shared a moment, our eyes locking in an understanding deeper than words, a connection bolstered by both courage and vulnerability. But as the door creaked open, cutting through the intimacy of our exchange, I felt a chill run down my spine.

Ethan's father re-entered, but he wasn't alone. Madison stood beside him, her presence cutting through the moment like a knife. She was the last person I wanted to see, her expression a perfect mix of confusion and condescension.

"I didn't realize we were having a party," she said, her voice dripping with sarcasm. "I thought this was a family discussion."

Ethan stiffened beside me, the moment of triumph evaporating like mist in the morning sun. "Madison, what are you doing here?"

"I came to find you," she replied, glancing between us, her eyes narrowing slightly. "And it seems I walked in at a rather inconvenient time."

I exchanged a quick glance with Ethan, the tension between us suddenly feeling more charged than ever. "Inconvenient doesn't begin to cover it," I muttered under my breath.

Madison stepped further into the room, the air thick with unspoken challenges. "You're making quite the scene, Ethan. It would be a shame if this got out."

Ethan's jaw clenched, and I felt a surge of protectiveness on his behalf. "What do you want, Madison?"

"Just a chat," she said, her voice laced with honeyed sweetness that did nothing to disguise the underlying threat. "After all, family matters are best discussed among family, don't you think?"

I could sense the weight of impending conflict swirling around us, a storm ready to break. And as the shadows closed in once more, I couldn't shake the feeling that this was only the beginning of a much larger battle.

Chapter 23: Madison's Return

Ethan and I stood under the vibrant canopy of autumn leaves, a warm golden glow filtering through the branches overhead. The air was crisp, filled with the scent of pumpkin spice lattes wafting from the nearby café, where laughter bubbled like the effervescent drinks we all craved. This season, my favorite, had always felt like a cozy embrace, a promise of comfort and change intertwined. But as I leaned against Ethan, our hands clasped together, I sensed a chill that had nothing to do with the impending winter.

"You're thinking too much again," he said, the corners of his mouth lifting into that infuriatingly charming grin that made my heart flutter against all reason.

I rolled my eyes playfully. "Just because I'm not staring into the abyss of your perfectly sculpted jawline doesn't mean I'm overthinking. I'm simply... contemplating life. Like a deep philosopher. Or maybe just someone who forgot to check her caffeine levels."

His laughter was a warm blanket, wrapping around me as I tried to shake off the unease threading through my thoughts. "Well, philosopher," he teased, "let's find some coffee before your musings drive us into an existential crisis."

We were making our way toward the café when I caught sight of her—Madison—across the square, standing in the glow of the afternoon sun like a spotlight beckoning unwelcome attention. My breath caught as I watched her. Gone was the unsure woman who'd left town in the wake of her broken engagement with Ethan. This Madison was a polished version, her hair cascading like a waterfall of dark silk, and her clothes tailored to perfection, each piece accentuating her figure. But it was her smile that made me uneasy; there was an edge to it, like a blade concealed beneath the charm.

"What is it?" Ethan's voice pulled me back, and I quickly plastered a smile on my face.

"Nothing," I said too quickly, the word escaping my lips as I focused my gaze straight ahead, but I could feel the tension coiling between us.

"Uh-huh," he replied, his tone skeptical. "You're definitely lying. Your face says 'I've just seen a ghost,' and it's not the friendly kind."

Ignoring his teasing, I kept walking, but my mind raced, replaying the memory of Madison's departure. The silence that followed her exit had been heavy, the kind that settled in your bones and made every breath feel like a conscious effort. Now, she was back, and the air around us shifted, charged with something I couldn't quite place.

As if summoned by the universe's most unfortunate sense of timing, Madison sauntered over, her heels clicking against the cobblestones like a countdown to disaster. "Well, if it isn't my favorite couple," she chimed, her voice smooth like velvet laced with honey, yet I detected an undercurrent of something sharper. "I thought I'd find you here, enjoying the ambiance."

Ethan's grip on my hand tightened, the subtle change in his demeanor palpable. "Madison," he said, voice steady but cool, like the calm before a storm.

"Back in town for a bit of work," she said, flipping her hair over her shoulder with an ease that seemed practiced. "You know how it is. Some of us just can't resist the call of our hometown, no matter how far we wander."

Her gaze flickered to me, and for a moment, I felt as though she was examining a specimen under a microscope, searching for weaknesses. I straightened my back, squaring my shoulders as if I could ward off her scrutiny.

"I thought you were done with all this," I said, attempting to sound casual, though my heart raced. "You moved to the city, didn't you? Big corporate world and all that?"

Madison's laughter danced in the air, too bright, too rehearsed. "Oh, honey, you know how it is. The city never stops calling, but I felt a pull back here. Must be the autumn air." She took a step closer, her eyes sparkling with mischief. "Besides, there are just so many old friends to reconnect with. Isn't that right, Ethan?"

I could practically feel the electricity crackling between them, an unwelcome spark igniting the air. "Yeah, well, I've got my hands full with work," Ethan replied, the slight hitch in his tone revealing his discomfort.

"Oh, come on," she prodded, her eyes narrowing slightly. "You've got to make time for friends. And you must admit, it's been a while since we all caught up. It'd be just like old times."

I could hear the unspoken challenge laced in her words, a not-so-subtle invitation to reenter the lives we had all once shared.

"Yeah, I guess we can always meet up for coffee," Ethan said, but I could hear the hesitation lurking beneath his easy tone.

Madison's smile widened, teeth flashing in the sunlight. "Perfect! I know the best little spot downtown. You'll love it."

And just like that, she spun on her heel and strode away, leaving a trail of unease in her wake. I felt a mixture of relief and dread flood through me, the tension leaving a bitter taste in my mouth.

"Well, that was... interesting," Ethan said, his eyes still on her retreating figure.

"Interesting is one way to put it," I replied, my heart racing. "What's she really doing back, Ethan? You know she's not just here for coffee and good vibes."

Ethan rubbed the back of his neck, a familiar sign of his rising tension. "I don't know. Maybe she's trying to find closure or something. It's been a long time."

But I could sense the weight of Madison's presence, an anchor dragging us into uncertain waters. The shadows of the past loomed large, and I feared that the cracks in our fragile relationship, once starting to heal, were about to deepen. I wasn't sure I had the strength to face Madison or whatever tempest she was bringing with her.

Ethan and I spent the next few days navigating the awkward tension that hung over us like a low-hanging fog. It felt as if the world had shifted, our laughter muffled by the weight of unspoken words and the specter of Madison looming over every interaction. We returned to our routines, but the comfortable rhythm we had established began to falter, and even mundane moments felt charged with uncertainty.

One afternoon, as we sat at our favorite café—an inviting little place draped in fairy lights and bustling with life—I noticed a group of people gathered near the entrance, their animated conversations rising and falling like waves. I sipped my mocha, trying to drown out the unease simmering beneath the surface, but my eyes darted toward the door as soon as it swung open.

Madison glided in, her presence slicing through the crowd like a hot knife through butter. She wore a fitted leather jacket, a sharp contrast to the soft, pastel hues that adorned the café. With her hair pulled back in a sleek ponytail, she radiated confidence, the kind that made my heart race in an entirely uninvited way. She was magnetic, pulling attention effortlessly, and I could feel the collective gaze of the café shift toward her.

"Ah, look who it is," Ethan said, his tone light, but the tension in his shoulders betrayed him. "Just what we needed."

"Can we pretend we didn't see her?" I asked, sinking lower in my seat. "I don't think my heart can take another round of her charm offensive."

"Too late for that," Ethan replied, eyes narrowing as he tracked her movements. "Looks like she's headed this way."

I forced a smile, but it felt more like a grimace as Madison approached, her eyes sparkling with a hint of mischief. "Ethan! What a lovely surprise," she exclaimed, as if our presence here was the most fortuitous encounter in the world.

"Madison," he replied, his voice steady. "What brings you here?"

"Oh, just the usual," she said, casually waving a hand as if dismissing the question. "The ambiance, the coffee—how could I resist? And it seems I found you two enjoying the fine art of avoidance."

I shot Ethan a look that said, "Do something," but he merely raised an eyebrow, clearly torn between amusement and discomfort.

"Nothing to avoid here, just a normal afternoon," I managed to say, injecting as much cheer into my voice as I could muster. "You know, sipping coffee, enjoying life. The usual."

She leaned in closer, lowering her voice conspiratorially. "You know, it's really great to see you both together again. I'd hate for there to be any... awkwardness." Her smile widened, the glint in her eyes suggesting a level of glee that made my stomach churn.

"Thanks," I replied, trying to sound nonchalant. "We're fine."

"Good, good," she said, nodding, the sincerity dripping from her words like syrup. "So, any plans for the weekend? I hear there's a new art exhibit opening downtown. I think you both would love it."

Ethan opened his mouth, but I jumped in first, unable to let him agree to anything that might involve Madison monopolizing our time. "Actually, we're busy this weekend. A lot of... things to catch up on, you know?"

Madison's expression didn't falter, but I could sense the slight tightening of her jaw. "Oh, come on! You can't possibly have plans that are more exciting than a night out at an art exhibit," she coaxed, her voice silky, each word laced with persuasion.

"Actually, I was thinking we might binge-watch a show," Ethan interjected, his eyes darting to mine for support. "You know, the kind of riveting drama that keeps us on the couch."

Madison laughed lightly, but I noticed the subtle way her smile faltered for a fraction of a second, a fleeting crack in her carefully crafted facade. "Oh, I can't let you miss out on this. Trust me, it'll be the talk of the town. And who knows, maybe there's a piece that'll really inspire you both."

Ethan looked at me, his expression caught between wanting to stand his ground and the undeniable pull of Madison's magnetic energy. "Maybe we'll think about it?" he offered hesitantly, glancing at me as if I could conjure up a reasonable excuse.

Before I could protest, Madison's phone buzzed, pulling her attention away. "Excuse me for just a moment," she said, her smile still in place as she stepped a few feet back to take the call.

"Ethan," I hissed, leaning closer. "She's not going to let this go. She's probing, and if we don't set boundaries now, she'll just worm her way back into our lives."

"I know," he replied, his voice barely above a whisper. "But it's just coffee. It doesn't mean anything."

"Sure, but it's Madison," I said, frustration bubbling to the surface. "She doesn't do anything without a motive."

Ethan opened his mouth to respond, but before he could, Madison returned, her conversation evidently finished. "So, what do you say? Art exhibit this Saturday? I promise it'll be fun!"

My heart raced as I exchanged a glance with Ethan, who hesitated, clearly torn. "We'll let you know," he finally said, and I could almost feel the tension ebbing, if only slightly.

Madison's smile faltered for just a moment, and I caught a flicker of disappointment in her eyes, quickly masked by that practiced charm. "No pressure! I'll be around." With a final, lingering glance at Ethan, she turned and strolled back toward the entrance, her heels clicking in rhythm with the growing anxiety coiling in my stomach.

As the door swung shut behind her, the café seemed to exhale, the atmosphere lightening as if the weight of her presence had been lifted.

"Well, that was cheerful," I said, taking a deep breath as if to shake off the lingering remnants of her presence. "What do we do now?"

Ethan sighed, running a hand through his hair, a gesture that always made my heart flutter. "I guess we play it by ear. But I don't want you to feel uncomfortable. We can avoid her if you want."

"No," I replied, my heart thumping heavily in my chest. "That's just it. It feels like we're playing defense instead of enjoying each other's company. I refuse to let her dictate our lives."

"Then we make our own plans," he said, his voice firm. "Let's do something just us this weekend. How about a hike? We could pack a picnic and escape for a bit."

The thought warmed me. The idea of us, surrounded by nature, the sunlight filtering through the trees, seemed like the perfect antidote to the chaotic energy Madison brought. "I'd love that," I said, a smile creeping onto my face.

"Good," Ethan replied, relief washing over him. "It'll be just us, away from all... this."

As we settled back into our coffee and conversation, the comfort of familiarity slowly returned. Yet, I could still feel Madison's shadow lurking, a reminder that the battle lines had been drawn, and I wasn't sure if I had the strength to hold my ground against a storm.

The sun peeked through the curtains, casting a soft glow across our little living room as I attempted to shake off the lingering shadows of last night's coffee debacle. Ethan was in the kitchen, humming a tune while the scent of freshly brewed coffee wafted through the air. I savored the warmth of our shared space, the memories of laughter and quiet moments flooding back like a comforting tide.

But every time I glanced at the vibrant, sunlit window, I felt a twinge of anxiety clawing at my insides. Madison's presence loomed large, an unwelcome guest at the feast of my thoughts. Just when I thought we'd put distance between us, she had managed to infiltrate our lives like a persistent stain that wouldn't wash out.

"Good morning!" Ethan called, his voice bright as he emerged from the kitchen, a steaming mug in each hand. He handed me one, our fingers brushing in a way that sent a shiver down my spine. "Coffee to fuel your day. I hope you're ready to conquer the world."

I smiled, though my heart wasn't in it. "Conquer? More like just trying to survive the day without running into a certain ex who thrives on chaos."

He laughed, the sound rich and warm, and it made me feel a little lighter. "Madison doesn't stand a chance against you. You've got this."

"Thanks for the vote of confidence," I replied, but deep down, the nagging feeling of uncertainty clawed at me. I took a sip of the coffee, the familiar bitterness grounding me momentarily. "But what if she decides to crash our plans this weekend? She has a way of showing up where she's least wanted."

Ethan's expression shifted, a flicker of concern flashing across his face. "Then we'll handle it. Together. Just like we always do."

I nodded, but my mind raced. The hike we had planned felt like a refuge, a chance to escape the storm brewing around us, but would it really be enough?

After breakfast, we decided to take a walk in the nearby park. As we strolled hand in hand, the leaves crunched beneath our feet, a delightful symphony of autumn. The sun filtered through the trees, casting dappled shadows that danced playfully on the ground. For a moment, everything felt right.

"Remember when we used to come here as kids?" Ethan mused, his eyes sparkling with nostalgia. "We'd race to the swings, and whoever lost had to push the other until they felt like they were flying."

"Right? I think I lost more often than I'd like to admit," I replied, laughing. "But you were always so generous with the pushing. I think I still have a few scars from those days."

"I thought we agreed to never speak of the playground incident again?" he teased, his expression shifting to mock seriousness.

I gasped dramatically. "I'll have you know that my fall was entirely due to your overenthusiastic pushing! I still bear the emotional scars of that day."

"Emotional scars? Really?" he said, mock disbelief dancing in his tone. "You might want to work on that before our hike."

"Please. The only thing I need to work on is not letting Madison derail my life," I replied, my voice quieter, the weight of my thoughts creeping back in.

"Let's focus on today," he suggested, squeezing my hand. "We'll deal with Madison when the time comes."

Just then, a familiar figure came into view, jogging through the park with an easy grace that made my heart sink. It was Madison, her ponytail swinging as she approached, a bright smile plastered on her face. I froze, feeling the tension roll off Ethan beside me.

"Ethan! Fancy seeing you here!" she called out, her voice dripping with feigned cheerfulness as she slowed her pace, her eyes darting between us. "And you brought your... friend."

"Madison," Ethan said, his tone careful. "We were just enjoying a walk."

"Clearly." Her eyes sparkled with mischief, a predatory glint that made my skin crawl. "What a lovely day for it. Mind if I join?"

"Actually," I interjected, my voice steady as I felt Ethan's tension beside me, "we were just about to head to the trail. It's quite secluded."

Her smile faltered for just a moment before it returned, but this time it felt forced. "Oh, I adore a good hike! Mind if I tag along? I could use the fresh air."

I felt Ethan stiffen beside me, the atmosphere thick with unspoken tension. "Uh, it might be a little cramped," he said, the unease creeping into his voice.

"Nonsense!" Madison chirped, her tone too bright, too eager. "Besides, I promise I won't talk too much. Just the right amount of friendly banter to keep it interesting."

I shot Ethan a look, my heart racing. "I think we'd prefer it quiet. The whole point is to escape."

Madison stepped closer, her smile narrowing, eyes flickering with something darker beneath the surface. "Oh, come on. It's been ages since we all hung out together. You wouldn't want to miss out on the fun, would you?"

Ethan glanced at me, uncertainty clouding his expression. "Maybe we can plan something else another time?" he suggested, clearly trying to find a way out of this spiraling situation.

Madison laughed, a sound that rang hollow. "You're both so adorable, trying to avoid me. But I assure you, I'm not going anywhere. And who knows, maybe we can rekindle some old friendships?"

A shiver ran down my spine as her words lingered in the air, thick with unspoken implications. I could feel the way Ethan's jaw tightened, the lines of his face hardening as the tension thickened around us.

"Madison," I said, trying to keep my voice steady despite the growing dread. "We really don't want to—"

"Oh, please," she interrupted, her tone suddenly sharp. "You think you can just pretend I'm not here? That I don't exist?" Her gaze locked onto Ethan, fierce and unwavering. "But I'm back, and you two are going to have to deal with me. Like it or not."

Before I could respond, a sudden commotion erupted from the other side of the park, drawing our attention. A group of children had gathered near a fountain, shrieking in delight as a frisbee soared through the air, narrowly missing a couple sitting on a nearby bench. But my heart was racing for another reason entirely. In the chaos, I caught sight of Madison's eyes, sparkling with something sinister, something that whispered of ulterior motives.

"I don't mind a little excitement," she said, her voice low, barely masking the predatory edge. "Let's see just how far we can push this friendship."

Ethan's hand tightened around mine as we exchanged a look, the unspoken understanding crackling between us. But before we could formulate a plan or a way out, Madison leaned in closer, her voice dropping to a conspiratorial whisper. "You'd better be ready, because I'm not going to let this go. Not now, not ever."

And with that, the world around me spun, the vibrant colors of autumn dimming as dread settled in my chest like a stone. I took a step back, feeling the ground shift beneath me, and as I did, I heard her laughter—a chilling, melodic sound that seemed to echo through the trees, promising trouble ahead.

The shadows deepened, and the fragile thread of our reality hung in the balance, teetering on the edge of chaos.

Chapter 24: The Break

The scent of fresh lilies wafted through the air, mingling with the faint hint of citrus from the cocktails being served at the grand gala. The venue was transformed into a shimmering wonderland of twinkling fairy lights and ornate decorations, a far cry from the ordinary town we called home. This annual charity gala was the epitome of our community's social calendar, where the town's elite donned their finest attire, eager to parade their wealth and influence. As Ethan and I entered, I could already feel the weight of expectations pressing down on me, heavier than the layers of taffeta and silk I wore.

Ethan looked dashing in his tailored navy suit, the kind of outfit that hinted at his understated charm. I glanced at him out of the corner of my eye, a small smile curling on my lips as I adjusted my strapless dress, feeling its soft fabric hug my body just right. We had rehearsed our entrance in the car, but now that we were here, I felt a mix of anticipation and trepidation. I had imagined this evening as a romantic evening filled with laughter and whispered secrets, not as a stage for the hidden tensions that had been brewing for weeks.

We wove through the crowd, exchanging pleasantries with acquaintances and soaking in the atmosphere, but I could sense something simmering beneath the surface. It wasn't long before Madison emerged, like a specter from the past. She glided toward us with an air of confidence, her sleek black dress accentuating every curve, her smile practiced but icy. As soon as her gaze locked onto Ethan, the air around us thickened, and I felt the spark of tension ignite.

"Ethan!" she exclaimed, a bit too cheerfully for my liking. She reached out, her fingers brushing his arm as if it were an involuntary gesture. "I was hoping to see you here. This event just wouldn't be the same without you."

I shifted my weight, my heart thudding in my chest as I stood there, a reluctant spectator to this familiar dance. Ethan was caught off guard, and I could see the flicker of discomfort in his eyes, though he masked it well.

"Madison, good to see you," he replied, his voice steady but lacking the warmth I had hoped to hear. I crossed my arms, feeling the bile rise in my throat as she leaned closer, whispering something into his ear that I couldn't hear. Whatever it was, it sent a ripple of tension through him. He stiffened, his expression faltering as I caught a glimpse of the uncertainty written all over his face.

That's when it happened. A surge of possessiveness washed over me, igniting an impulse I hadn't anticipated. Before I knew it, I was stepping forward, my heart racing, and confronting the very embodiment of my insecurities.

"Ethan," I said, my voice steady but my heart pounding, "can we talk?"

Madison's laughter tinkled, laced with a mocking edge. "Oh, sweetheart, don't mind us. We're just catching up on old times."

The smirk on her face felt like a dagger to my gut. I could almost hear the crowd's collective intake of breath, as if they were all waiting for the impending explosion. "Old times? Is that what we're calling it now?" I shot back, the heat of confrontation igniting my resolve.

"Let's not do this here," Ethan said, his eyes darting between us, a hint of panic flickering in his gaze.

But the adrenaline coursing through me clouded my judgment. "No, Ethan. I need you to understand that this—" I gestured wildly at Madison, who stood there with an infuriatingly composed expression, "this isn't just a harmless chat. She knows how to get under your skin. You can't let her pull you back in."

Madison's eyes sparkled with amusement as she crossed her arms, clearly relishing the drama unfolding before the onlookers. "Aw, how sweet. You're worried about your boyfriend's feelings? How charming." Her voice dripped with sarcasm, and it only fueled my anger.

"You think this is charming?" I shot back, my voice rising, the cool elegance of the gala starting to crack. "You think manipulating him is some kind of game?"

Ethan's hand found mine, squeezing gently as if trying to tether me to sanity, but the moment felt electric and all-consuming. The murmurs from the crowd intensified, fueling the fire. "Let's go," he pleaded, but it felt too late. The words hung in the air, heavy and irrevocable.

"No! Not until you stand up for yourself," I insisted, frustration bubbling over. "You have to choose. It's either her or us. You can't have it both ways."

Madison stepped closer, her eyes narrowing. "You're making a scene, and it's quite unbecoming. Just remember, Ethan and I have a history. You might want to consider that before you go throwing accusations around."

Her words hit me like ice water, chilling my resolve. The weight of her presence seemed to envelop us, and for a brief moment, I wondered if I was fighting a losing battle. Would he choose her? Would he see her as the better option, the one who had somehow always managed to slip back into his life when I least expected it?

"History?" I echoed incredulously. "History doesn't mean a damn thing if it's built on manipulation and lies! You deserve more than that, Ethan!"

The escalating tension cracked like a lightning bolt, and for a heartbeat, I feared the outcome. The whispers grew louder around us, the weight of judgment hanging in the air, suffocating. I caught a glimpse of our reflections in the ornate mirror beside us, two people on the verge of collapse, caught in a web of feelings that were as tangled as the strands of my hair cascading down my shoulders.

"Stop," Ethan said, raising his voice above the din. "Both of you."

The words reverberated through the hall, halting the ongoing murmurs and shifting the focus back to us. My heart stuttered as I met his eyes, desperate for reassurance, but all I saw was confusion and conflict. In that moment, it felt like everything was slipping away, and I could almost hear the cracking of our foundation beneath the weight of unresolved issues and simmering tensions.

As the gala continued around us, a chaotic tapestry of color and sound, I stood on the precipice of something monumental—a fight that felt more like a reckoning. I wondered if this was the moment that would define us, a turning point that could either shatter everything I believed in or bring us closer than ever before. Would we rise from the ashes, or would this be the end of us?

The tension in the air crackled like the electric hum of anticipation before a storm, and for a moment, I forgot where I was. My heart thumped in my chest, a relentless drumbeat urging me to confront the chaos spiraling around us. Ethan's eyes darted between Madison and me, and I could see the conflict brewing within him, a tempest he was trying to navigate. My breath caught in my throat, thick with the scent of despair and the sharp tang of adrenaline.

Madison, smug and triumphant, took a step closer to Ethan, her voice low and coaxing. "Come on, Ethan, don't let her rattle you. You know I've always had your back." Her fingers brushed lightly against his forearm, a gesture so deceptively innocent that it made my stomach churn.

I wanted to hurl the nearest cocktail glass at her, but I opted for words instead, feeling the power they wielded when wielded with conviction. "Ethan, you're not a pawn in her game. You're not some trophy she gets to flaunt around to remind everyone of her past victories." My voice was steady, but the emotion underneath trembled like a taut string ready to snap.

"Can you keep it down?" Ethan whispered, urgency lacing his words. His brows knit together, and for a brief moment, I felt the flicker of solidarity, but then it dimmed under the weight of Madison's presence. "This isn't the place."

"Not the place?" I laughed, incredulous. "We're surrounded by a hundred witnesses! You think she cares about this place? She thrives on it." The words escaped my lips with a fierceness that surprised even me. "You're better than this, Ethan. You deserve to be with someone who uplifts you, not someone who stabs you in the back every chance she gets."

His jaw tightened, and I could see the gears turning in his mind. "That's not fair," he said, his voice a mixture of frustration and confusion. "You don't know what I'm dealing with here."

"Right, because allowing her to worm her way back into your life is the solution," I shot back, my heart racing. "You think she's here for you? She's here for the spotlight, and you're just another accessory."

Madison smirked, reveling in the drama unfolding. "Oh, sweetie, you're being quite theatrical. Is this how you plan to win him over? By putting on a show?"

"You don't know anything about me," I retorted, barely managing to keep my voice from shaking. The crowd's attention was a tangible thing, a living entity that made every word feel like a performance.

"Actually, I know a lot," she replied, her tone deceptively sweet. "I know you're desperate for his attention, and it's kind of pathetic."

A nerve in my temple throbbed at her insinuation, and I was on the verge of retaliating when Ethan stepped in. "Enough!" His voice boomed, startling even the onlookers who had been gleefully soaking in the tension. "We're not doing this here. Not tonight."

His intervention was like a bucket of cold water splashed over my fiery resolve. I stepped back, blinking against the sudden rush of emotions. "Ethan, you can't just—"

"No, you listen to me." His gaze locked onto mine, a mix of vulnerability and frustration flashing behind his blue eyes. "You're both important to me, but I need you to trust me. I need you to step back for a moment."

The moment hung thick in the air, like a suspended note waiting to resolve. I searched his face for understanding, for any sign that we were still on the same page. Instead, I found confusion, a reflection of my own. "Trust you?" I echoed, the word heavy on my tongue. "This isn't about trust; it's about choice. It's about you choosing her, or choosing me."

He sighed, the weight of the world visible in his expression. "It's not that simple. You both know that."

"No, we don't know that," I insisted, feeling the ground shift beneath me. "It feels pretty damn simple from where I'm standing. You can either walk away from the person who's been playing with your heart for years or stick around for someone who's actually invested in you."

Madison's eyes sparkled with amusement, a predator ready to strike. "And look where that's gotten you," she shot back, waving her hand dismissively. "Dramatic moments at galas? That's not exactly a glowing endorsement for your relationship."

"Shut up!" I spat, but her laughter echoed in my ears, mocking and triumphant. I could feel the crowd shifting, a tide of judgment rising, and the knot in my stomach tightened.

"Guys, please!" I heard someone call from the fringes, their voice muffled by the chaos. It was someone I recognized, a friend from college, but their concern felt futile against the storm brewing.

Ethan looked between us, exasperated. "This is not how I wanted tonight to go. You two are acting like children, and I can't handle it!"

In that moment, I felt something shift, a subtle crack in the foundation of our relationship that I had thought was unshakeable. The emotions roiling inside me bubbled up, threatening to spill over, but I took a deep breath and tried to steady myself. "Ethan, I'm just trying to protect what we have," I said, my voice softer now, tinged with desperation.

"Protecting me? Or protecting yourself?" he challenged, his words a slap that sent heat to my cheeks. "It feels like you're fighting me instead of for me."

Madison's lips curled into a satisfied smile as if she knew she had struck gold. "You see that, right? She's making this all about her. You're the prize in her little game."

I gritted my teeth, unwilling to let her words poison the conversation further. "I'm not making this about me. I'm trying to show you that you're being manipulated, Ethan. Can't you see that?"

"Maybe I don't need saving," he retorted, the frustration boiling over. "Maybe I can handle my own life without either of you telling me what to do."

The silence that followed was deafening, punctuated only by the clinking of glasses and murmurs from the crowd. I felt my heart drop, a lead weight in my chest. His words felt like a knife, slicing through the fragile hope I had nurtured.

Madison stepped closer, her voice low and sultry. "You see, Ethan, she doesn't really understand you the way I do. She's just scared of losing you, and that's a different kind of love."

I opened my mouth to protest, but the words failed me. The vulnerability I felt in that moment hung in the air, and I struggled to hold my ground. All I wanted was for him to look at me the way he once had, with admiration, with certainty. But there was only doubt swirling between us, and the realization crashed over me like an unforgiving wave.

Maybe I had fought too hard for something that was already slipping away, and I could feel the darkness creeping in, threatening to consume everything I had built. I just hoped that somewhere within this tempest, Ethan could find his way back to me before it was too late.

The silence that settled around us felt like a heavy fog, thickening with each moment as I stood there, trapped between Madison's smirk and Ethan's troubled gaze. The crowd, once a vibrant backdrop of laughter and light, now felt like a hostile audience, eyes wide and hungry for drama. I could almost hear their whispers, the speculative tones of friends and acquaintances keen on dissecting our confrontation like a prized specimen.

"Look, can we just take a breath?" Ethan said, his voice taut with a mix of frustration and desperation. The strain in his tone sent a shiver through me, and I felt my heart waver like a candle in a windstorm. "This isn't the way to handle things."

"Oh, so now I'm the problem?" I shot back, feeling the sting of betrayal seeping into my words. "Is that what you really think, Ethan? That I'm the villain in this story?"

Madison clapped her hands, her laughter ringing out like a wind chime caught in a storm. "You've got it all wrong, darling. I'm the one with the history here. You're just a fleeting moment in his life—a pretty little distraction."

Ethan clenched his jaw, clearly torn between the two of us, and my heart sank further. "You don't get to talk about her like that," he said, his voice strained. "You're not some hero in my life, Madison. You're the ghost I'm trying to move past."

Her smile faltered for a split second, and in that blink, I saw an opportunity—a glimmer of hope. "See, Ethan? You don't owe her anything. You owe it to yourself to make the right choice."

"Do I?" he replied, a hint of doubt creeping into his tone. "I don't know what that is anymore." The admission hung in the air, heavy with the weight of unspoken fears.

Madison leaned in closer, her voice low and sultry, as if trying to seduce him back into her orbit. "You really think she knows you like I do? That she can understand the pressure you're under? I mean, come on, this is a charity gala, not a therapy session."

"Maybe it should be," I snapped, feeling the frustration bubble up once again. "Because if you had any decency, you'd back off."

Ethan's eyes darted between us, and the tension crackled like static electricity. "Both of you, please," he said, his voice rising above the murmurs of the crowd. "This is insane."

"Insane?" I echoed, incredulity washing over me. "What's insane is letting her manipulate you like this. You think she cares about you?"

"Of course I care about him," Madison interjected, feigning innocence. "I've always been there for him. That's what friends do, right?"

"Right, friends," I replied, my voice dripping with sarcasm. "Friends who swoop in whenever they feel threatened by someone better."

Ethan's eyes narrowed, and I could see the conflict etched on his face. "I'm not some prize to be won!"

"Then stop acting like one!" I retorted, the heat rising in my chest. "You have a choice, Ethan. You can either stand up for yourself or keep being her puppet."

Madison rolled her eyes, an exaggerated gesture that made my blood boil. "You're both exhausting. How about we take a step back and let Ethan decide who he wants to be with? After all, it's not like you're going to take him anywhere special with your little 'distraction' act."

"Distraction?" I hissed, my heart racing. "This isn't a game for me. This is my life, and I want you out of it."

"Isn't that sweet?" Madison purred, the malice hidden behind her sugary tone. "But, you know, love isn't always enough. Sometimes it's about practicality. And let's face it, Ethan and I have a connection that runs deeper than what you two have."

"Is that why you're here tonight?" I asked, the words slipping out before I could stop them. "To remind him of the past while pretending to care about his future?"

The silence that followed was deafening. The crowd shifted, an undercurrent of tension rippling through the onlookers, and I could feel their anticipation building, waiting for the next dramatic turn.

Ethan ran a hand through his hair, a gesture of frustration that made my heart ache. "This isn't how I wanted to spend tonight, and it's certainly not how I wanted to feel. Can't we just...?"

"Can't we just what?" I interrupted, the bitterness creeping into my voice. "Pretend everything is fine? Act like you're not being pulled in two different directions?"

"Maybe that's exactly what you should do," Madison chimed in, her smile triumphant. "Pretend this isn't happening. Pretend you're not losing him to someone who understands him better."

The sting of her words hit me harder than I expected, and I fought to maintain my composure. "Ethan, you deserve someone who believes in you, not someone who thrives on tearing you down. You're so much more than her shadow."

The atmosphere shifted, palpable tension suffocating me as Ethan glanced back at Madison, his expression indecipherable. "I need to think," he finally said, turning away from us both.

"Think?" I echoed, incredulous. "You're going to just walk away?"

He paused, his shoulders tense, the weight of the world pressing down on him. "I'm not walking away from you. I just need some space to figure this out."

Madison smirked, her victory almost palpable as she sidled closer to him. "Take your time, Ethan. I'll be right here."

My heart sank as I watched him take a step back, the distance between us feeling insurmountable. "This isn't a game, Ethan," I called out, desperation creeping into my voice. "Don't let her manipulate you. You're stronger than that."

He hesitated, and in that moment, a flicker of doubt crossed his features, a brief glimmer that made me hope. But before I could seize the moment, Madison whispered something to him, a conspiratorial tone that made my stomach churn. His expression shifted, and I could see the wall between us begin to rise once more.

The gala swirled around us, the music fading into a murmur, but all I could focus on was Ethan's retreating figure. The world felt like it was spinning out of control, and I wanted nothing more than to reach out, to pull him back, to remind him of the moments we had shared—the laughter, the late-night conversations, the dreams we had woven together like threads in a tapestry.

But the distance felt infinite, and the anger simmering in my veins clashed violently with the love I held for him. "Ethan!" I shouted, the word tearing from my throat, raw and ragged. "Please!"

He turned slightly, but the flicker of recognition in his eyes quickly dimmed. "I'll be back," he said, his voice a mere whisper, a promise that felt hollow. And then he was gone, swallowed by the crowd, leaving me standing on the precipice of despair.

Madison's laughter rang out behind me, a haunting melody that filled the space he left behind. "Looks like you're all alone now, darling. Did you really think you could win him over so easily?"

I clenched my fists, fighting against the flood of emotions threatening to drown me. "You won't keep him," I warned, my voice steadier than I felt. "He deserves better than this."

"Oh, sweetie," she cooed, the condescension dripping from her words. "Better is subjective, and I happen to know what he needs. Maybe you should learn to let go."

As the gala continued around me, laughter mingling with the clinking of glasses, I felt the ground shift beneath my feet, the walls of my carefully constructed world beginning to crumble. A storm was brewing within me, and I was standing at the edge of it, teetering between hope and despair.

Just as I thought the evening couldn't get worse, a voice called out from behind me. "Excuse me, are you...?"

I turned to see a familiar face approaching, but before they could finish their sentence, I caught sight of Ethan across the room, locked in conversation with Madison. Something was exchanged between them—an intimate glance, a slight smile—and in that moment, my heart shattered.

I felt the world tilt dangerously, as if the ground had opened up beneath me. Panic surged through me, and I rushed toward them, desperate to reclaim what I feared was slipping away forever. But before I could reach him, I heard a voice—a deep, resonant tone that made my blood run cold.

"Ethan, we need to talk."

It was the kind of voice that demanded attention, and as I turned, my heart raced in my chest, a frantic drumbeat echoing in my ears. This was not how it was supposed to end. I had fought too hard, loved too deeply, to let it slip through my fingers now.

As the words echoed in my mind, I felt the ground beneath me shift again, and I knew, in that moment, everything was about to change.

Chapter 25: Picking Up the Pieces

The days following the gala slip through my fingers like water, each moment tinged with a potent mix of regret and heartache. The air feels different now, charged with an unspoken tension that weighs heavily on my chest. I can still see Ethan's face, twisted in that moment of shock when I walked away, the glittering lights of the gala fading into the distance behind me. He tried to call, text, even leave voicemails that likely dripped with desperation, but I've sealed myself off like an old letter left unopened. The only sound I allow into my world is the gentle lapping of water against the shore, a soothing rhythm that echoes my turmoil.

Returning to the lake feels both like a sanctuary and a prison. It's a place I've always turned to for solace, where the familiar scent of pine mingles with the cool, damp earth beneath my feet. Here, I can breathe. I settle onto the same weathered dock where summer days once slipped by in a haze of laughter and sunlight. The planks creak beneath me, each groan a reminder of time passing and moments lost. I gaze out across the water, watching the sun dip lower in the sky, painting the horizon with strokes of orange and pink. It's beautiful, yet all I can think of is how Ethan's warmth seemed to disappear the moment I needed it most.

With each passing hour, I wrestle with my emotions, replaying our last conversation in my mind like a broken record. How did it come to this? I thought we were building something real, something sturdy enough to withstand the storms of our lives. But the truth is, Ethan and I seem to be caught in a cycle of miscommunication and hurt feelings, each of us too stubborn to admit when we're wrong. I let out a frustrated sigh, the sound carrying over the water, as if the lake itself could absorb my pain.

As dusk settles, a shiver runs through me, not just from the evening chill but from the memories that haunt me. I can almost hear Ethan's laughter, see the way his eyes sparkled with mischief. It gnaws at me, this longing mixed with anger. I know I should reach out, let him know how I feel, but the hurt feels too fresh, too raw. Instead, I drown myself in thoughts of everything we've built, the late-night talks, the quiet moments shared in the kitchen over steaming cups of coffee, our dreams intertwining like the vines climbing the trellis in my grandmother's garden.

When I finally decide to head home, the last light of the day barely glimmers on the surface of the lake. My heart is heavy with the weight of unspoken words, and my mind is a whirlwind of confusion. The house feels different as I step inside, the familiar smell of lavender and vanilla clinging to the air, yet it feels hollow without Ethan's presence. I find myself wandering through the rooms, almost aimlessly, until I reach the small desk in the corner, my sanctuary of sorts. Among the clutter of papers and half-finished sketches, I spot it—a letter.

The envelope is neatly folded, the handwriting instantly recognizable. My heart leaps, then sinks. I hesitate, fingers trembling slightly as I pick it up, the paper cool against my skin. It feels like a lifeline thrown to a drowning person, yet I'm terrified to open it. What could he possibly say? With a deep breath, I unfold the letter, the scent of ink and paper wrapping around me like a warm embrace.

His words tumble out in a rush of ink and emotion, raw and unfiltered. He lays bare his soul, revealing fears that I never knew he harbored—the weight of his past mistakes, the looming shadow of inadequacy that has followed him through life. He speaks of his love for me with a vulnerability that sends shivers down my spine. It's as if he's peeling back layers of himself, exposing the very essence of who he is, flaws and all.

"I'm scared," he writes, "scared that I'm not enough for you, that I'll never be the man you deserve. I've messed up, I know that. But you're worth fighting for, and I'm not ready to give up on us." Each line draws me in deeper, the sincerity in his words unraveling the knots in my heart.

Tears prick at my eyes as I read on, the weight of his honesty crashing over me like a tidal wave. He acknowledges the pain we've both felt, the moments when we could have bridged the gap between us if only we'd been brave enough to speak our truths. He admits his mistakes, but also insists that the love we share is real, that it's flawed but beautiful in its imperfections.

And just like that, something shifts inside me. The anger that felt so solid begins to dissolve, replaced by the recognition that love isn't perfect. It's messy, complicated, and often tangled in miscommunication. But maybe, just maybe, that's enough. I close my eyes, envisioning Ethan's face, the warmth of his smile, the way his laughter dances in the air, weaving through my memories like a comforting melody.

With the letter still cradled in my hands, I feel a flicker of hope igniting within me. Perhaps it's time to pick up the pieces, to stop letting fear dictate my choices. Maybe it's time to embrace the chaos of love and everything that comes with it, even if it means facing the truth that I've tried to avoid for too long.

As the sun sets and the shadows stretch long across my living room, I find myself clutching Ethan's letter like a talisman, the weight of it grounding me in a sea of uncertainty. The air feels charged with possibility, a stark contrast to the heaviness that had clung to me since the gala. I read the letter again, savoring the nuances of his thoughts, the way he wrestles with his fears. Each sentence seems to shimmer with a truth that pulls at the corners of my heart, inviting me to step beyond my anger.

The promise of a fresh start tingles in the air, urging me to consider the next step. Yet, the reality of our situation gnaws at me—how could we come back from this? I chew my lip as I walk to the kitchen, my mind racing with possibilities. As I pour myself a glass of water, the coolness of the glass brings a brief moment of clarity. I take a deep breath, letting the coolness wash over me, hoping it will help me process what I feel.

Suddenly, the shrill ring of my phone cuts through the silence, sending my heart into a minor panic. I glance at the screen, and my stomach flips—it's Ethan. My instinct is to let it go to voicemail, to maintain the fragile barrier I've built, but curiosity holds me captive. I pick up the call, my voice steady yet laced with an undertone of uncertainty.

"Hey," he says, and I can almost picture him on the other end, hands shoved deep in his pockets, nervously pacing like a caged animal.

"Hey," I reply, trying to keep my tone neutral. The silence that follows is thick, almost palpable, as if the weight of our unspoken words fills the space between us.

"Did you get my letter?" His voice is tentative, as if he's tiptoeing over a minefield.

"I did," I admit, my heart racing.

"And?" His breath catches, a telltale sign of his anxiety.

I glance out the window, the dusky sky painted in hues of deep indigo. "You really bared your soul, didn't you?" I manage to inject some levity into my tone, hoping it will lighten the mood.

He chuckles, a sound so familiar yet achingly distant. "Yeah, well, that's what happens when you're trying to dig yourself out of a hole."

We share a moment of laughter, a brief respite from the tension, and I can feel a crack forming in the wall I've built around my heart. "It was...raw," I say slowly, searching for the right words. "And honest. I can't say I expected that from you."

"I've got layers, you know," he replies, his voice lightening. "Like an onion. Or a cake. You choose."

"A cake sounds more appealing," I tease, leaning against the counter. "What kind of cake are we talking? A rich chocolate, or something more delicate, like a lemon chiffon?"

"Definitely a chocolate cake. With sprinkles on top, obviously. I'm all about the extravagance," he says, his voice growing playful.

Laughter bubbles up inside me, surprising me with its suddenness. "Sprinkles? How very avant-garde of you."

"Hey, I aim to impress," he replies, and I can almost hear the smirk on his face. The light banter opens a window of warmth between us, and for a fleeting moment, the distance created by hurt and misunderstanding fades into the background.

But the laughter soon gives way to the weight of reality, the comfort of cake talk disintegrating as I gather my thoughts. "Ethan, the thing is, I don't know if we can just laugh our way out of this. There's a lot we need to unpack."

"I know," he sighs, the playfulness slipping from his voice. "I just—I want to make this work. I don't want to lose you."

The sincerity in his tone stirs something deep within me, an ache for the connection we once had, the dreams we had woven together. "What does 'making it work' look like for you?"

"Honestly? I think it starts with us being honest about everything—no more hiding, no more pretending. I don't want you to feel like you can't talk to me, like you have to hold everything in."

I chew on that for a moment, weighing his words against the memories of our past misunderstandings. "It's just so easy to slip into that, isn't it? Pretending everything is okay when it's not."

"Exactly. But I want to be the person you can rely on, not someone who adds to your burdens."

I swallow hard, the lump in my throat a mixture of emotions. "And what if you are that person? What if you're already doing the opposite?"

Silence stretches between us, each second ticking by like a clock counting down to something monumental. "I guess it's about being brave, right?" he finally says, his voice softening. "Brave enough to face the mess we've made together."

"Bravery seems overrated sometimes," I say, trying to inject a little levity. "It would be nice if we could just, you know, hit a reset button and pretend like none of this ever happened."

"If only," he replies, his tone teasing but laced with sincerity. "But where's the fun in that? We need to embrace the chaos. That's how we learn."

"Embracing chaos sounds exhausting," I say, half-joking, yet feeling the weight of truth in my words.

"Yeah, but it also sounds like us," he replies, a hint of determination in his voice. "What do you say we tackle it together? You and me against the world?"

I close my eyes, picturing him standing there, a goofy smile plastered across his face, as if he were offering me a partnership in this beautiful mess we call life. The warmth of his proposal melts the last remnants of my hesitation, and I find myself smiling, a small spark of hope igniting in my chest.

"Alright, Ethan. Let's do this."

His breath hitches slightly, a sound of relief that echoes through the line. "You won't regret it."

"Famous last words," I say, a playful challenge lacing my tone, and the tension that has hung over us begins to dissipate.

We share a moment of laughter, and in that brief exchange, I realize that while love may not be the tidy fairytale I once dreamed of, it is something raw and real, just like us. And maybe, just maybe, that's more than enough.

The morning light filters through the window, illuminating the kitchen with a golden glow that feels almost ethereal. I stand by the counter, cradling a mug of coffee, the warmth seeping into my palms like a gentle promise of a new day. The air is thick with the aroma of freshly brewed coffee, mingling with the sweet scent of vanilla candles I've taken to lighting as a small act of self-care. Today feels different, and not just because I'm wearing my favorite sweater—though it does have a way of making me feel invincible.

Ethan's words still echo in my mind, a constant reminder of our conversation. With every sip of coffee, I remind myself that I've agreed to embrace the chaos, to let down the walls I've built around my heart. Maybe I'm ready to face the messiness of our love. I take a deep breath, grounding myself in the moment, when the familiar ping of a text breaks the spell.

It's from Ethan. My heart skips, a blend of excitement and trepidation washing over me.

"Can we talk later? I found something."

What could he possibly have found? My mind races, each scenario more outrageous than the last. I imagine him uncovering a hidden treasure, or perhaps a long-lost letter from an ex—something that would throw another curveball into our already tangled web. I type back quickly, my fingers moving faster than my thoughts. "Sure. What did you find?"

His response is almost immediate, like he's waiting with bated breath. "I'll explain everything in person. Can you meet me at the park?"

I hesitate, the thrill of the unknown sending tingles up my spine. The park is where we first met, a serendipitous encounter that sparked the beginning of our story. "In an hour?" I type, trying to mask the flutter of nerves in my stomach.

"Perfect. See you soon."

As I sip my coffee, I feel a rush of anticipation mixed with anxiety. I think back to that day in the park, how our lives collided like two comets streaking across the night sky. The vibrant green of the trees, the laughter of children playing, and the sound of birds chirping created a symphony that had pulled me in. I can still picture Ethan, hands tucked in his pockets, casually leaning against the wooden bench, a smile dancing on his lips as he caught my eye.

Now, here we are again, on the precipice of something uncertain, but perhaps beautiful in its own right. I finish my coffee and change into something comfortable yet flattering—maybe today's the day I show him that I can embrace the chaos with style. The minutes tick by like slow-moving molasses, each second stretching as I throw on some jeans and a simple top, a flicker of hope igniting within me.

As I walk to the park, the world around me feels alive, each step buoyed by the promise of renewal. I find myself grinning like an idiot at the thought of what Ethan might reveal. What has he uncovered that could possibly change everything? My heart races with curiosity, fueling my pace until I finally arrive, breathless and slightly out of sorts.

Ethan stands by the fountain, his figure silhouetted against the sun, casting a long shadow across the grass. There's an intensity in his posture that sets my nerves on edge. As I approach, his eyes lock onto mine, and the world around us fades into a gentle hush.

"Hey," I say, trying to keep my voice steady despite the rapid beating of my heart.

"Hey," he replies, and there's a depth in his voice that sends a shiver down my spine. "Thanks for coming."

"Of course. You said you found something? What is it?"

He looks down for a moment, gathering his thoughts, and I catch a glimpse of his vulnerability—an unguarded moment that makes my heart ache. "I did some digging. You remember how we talked about being honest with each other?"

"Yeah, I remember," I say, the seriousness of our conversation settling over us like a heavy blanket.

He takes a deep breath, his gaze steady on mine. "I think it's time I show you my truth, too. Something about my past I've been too scared to share."

My stomach flips, a knot tightening as I sense the weight of his words. "What do you mean?"

Before he can answer, a child bursts into laughter nearby, breaking the tension momentarily. I glance over, grateful for the distraction, but Ethan's focus is unwavering, a storm brewing behind his calm exterior.

"It's about my family," he begins, his voice low. "There are things I've never told you—things I thought I could bury."

I nod, urging him to continue, the curiosity mingling with dread. "Okay."

He rubs the back of his neck, a nervous habit I've come to recognize. "When I was a kid, my family was...complicated. We moved a lot. My dad struggled with...well, everything. I think I've tried to shield you from that part of me."

"I understand," I say softly, encouraging him to keep going.

"But it's more than just my dad's issues," he says, his voice breaking slightly. "I had a brother—a twin, actually. He was...different. He had a lot of challenges, and I spent my whole life trying to protect him."

"Ethan, I—"

"Wait, let me finish," he interrupts, his gaze fierce, almost pleading. "When I went to college, things took a turn. I had to make a choice between my family and my future. I chose school, and I never looked back. I thought I was doing the right thing, but I left him behind."

His words hang in the air like a weight, a sudden chill creeping into the warm afternoon. The gravity of what he's sharing sinks in, and my heart aches for the burden he's carried alone for so long.

"I'm so sorry," I whisper, feeling the heat of tears prick at my eyes.

"And now, after everything that's happened between us, I can't keep this to myself any longer," he continues, his voice stronger now. "I need you to understand why I sometimes feel like I'm not enough."

"I don't want you to feel that way," I say, my voice trembling. "You're so much more than your past."

He meets my gaze, determination burning in his eyes. "But it's important you know. Because I'm scared that if you truly understand me, you might leave."

"I won't leave," I promise, desperation creeping into my tone. "We're in this together, remember?"

He hesitates, a flicker of doubt crossing his features. "I want to believe that, but there's something else. Something I didn't just uncover about my family."

The air grows thicker, an almost electric tension spiraling between us. I step closer, my heart pounding as his next words hang in the balance. "What is it?"

Ethan takes a deep breath, his expression shifting into something darker, something almost fearful. "My brother... he's not just my past. He's here. And I think he's been looking for me."

The revelation hits me like a thunderbolt, my mind reeling as the weight of his words sinks in. I open my mouth to respond, but the sound of footsteps interrupts, the rustle of leaves signaling someone approaching. My heart races as I glance over Ethan's shoulder, the reality of the moment crashing down like waves against the shore.

There, stepping into the clearing, is a figure I never expected to see—a shadow from his past emerging into our present, igniting a storm I can't yet comprehend.

Chapter 26: A New Beginning

The park is alive with the vibrant chaos of autumn. Leaves spiral through the air, casting dappled shadows on the path as they dance to the ground, each one a tiny celebration of change. I tread carefully, aware that my heart is not just racing from the chill in the air but also from the anticipation of what lies ahead. There's something magical about the way nature seems to mirror our own transformations, a reminder that endings can be as beautiful as beginnings.

When I spot Ethan beneath the towering oak where we had first bared our souls, my breath catches in my throat. He stands with his hands shoved deep in the pockets of his jacket, a familiar frown etched across his brow, but today, it feels less like a wall and more like a doorway. The sun hangs low, casting a golden hue around him, and for a fleeting moment, he appears almost ethereal—like someone who has stepped out of my dreams and into this tangled reality.

"Hey," I say, my voice barely above a whisper. It feels monumental, like a fragile bridge spanning the chasm between us.

He looks up, surprise flickering in his eyes, swiftly followed by that trademark smile of his, the one that had once melted all my reservations. "Hey yourself. Ready to talk?"

The weight of those words hangs in the air, thick and palpable. I nod, feeling the thrill of possibility curling in my stomach like the last remnants of summer, refusing to fade just yet.

We walk side by side along the winding path, the crunch of leaves beneath our feet punctuating the silence that envelops us. There's an unspoken understanding that today is different. No more rehearsed arguments or wallowing in regrets; today, we peel back the layers of hurt and fear that have piled up between us like autumn debris.

"I've missed this," I admit, gesturing at the world around us, the golden glow of late afternoon settling comfortably over the park. "Being here with you, just talking."

"Me too." His voice is a gentle murmur, and it sends a shiver down my spine, awakening feelings I had thought were buried deep within. "I've thought about it a lot. About us. And what we're doing."

We stop at a bench, the weathered wood a sturdy reminder of the countless conversations it has witnessed. I sit down, pulling my knees up to my chest, instinctively seeking comfort. Ethan takes a seat beside me, our shoulders brushing ever so slightly, igniting a spark that I desperately want to fan into flame.

"What do you want, Ethan?" The question slips out before I can hold it back, the urgency of it striking me like a sudden gust of wind.

He runs a hand through his hair, a gesture both anxious and hopeful. "I want to figure things out. I want to understand what went wrong and how we can fix it. I don't want to lose you."

His honesty washes over me, a balm for my weary heart. "I don't want to lose you either," I reply, my voice stronger than I feel. "But what if we can't fix it? What if the cracks are too deep?"

Ethan leans in, his intensity pulling me closer to him, both physically and emotionally. "Sometimes," he says softly, "the cracks are what let the light in. It's not about erasing the past; it's about learning from it, you know? We've both made mistakes, but we're not defined by them."

A flicker of hope ignites in my chest, battling the shadows of doubt. "So, what do we do now?"

He takes a breath, the weight of our shared history swirling in the air around us. "We take it one day at a time. We start over. With honesty. With courage."

His words hang there, a promise wrapped in vulnerability, and I can feel the warmth of his determination radiating toward me. It's infectious, and I find myself leaning into it, allowing myself to imagine a future where we navigate the tumult together instead of apart.

"Okay," I say, a smile breaking through my uncertainty. "One day at a time. I can do that."

"Good," he replies, his eyes brightening. "Because I'm not giving up on us."

There's a moment of silence where the world feels suspended, the beauty of our surroundings sharpening as if nature itself is holding its breath, waiting for us to take the plunge. I glance at Ethan, and our gazes lock—a connection deeper than the churning currents of our past, one that promises something new, something tender.

Suddenly, he breaks the moment with a chuckle, shaking his head as if shaking off the weight of our conversation. "You know, when we first met, I thought you were just going to be this quiet girl who hid behind her books."

I laugh, warmth blooming within me, delighted to see the playful side of him emerge. "Well, I thought you were just another jock who cared more about his hair than his heart."

His laughter mingles with mine, a lightness filling the space between us, puncturing the seriousness of our previous words. "Touché," he concedes, feigning offense, his hand clutching his chest dramatically. "But I've grown on you, right?"

"Like a stubborn weed," I tease, but there's a fondness in my tone, a recognition that beneath the layers of our flaws lies something beautiful.

The sun dips lower in the sky, and the chill in the air becomes more pronounced, but I barely notice. The warmth between us eclipses the autumn bite, each shared laugh melting away the edges of our uncertainties. Today is not just a chance to redefine our relationship; it feels like an invitation to discover who we could become—not just as a couple but as individuals who dare to open their hearts and embrace the unknown.

The shadows stretch long as the sun sinks lower, casting a warm, golden light that dances through the branches overhead. I can feel the softness of the leaves underfoot, the crisp air mingling with a sense of something blossoming between us. We laugh, trading stories about our lives, the moments that shaped us, and the random quirks that make us who we are. The weight of unspoken words is still there, but now it feels lighter, buoyed by shared memories and tentative hopes.

"I can't believe you used to believe in those ridiculous horoscopes," Ethan says, a teasing smile tugging at his lips as he nudges me playfully. "What was it? Something about love at first sight?"

"Hey, it was a very convincing article," I defend, feigning indignation. "Besides, you were all mysterious and broody. What was I supposed to think?"

He raises an eyebrow, leaning back against the bench, arms crossed over his chest as if guarding his secrets. "Broody? You mean deep and introspective, right?"

"Sure, let's go with that," I reply, unable to contain a smirk. "If by 'deep' you mean avoiding eye contact like it's a contagious disease, then yes, you were very deep."

Ethan chuckles, and I can see the tension ease from his shoulders, like the clouds parting after a storm. It's a revelation that he's still the same person I fell for—a little older, maybe a bit more jaded, but undeniably him. "Okay, fine. I'll admit, I was a little intense," he concedes. "But it's not my fault you made me feel things."

"Ah, so I'm the problem?" I say, feigning shock, though my heart leaps at his confession.

"Not a problem. More like... a delightful complication," he corrects, a cheeky glint in his eye.

"Delightful, huh?" I muse, tilting my head as I study him. "What else did I inspire in you? Anxiety? Existential dread?"

He shakes his head, laughter spilling from his lips. "A little dread, maybe. But mostly just an overwhelming urge to figure out how to get you to smile."

My breath hitches, caught somewhere between amusement and vulnerability. The honesty in his words washes over me like a gentle tide, erasing the distance we had built around our hearts. Just when I think we might linger in this light-hearted space forever, a shadow falls across his face.

"Seriously though," he continues, his tone shifting to something more earnest, "I've been doing a lot of thinking. About why we got so lost in the first place."

The air thickens, and I can almost feel the familiar weight of regret settle back in, but I refuse to let it anchor me. "We both made mistakes, Ethan. It wasn't just you."

"I know. But I think I was scared. Scared of being vulnerable, of letting you in. And then when everything blew up, I didn't know how to handle it."

I nod, feeling a pang of empathy for the boy I knew. "You were trying to protect yourself. I get that. But in the process, you pushed me away. And it hurt."

He looks down at his hands, the honesty in his expression turning somber. "I never wanted to hurt you. I just... I thought if I could just keep it all bottled up, I could keep you safe."

I reach out, placing my hand over his, grounding him with my warmth. "But you were hurting me anyway, Ethan. We're stronger together than apart."

He glances up, his eyes meeting mine, and for a moment, the world around us fades. The tension between us transforms into something electric, igniting a spark that feels both familiar and new. "You really believe that?"

"I do," I reply, conviction solid in my voice. "If we're going to make this work, we have to be honest. No more hiding."

His gaze flickers with uncertainty, and for a split second, I worry that my words might send him spiraling back into his shell. But then he takes a deep breath, and I can almost see the gears turning in his mind. "Okay, then. What do you want to know?"

The question hangs there, pregnant with possibility. I consider it, the weight of our past pressing against the edges of my mind. "What's the one thing you wish you could go back and change?"

He takes a moment, his brow furrowing in thought. "I wish I had just told you how I felt. I kept thinking you'd figure it out on your own, but I was so wrapped up in my own head that I never gave you a chance."

"That sounds familiar," I reply, a soft laugh escaping me despite the tension. "I could have used a little more clarity back then too."

Ethan's expression softens, the remnants of his earlier tension dissolving into a palpable warmth. "So, what do we do now? How do we fix this?"

"We start by being honest about everything—about our fears, our dreams, our ridiculous quirks," I suggest, my heart pounding as I speak. "We have to lay it all on the table, no more hiding behind walls."

"Alright," he agrees, a glimmer of excitement sparking in his eyes. "But I warn you, my quirks can be pretty bizarre. I may or may not have a thing for collecting spoons."

"Like silver spoons?" I inquire, my brow arched in mock disbelief. "Or just any spoon?"

"Any spoon!" he exclaims, and we both burst into laughter, the sound ringing through the crisp air, light and liberating. "I have this whole display in my room—it's a very carefully curated collection."

"Wow, Ethan. I always knew you were a man of taste," I tease, a grin stretching across my face.

He shrugs, a playful glint in his eye. "What can I say? I have a flair for the unique."

The banter continues, each exchange drawing us closer, peeling back the layers we had wrapped around ourselves for so long. I find solace in our laughter, the way it weaves through the tension like a thread of gold. Each story shared feels like a small victory, a step toward rebuilding the bridge we had once crossed with such ease.

As the sun dips below the horizon, the air grows cooler, but I'm wrapped in a warmth that has nothing to do with the season. It's the warmth of possibility, of new beginnings, and for the first time in a long time, I feel a flicker of hope kindling in my chest. We're no longer just two people standing on the precipice of uncertainty; we're partners in this dance, ready to step forward into the unknown.

The shadows deepen around us as twilight creeps in, painting the park in shades of indigo and burnt orange. The air is tinged with the scent of damp earth and fallen leaves, and it feels like nature is wrapping us in a cozy embrace, shielding us from the weight of the world beyond our bubble. As laughter spills from our lips, I can't help but feel the fragile threads of our connection weaving tighter, a tapestry of shared moments and budding hope.

"Okay, my turn for a weird quirk," I announce, leaning in conspiratorially, the thrill of vulnerability dancing on the tip of my tongue. "I'm a closet soap opera fan."

Ethan bursts into laughter, the sound bright and infectious. "No way! You? A soap opera fanatic? I would've pegged you as the documentary type."

"Guilty as charged!" I say, throwing my hands up in mock defeat. "But sometimes, after a long day, I just need to watch people make terrible life choices while I eat ice cream. It's therapeutic."

He shakes his head, still chuckling. "Alright, I can't argue with that logic. My guilty pleasure is... getting lost in cheesy rom-coms."

"Cheesy rom-coms?" I feign shock, hand over my heart. "Ethan, I never took you for a hopeless romantic."

"Hopelessly romantic?" he retorts, a mischievous glint in his eyes. "Let's not get carried away. I just appreciate a good love story, you know? Like the kind where the guy finally figures out how to not screw everything up."

"Touché," I concede, laughing. "We should have a movie night, then. I can teach you about the beauty of dramatic plot twists, and you can show me how to appreciate the subtleties of Hallmark magic."

"Deal," he says, a warmth spreading across his face. "But be warned, I may require popcorn and a heartfelt confession by the end."

As we joke back and forth, I can feel the walls between us crumbling, revealing the genuine affection buried beneath the rubble of our past. I study his face, illuminated by the fading light, and I realize that this is the Ethan I remember—the one who could make me laugh even in the darkest moments.

"Okay, enough about us," I say, suddenly serious. "What do you want in life, really? Not just the cute quirks and movie preferences. What do you want for yourself?"

He pauses, his expression shifting into something more contemplative. "I want to feel like I'm doing something that matters. Something that has purpose. I want to help people, you know? But I keep getting lost in my own fears."

I nod, the weight of his words settling between us. "I get that. It's so easy to get caught up in the noise, to let fear dictate your choices."

"Exactly," he says, his voice firm yet laced with vulnerability. "But I think I've realized that I don't want fear to control me anymore. Not when it comes to you."

The moment hangs heavy in the air, and I can feel the pulse of something profound thrumming between us. "So, what's stopping you?"

His gaze locks onto mine, and I can see the fire igniting in his eyes. "Nothing," he says simply. "Nothing is stopping me anymore."

Just as the promise of something beautiful blooms, my phone buzzes violently in my pocket, a stark reminder of reality. I pull it out, glancing at the screen, and my heart plummets. Madison's name flashes across it, and the familiar knot of dread tightens in my stomach.

"Who is it?" Ethan asks, a shadow passing over his features.

"Madison," I reply, my voice strained. "I should probably answer."

"Maybe it can wait?" he suggests, his expression shifting from concern to frustration. "We were having a moment here."

"I know," I sigh, torn between the bliss of this connection and the nagging urgency of my best friend's call. "But what if something's wrong?"

"Then you handle it and come back," he says, his tone firm yet gentle. "We've made progress, and I don't want to lose it over a phone call."

I nod, but the anxiety is already bubbling up inside me. With a deep breath, I swipe to answer, bracing myself for whatever news awaits. "Hey, Madison, what's up?"

"Emily! You need to get over here now," she says, her voice laced with urgency. "It's about Ethan."

My heart races as I exchange glances with him. "What do you mean? What's wrong?"

"I can't explain it all over the phone, but you need to see this. Please."

The weight of her words slams into me like a freight train, and I'm already scrambling for my bag, adrenaline coursing through my veins. "I'm on my way."

I hang up and look at Ethan, whose expression has darkened. "What did she say?"

"I don't know," I admit, panic rising. "But it sounds serious. I have to go."

"Emily, wait," he says, grabbing my wrist. "You can't just run off like this. We were finally getting somewhere!"

"I know!" I shout, frustration spilling over. "But this is Madison! I can't leave her hanging."

He releases my wrist, stepping back as if my urgency has created a chasm between us once more. "Fine, but I want you to promise me something."

"What?"

"Promise you'll come back. I won't let you disappear again."

"I promise," I say, the sincerity of my voice piercing through the uncertainty that looms over us. I take a step back, the distance feeling heavier than the weight of the world.

As I turn to leave, the night wraps around me like a cloak, the park fading into the backdrop of my thoughts. The trees whisper secrets in the wind, and the shadows deepen with each step I take away from him, each heartbeat echoing in the silence. My mind races with questions, doubts, and the lingering warmth of our conversation.

What could Madison possibly have to say about Ethan? My heart thumps in my chest, a frantic rhythm urging me to hurry. I dash through the park, the chill in the air biting at my skin, but it's not the cold that sends shivers down my spine. It's the uncertainty that claws at the edges of my mind, twisting and turning, making me dread what I might discover.

Just as I reach the street, the air crackles with tension, and a figure steps out of the shadows ahead. My breath catches in my throat. It's Madison, her eyes wide with panic and something else—something darker.

"Emily," she breathes, her voice trembling. "You have to see this now."

And before I can process her words, she takes my hand and pulls me toward the dimly lit alleyway behind the park. The weight of dread settles heavily in my stomach, and as I glance back over my shoulder, I catch one last glimpse of Ethan, standing alone under the fading light, the uncertainty in his eyes mirroring my own.

Chapter 27: The Final Confrontation

The sun hung low in the sky, casting a warm, golden hue over Main Street, its light filtering through the fluttering leaves of the oak trees lining the sidewalk. I stood there, a pulse of adrenaline thrumming in my chest, each beat a reminder that everything was about to change. It was as if the air itself thickened with tension, a palpable energy that wrapped around me like a second skin. My heart raced, not just from the confrontation ahead, but from the knowledge that I had finally taken a step toward reclaiming my own narrative, my own future.

Madison's silhouette cut through the late afternoon crowd, a tempest in a sea of calm. Her eyes, typically a soft shade of hazel, now flashed with a stormy intensity. The vibrant colors of the shops around us faded into a blur as I focused on her, and the world shrank to the narrow space between us. I could practically hear the collective gasps of the bystanders, a mix of shock and intrigue as they paused to witness the scene unfolding before them. But all I could feel was the weight of her words, heavy and accusing, sharp as the autumn air.

"You think you can just waltz back into his life after everything?" she spat, the bitterness lacing her voice like poison. "You've ruined everything, you know that? Ethan was happy before you decided to swoop in like some fairy-tale princess, stealing his future right from under his nose."

I felt the anger flare in my chest but fought to contain it. This wasn't about me; it never had been. "Madison," I said, my voice steady despite the tremor of emotion that threatened to rise. "Ethan made his choice. It wasn't me who pulled him away from you. It was the lies you both built your relationship on."

Her laugh was a harsh, jagged sound that shattered the stillness around us. "Lies? You think you know everything? You have no idea what we went through." She stepped closer, her hands clenched into fists at her sides, trembling with the weight of unshed tears. "He was supposed to be with me, to build a life together, and you—"

"Am I just a scapegoat for your own failure?" I interrupted, the words tumbling out before I could second-guess them. "You cling to this idea of what your life should have been, but life doesn't work that way, Madison. You can't hold onto someone who's already chosen to leave."

Her eyes widened, a flash of vulnerability breaking through her armor, but it was gone in an instant, replaced by the fierce determination that had always characterized her. "You don't know the first thing about what we had. You only see what you want to see," she retorted, but the crack in her facade lingered, a flicker of uncertainty beneath her bravado.

I took a breath, grounding myself in the reality of the moment. "You're right. I don't know everything. But I know that love isn't about possession or control. It's about support and growth, and you've suffocated him with your expectations."

Madison's expression morphed, the anger fading, revealing a rawness that made my heart ache for her, even as I stood my ground. "You think you can just take his heart and walk away unscathed? Love isn't a game, and you'll lose. You'll always lose."

The words hit me harder than I expected, a reality I had been grappling with since the moment I re-entered Ethan's life. But there was a strength in me now, a clarity that hadn't been there before. "I'm not trying to take anything from him. I just want to help him find his way back to himself. If that's a loss for you, then so be it. I can't be held responsible for your inability to let go."

Madison's face twisted with a mixture of disbelief and sorrow. "You think you're so noble, don't you? Like you're saving him from me. But what if he doesn't want to be saved? What if he's happy where he is?"

My breath caught, the sharpness of her words cutting through the warm veneer of the day. "Is he? Or are you just projecting your own desires onto him? You can't manipulate someone into loving you. It has to be genuine, or it'll fall apart, just like your relationship did."

Silence fell between us, heavy and unyielding. The crowd around us faded into a dull hum, their curiosity turning into something more uncomfortable, like spectators watching a storm unfold. Madison's shoulders sagged slightly, and for the first time, I caught a glimpse of the girl she once was—the girl who loved fiercely, who believed in forever.

But even that flicker of vulnerability was quickly smothered by her pride. "You're delusional if you think this is over," she warned, her voice low but edged with desperation. "Ethan and I will work this out. I won't let you ruin everything we built."

I held her gaze, my heart aching for both of us, knowing that sometimes love isn't enough to patch the cracks in a broken relationship. "Maybe it's time to build something new, Madison. For both of you."

She flinched at my words, a flash of anger sparking in her eyes, but I could see the conflict swirling within her, a battle between what she wanted and what she needed. And just like that, with a final huff of indignation, she turned on her heel and stormed away, leaving me standing there amidst the bustling street, a swirl of emotions whirling through me like the autumn leaves dancing in the wind.

As I watched her retreating figure, I felt an unexpected weight lift from my shoulders. The power she once held over me, the sway of her anger and hurt, was fading. It wasn't that I wished her ill; it was more that I understood the necessity of letting go, for her sake as much as mine. And as I turned to leave, the warmth of the sun felt more inviting than ever, a promise of new beginnings and uncharted paths waiting just beyond the horizon.

The streets felt both foreign and familiar as I navigated the sidewalks, my mind still buzzing from the confrontation with Madison. Main Street had always been my favorite part of town, a patchwork of quaint shops and coffee houses where laughter mingled with the aroma of freshly brewed coffee. But today, it felt charged, as if the air itself hummed with the energy of new beginnings and lingering shadows. My feet carried me past the bakery, where the scent of cinnamon rolls wafted out like a warm embrace, but I couldn't linger; I had a meeting with Ethan that demanded all my attention.

He had agreed to meet at our usual spot, a cozy little café tucked away from the hustle and bustle, where the baristas knew our orders by heart. As I pushed through the door, the little bell jingled overhead, announcing my arrival. The dim lighting and rustic decor wrapped around me, instantly soothing the jagged edges of my nerves. I spotted him at a corner table, his brow furrowed in thought as he absentmindedly stirred his coffee. A pang of affection hit me, accompanied by a wave of worry. How had we gotten here?

"Hey," I said, sliding into the chair opposite him. The moment I spoke, he looked up, and a tentative smile broke across his face, a light that momentarily chased away the shadows of our earlier conversations.

"Hey," he replied, his voice warm, though there was an underlying tension in his gaze. "I wasn't sure you'd show up after... everything."

I shrugged, feigning nonchalance while my heart raced. "What can I say? I like a challenge."

He chuckled softly, the sound both comforting and unsettling. "You're brave, I'll give you that. Madison didn't make it easy, did she?"

"No, she didn't," I said, searching his eyes for a glimmer of understanding. "But I'm not here to talk about her. I want to talk about us. I need to know where you stand."

Ethan's expression shifted, a shadow crossing his features as he looked away, stirring his coffee with newfound intensity. "I don't want to hurt you," he said finally, his voice barely above a whisper. "I just... I'm not sure if I can choose."

The admission hung between us, heavy and suffocating. My heart sank. "You mean you're not sure if you want to choose me?"

He met my gaze, his eyes filled with uncertainty. "It's not that simple. I care about you, but Madison and I have a history. It's hard to just erase that."

"History doesn't define the present," I argued, my voice gaining strength. "You're not bound to her because of what you've shared in the past. You deserve to be happy, Ethan—truly happy. And that means making a choice that's right for you, not out of obligation or fear."

He leaned back in his chair, arms crossed over his chest as if shielding himself from the truth I laid bare. "You make it sound easy. Like it's just a matter of flipping a switch."

"I know it's not easy," I countered, my heart racing with the fear of rejection. "But sometimes, the hardest choices lead to the most rewarding outcomes. You can't let Madison's expectations trap you in a life you don't want."

Ethan sighed, running a hand through his hair, frustration etched in his features. "And what if I don't know what I want yet? What if I'm still trying to figure it out?"

"That's okay," I reassured him, leaning forward to bridge the emotional gap. "But it's not fair to string either of us along while you do. You owe it to yourself, and to both of us, to be honest about your feelings."

He looked at me, the weight of my words settling into the space between us. "I just don't want to hurt her. She's been through a lot."

"She'll hurt regardless if you're not truly with her," I pointed out gently. "Staying for someone else's sake is a form of betrayal to yourself. You have to be authentic to find real happiness."

His eyes flickered with something akin to hope, and for a moment, I thought he might break through the barriers that had held him captive for so long. But just as quickly, the walls returned, fortified by fear and uncertainty. "I need time to think," he finally said, the distance in his voice like a chill sweeping through the warmth of the café.

I swallowed hard, the truth settling in my stomach like a stone. "Time? Or just more avoidance?" I asked, the sharpness in my tone surprising even me.

"I'm not avoiding anything," he shot back, the defensiveness creeping into his voice. "I'm just trying to figure out my life."

"Your life? Or the life you think you should want?" I pressed, refusing to back down. "You're a good person, Ethan, but you can't be everyone's savior. That's not your job."

His frustration boiled over, the tension in the air shifting like a sudden gust of wind. "You think I don't know that? You think I don't feel trapped? You're painting me as this helpless victim, but I'm not. I have choices!"

"Then make one!" I exclaimed, the heat of the moment igniting a fire within me. "Stop waiting for the perfect moment to decide. Life isn't waiting for you to catch up."

The silence that followed was heavy, punctuated only by the soft clinking of cups and the hum of conversation surrounding us. I could see the internal struggle flickering across his face, an emotional tug-of-war that threatened to tear him apart.

"Why is it so hard for you?" I challenged softly, my tone shifting to one of understanding. "Why do you feel like you owe Madison something when it's clear you're not happy?"

"I don't know," he said, the fight draining from his voice. "I guess I just don't want to be the bad guy. I don't want to break her heart, but I don't want to lose you either."

"Then don't," I replied, my voice steady. "You don't have to break anyone's heart to find your own happiness. You just have to be honest about what you want."

Ethan leaned back, his eyes searching mine as if trying to decipher some hidden message. The weight of his uncertainty still hung in the air, but beneath it, I sensed a glimmer of resolve starting to form, like the first rays of dawn pushing through the remnants of night. Whatever choice he made, I knew I had given him something important—a nudge toward the truth, a chance to confront his fears head-on.

But deep down, I wondered if that would be enough.

The clamor of the café faded into the background, leaving a tightness in my chest as I absorbed the uncertainty flickering in Ethan's eyes. The sunlight streaming through the window illuminated the table between us, casting a soft glow on the crumpled napkin adorned with my nervous doodles—swirls and stars, a chaotic reflection of my racing thoughts. I could feel the pressure building, an invisible force urging me to either push for clarity or retreat into the safety of silence.

"Ethan," I said, my voice softer this time, "you don't have to play the hero. It's okay to want something different, something more. You can still be a good person without sacrificing your happiness for someone else."

He looked at me, a hint of vulnerability breaking through his usually confident demeanor. "I've always felt like I had to be the one who keeps everything together. If I don't hold onto Madison, who will? She needs me."

"But do you need her?" I countered gently, aware of how this delicate question could shift the dynamics between us. "What do you need?"

His gaze dropped to the table, and for a moment, the tension between us seemed to unravel. "I don't know," he admitted, his voice barely above a whisper. "I've always put others first. It's easier that way, isn't it? Less messy."

"Life is messy," I replied, leaning in as if our connection could bridge the chasm of uncertainty that lay before us. "But that's what makes it beautiful. If you keep avoiding the mess, you'll never find the clarity you're looking for. You deserve to feel something real, Ethan."

He sighed, the weight of my words hanging in the air like the aroma of fresh coffee—inviting yet heavy. "It's just... I can't help but feel guilty. Madison has always been there. I feel like I'm betraying her if I let go."

"Sometimes, letting go is the bravest thing you can do," I said, my heart aching for both of us. "You're not responsible for her happiness, and she's not yours. You're both too smart to keep dragging this out."

Ethan's brow furrowed as he considered my words, the tension in his shoulders slowly easing. "And what if she doesn't see it that way? What if I lose her forever?"

The thought sent a chill down my spine. "But are you losing her, or are you just freeing yourself to find out who you really are without her?"

He paused, his gaze sharpening. "You make it sound so simple."

"Nothing is simple," I replied, the edge of frustration creeping into my voice. "But it's worth the risk. Life is full of uncertainty. You can choose to live it authentically, or you can stay trapped in a cycle that doesn't serve you. What do you really want?"

He hesitated, uncertainty swirling in his eyes as if my question had opened a door he wasn't ready to walk through. I could see him grappling with the weight of that choice, and I wished I could ease his burden, to give him the clarity he sought.

"I want..." he started, his voice trailing off as he leaned back in his chair, his expression one of deep contemplation. The moment hung between us like a fragile thread, ready to snap at the slightest movement.

Just as I was about to reach out and reassure him, the café door swung open with a crash, drawing our attention. Madison stood framed in the entrance, her expression a mix of determination and vulnerability. The sunlight spilled behind her like a spotlight, illuminating her as she stepped inside, an unexpected figure in this unfolding drama.

"I knew I'd find you here," she announced, her voice carrying an edge that sent a ripple of tension through the café. People turned to look, a wave of awkward curiosity rippling through the crowd.

Ethan's eyes widened, a mix of surprise and apprehension coloring his features. "Madison, wait—"

"No," she interrupted, striding forward with a fierce energy that demanded attention. "We need to talk. Now."

I felt the air shift, an uncomfortable tightness wrapping around us as she approached our table. The café's lively hum faded into an eerie silence, as if the universe held its breath, waiting for the inevitable confrontation.

"Madison, this isn't—" Ethan began, but she cut him off again, her voice rising above the quiet din.

"I'm not leaving until we sort this out," she insisted, her gaze fixed on Ethan with an intensity that burned through the air. "You can't just waltz back into my life and then run off with her. That's not how this works."

My heart raced as I exchanged glances with Ethan, whose expression shifted from surprise to guilt. The warmth of our earlier conversation dissipated like steam in the chilly air.

"Madison, please, let's talk this through," Ethan pleaded, the tension in his voice rising.

"No more talking!" she shot back, her eyes flashing with a fire that spoke of hurt and betrayal. "You owe me answers. You can't keep stringing us both along!"

Ethan glanced at me, and I saw the turmoil reflected in his eyes, the tug of loyalty battling against his desire for freedom. "I didn't mean to hurt you," he said, desperation edging his tone.

"Then show me," she challenged, crossing her arms defiantly. "Show me that you mean it. Because right now, all I see is a coward hiding behind someone else's feelings."

"Stop!" I interjected, my voice rising above the din of confusion. "This isn't about cowardice. It's about being honest."

Madison turned her piercing gaze on me, a flicker of anger and pain cutting through her façade. "And who do you think you are? Playing the hero in our story? You think you know what's best for him?"

"I'm not trying to be a hero," I replied, standing my ground. "I just want him to be happy, even if that means letting go."

The words hung heavy in the air, and for a moment, it felt as if time stood still. The tension was a taut string ready to snap, and I braced myself for the aftermath.

Madison's expression shifted, a mixture of sorrow and determination flickering in her eyes. "You may want him to be happy, but I can't just let him go without a fight."

Ethan's gaze darted between us, confusion and dread written across his face. "Madison, please—"

But before he could finish, Madison reached into her bag and pulled out a small, crumpled envelope, holding it up as if it were a weapon. "Then let's see what you really want," she said, her voice steady despite the tremor in her hands. "Because I have something that will change everything."

The café seemed to hold its breath, the tension thick enough to cut. I could feel my heart racing, a surge of anxiety flooding through me. Whatever was in that envelope could shatter the fragile truce we had built.

Ethan's face paled, and I braced myself, uncertain of what revelation was about to unfold. The air was electric, charged with uncertainty, and as I stared at Madison, a chill ran down my spine. I had the sinking feeling that whatever she was about to reveal would change everything—once and for all.

Chapter 28: Love and Light

Ethan's kitchen smelled of fresh coffee and cinnamon, the aroma curling around us like a warm hug as I stirred the batter for pancakes. The light streamed in through the window, bathing the room in a golden hue that felt almost ethereal. I whisked with purpose, letting the rhythmic motion ease the lingering tension that sometimes crept in, the kind born from years of misunderstandings and shadows. Each swirl of the spoon was a promise, a reaffirmation of the trust we were trying to build again. The quiet moments—like this one—became the threads weaving our new life together, each breakfast a stitch reinforcing the fabric of our relationship.

"Are you sure that's enough sugar?" Ethan's voice was playful, laced with a teasing tone that made me smile, the corners of my mouth lifting before I even turned to face him. He leaned against the doorframe, his arms crossed, a half-smirk playing on his lips as he watched me with those deep, inquisitive eyes. They always held a spark of mischief, as if he were perpetually amused by my attempts to concoct something edible.

"It's the secret ingredient, I swear," I replied, my tone light, attempting to sound confident despite my inner turmoil. The truth was, my cooking skills were as shaky as our past. But this was different. I could feel it in the air, thick with the scent of possibility. This wasn't about impressing him; it was about us.

"Your 'secret' could easily be mistaken for a sugar bomb," he shot back, stepping into the kitchen and getting closer. The warmth of his presence wrapped around me, igniting a flutter in my chest that I'd longed to feel again. It was intoxicating and terrifying all at once.

"Are you trying to imply that I'm trying to poison you?" I raised an eyebrow, my playful retort barely masking the vulnerability hiding just beneath the surface. It was a joke, one we both shared, but I could sense the edge of seriousness that lurked beneath my words.

Our history was a tapestry of trust eroded by secrets, and sometimes, I still feared the ghosts of our past would come back to haunt us.

"Maybe just a little," he chuckled, stepping back as I tossed a handful of flour in his direction, which he dodged with a deftness that belied his tall frame. We both erupted in laughter, the sound echoing off the kitchen walls, filling the room with a lightness I had forgotten existed between us. It was easy, too easy, but I embraced it wholeheartedly. It felt like we were finally beginning to dance to the same rhythm again, even if we occasionally stepped on each other's toes.

As the pancakes sizzled on the skillet, I stole a glance at him, his silhouette framed by the morning light, and I marveled at how different everything felt. There was an openness in the way he stood, as if he were shedding the weight of his past burdens right there in my kitchen. It was like watching a flower bloom, slowly unfurling petal by petal, revealing the colors hidden within.

"Do you ever think about how crazy life is?" I asked, flipping a pancake with more confidence than I felt. "Like, we were in such different places not too long ago, and now here we are—making breakfast together like we've been doing this forever."

His smile faded slightly, replaced by a thoughtful expression that made me hold my breath. "Yeah, I think about it a lot. Sometimes it feels like we're two puzzle pieces that finally fit, and other times... it's like we're still trying to figure out the picture."

His honesty struck me, cutting through the lightness like a knife. I wanted to push away the doubt that lingered in the air, the uncertainty that haunted our laughter. "It's okay to take our time, you know? We don't have to rush into anything," I said softly, a quiet reassurance that mirrored my own hopes.

"Taking our time sounds perfect," he agreed, a glimmer of relief dancing in his eyes. "As long as I get pancakes, I think I can handle the slow approach."

BRIDGING THE UNSEEN

We finished breakfast with light banter and stolen glances, the kind that sparked with unspoken feelings and the promise of what was to come. Afterward, we cleaned up together, our movements falling into a comfortable rhythm, and I felt the corners of my heart begin to soften. The past still loomed over us like a specter, but we were learning to navigate it, step by cautious step.

Once the dishes were washed, Ethan leaned against the counter, watching me as I wiped my hands on a towel. "So, what's next for us?" he asked, his tone shifting to something more serious, a glint of hope intertwined with uncertainty. It was a question that hung in the air, fragile yet heavy, as if it contained the weight of our future.

I paused, considering the best way to answer. "I think... I think we just need to keep being honest with each other. No more secrets, right? Just love and light. That's the goal."

He nodded, the corners of his mouth lifting into a small smile that made my heart race. "Love and light, huh? Sounds like a cheesy motto, but I think I can get on board with it."

"It's our motto now," I declared, grinning back at him. "We're the authors of our own story. Let's make it a good one."

And with that, a new chapter of our lives began to unfold, written in the laughter that echoed in the walls of my kitchen, the lightness of our spirits soaring high above the burdens we had carried for too long. The world outside still held its judgments, the whispers of our past trailing behind us like shadows, but in this moment, it didn't matter. All that mattered was the warmth radiating between us, the soft laughter dancing in the air, and the promise of new beginnings.

The sun hung low in the sky, casting a warm golden glow across the town as Ethan and I strolled down the main street, hand in hand. The air was filled with the scent of blooming lilacs and fresh-cut grass, wrapping around us like a soft embrace. We passed the little café where we'd spent many afternoons, our conversations punctuated by laughter and the clinking of coffee cups. It felt like an eternity ago, that past life of uncertainty and half-hearted attempts at connection. Now, each step together was infused with a lightness I had almost forgotten existed.

"Do you remember the first time we came here?" I asked, my voice laced with nostalgia. "You spilled your coffee all over that cute waitress's apron."

"Hey, that was a strategic move," he retorted, feigning offense, his eyes sparkling with mischief. "I had to make a lasting impression. What better way than to give her a story to tell?"

I rolled my eyes playfully. "I think she still talks about the guy who tried to flirt while mopping up coffee from her shoes."

"Mission accomplished, then!" he laughed, and I couldn't help but join in, the sound mingling with the gentle hum of the town around us.

As we continued walking, I noticed the familiar faces of our neighbors passing by, their gazes lingering just a second longer than usual. I felt the prickle of their judgment, a reminder that the whispers of our past still echoed in the streets. But with Ethan beside me, those stares lost their power. We were forging our own path, and I was determined not to let anyone derail us.

"Let's grab ice cream," I suggested, glancing toward the brightly painted shop that had become a staple of our summer afternoons. "I need something sweet to balance out the bitterness of small-town gossip."

"Agreed," he replied, a grin spreading across his face. "But I'm getting the biggest scoop they have. It's time to celebrate our newfound status as 'the couple that survived the scandal.'"

I laughed, shaking my head. "You're not serious."

"Oh, I'm dead serious. We deserve a trophy for that. Ice cream is just the first step. I might even consider naming a street after us," he quipped, his tone dripping with playful mockery.

We entered the shop, the bell above the door chiming cheerfully. The air was cool and heavy with the scent of sugar, and I felt my heart swell with delight. We approached the counter, and Ethan eagerly scanned the array of flavors, his excitement palpable.

"Okay, I'm thinking double chocolate fudge brownie with extra sprinkles," he declared, grinning like a child on Christmas morning.

"Too predictable," I teased, nudging him with my shoulder. "You've got to think outside the box. How about lavender honey? It's unique, just like us."

Ethan raised an eyebrow, considering my suggestion. "Lavender honey? Are we still talking about ice cream, or have we stumbled into a spa retreat?"

"Hey, don't knock it till you try it!" I shot back, determined to coax him out of his comfort zone. "I mean, we're all about new beginnings, right?"

"Fine, I'll be brave. But only if you promise to share your scoop of chocolate peanut butter bliss," he countered, a mock-seriousness settling on his features.

"Deal!" I laughed, feeling the ease of our banter wash over me. It felt good—no, it felt great—to be lighthearted again, to savor these moments of joy without the weight of past mistakes.

As we made our way back outside, our cones in hand, the sun began its descent, painting the sky with hues of pink and orange. We found a bench near the park, and I sat down, savoring the first bite of my lavender honey ice cream. The flavor was unexpected, floral yet comforting, and I watched as Ethan dug into his chocolate peanut butter bliss with the enthusiasm of a kid at a birthday party.

"You should really try this," he said, holding out his cone toward me, his eyes sparkling with mischief. "It's like a party in your mouth. Want a taste?"

"Only if I can have a taste of your lavender honey," I countered, my heart swelling at the simple intimacy of our exchange.

"Deal," he replied, and as our cones met in a small clink, I felt a spark of something that reminded me of the magic we had once shared. The kind of connection that was tender yet electric, sparking with the potential of what was to come.

"So, what's the plan for the rest of the weekend?" I asked, licking the melting ice cream that threatened to drip onto my hand.

"Well, I thought we could finally check out that hiking trail everyone's been raving about. You know, the one with the breathtaking views?" He leaned in closer, his enthusiasm contagious.

I tilted my head, considering his suggestion. "Are you sure you're ready for an adventure? I mean, what if we get lost? The last thing I want is to be the girl who drags the great Ethan Thomas into the wilderness and gets us hopelessly turned around."

"Then I'll just charm the trees into showing us the way," he joked, but his eyes sparkled with a hint of genuine excitement. "Come on, it'll be fun! Just imagine us, surrounded by nature, laughing at our own clumsiness as we stumble through the underbrush."

"You do realize you're describing a scene straight out of a rom-com, right?" I said, smirking as I imagined us in such a ridiculous situation.

"And I'd say we're pretty much a rom-com at this point," he replied, a cheeky grin on his face. "Complete with a whimsical soundtrack and a dramatic plot twist at every corner."

I took a moment to consider it, the idea of a hiking trip sending a thrill through me. "All right, you've convinced me. Just promise to not let me fall off a cliff or anything," I said, rolling my eyes as I leaned back against the bench, letting the last rays of sunlight warm my skin.

"Cross my heart," he replied, lifting a finger to his lips in mock solemnity. "You'll be perfectly safe with me, even if I have to pull you back from the edge of oblivion."

We both burst into laughter, the sound ringing out like music in the twilight, resonating with the warmth of our shared hopes and dreams. It was an adventure waiting to unfold, a promise of new beginnings as vibrant and unpredictable as the colors streaking across the sky. In that moment, I felt truly alive, ready to embrace whatever lay ahead—together.

The next morning dawned bright and clear, the sunlight filtering through my bedroom window, casting a warm glow over everything it touched. Ethan had spent the night, and I woke to the comforting rhythm of his breathing beside me, a sound I never wanted to forget. As I turned to face him, I couldn't help but smile. He looked peaceful, tousled hair falling over his forehead, lips slightly parted as if he were caught in a dream of endless possibilities.

I carefully slid out of bed, careful not to disturb him, and tiptoed into the kitchen. The aroma of fresh coffee filled the air as I prepared to start the day. There was something exhilarating about the routine we were carving out, something comforting in the mundane tasks that now felt rich with potential. I poured two cups, relishing the rich, dark brew, and considered what we had planned. The hike was on the agenda, a chance to immerse ourselves in nature, to escape the weight of our past and step into something new together.

As I poured a splash of cream into the second cup, my phone buzzed on the counter. I glanced at the screen, my heart dropping when I saw the name flashing there: Sarah. She was my closest friend, but her calls rarely held good news these days. I hesitated, a lump forming in my throat as I accepted the call.

"Hey," I answered, trying to sound upbeat. "What's up?"

"Hey, I just wanted to check in on you," she said, her voice tight with concern. "I heard about the incident at the park yesterday. The whole town is buzzing."

The weight of her words pressed down on me, and I clenched the phone tighter. "What incident?" I asked, trying to mask the anxiety creeping into my tone.

"The police were called because someone saw you and Ethan together, and they were worried. You know how people are around here. They love a good drama," she replied, her voice laced with sympathy. "I thought you should know."

A wave of frustration washed over me. "Of course, they'd twist it into something dramatic," I muttered, glancing toward the bedroom where Ethan still slept, blissfully unaware. "We're just trying to move forward, but it feels like we're always being pulled back into the past."

"I know it's tough," she said softly. "But you two are trying to build something real. Just keep your heads up. Ignore the noise."

"Yeah, easier said than done," I sighed. "Thanks for letting me know. I'll talk to you later."

After ending the call, I stood still for a moment, letting the reality of our situation settle in. The walls of my sanctuary felt like they were closing in, and I took a deep breath, forcing myself to shake off the weight of the gossip. This was our life, and I was determined not to let anyone else dictate how we lived it.

I finished preparing the coffee and set it on the bedside table, watching Ethan as he stirred awake, a sleepy smile breaking across his face when he spotted me. "Good morning, sunshine," he said, his voice gravelly with sleep.

"Morning! I brought you coffee." I leaned down to kiss him, savoring the warmth of his body against mine. "We have a slight hiccup with our plans today."

"Oh? Do tell," he said, taking a sip from his cup and raising an eyebrow.

"Sarah called. Apparently, the town is buzzing again. They're worried about us. Someone saw us at the park yesterday and decided it was worth calling the police."

Ethan's expression darkened, and he set his cup down with a thud. "Seriously? Can't people mind their own business for once?"

"Exactly," I replied, frustration rising in my chest. "But it feels like they're trying to drag us back into the chaos, and I don't want that. I just want to be with you and enjoy what we have."

He reached for my hand, squeezing it tightly. "Then let's not let them ruin our plans. We'll go for that hike and let the world spin on without us for a while. We deserve that."

The fire in his voice made me feel a little lighter, and I nodded, determined not to let anything steal our joy. We finished our coffee and dressed for the day, my heart racing with anticipation of our adventure. The air outside was crisp, invigorating, as we stepped into the sunlight.

The drive to the trailhead was filled with laughter, the kind that bubbled up effortlessly between us. I felt a thrill of excitement as we parked and made our way to the entrance of the trail. The trees loomed tall and majestic, their leaves whispering secrets to one another, and I felt the world quiet around us as we ventured deeper into the woods.

Ethan led the way, his long strides carrying us over the uneven terrain. I took in the sights, the bursts of wildflowers splattered across the ground like nature's confetti, and the sounds of birds chirping overhead. Each step felt liberating, washing away the doubts that had crept in with the morning light.

"You know," he said, glancing back at me with a playful grin, "I'm starting to think that this hike might be more than just a stroll in the woods. It could be a pivotal moment in our story."

I laughed, matching his pace. "Pivotal? Really? You're laying it on a bit thick, don't you think?"

"Hey, I'm just trying to emphasize the significance of this adventure," he replied, mock-serious. "There could be metaphors, like conquering mountains or overcoming obstacles."

"Or slipping on rocks and falling face-first into the dirt," I countered, remembering my own tendency to trip over my own feet.

Ethan chuckled, and for a moment, it felt like nothing could touch us. But just as we rounded a bend in the trail, a strange noise broke the harmony of our laughter. It was faint at first, like a low murmur. My instincts kicked in, and I slowed my pace, glancing around.

"What's that?" I asked, my heart racing.

Ethan's expression shifted as he strained to listen. "I don't know. It sounds... odd."

As we approached a clearing, the noise grew louder—shouts, urgent and panicked. Our laughter faded, replaced by a sense of foreboding. We exchanged uneasy glances, and I could feel the tension building between us.

"What if it's just hikers?" I suggested, attempting to quell the anxiety creeping into my mind.

"Let's check it out," Ethan said, his voice steady but laced with an undercurrent of concern. We edged closer, the trees parting to reveal a scene that stopped us in our tracks.

A group of people stood gathered around something—or someone—on the ground. Their faces were grim, and the atmosphere was thick with a sense of urgency. The murmur of voices heightened my anxiety, my heart pounding as we took a cautious step forward.

"Is that...?" I started, but Ethan grabbed my arm, his grip firm, grounding me as we moved closer.

In the center of the crowd, a figure lay sprawled on the ground, a dark pool of crimson forming beneath them. My stomach dropped as I took in the sight, the reality of the moment crashing down like a wave. The noise in my ears dulled, and my mind raced with disbelief.

"Oh no," I whispered, horror creeping into my voice.

Ethan's grip tightened as he pulled me back slightly, the reality of our world shifting beneath our feet. Just then, a familiar face broke through the crowd, panic etched across her features.

"Call 911!" Sarah yelled, her voice slicing through the tension like a knife. "We need help!"

I froze, the world around me blurring into a haze. I felt Ethan's presence beside me, steady and reassuring, but my mind was spinning. The tranquility of our hike had shattered in an instant, replaced by chaos and fear.

"Who is it?" I gasped, searching the faces around us for answers.

But as Sarah turned, her eyes wide with dread, I felt my breath hitch. And just like that, the bright future we had been so eager to embrace slipped away, leaving only the echo of uncertainty and dread in its wake.

Chapter 29: A Promise in the Rain

The air was thick with the scent of wet earth and impending transformation, a palpable mix of petrichor and nostalgia that wrapped around me like a familiar embrace. Each raindrop danced in a chaotic rhythm against the surface of the lake, sending ripples cascading outward, as if the very essence of our past was striving to resurface, to remind me of the heartbeats and whispered secrets shared in this very spot. The world around us was blurred—a hazy fusion of grays and greens, colors muted by the heavy clouds that loomed overhead. Yet, in that darkness, I felt a spark ignite within me, an electric current threading through the storm.

Ethan stood beside me, an anchor against the tempest, his warmth a stark contrast to the chill seeping into my bones. His hair clung to his forehead, beads of rain tracing their way down his chiseled jawline. I marveled at how he could look so utterly composed, even as the weather raged around us. His presence grounded me, filling the spaces of my uncertainty with unwavering confidence. With each passing moment, the weight of our shared history pressed upon my chest, but there was a freedom in our closeness that made me want to laugh, to cry, and to scream all at once.

"Why do you always pick the worst weather for these heart-to-hearts?" I teased, my voice barely rising above the patter of rain. I had long since stopped caring about the drenched fabric clinging to my skin; in this moment, I felt alive.

He chuckled, a low sound that cut through the storm, a beacon of light amidst the dark clouds. "Because I want to make sure you remember how hard I fought to get you back." His smirk sent a flutter through my heart, the kind that reminded me how easy it was to fall for him, even in the most unpredictable of circumstances.

I bit my lip to stifle my laughter, my eyes locked onto his. "So, you're saying you plan to get drenched every time you want to profess your undying love?"

"Hey, a little rain never hurt anyone," he replied, shifting closer, the space between us dwindling. "Besides, it makes me look ruggedly handsome, don't you think?" He struck a mock-heroic pose, lifting his chin and flashing a grin that made my heart do somersaults.

"Ruggedly handsome? More like doused rat." I giggled, but my breath caught in my throat as he stepped forward, the playful banter melting into something far more serious. The mood shifted like the winds whipping around us, pulling me closer into his orbit.

"I promise you," he murmured, his voice low and serious, cutting through the sound of the rain. "I'll never stop fighting for us." His eyes were intense, brimming with an emotion that made me both anxious and exhilarated. Those words hung in the air between us, electric and charged, and I could feel the unspoken weight of what they meant.

In the moments that followed, I was lost in his gaze, entranced by the depth of what lay beneath the surface. It was as if he could see every fracture, every scar I had concealed beneath layers of bravado. The rain blurred the lines between us, erasing the past and reshaping our future. "Do you really mean that?" I asked, the sincerity of my tone surprising even me.

"Always," he said, his voice steady, like the heart of a storm. "No matter how many obstacles we face, I'll stand by you. We'll navigate this together."

My breath hitched as I stepped back, breaking the spell for a moment, my heart racing. "You say that now, but what if the storm doesn't pass? What if we're swept away?" I couldn't help but voice the doubts that clawed at the edges of my mind. I had been left before, my heart discarded like a broken umbrella, and the memory of that pain felt raw and fresh.

Ethan reached for my hand, his grip warm and reassuring. "Then we'll build our own shelter. We'll make a home wherever we land, rain or shine." His confidence resonated with me, filling me with a warmth that chased away the chill of uncertainty.

I could see the truth in his eyes—the promise of everything we could be, tethered by shared dreams and unyielding trust. The lake, once a backdrop for heartbreak and loss, shimmered with potential, its depths mirroring the complexity of our emotions. With every drop that fell, I felt lighter, as though the storm was washing away the remnants of fear I had clung to for too long.

But as I stood there, soaking wet and vulnerable, I realized that this wasn't just a promise made in the rain. It was a commitment to weather the storms, to embrace the chaos and uncertainty together. I took a step closer, letting the rain drench me completely, surrendering to the moment and to him.

"Then let's make a deal," I said, my voice firm, emboldened by the storm surrounding us. "If we're going to do this, we're going to do it fully. No holding back, no second-guessing. We take each day as it comes, together."

He grinned, that mischievous spark igniting in his eyes. "Deal. But you have to promise not to let me drag you into too much trouble."

"Trouble? With you? I'd be worried if I wasn't," I replied, a teasing glimmer in my gaze. The laughter that followed mingled with the rain, a melodic symphony that drowned out my worries.

Together, we stood beneath the turbulent sky, two souls anchored in a world of uncertainty, and I realized that in this moment, we were not merely surviving the storm—we were learning to dance in the rain.

The rain intensified, a curtain of droplets that blurred the world around us, creating a soundscape reminiscent of a thousand heartbeats echoing through the night. I felt exhilarated, each raindrop a tiny reminder of our shared resolve. It was absurd, really—here we were, two adults caught in a downpour, lost in our own little bubble of chaos. But it was also a reprieve from the weight of expectations and the noise of the world. It was just us.

Ethan's smile was infectious, a glimmer of hope and mischief that contrasted sharply with the heavy clouds. "You know, if I had known this was how our relationship was going to play out—rainstorms and all—I would've invested in a better umbrella," he said, shaking his head dramatically, sending water flying in all directions.

I laughed, unable to suppress the joy bubbling up inside me. "I think the lack of an umbrella is the least of our problems, don't you? But hey, if you ever want to invest in one, I can definitely help you pick one that matches your eyes."

"Wow, so now I'm just a color scheme to you?" He raised an eyebrow, feigning offense. "Next, you'll tell me you want matching rain boots."

"Only if you promise to wear them. That way, I can make fun of you later." I nudged him playfully, reveling in the warmth of his presence. It felt like we were on a reality show, caught in a moment of absurdity, our lives reduced to playful banter and soaked clothes.

But beneath the laughter, there was a truth simmering, a realization that clung to me like the moisture in the air. We were here, together, and despite the past that tried to haunt us, this moment felt electric. My heart swelled with a mix of fear and hope, both dizzying and invigorating.

"Okay, let's get serious for a moment," Ethan said, his tone shifting as he took a step back, creating a distance I wasn't sure I wanted. "This... whatever this is between us, it's real. But it's not just going to fix itself because we want it to."

His words cut through the lightheartedness, reminding me of the challenges that loomed ahead. The playful banter slipped away, leaving a space filled with the unspoken weight of our relationship.

"I know," I replied softly, my heart racing. "It's just... sometimes, it's easier to pretend everything is fine."

"Pretending doesn't really get us anywhere, does it?" he said, his gaze unwavering. "We need to talk about the future. What do you see for us?"

I shivered slightly, though it wasn't just from the cold. The thought of a future seemed daunting, a swirling fog of possibilities that both excited and terrified me. "I want to believe it can be something good," I said, cautiously choosing my words. "But what if we're just repeating old patterns? What if I mess this up again?"

Ethan stepped closer again, his warmth enveloping me like a shield against my worries. "You're not going to mess this up. Not this time. We've both changed, right? We're not the same people we were when this all started."

"That's true," I conceded, my heart softening at his words. "But what if we're too different now?" The fear of growing apart while trying to rekindle something precious weighed heavily on my chest. "What if we can't find common ground?"

He shook his head, a gentle smile playing on his lips. "That's the beauty of it. We're not meant to be the same. We're two people finding our way. It's messy, and it's complicated, but that doesn't mean it's not worth it."

His voice resonated deep within me, stirring something I had tried to suppress for so long. "You're right," I said, a hint of defiance sparking in my chest. "I want this, Ethan. I want us."

"Then let's figure it out together," he said, his voice low and firm, each word coated in sincerity. "Starting now. No more hiding. We take our fears and face them head-on."

Just then, a loud clap of thunder boomed overhead, causing me to jump. "Great timing, Mother Nature," I joked, though the fear in my chest was real.

Ethan laughed, his eyes dancing with mischief again. "Well, if we're going to face our fears, we might as well do it with a bang, right?"

I couldn't help but chuckle at his audacity, the way he turned my anxious thoughts into something light. "You're unbelievable," I said, shaking my head in disbelief.

"I prefer the term 'endearingly insane,' but I appreciate your feedback." He winked, his playful demeanor lifting the tension between us, reminding me of the joy we could still share.

The rain continued to fall, an unwavering rhythm that kept the world at bay, and for a moment, I let myself believe that we could conquer whatever lay ahead. It was exhilarating, liberating, and terrifying all at once.

We stood there, inches apart, the rain mingling with the unspoken promises that hung between us. It was as if the universe conspired to keep us exactly where we needed to be—together, in this moment, amidst the chaos.

As the thunder rumbled again, I felt a rush of determination surge through me. "You know what? Let's stop worrying about the future," I declared, my heart racing with the audacity of it all. "Let's just focus on today. Tomorrow can wait."

"Now that's the spirit," Ethan said, his smile infectious. "What do you want to do right now? Other than get soaked?"

"I don't know," I said, glancing around the rain-soaked landscape. "Maybe we should make a splash? Literally."

With a mischievous grin, Ethan took my hand, and before I could process what was happening, he was pulling me toward the water's edge. "Oh no, you don't!" I squealed, laughter spilling out of me as he tugged me along.

We both burst into the lake, laughter echoing off the surface as the cold water enveloped us, invigorating and refreshing. In that moment, everything felt possible—the worries, the doubts, the fears—they were washed away in the laughter and the joy of being alive. The world may have been shrouded in darkness, but in that lake, we were illuminated by our shared laughter and promises.

"See? This is so much better than a serious conversation," he shouted over the sound of the rain, his laughter mingling with mine, creating a symphony of joy and abandon.

And for the first time in what felt like forever, I didn't just hope for a better future—I felt it in my bones. We were building something beautiful, one moment at a time.

The laughter echoed through the air, mingling with the sounds of the rain as we splashed through the water, an impromptu dance against the backdrop of nature's wild symphony. Ethan lunged toward me, his expression a perfect blend of mischief and delight, and before I could react, he scooped me up, the cool water splashing over us like a shower of glistening diamonds. "You're in trouble now," he teased, his voice light yet filled with a promise of chaos.

"Put me down, you maniac!" I shrieked, half-laughing, half-trying to sound serious as he twirled me around, the world spinning in a whirl of raindrops and exhilaration. "What are you, a romantic pirate? Next, you'll be claiming this lake as your treasure!"

Ethan paused, eyebrows raised in mock contemplation. "A pirate, huh? Well, I could use a crew. You in?" He set me down but kept his grip on my waist, his hands warm against my damp skin, a grounding force in the playful whirlwind.

"Only if you promise not to make me walk the plank," I shot back, a grin spreading across my face. The moment felt electric, the kind of connection that didn't just bounce off the surface but seeped deep into the marrow of my bones.

"Oh, I don't know," he mused, his gaze playful yet calculating. "Walking the plank could be a fun way to see if you're actually as buoyant as you claim. Or do you float better than you swim?"

BRIDGING THE UNSEEN

I rolled my eyes, splashing water at him. "If you're going to make me float, at least offer me a cocktail first."

"Only if it comes with an umbrella," he quipped, and I couldn't help but laugh again, my heart racing not just from the cold but from the sheer joy of being in this ridiculous moment with him. The rain fell steadily, but it felt like a cleansing of sorts—washing away the fears, the doubts, and the hesitations that had crept into my mind.

But just as I began to relax into the joy of our silly exchange, a dark shadow of uncertainty flickered at the edges of my mind. I looked up at the stormy sky, the clouds swirling ominously, the distant rumble of thunder growing closer. "Ethan," I said, my voice suddenly serious. "What if this is just a fleeting moment? What if once the rain stops, everything goes back to how it was before?"

His expression shifted, the lightness fading for a moment. "Then we make sure it doesn't," he replied firmly. "We're not going back. This is a new chapter, and we're the ones writing it."

I wanted to believe him. My heart yearned for that future—a future where we could laugh freely, where our connection could thrive. Yet, the memories of pain, of hurt and loss, loomed like specters just out of reach. "You say that now, but what happens when reality hits? When life decides to throw curveballs at us?"

He stepped closer, his gaze unwavering. "Life is always going to throw curveballs, but it's how we handle them that counts. You and I, we're a team. And I'm not going anywhere."

Before I could respond, a particularly fierce gust of wind whipped through the trees, sending a shiver down my spine. The atmosphere changed, the lightness of our moment suddenly feeling heavy with anticipation. It was as if the world had paused, waiting for something to happen.

"Did you feel that?" I asked, instinctively stepping back. The playful spark had dimmed, replaced by a tangible tension that settled between us like fog.

Ethan nodded, his brow furrowing. "Yeah. It feels... different. Almost like something is about to happen."

Just then, the ground trembled slightly beneath us, and I glanced at him, my heart pounding. "What do you mean by 'something'? What are you talking about?"

"It's probably nothing," he said quickly, though the way his voice wavered suggested otherwise. "Maybe it's just the storm—weather can be unpredictable."

"Or maybe it's something more," I suggested, a hint of nervousness creeping into my voice. "What if it's a sign?"

"Signs don't usually come with thunder and lightning," he chuckled, but I could see the doubt in his eyes. The moment hung heavy between us, charged with an unspoken worry that neither of us wanted to acknowledge.

Suddenly, a sharp crack of thunder echoed through the sky, and I instinctively grabbed his arm, my heart racing. The world felt precarious, as if everything we'd just built in this fleeting moment was now teetering on the edge of chaos.

Ethan turned to me, his expression serious. "No matter what happens, we face it together. Okay?"

I nodded, swallowing hard. "Together," I echoed, but my voice felt small, lost in the encroaching darkness.

Before we could dwell on it any longer, a flash of lightning illuminated the lake, the bright light slicing through the shadows, revealing the world in stark relief for just a heartbeat. And in that heartbeat, something moved in the water—a shadow, large and undulating, lurking beneath the surface, sending a ripple of unease through me.

"Did you see that?" I gasped, my voice barely a whisper, the realization that something was out there sinking into my bones like ice.

Ethan's expression turned grave. "What the hell was that?"

I glanced back at the water, the surface calm now, but I could still feel the weight of whatever had stirred beneath. "I don't know," I admitted, fear creeping into my voice. "But I think we should—"

Before I could finish, the surface of the lake erupted, and a massive shape surged upward, breaking through the water with a ferocious splash that sent waves crashing over us. My heart raced as I stumbled back, grasping Ethan's arm for balance, both of us caught in the moment, our laughter and joy replaced by a sharp gasp of shock.

What emerged from the water was not what I had expected—a creature unlike anything I had seen before, sleek and glistening, its eyes piercing and intelligent, meeting mine with an unnerving intensity. It was mesmerizing and terrifying all at once, a creature born from the very depths of the lake, its presence an enigma that defied explanation.

"What is that?" I breathed, feeling the thrill of fear mixed with wonder wash over me.

Ethan's grip tightened around my waist, pulling me closer as the creature arched its back, gliding gracefully in the rain-soaked water. "I have no idea," he whispered, awe and fear flickering across his face.

The world around us faded into a blur, the only thing that mattered now was the creature before us, and as it moved, I realized that this was not just a moment—it was a turning point. Everything we had fought for, everything we hoped for, could hinge on what happened next.

And as I looked into the depths of its eyes, I knew the storm was only just beginning.

Milton Keynes UK
Ingram Content Group UK Ltd.
UKHW040257181024
449757UK00001B/91